Allies AND Outcasts

THE BLOOD FATE SERIES (BOOK TWO)

ANDALEE BROOKE

Copyright © 2024 Andalee Brooke

All rights reserved.

No portion of this book may be reproduced in any form without permission from the publisher, except as permitted by U.S copyright law.

For permissions contact: authorandaleebrooke@gmail.com

Formatted by ReignFormatting

In loving memory of my Nana, who taught me how to read and gave me her love of books.

This one's for you.

♥

Content Warning

Please note that this version of Fangs and Paws has more mature themes than the other version. This version includes more graphically descriptive sex scenes as well as adult language. If this makes you uncomfortable, I would suggest reading the other version as it has more of a PG-13 rating. It has a slightly different cover, and no content warning.

Now, if that doesn't bother you and that's exactly the reason you bought this version...

Enjoy.

Andalee Brooke

One

DRAKEN

FOURTEEN YEARS AGO

"You're reading us a story tonight, right, Daddy?" Crystal asks as I help her wriggle into her pyjamas.

"I suppose I am," I reply, pulling the soft pink top down, making sure I don't put it on backwards … again. "Come on now, right foot," I say whilst encouraging her to put on the matching pink pants.

She grabs my arm to balance herself, then clumsily places one foot in a leg hole.

"Good job! Now the left … perfect!" I applaud, grinning as she smiles up at me, purple eyes sparkling with triumph.

"Reese and Heaf made Mama m-mad," Ruby says softly

as I turn to help her out of the tub and wrap her in a towel that engulfs her tiny body.

"Yes, yes they did," I agree as I set her down to finish drying her off. "Cici, don't run off, we need to run a comb through that hair."

"Okay ..." Crystal huffs as she sits in front of Alice's vanity, crossing her arms with a pout.

Oh, the woes of a five year old.

As if on cue, Alice's voice echoes from downstairs.

"What do you mean, 'Why can't a maid do it?!' You two made this mess, you two are gonna finish moppin' it up, then you're both takin' a bath. After that, you can clean my bathroom from top to bottom!"

I bite my bottom lip to keep myself from chuckling as the two boys whine in protest.

"Hey, how come we had to take a bath? Reese and Heath are the dirty ones!" Crystal asks in an annoyed tone.

"Yeah, h-how come?" Ruby echoes as I finish zipping up her red feetie pyjamas. Even though she's three years old, she still fits in size 2-T clothes, with plenty of wiggle room.

"Because you needed a bath either way, and your Mum wanted me to bathe you two in a clean tub before those boys get in and sling mud all over the place," I reply with a sigh.

Reese and Heath had decided it would be a bright idea to ride their bikes through the mud, then get off and have a 'mudball fight, since there wasn't any snow' – coz, of course that's a reasonable excuse – and then trampled mud all over Alice's freshly mopped kitchen. Although Alice does most of the cooking and cleaning daily, we have a maid service come out once a week to deep-clean the entire house.

The boys were currently learning that living a life of luxury doesn't mean we'll always pay someone to clean up after them. While Alice supervises, I'm left with the duty of getting the girls bathed and ready for bed.

"Remember, to do it soft," Crystal instructs as she hands me her glittery-pink, wide-toothed comb.

"Soft soft," Ruby echoes, taking a seat beside her sister on Alice's bench, as they look at each other in the mirror.

"Yes, yes, I know. I'll try my best, Princess," I promise.

Apparently I comb harder than their Mummy and 'don't do it right.'

Combing Ruby's hair is easy, as her hair's straight and baby fine like mine, though it's chestnut brown like her mother's. She also never protests, she's only mimicking Crystal because she's in agreement with her sister in all things as of late. Crystal, on the other hand, has my silvery-blond colour, but her mother's thick, coarse, waves and curls. It doesn't help that she's such a tomboy, and her hair's usually a knotted mess or, as Alice calls it, 'a rat's nest' after playing outside. Thankfully, neither she nor her sister participated in the mudball fight.

I would just do Ruby's first, since her chin length bob would take mere seconds, but she would immediately ask for me to comb it again after I finish with Crystal, anyway, and I decided to leave her for last. So, I began parting Crystal's elbow-length hair and spraying it with detangler. It hardly seemed to make a difference, but Alice insisted on using it, anyway.

"Ow!" Crystal yowls, causing me to jump and nearly drop the comb.

"I haven't even touched your head with it yet!" I shout, already beginning to feel exasperated.

Crystal's nose crinkles as she begins to giggle hysterically, and I have to fight the smile threatening to form on my lips as I shake my head at her reflection.

"Ow!" Ruby mimics, covering her head with her tiny hands and grinning from ear to ear. This causes them both to erupt into laughter, and I place my hands behind my back raising an eyebrow at them in the mirror.

"What're you doing, Daddy?" Crystal giggles, looking up at me.

Those precious purple eyes have way more power over me than they should. If they were turquoise, they would be identical to her mother's. Mischievous sparkle and all.

"What d-doing, Daddy?" Ruby echoes, my own shade of grey staring up at me through her big doe eyes, framed by long lashes.

If Ruby was blonde, she'd be my mother's clone.

Bloody hell, who am I kidding? They both have me wrapped around their little fingers.

I have no idea how, but I somehow manage to keep my composure as I look down at them with what I hope is a disapproving stare.

"Are you two quite done?"

They nod, but giggle again.

"Right, sit up straight then."

Luckily, Crystal is distracting herself by making faces at Ruby in the mirror as I work through the largest tangles. Ruby squeals with joy before attempting to copy her, making Crystal laugh in return. Soon, Crystal's long locks are tamed, and I finish combing Ruby's in no time.

"Right, who's ready for a bedtime story?" I ask after wiping up any lingering splatters of bath water from the floor.

"Me!" my daughters shout in unison, both jumping up and down with excitement.

"Last one in the bed is a rotten egg!" I say, stifling a laugh as they both screech and run down the hall.

I glance over the bathroom one more time, making sure everything is as clean as it can be before the two little goblins come to dirty it. Even though it's about to be dirtied anyway, Alice would've choke-slammed me if I left it a mess.

"Hurry up, Daddy!" Crystal calls from down the hall.

"Hurry, hurry!" Ruby echoes.

Satisfied, I turn off the bathroom light and make my way to the girls' room.

"Reese Scott! Do not sword fight your brother with the mop! Clean only!" I hear Alice shout from downstairs, followed by two disgruntled groans.

I bite my lip, shaking my head with a smile as I close the girls' bedroom door behind me.

"They in big t-twouble." Ruby whispers to a giggling Crystal, who nods in response.

"Indeed, but pay them no mind. Why don't you two go pick out a book?" I say, sitting on the foot of the queen size bed they'd recently started sharing.

After Ruby outgrew her cot, or crib, as Alice likes to argue, she begged to sleep with Crystal, even though we offered to buy her a 'big girl bed' of her own. Crystal seemed delighted at the idea, so Alice and I figured we'd let them share until they decide they no longer want to.

"You're the rotten egg, Daddy! We beat you!" Crystal declares triumphantly over her shoulder as she points a finger at me.

"B-beat you!" Ruby giggles, mimicking her point.

"You two are too fast for this old man to keep up with," I sigh, slouching in mock defeat, which causes them to erupt in another fit of giggles. "Well, I guess I can't read you a story if I'm a rotten egg …" I say with exaggerated disappointment, beginning to stand.

"No, no, no!" they shout in unison, each taking one of my hands to keep me from moving.

"Oh? You two still want this old slowpoke to read you a story?" I ask, feigning surprise.

They both begin to nod vigorously before rushing over to the bookcase against the opposite wall. I chuckle as I sit back down, awaiting their decision. They each pick up and discard a few books, before Crystal's little brow furrows in thought as she sets down the last book she'd picked up.

"Daddy?"

"Yes, Princess?"

"Can you tell us where vampires come from?"

I blink in genuine surprise, as Ruby nods in approval, putting down her own book.

"Where they c-come from, Daddy?"

"Well," I exhale, trying to think of how to respond, "I suppose I can tell you."

The edited version. So your Mum doesn't burn me to a crisp.

They both grin and run to scramble onto the bed. After tucking them both in, and making sure they each have their favourite stuffy to cuddle, I sit at the edge of the bed and think of where to start.

"Let's see …" I mumble, running a hand through my hair as I try to assemble my thoughts, "this is all legend, okay? Do you know what that means?"

"Mama says legends are stories that are maybe true or maybe not," Crystal replies, as Ruby nods in agreement.

"Well, I suppose that is an accurate description," I nod with a smirk; that's an Alice answer if I've ever heard one. "Okay, well here is the legend of the first vampire as I heard it from my mum a long time ago."

"Nan?" Crystal asks as Ruby blinks up at me with questioning eyes from behind a colourful stuffed unicorn.

Although they were never able to meet my mother, they still lovingly referred to her as their Nan when she was brought up in conversation. I knew it's what she would've wanted to be called had she lived to meet them, and it makes my heart happy to keep her memory alive this way.

"Yes, your Nan. She told it to me when I was younger."

"Were you little like us?"

"I was a tad bit older than the twins when I asked about it, actually."

"G-guardian fox, Daddy." Ruby mumbles, her voice muffled by the rainbow mane she has buried her face in, lifting a small hand to point at the little fox shaped nightlight at the bottom of the wall between their bed and the door.

"Ah, yes. Of course."

I nod, getting up to flip the little switch, causing an orange glow to form around the little glass fox as I switch off the bedroom light. It's a well-loved gift from their godfather, who thought it a perfect theme for the first Fox baby Alice and I introduced to the world. Truthfully, I think Crystal has outgrown it and allows it to stay on for Ruby's sake.

Crystal was never really afraid of the dark; she mainly likes the nightlight because it's a cute decoration. Ruby, on the other hand, is petrified of the dark. She was probably worried I would forget to turn it on if she fell asleep during the story, and she'd wake up to a frightening pitch-black room.

"Alright, our guardian fox, destroyer of darkness, is lit, shall we begin?" I ask, sitting back down to face the girls.

Ruby's face is still buried in her stuffed unicorn, but I can tell by her eyes she's smiling when she nods at me. Crystal snuggles her stuffed pink kitty to her cheek, patiently smiling up at me.

"This story is about Ambrogio the Adventurer."

"Ambwoshio?" Crystal asks, wrinkling her nose in confusion. The word is a bit tough for her to pronounce, despite her ability to speak clearly at an early age.

"Yes." I chuckle, "The Adventurer who became the first vampire."

They glance at each other in excitement before looking back up at me, waiting for me to continue.

"Long ago," I begin, "Ambrogio the Adventurer heard of an oracle who lived in the city of Delphi. Do either of you know what an Oracle is?"

"They t-tell the f-future." Ruby whispers as Crystal nods in agreement.

"Very good. You are both your mother's children." I say with a smile.

They grin, but remain quiet.

"Ambrogio sought to have his future told by this particular Oracle, for she was widely known for her predictions always coming true. She lived in a temple that was built to worship the sun god, Apollo. One night, after a very long journey, Ambrogio found the Oracle preparing a ritual to honour Apollo the next morning.

"He told her of his request, and the Oracle agreed, closing her eyes as she began to meditate until she was in a trance-like state. When she finally opened her eyes, they were filled with fear as she began to chant,

The curse.
The moon.
The blood will run.

"Confused, Ambrogio tried to ask her for specifics, but the Oracle was known for talking in riddles and never giving direct answers, so his attempts were in vain."

"Why?" Ruby asks, tilting her head in curiosity.

"Because women were difficult even back then, Princess."

"I'm t-telling Mama."

"Do you want me to live to tell the rest of the tale?"

"Shush, Ruby!" Crystal chastises, bringing a finger to her lips.

"Otay, Otay! I w-won't tell her," Ruby giggles.

"Anyway," I stifle a chuckle before continuing, "Ambrogio tried to have the Oracle tell him more, but she would not. After many failed attempts at trying to get her to speak, he left. Unable to sleep, he walked aimlessly as he tried to gather his thoughts and make sense of what she said. But it was no use. Eventually, morning came and he still hadn't slept a wink.

"Exhausted and frustrated, Ambrogio decided to make his way back to the temple to try and reason with the Oracle again. When he arrived, he happened upon a maiden who looked eerily like the Oracle, except her hair was black instead of the Oracle's silvery white. She was gathering herbs, and didn't notice him until he startled her with his voice. He learned her name was Selene."

"Like my middle name?!" Crystal asks excitedly.

"Yes, although yours is spelled like that singer your mum likes, this story is also what inspired her to pick that name."

"Cool!" Crystal says with a small smile, as she waits for me to continue.

"Ambrogio learned that Selene was the Oracle's sister. She helped keep the temple and prepare the rituals. They talked the rest of the day and Ambrogio's worries were replaced with the blooming romance of love at first sight. He continued to visit Selene every morning, and she quickly fell for him as well."

"Ew." Crystal says, scrunching up her nose in disgust.

"Aw …" Ruby sighs, eyes twinkling with admiration.

"That's right, Cici. Boys are very ew."

I nod in approval, hoping Ruby catches on but, of course, this is the one time she doesn't copy her sister when I'd like her to. Crystal giggles, as Ruby shyly hides behind her stuffy.

"After many blissful days of getting to know one another," I continue, "Ambrogio finally worked up the courage to ask Selene if she would be willing to leave Greece and return with him to Italy. He promised to marry her, and to take her on many adventures all over the world. Selene happily agreed. Not wanting to waste a single second, they made plans to meet in the morning to prepare for their departure.

"Little did they know that the sun god, Apollo, had been watching them. Selene was his favourite servant, and he did not want to lose her. Overcome with jealousy and rage, he appeared to Ambrogio as he made his way back to his boat. Apollo placed a curse upon Ambrogio, making his skin burn in the sun, so he'd never be able to walk in the daylight ever again.

"Completely distraught over the idea of not being able to meet with his beloved Selene in the morning as planned, he decided to do the unthinkable and seek out Hades, god of the underworld, to make a deal as a last resort. He was terrified Selene would think something happened to him, or worse, that he had left without her, so he was willing to bargain anything if it meant he could fulfil his promise to meet with her."

I stifle a smile as the girls exchange a worried look.

"Ambrogio found a cave that led to an underground temple for Hades. After Ambrogio begged for a bargain to aid him, Hades appeared and listened to his story. He agreed to give both Ambrogio and Selene shelter under his protection if Ambrogio would steal Artemis's silver bow for him."

"Artemis is Apollo's sister, right?" Crystal asks quietly.

I nod.

"Uh-oh …" Ruby mumbles as she cuddles closer to her sister.

"Hades told Ambrogio that, in order to get Artemis's attention, he had to leave out a sacrifice she would deem worthy, so he loaned him a wooden bow to hunt with in the meantime. Before Ambrogio could agree and take it, Hades told him that he must take his soul as collateral until he brought the silver bow. If he failed, he would have to stay in the underworld as his subject forever.

"Reluctantly, Ambrogio agreed and allowed Hades to rip his soul from his body, deeming it a worthy sacrifice to have the chance to be reunited with his Selene again. And that, my dears, is the piece of the story that led to people believing that vampires don't have souls."

"B-but, we do got souls?" Ruby asks, cautiously.

I nod, and she and Crystal sigh in relief.

"We do, my loves. Don't fret," I say as I pat them each on the leg in assurance.

My heart swells as I notice Ruby taking Crystal's hand in hers, and watching Crystal clasp it back forces me to clear my throat of the emotion the sweet gesture causes before I can continue.

"Ambrogio used the wooden bow to shoot a swan to offer as a hunting trophy to Artemis. And-"

"Aw, no!" Ruby gasps, her big eyes shining with emotion.

Damn it, I should have omitted that bit.

"It's okay, Ruby. I promise. It's no different than how we get our meat to eat," I try to explain without stumbling over my words.

"Did it hurt?" she asks barely above a whisper.

"Ah, no. The bow Hades loaned him made it so it doesn't hurt when the swans go to heaven," I lie.

Ruby nods in satisfaction, but still seems sad as she looks

down to pet her unicorn for comfort. Crystal gives me a doubtful look, and opens her mouth to question me. When I shake my head once, she catches on, and closes her mouth. But, as she glances at Ruby, her brow remains furrowed in obvious irritation. I raise my eyebrows at her, and she rolls her eyes before settling back into her pillows. She looks so much like Alice when she does that, I have to stop myself from grinning so I don't encourage the behaviour.

"Ambrogio used the swan's feather and blood to write a note to leave for Selene, and-"

"That's metal as fuck." Crystal interrupts, grinning.

"Wha- Where did you hear that?"

"I heard Heath say it after Reese said books are just tattooed dead trees."

"Those two little-"

I pinch the bridge if my nose and sharply exhale as I try to calm myself. Finally, I clap my hands together, then look up at her. Crystal and Ruby are both looking at me in amused confusion.

"That's a naughty word, don't say it again. I'll be talking to the boys about it."

"Which one?"

"The one you said at the end of the sentence."

"You and Mama say it all the time!" Crystal protests.

"All the t-time!" Ruby echoes, nodding in agreement.

"Yes, and it's a grown up word, although Mummy and I will try not to say it as much. Anyway, do you want me to finish this story or not?"

"Fine."

"F-fine."

"Right," I nod, "Selene found the note the next morning and was heartbroken. She wasn't angry at Ambrogio, but was very understanding despite her despair. She decided to keep serving at the temple as normal as to not anger Apollo any further, but she secretly held onto hope that she and Ambrogio would have their happily ever after.

"Ambrogio slayed a swan for forty-four nights, and would offer it to Artemis after writing Selene a love letter. He secretly hoped he would earn Artemis's approval and not have to steal her bow. However, on the forty-fifth night, he was down to his last arrow and missed his target. Ambrogio fell to his knees in despair, and wept because he had no swan to offer to Artemis, and no blood to write a letter to Selene.

"Artemis appeared before him and told him she admired his devotion, then asked why he was weeping. Ambrogio explained his situation, leaving out bits of the truth, and begged to borrow her silver bow to write Selene one more letter."

"Why didn't he just ask for a pen? Did he have paper? Why did-"

I hold out a hand to stop Crystal's seemingly never-ending flow of questions.

"I don't know, Cici. Ask the Greeks."

She raises an eyebrow, probably preparing to ask another question, but I continue the story before she gets the chance.

"Artemis took pity on Ambrogio, and allowed him to borrow the silver bow. Feeling like he wouldn't have a such chance again, Ambrogio tried to flee back to Hades with it. After realising she'd been tricked, Artemis pursued him until she struck him down.

"Ambrogio kept his head down in guilty defeat, and handed her the bow to await his punishment. When Artemis probed him for an explanation, Ambrogio finally admitted the entire story, not withholding any of the truth this time. Artemis took pity upon Ambrogio again, and told him she could make him a better deal than the one he made with Hades, and that this was his last chance.

"Ambrogio thanked her for her mercy, then asked what she required from him. Artemis stated that he and Selene would have to worship and devote the rest of their lives to her, and that every female follower of Artemis had to remain a virgin. That meant Selene and Ambrogio could never touch and-"

"What's a virgin?" Crystal asks, and I mentally kick myself for not omitting this bit as well.

Alice is going to kill me.

"Ahem, it's ah … a woman that hasn't … had babies yet," I stammer, running a hand through my hair nervously at their questioning stares. "So, basically Ambrogio and Selene could never get married or have babies. They could only be friends."

They both still look a little confused, but nod, much to my relief.

"Ambrogio agreed. Even though it was a hard price to pay, at least he and Selene could live safely together. After receiving his oath, Artemis gave Ambrogio powers of a hunter second only to her own. His strength, speed, and all his other senses heightened, his eyes turned red and he grew fangs. The goddess explained he could draw power by using his fangs to drink blood and retain the life force of animals and humans. She also made him immortal, so he no longer had to worry about Hades holding onto his soul. The hunting goddess herself provided him with blood to leave a final note for Selene, instructing her to meet him at the docks and board a specific ship that would lead to the sanctuary of Artemis's temple.

"Selene read the note, and hurried to the docks before the sun rose, as to not gain any attention from Apollo. She boarded the ship and found a coffin inside. The captain, a fellow female follower of Artemis, instructed her to not open it until the sun went down again, and told her Ambrogio was safe and well in there. Selene was confused, but agreed and stayed by the coffin as the ship departed and made its way to Artemis's temple in Ephesus. And that, my dears, is where the legend of vampires sleeping in coffins comes from."

"It protected Ambwoshio from the sun ..." Crystal mutters.

I nod.

"After the sun set, she freed Ambrogio and they had a joyous reunion. Though he longed to kiss her, he couldn't. They tried to find the positives and plan out the rest of their lives together. When they arrived at Ephesus, they found a cave to keep Ambrogio safe from the sun during the day, and would come out to worship Artemis every night. They lived as happy as they could be, despite the platonic rules of their relationship."

"What's Puhtonic?" Crystal asks.

"Just friends, zero romance."

"Oh."

"Anyways, thanks to his immortality, Ambrogio stayed young while Selene grew old. Artemis appeared to Ambrogio once again when she found him weeping over Selene's dying body. Artemis admired his years of devotion to her, but also his devotion to loving Selene despite her strict rules. She decided to reward him with a final deal.

"She instructed him to break her rule of no touching to bite Selene and drink some of her blood, then to bite his wrist to offer his own blood to Selene to drink. Ambrogio hesitated, but agreed once Selene weakly begged him to do it. A lot of vampires believe this was the first Blood Fate to ever happen, and that Artemis's power was enough for them to not need an enchanted goblet to drink from.

"The moon seemed to shine brighter than it ever had before, and Selene's body began to glow a bright, pure white. Temporarily blinded, Ambrogio began to panic until the glow faded, revealing a youthful Selene in his arms. She looked just as young and beautiful as the day he first saw her, only she was still glowing, and robes of white and silver had replaced her clothes. She wore a tiara and other jewellery made of moonstones and opals.

"Selene's eyes fluttered open, and Artemis explained that she was now the goddess of moonlight. Ambrogio could now touch her, and claim her as his bride. Selene used her powers to bless him with that ability to walk under the sun and not be harmed again, although she could only leave the realm of the gods and come to visit him on earth at night afterward. Ambrogio also had to accept that he would have to recharge for a whole day after feeding from blood, as penance for being able to enjoy the sun again. For no hunter should be that powerful and be able to roam the earth day and night. He would be unstoppable.

"That is the origin story of why we have to recharge after feeding from blood, obviously. Every night, he would wait for her under the moon, and it is said that, together, they created the vampire race with their children."

"Wow." Ruby whispers, excitement gleaming in her now heavy eyelids.

"That was cool," Crystal nods, "Now what about the first Dhampir?"

"That, I'm not sure of. I'll have to get back to you," I chuckle, watching them each yawn. "Time for bed anyway, you two are tired."

"How many kids did Anbwoshio and Selene have?" Crystal asks, trying to hide how sleepy she is.

"Not sure, love."

"Where do babies come from?"

I freeze, and it takes a moment for me to register what she just asked. Even though they're both obviously tired, they're both staring at me to await an answer. I feel as though my brain has glitched, taking a few seconds to get my mouth to work again.

"The deal was one story. It's bed time." I finally stammer.

"Just one more!" Crystal protests.

"Nope, your mother can tell you that one. As I said, it's time for bed, girls."

Alice is definitely going to kill me, now.

"But-"

"Bed!"

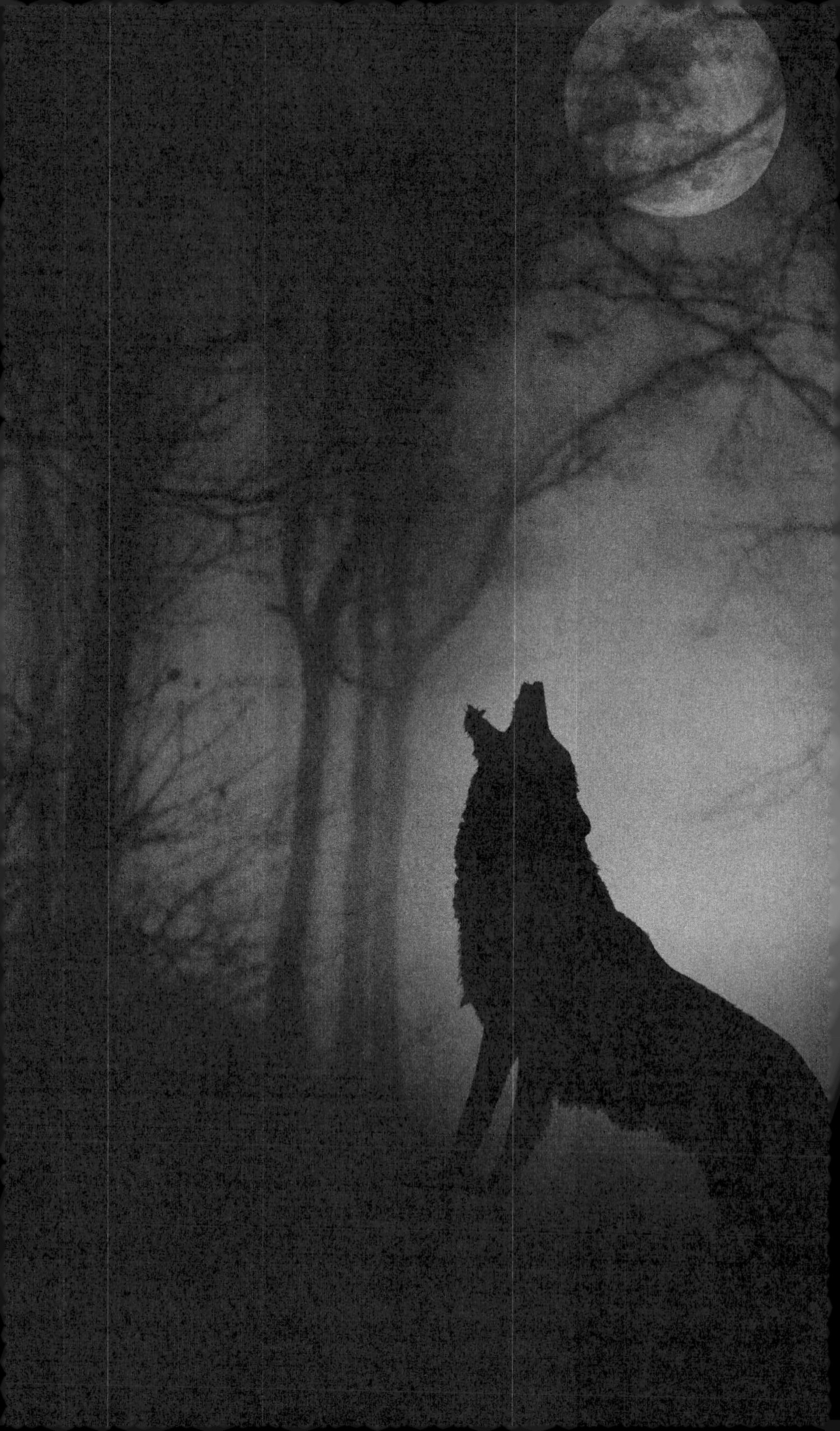

Two

CONAN
THIRTEEN YEARS AGO

"You wanted to see me, Dad?" I ask, trying to hide my nervousness.

Usually when Dad calls for me, I'm in trouble. I could've pretended to not hear him when he called, but I know he'd be twice as angry if he had to come get me.

And if he thought I was ignoring him on purpose …

I suppress a shiver at the thought.

"Yes, come here, boy." Dad says, beckoning me closer to his recliner.

He doesn't seem mad, but he does look serious. There's an unfamiliar gleam in his eyes that I can't quite place. I obediently walk up to stand in front of him. Even sitting down, he seems so big.

I wonder if I'll ever be that big ...

I try to stand straight and not fidget. Dad hates when I fidget. I shove my hands into my shorts pockets, deciding it's the safest place for them.

"Your mother told me you were asking about where werewolves come from," Dad says, leaning forward in his chair.

The side of his mouth looks like it almost wants to twitch up into an almost-smile. He doesn't seem angry at this question, so I decide it's safe to nod.

"Well," he leans back, smirking a little, "I told your mother that, if you're old enough to ask, you're old enough to know. She babies you too much for my liking, anyway."

"I'm seven! Not a baby!" I reply angrily, removing my hands from my pockets to fold my arms across my chest.

I feel the wrinkle in my brow shifting from anger to confusion as Dad chuckles. He hardly ever laughs. It's weird when he does.

"That's right, you're a big boy. Sit down and I'll tell you our supposed origin story."

He gestures to the floor, and I hesitantly sit down, cross-legged. Ma always likes me to sit in her lap, or next to her when she tells me a story, but Dad never does. I wonder why that is but, at the same time, it'd be really awkward if he started now. All I can do is hope he's okay with how I'm sitting so I won't get fussed at.

"Um, is this a real story, or a legend?" I ask quietly.

"Honestly," Dad shrugs, "that's up to you to decide, son. Every Alpha I've known has told this story, including my father, so there must be some truth to it."

I nod. Dad respects Nonno Alessandro a lot. So, if he told Dad this story, it must be real.

"It all started with the king of Arcadea, Lycaon. Like his father before him, King Lycaon was a feared but fair leader to the people of Arcadea. You remember who Zeus is from your Greek books, right?"

I nod.

"Very good," Dad nods in approval, and I feel a bundle of happiness flutter in my chest. "King Lycaon used to warn the people of Arcadea to always be on their best behavior as if Zeus was watching, because he was known to disguise himself as a human peasant and walk among them."

"Like a spy?"

"Sort of, yes. I suppose you could think of it like that. However, a group of troublemakers doubted this, and wanted to see if it was true. Probably what we would consider lawless rogues who just wanted to do whatever the hell they wanted with no sense of order. They assumed it was a scare tactic to make them be kinder to the unfortunate.

"One day they noticed the king serving this luxurious meal to a lowly beggar, and decided to test for themselves if this was Zeus in disguise. They were sure this was a plot King Lycaon had come up with to prove his point, for what king serves anyone, especially a lowly peasant? So, they waited for King Lycaon to get distracted, and served the man the roasted flesh of a prisoner, for only a god would be able to tell the difference between the meat of man and beast."

"Ew, there wasn't a less gross way to test that?" I ask, my nose wrinkling at the thought.

"Times were very different back in the old days, son. Now, quit interrupting me."

"Sorry," I mumble quietly, and imagine my lips being zipped like they do sometimes in cartoons, to help me stay quiet.

"The beggar, indeed, turned out to be Zeus and, angered

by their trick, he quickly shed his disguise and showed them his true form. As they begged for mercy, he struck them all with lightning on the spot. Startled, King Lycaon rushed over to find out what had happened. He was embarrassed by his people, and knelt before Zeus to ask for forgiveness.

"Zeus didn't blame King Lycaon. In fact, as a reward for the years of devotion the king had given him, the god decided to bless King Lycaon with gifts to help him be a better leader and command the respect and fear of Arcadea. He granted him the ability to shapeshift into a wolf, so he could lead his people as an Alpha leads his pack.

"Knowing he would need more than just the abilities of an average wolf, Zeus sought help from the moon goddess, Selene. Selene agreed to make him a child of the moon, and blessed him with gifts. Although his transformations would be painful at first, he would be bigger, stronger, and faster than the average wolf. His strength and all his senses would be heightened when he was in human form, as well. All these gifts would be passed down to any of Lycaon's children.

"Selene requested he and any other of her wolves blessed by the moon show their devotion to her by staying in their wolf form for the entirety of each night with a full moon. She also explained the wolf was a part of Lycaon, but also its own wild, untamed being. Lycaon would have to slowly earn its respect. Each transformation would be less painful as the bond with his wolf strengthened, and he would gain more control over his wolf form as he and his wolf slowly became in sync. The same would apply to all future wolves blessed by the moon."

I blink up at him a little absentmindedly when I notice he's done speaking.

"And that's supposedly where we come from," Dad says,

a cocky smirk spreading across his face as he reclines farther into his chair.

"Hm," is all I can think of to respond with.

I'd started to lose interest halfway into the story, but knew better than to interrupt Dad again or to leave before he was finished.

"Don't you have any questions?"

"Not really. The whole thing was kinda weird."

"Weird?!" Dad sits up straight, "It's your history!"

"Can I go play Pokémon now?" I ask, excited as I remember I have the newest game from my recent birthday.

"Wha-? *Pokémon?*" Dad stammers, then rubs his face in obvious annoyance.

For a moment I'm scared he's going to punish me by taking away the game and my heart sinks to my stomach.

"Whatever. Go on then. I shouldn't be surprised," he grunts, laying back in his chair to pick up the TV remote.

I know better than to stick around, and dart back to my room before he can change his mind.

CONAN

SEVEN YEARS AGO

I double over in pain, dropping the armful of firewood I was carrying. Every bone in my body hurts, and I swear I heard a sickening crack when I bent over. My head is pounding, and I can only close my eyes and grit my teeth, waiting for it to pass.

"Conan?!" I hear my mother yell, her voice full of concern.

All I can do is stay perfectly still, afraid I'll fall to my knees if I move a muscle. I don't dare even open my eyes, but

I hear her rush down the patio steps toward me. The pain subsides for a moment but, as soon as I start to open my mouth, another sickening crack sounds from my back. Once again, I place my hands on my knees, breathing heavily as I try to steady myself.

"Conan, what's wrong?!" Mom shouts, even though she's standing right in front of me.

"Hurts," I manages to rasp out.

Even though it's a chilly autumn night, I suddenly feel hot all over and I'm beginning to sweat as if I'm in a sauna.

"*What hurts, son? Tell me!*" Mom cries out in Italian, gently placing a hand on my back.

"Everything," is the only word I can manage to squeeze out through my gritted teeth.

My hair's sticking to my forehead, and I feel my shirt beginning to stick to my skin as I continue to sweat buckets.

"Oh my God, you're going through your first Change," she says, and I can hear the bewilderment in her tone.

"Camilla, is everything okay? Should I get Red?" I hear Cora, the mate of our pack's Beta, ask.

"Go get Luther, I think Conan's about to shift for the first time," my mom answers as she continues to rub gentle circles on my back.

"What? He's only thirteen! Are you sure?!"

"Look at him, Cora!"

I hear Cora gasp as my bones begin to crackle and pop again, and I finally surrender and fall on my knees, my hands grabbing fistfuls of dirt and dead leaves.

"I'll get him right away!" I hear Cora call out as the sound of her retreating footsteps fades away.

"Lay on the ground if you have to, *figlio*," Mom says in a soft, soothing voice as she tries her best to comfort me.

Her voice broke on the Italian word for son, though she's trying her best to sound calm.

"Hurts to move, Ma," I choke out, and open my eyes to find my fingernails are turning black and growing more pointed.

"I know, I know. It's only this bad the first time," she replies in a tone barely above a whisper. "I can't believe my baby is shifting already."

My teeth begin to ache, and I wince as I run my tongue over them, noticing that I now have four very sharp, very pointy canines.

"Let me see your eyes, Conan."

Her soft, warm hands gingerly cup each side of my face as she slowly angles my head to look up at her. I flutter my eyes open for a moment, then squeeze them shut as another wave of pain rolls through my body.

"They're gold, your wolf is definitely coming out," she confirms before kissing my forehead, her lips cool against my feverish skin.

"Well, guess it's true after all," I hear Dad say in obvious amusement, his heavy boots crunching the leaves as he gets closer. "Oh, stop coddling him, Camilla!" he grunts his annoyance, sounding like he's less than a foot away from me now.

"He's going through the Change at *thirteen*, Luther!" Mom snaps back.

"And? He's always matured quick for his age, it only makes sense. The Alpha blood running though him is making sure of that."

"He's still just a boy!"

"It's a natural part of our lives!"

"And it's scary for all of us when we go through it the first time!"

"No one coddled me, and I turned out just fine. Quit babying him. He's thirteen, not *three*."

I grit my teeth as my head continues to pound, all the yelling making it worse.

Why can't they argue somewhere else?

"Hey," Mom mumbles as she brings her face closer to mine, "I'm right here, okay? I'll force myself not to change until you're done, then you can follow m-"

"Oh, for God's sake, you babying him is just going to freak him out more! Just let him finish then catch up to the rest of the pack!" Dad chastises.

"I will *not* leave him like this, Luther!" Mom snarls back, the undertones of her wolf's growl lining her voice.

It's a full moon, so everyone's going to change soon if they haven't already. Everyone's wolf is closer to the surface than normal during this time, and our primal instincts create a blurred line with our humanity at times.

An awkward silence follows, and I can only assume they're having a stare-off. Mom is usually pretty submissive to Dad when he gives an order as Alpha but, on the rare occasions she finds it necessary to stand up to him, she's the only one who can question his authority and live to tell the tale.

I was just supposed to be gathering firewood for the pack bonfire, not starting a family feud.

Guilt pools in my stomach as I pant between the surges of pain. A few minutes go by without more bones cracking, so I use the opportunity to speak.

"Go ahead, Ma..." I pant, "I'll catch up."

"No, I'm staying right here with you. I'll be with you the whole time. Your new wolf is going to be confused and scared, but he'll recognize Rosa as his mother. I'll lead you to the pack."

I wonder what my wolf's name is ...

Both of my parents' wolves have "R" names, Rosa and Rocco. I try to distract myself by wondering if my wolf will continue the theme.

"This is the only time you'll be babysitting him during a Change, Camilla," Dad says, the warning clear in his tone.

I hear Mom snort in response, but she doesn't argue. Dad's heavy footsteps move away, and I swear I feel my body relax a bit, despite the pain.

"Okay, so try to listen to your wolf. It's more a *feeling* than listening, but you'll know what I mean. Don't fight it, just try your best to flow with the shift. Easier said than done, I know."

"Don't feel anything except pain," I grunt, my body completely slick with sweat from head to toe.

"I know, I know. But it'll pass. It'll still hurt the next few times, but each time will be easier than the last and, before you know it, you'll be able do it with no pain at all!" she says in the most optimistic voice she can muster.

"This sucks," is the best I can manage in response.

Mom lets out a humorless laugh.

"I know, *figlio*. I know." She begins to rub circles on my back again. "I guess I shouldn't be so surprised, since you're already on your way to growing a damn mustache …"

I would've laughed if it wouldn't have made the pain worse.

"Here," I hear the sound of fabric ripping as she drags a clawed finger down my back, careful not to slice any of my flesh. "Let's get this off. It'll make it easier."

I raise my arms one at a time to let her finish pulling off the remains of my shirt. She starts to say something else, but my mind drowns it out as the presence of my wolf begins to engulf me.

Nero.

My parents weren't kidding when they said I would just *know* my wolf's name. In my mind's eye a feral, black wolf begins to pace with restlessness. I feel him come closer and closer to the surface until finally, he breaks loose.

Werewolves never remember much when they first shift. We're wild animals until our souls grow a proper bond with our wolves and the two halves of our being become one. But a few hazy feelings stand out in the fog. I remember my mother's scent comforting me. I remember following Rosa on shaky legs. I remember the rush of freedom once I got used to being on four legs for the first time and was able to run. I remember feeling Rocco's irritation as I wandered away from the pack to explore on my own.

CONAN

PRESENT DAY

A wave of nostalgia washes over me as I pass through a lot of the areas I explored as a wolf that first time. It was about this time of year, too. The lone wolf life seemed more appealing to me from the very beginning, much to my dad's dismay.

Through Nero's eyes, I see a familiar stream ahead. I drink some water, then make my way back toward the little cabin I turned into a bachelor pad, only shifting back into my human form when I reach the back door.

I take a quick shower and pull on a pair of sweatpants before heading to my front door to retrieve a few packages I'd noticed through my wolf's eyes. Back inside, I begin to open the packages to ensure each contains the correct items. I'm pleased to see the stuffed panda I ordered arrived this time. Last time I ordered it, I received an email claiming it'd been delivered but never received the package. Luckily, the vendor sent a replacement free of charge after I emailed to explain the situation.

I rub my thumb over the soft, faux fur and can't hold back a small smile. I'd ordered it because it has large, purple eyes to match its purple, instead of black, markings. The eyes reminded me of my daughter's, and I had to get it for her. Of course, they reminded me of her mother, too. I set the toy on my couch and open the next parcel.

I have no idea when, or if, Crystal will let me see Lila, but I want to buy things for her, anyway. Even if I have to mail them to Crystal, I want to provide for my child in some way. I know Crystal doesn't need money, considering I met her father in a lavish limousine, but I still want Lila to have something from me. Both my human and wolf sides feel the primal urge to provide for her.

Nero has been restless ever since I last saw Crystal. I've kept my vow to not contact her, to wait for her to contact me first, but Nero doesn't understand. He just wants his pup and her mother here where he can see and protect them at all times. A month has passed since I saw, felt, and spoke to Crystal in the woods that night, and he's been a pacing, anxious mess since. As for me, I've thought of nothing else since. Those last words and that last kiss replay in my mind on repeat. I even dream about it—when I can actually sleep. Shifting and going for a run through the woods helps a little, but it barely takes the edge off.

When I'm sure all Lila's things arrived, I put them all in the largest box and place it between the living room wall and the couch. I toss the remaining boxes into the recycling bin before plopping myself in my recliner and turning on the TV for a little background noise as I lean back and go through pack-business emails. I'm in the middle of organizing them by time sensitivity when my ears pick up a familiar name on the tv.

No way.

I glance up from my phone to look at the television screen and immediately feel my blood begin to boil as I notice a familiar, heavily tattooed vampire being interviewed on some talk show. Again.

"Are you going to continue going by your name, or do you think you'll form a band under a different name some day?" the interviewer asks.

"Nah, Victor Thorne has a nice ring to it. I'll keep my birth name as my stage name."

Seriously? Am I just going to start seeing this prick's face everywhere now that's he's gained more fans?

Growling, I reach for the remote before the sound of another familiar name causes me to freeze.

"You told us your best friend was featured in your newest song. Crystal Fox, right?"

"Yep."

"Daughter of billionaire Draken Fox?"

"That's her."

I feel the breath leave my lungs as my heart begins to ache. I can't even force myself to look at the TV, and I just stare at the remote on the side table.

"And you're *just* best friends?" the reporter baits, sounding a little skeptical.

At that, a snarl erupts from my throat and I glare at the screen.

Victor rolls his dark blue eyes.

He chews on his lip ring, as if debating his next words before replying, "Our personal lives are nobody's business."

I knew there was nothing but platonic love between them. Crystal revealed to me one of her most vulnerable secrets the night she told me all about how they mistakenly thought they were mates when they were younger. After a vampire's Blood Fate ritual was unsuccessful, any sexual or romantic desire was lost between the vampires. They'd been best friends since childhood, and their love went back to that platonic level of love, and would never be anything more. But both the question and how Victor didn't exactly deny it pissed Nero off.

Okay, so it pissed me off, too; call me a caveman. Whatever. Whether she accepted it or not, every instinct in my body viewed Crystal as *mine*, and it pained me the world didn't know it.

"Well then, I guess you won't leak the secret of how Mr. and Mrs. Fox both manage to stay looking so young?" the host chuckles, a little nervously.

"I'm afraid not." Victor says with a smirk.

Draken and Alice Fox don't look nearly old enough to be parents of grown children because they're vampires. Hell, the thought of them being grandparents is even weirder. I know vamps don't live forever, but they age even slower than werewolves—in looks, anyway. They could easily pass for Crystal's older siblings. They don't have the usual telltale signs of Botox or plastic surgery, so I'm sure they're plagued constantly by jealous humans about how they maintain their youthful looks.

"Well, how about we cut to the video you and Crystal made for your Metal Blog?" the host asks as he gestures to a screen behind them.

"Let's," Victor agrees, lazily threading his fingers behind his head as he leans back in his chair.

The screen comes to life, advertising Victor's name for the Metal Blog website, then I feel my heart skip a beat as a video begins to play of Crystal sitting next to Victor.

"Victor Thorne here, back with a new single that'll be

dropping next month, and you guys will be the first to hear it, here on my blog. I'd like to give a special thank you to my subscribers for giving me a reason to offer a sneak peek to any of my work. It makes me feel like I might be an actual rock star now," Victor chuckles, and Crystal scrunches her nose in annoyance before swatting his arm.

"You *are* a rockstar!" she says, failing to hide a smile as Victor pretends to cringe in pain.

"Anyway, this abusi— I mean, *lovely* lady next to me is my best friend and has been kind enough to lend me her vocals for this new song," Victor says as Crystal nervously fidgets but smiles at the camera.

I can't see her hands, but I know she's spinning her opal ring around her right forefinger. She does it whenever she's nervous.

Victor continues to describe whatever his stupid song is about, as his hands slowly lift a piece of paper that says, *"Help, she beats me when I don't sing good enough."* He keeps a straight face as he continues on about the meaning behind his song and, at first, Crystal is too busy fidgeting to notice.

I take the opportunity to just stare at her. She has on little make up, black-winged eyeliner and pink lip gloss. I can almost taste her lips as I remember the vanilla on my tongue when I kissed her last. Any lip gloss or Chapstick she bought was always vanilla flavored. I snap out of my hypnotic state when I see her jerk her head to the side, realizing what the sign says as she scrunches up her nose again and rips the paper from him. He laughs while she balls it up and proceeds to throw it at his head.

"How's *that* for abusive?" she snaps.

God, what I would pay to have her scrunch up her nose all cute at me.

I'd gladly take any insults or objects she'd throw at me, just to be in the same room as her again.

After their squabble, Victor grabs a guitar while Crystal adjusts one of the two microphones in front of them.

Can I really handle hearing her sing? I should just change the stupid channel. Or turn the damn TV off. Right now, before it starts to hurt too much.

My chest aches, and I know I'm torturing myself, but I can't quit watching. This is the closest I can get to seeing and hearing her after being deprived of her for over a month. It's bittersweet, but I'll take any dose of her I can get, no matter how painful it is.

Victor starts to sing; the bastard is talented, but I don't even bother with whether I like his music or not. I just stare at Crystal. I stare at those purple eyes I was just thinking about. I stare at that lower lip I want to nip and taste. I stare at the long, silver locks I want to run my fingers through. I've just started to imagine what those locks feel like when I grab a fistful to pull her into a kiss when she starts to sing the chorus with Victor, shaking me out of my naughty daydreams.

They sing in perfect harmony, then Victor shuts up and lets her sing a few lines by herself before taking back over. Her voice still gives me goosebumps every time I hear it. Nero is just as entranced. He finally seems to be at ease, focused solely on her as she sings. I share his pride as we continue to watch her. I'm so damned happy to hear that voice again, even Victor's stupid singing doesn't ruin it for me.

All too soon, the song is over.

"We hope you guys enjoyed the sneak peek of my new song, Embers. Thank you for watching!" Victor says with a wink.

"Bye!" Crystal gives an awkward little wave before the screen goes black.

The camera is now positioned on current Victor as the audience of the show cheers. The host claps his hands with a smile, and Victor gives a polite nod in thanks.

"You both sounded wonderful! Can't wait to hear that bad boy on the radio!" the host exclaims happily.

"Thank you. Without Crystal it would've been—" Victor's voice is cut off by the loud censoring bleep sound as a black bar covers his mouth. "Whoops, sorry," he chuckles.

"It happens," Host Guy laughs nervously and tugs at his shirt collar. "So, can we expect to hear more from Crystal soon when it comes to music?"

I sit up straight then lean forward, curious to know if my baby mama is about to become a rock star herself.

"I've tried to persuade her, but no," Victor says as he shakes his head, looking exasperated. "For now, I'm lucky when she agrees to lend her voice here and there. She has no desire to pursue a musical career of her own."

"That's a shame! She has the voice of an angel!"

That she does. I know Crystal could easily become a rock star if she wanted to. She could easily leave Victor in the dust, but I'm not surprised to hear she still has no desire to make a career out of it. She told me before she didn't mind playing small gigs every now and then, she just always needed a cigarette after to calm her nerves from stage fright. Part of me is relieved to know I won't have to worry about seeing her in every form of media, it would sting as a reminder that she's not ready to talk to me yet.

"And you're releasing the song on all streaming platforms on Halloween, right?"

"Yes, we wanted to release it on our favorite holiday," Victor agrees.

I glance at the date on my phone and feel a pang of guilt that I only just realized what time it is.

It's just a little past midnight ...

This is a rerun, so I'm not sure when they recorded it but, technically, as of a few minutes ago, Halloween is tomorrow. Which means ...

Crystal's birthday is today.

I lift my phone back up and swipe my finger to unlock the screen, then open my contacts. I scroll down to the name "Fangs" and hover my thumb over the button that will open a new text message.

I promised her I wouldn't contact her until she contacted me first. But ... I also want her to know I remembered her birthday ...

I let out a frustrated sigh as I weigh my options. Would she be upset if she thinks I forgot her birthday? Would she be mad if I only texted her a quick happy birthday? Would she rather I just kept my word and not text her, even though I remember?

Which would piss her off more?

After mentally debating myself for what feels like forever, I finally decide to go ahead and risk her anger by texting her.

> Hey, I know I promised I wouldn't contact you until you contacted me first, but... I'd feel like even more of a douchebag if I didn't let you know I remembered what today was.

> Happy birthday, Crystal.

> You don't need to respond, I'll understand if you don't want to.

I don't know how many times I reread that message before I finally have the guts to press the send button. My stomach twists with anxiety as I put my phone back into my pocket, hoping I made the right choice.

I miss her so much, and everything in me and my wolf aches to make her happy. I would do anything to repair the damage I've done. I crave her touch, her scent, her taste so much it's painful at times.

I'd also do anything in this world to have Lila in my arms again. I never knew it was possible to miss someone so much, someone I'd only met once in my life. The idea of Crystal rejecting me forever hurts in more ways than I could ever explain, but the idea of never seeing my daughter again is insufferable. I loved that little girl with all my heart at first sight, before I even knew her name.

I glance at the box containing all the baby items I just ordered. I hope one day, they'll all be put to use and Crystal will allow me to be there in person to see that happen. As I glance around the silent room, I realize just how empty this small house really is.

CRYSTAL

PRESENT DAY

"Are you absolutely *sure.* you want to do this?" Mom asks for what feels like the millionth time.

"I'm sure." I reply.

"Okay, you're the birthday girl," she says with a shrug as she turns to pick up a comb on the bathroom counter.

"If I hate it, I can just grow it back right?" I shrug back as I stare at her in the mirror of her bathroom vanity.

She nods once, running the comb through my hair as she begins to divide it into sections.

"Of course, baby. But, why the sudden urge to chop all your hair off *now*?"

I sigh and feel her hands pause, probably wondering if I'm having second thoughts, as I stare at my feet.

"I dunno …"

I stare at the freshly applied black nail polish Ruby recently applied to both my and Lila's toenails, focusing on the flecks of rainbow glitter mixed inside the color as I try to gather my thoughts.

"I just want a change, I guess," I mumble before finally looking up to meet Mom's gaze in the mirror. "Plus, I've just been so depressed that I haven't really felt like taking care of myself, much less fixing my hair. Lila matters more, anyway."

Her turquoise eyes shine with emotion as she ponders what I've said, then she clears her throat as she continues to comb my hair. I think she's only doing it keep her hands busy and distract her from crying. I know it hurts her to see me in pain, but I don't want to lie to her either.

"I know you've been through a lot, baby …" she begins as she sets down the comb and begins to run her fingers through the curly waves that reach my hips. "It's understandable. I get it. And of course, Lila is important. You're a damned good mother to her, but you need to take care of yourself, too."

She yanks a few strands to grab my attention. I scowl at first, but can't help softly smiling at her aggressive form of affection.

"And I'll fix your hair *anytime* you don't feel like it, Cici," she adds softly as she smooths her hand over my scalp.

My heart warms at her words, and my smile widens with genuine appreciation.

"I know, Mama. I still want to try it out, though. I look at it as a stepping stone to fresh starts."

Nodding, she picks up a pair of scissors and looks up to lock eyes with my reflection.

"Alright, sweetheart. I just wanted to make sure my little girl wasn't having a midlife crisis at 19, what with the new nose ring and urge for a new haircut," she says with a chuckle as her eyes glance down to the small stud in my nose – my birthday present to myself.

"Haha, you're so funny," I say dryly as I roll my eyes, but still find myself smiling.

"You know I'm just kiddin', baby."

"I know, Mom."

"Okay, so you're set on the Pixie Cut still?"

I nod, and hold my breath as she starts to cut my hair.

"You got it," she replies, and I watch my long locks begin to pool at my feet.

"I think we're done," Mom says as she trims one more piece of my bangs, then moves out of the way so I can see myself in the mirror.

My lips part in surprise at this weird new version of me. I lift my hand to rub the stubble at the base of my neck, noticing how cold it now feels. My head also feels as if it lost ten pounds.

"Here," she hands me a handheld mirror so I can turn around and look at the back. "Whatcha think?"

"I love it," I say with a grin.

It's strange, but a good strange. I can't stop running my

fingers through what's left of my hair, the sensation alien to my fingers.

"You look *just* like her," Mom mumbles, her eyes widening in surprise.

"Huh?" I ask, giving her a confused look as I set down the mirror.

"Christa! You look *just* like her! You and Ruby both favor her, but your thick hair is from me, and I guarantee your eyes would be identical to mine if they weren't purple. But now, with your hair cut like that …"

She quickly walks out of the bathroom to go grab a picture frame from her dresser. When I follow, she hands it to me, and I look at the familiar black-and-white photograph of my paternal grandmother. I've seen the picture thousands of times, but now I see what Mom's talking about.

Christa Fox had a short haircut, called a "Titus Cut" in the 1800s. It was similar to a pixie, and very odd for women during that time period. Ruby and I both had her upturned, elven nose, and full, pouty lips. I had her blonde hair color, Ruby's hair was brown but with her straight, baby-fine texture. Ruby also inherited her large, gray, doe eyes and pale skin, just like Dad. So, despite her hair being long and brown, we always figured that, of the two of us, Ruby looked more like her. But now I see myself in that photograph. I feel my heart swell with pride as I gently rub a finger over the glass frame.

"Why did Nan keep her hair short?"

"Remember it's called a Titus Cut? Or *coiffure à la Titus*, Apparently, it was done as an act of rebellion during the French revolution to imitate how executioners would shave victims before ending their lives by guillotine. They'd even wear red scarves to symbolize the cut on the neck.

"Christa's friend was a widow thanks to a false charge

that earned her husband a death sentence by guillotine. She cut her hair in support—to match her friend's—and kept the cut until the day she died, despite your grandfather's disapproval," Mom explains, taking the picture back from me to look at it herself. "Ironic isn't it? Since she died by beheading, even though it was by a cursed blade rather than a guillotine …"

I nod somberly. Thanks to many bedtime stories, Nan always seemed to be the perfect role model for women when it came to progressive thinking.

"I wish I could've met her." I say softly.

"You and me both, baby," Mom says as she places the picture back on her dresser. "She sounded like a hell of a woman."

"Total badass," I agree, feeling even more proud of the fact I could now see more of a resemblance to her in myself.

"Well, I'm gonna get started on your birthday dinner. Why don't you go relax, hm?" Mom says, squeezing my shoulder on the way out.

I nod at her, then find myself staring at the picture in silence long after I hear Mom descend the stairs.

"I can't help but wonder if you'd be proud of me …" I whisper, spinning my opal ring as if nervous she's going to answer back. "Dad says you would've loved me despite the fact I'm a dhampir, and I believe him … But, would you have accepted your great-grandchild?"

I stare at her beautiful face in silence for a few more seconds. Although it was the norm for people to have serious expressions rather than smile in photographs back then, her kind eyes, which remind me so much of Ruby's, send a sense of peace washing over me.

"I'd like to think so."

I kiss the tip of my fingers, then press them to the glass over her cheek, before leaving my parents' bedroom.

After peeking in the nursery to find Lila napping, I head to my room.

I need to answer my birthday messages.

I'd left my phone on Do Not Disturb since last night, knowing I'd have several notifications during the night. When I woke up, I did my usual morning routine for Lila and completely forgot about it. Then I'd been too busy rehearsing in my head how to propose the idea of my haircut to my Mom, and we'd begun cutting my hair after leaving Lila with Ruby.

I walk to my nightstand and unplug my phone from the charger before taking a seat on my bed. I unlock my phone, switch off the Do Not Disturb feature, and watch as a flood of missed texts and phone calls begins to light up my notifications.

Victor and the twins had this annoying ritual of spamming my phone with texts filled with emojis. It annoys me so much and brings them so much joy, they decided to carry over the ritual to Ruby's birthdays as well. Sometimes Baylor was even rude enough to join in the fun. Over 400 text messages show up, and I roll my eyes. I compose a text message to be sent as a group chat to the four of them, so they'll all receive my "thanks" at the same time.

> Y'all texted me the birthday cake emoji a hundred times each?!

After I finish going through a few other messages, one name makes my heart skip a beat when my thumb lands on it mid scroll. Three new messages from "Paws."

He said he wasn't going to contact me until I was ready ...

Part of me is annoyed, but part of me is also relieved, which kinda annoys me more. I bite my lip and slowly exhale through my nose as I open the messages. I find my annoyance melting away as my heart begins to flutter and my cheeks warm.

He remembered my birthday ...

CONAN

I grunt in annoyance when my phone vibrates in my pocket as I finish loading my dishwasher.

Dad can wait five fucking seconds.

After adding the dish detergent, I slam the dishwasher door closed a little too hard before fishing my phone out of my pocket. Dad has been on my ass to finish some paperwork for the pack before November 1st, and was unhappy when I reminded him I still had a day left in October.

My scowl turns into a startled gasp when I read the name "Fangs" in my notifications. I hurriedly open the text, heart pounding with anticipation of her response.

FANGS

> Thank you.

• • •

Three dots appear to show me she's still typing, and I feel my heart skip a beat as I watch them, waiting to see what else she possibly has to say since, I hadn't expected her to answer at all, especially with something as polite as a simple, "Thank you."

Fangs

> You're still totally a douche bag tho :P

I blink, then scoff. I reread it, then find myself chuckling.
Okay, I totally had that one coming.
Let's see if she'll carry on a conversation with me ...
I fidget my thumbs for a second before typing back:

> Okay, I deserve that.

> Would it be too much to ask how you and Pup are doing?

I chew on my lower lip as I watch the three dots appear again, my stomach doing somersaults thanks to my nerves. It doesn't take her long to respond with one word.

• • •

FANGS

> "Pup"?

Ah, she doesn't know I call her that.

I feel my cheeks and neck warm a bit before I begin to type back:

> Just a nickname I came up with for her before I learned her actual name.
>
> I'm still unsure of how to spell it, btw...
>
> Lila? Lyla?

I hope she isn't bothered by the "Pup" comment ... It's a term of endearment used by wolves, but I could see how it might be off-putting to her.

There's a long pause that worries me I pushed the boundaries before the three dots have relief flooding through me.

FANGS

> Your first guess was correct. It's Lila.
>
> Lila Hope.
>
> I think Pup is cute, though <3

> I've gotta go get ready for my birthday dinner, but I'll talk to you later, k?

I blink once, twice, then finally reread the last sentence before the third blink.

I had read that correctly.

She said she'll talk to me later!

I have no idea if she means it, or only said it to be polite, but I don't care. Her responding in general was a success. I was pleased to learn Lila's middle name, too. Hope has been the emotion driving me to carry on. Nero is blooming with pride over our new information about Pup, and is more anxious than ever to see her.

Small steps, we don't wanna scare her mother away.

Nero huffs, but reigns in a very small amount of the eagerness he was trying to push on me. I reread the message one more time, grinning to myself as I compose a reply.

> I love her name.
>
> I'll be happy to hear from you anytime.
>
> I'll leave you alone now, but here's a little birthday gift I made for you. Hope you like it.

I copy and paste the playlist I composed for her and hit send. I stare at the screen for several minutes before I gave up on waiting for a reply.

I hope she likes it.

I couldn't sleep worth a shit, so I spent all night and most of the morning creating a playlist of songs to show Crystal how I really feel about her.

Oh yeah ...

I take my phone out, and quickly add:

Fangs

> The last song is for Pup.

I slip the phone back into my pocket and let out a slow, shaky breath. Staind has been one of my favorite bands for as long as I can remember, and a few of the songs to Crystal were by them. I stumbled upon their song, Zoe Jane by accident. It was written by the lead singer for his daughter, and perfectly captures every emotion I've felt in my brief time as a father.

I know how much music means to her, so I can only hope she takes the time to listen to the whole thing. I hope she listens to every lyric and knows just how much I really love her and Pup and want to make things right. If this doesn't help win her back ... I don't know what will.

Three

BAYLOR

"It's got to be around here somewhere …" I mumble to myself as I scan the countless rows of books for what feels like the millionth time.

After looking through the top rows yet again, I sigh and begin to climb down the step ladder.

Maybe it's on the very bottom?

Once both feet are on the floor, I squat down to look at the bottom row. I don't think it'll be here, but it doesn't hurt to check in case someone misplaced it.

"Whatcha doin'?" a voice asks from behind, nearly making me jump out of my skin. I roll my eyes as the familiar mischievous chuckle confirms the speaker's identity.

"Can you *not* sneak up on me like that?!" I cry as I turn around to face my tiny, fawn-haired coworker. Her blue eyes are still sparkling with joy at my expense as she raises her hands in a placating gesture.

"Sorry!"

"Are you?"

"No."

I pinch the bridge of my nose, exasperated as she begins to chuckle again.

"Ha. Ha. *So* funny, Ella."

"Whatever, scaredy cat. Are you gonna tell me what you're looking for so I can help or what? I see you've got your reading glasses on, so this is obviously some serious business," she says with a wink.

"Any idea where the story of the original vampire and werewolf feud went?" I take off my glasses to rub away a smudge with my shirt. "I know it's somewhere in the Greek mythology section, but …"

"It's not in this section?" She furrows her brow in confusion and looks toward the shelves I just combed through, tapping a crimson painted nail against her chin.

"I've checked and rechecked."

"If I look and it's there, you're buying me lunch tomorrow."

"Fine."

I step aside as she stands on her tiptoes to browse the titles on the book spines just a smidge out of her reach.

"Good luck," I scoff, "I've picked that shelf apart and-"

"Found it."

I blink in surprise as she holds up a book, her smirk threatening to take over her entire face.

"Where?!"

"On the shelf, duh."

"I hate you."

"Looks like you're treating me to Mr. Clucky's Chicken Wings tomorrow!" she crows as she hands over the book with a triumphant grin.

"You sound like Vic," I mutter under my breath before blowing dust off the ancient volume.

"Are you saying me and Victor Thorne have the same taste?"

"Uh, yeah. He's literally obsessed with that place."

I gently open the book and begin to flip through its yellowed pages, handling it carefully so I won't add more tears than it already has. I feel Ella staring a hole into my head, so I glance up and raise an eyebrow, pushing my glasses back up the bridge of my nose.

"What?"

"You have to formally introduce us one day."

"You've already met him!"

"Not formally! I've only seen him a few times when he's come to pick you up."

"Yeah, yeah. Okay," I grunt as I make my way over to a nearby table to find a seat.

"Yes!" She claps her hands together in what can only be described as giddy delight.

"Can you go fangirl somewhere else and let me read in peace, woman?!"

She rolls her eyes then walks to stand in front of me, placing a hand on each of her hips. I have to stifle a snort because she's so short she barely stands taller than me when I'm sitting down.

"Mr. Clucky's. Tomorrow at noon. Don't forget."

"Yeah, yeah," I say again.

She points two fingers toward her eyes, then back at me as

if to say, "I'm watching you," before strutting out of the library.

Each of The Ravens' locations includes a well-stocked library with countless books and documents from several different eras. With all the recent events in my friends' lives, I wanted to find the earliest documented story of why vampires and werewolves hate each other so much. Since today was pretty slow for a work day, I decided to come by before I head home and see what I can learn.

I've heard bits and pieces of different origin stories from all over concerning their feud. It's no surprise that different countries have their own versions. But I wanted to find the earliest written history that *could* be found, and my research so far has pointed me to the Greek mythologies. Surely there'd be more truth to those stories than the others I've heard?

As I gingerly flip through more pages, I can't help feeling an excited anticipation at the thought this story just might be the root of all our wars throughout the years.

Let's see ...
Vampire Origin Story, I've already read that one.
Werewolf Origin Story, already read that one too ...
Aha. Here it is.
The Origin of Their Feud ...

Some of the translations are a bit tricky to read but, apparently, it all began with Callisto, daughter of King Lycaon, and Alonzo, son of Ambrogio.

Since Zeus asked Alonzo's mother, the moon goddess, Selene, to bless and watch over the werewolves, there was no feud between them and the vampires at that time. Therefore, if they wanted to become romantically involved, it was perfectly fine.

Callisto and Alonzo planned to marry, and their fathers

were thrilled to see what kind of powerful offspring the two would create. Considering Callisto and Alonzo each possessed different powers from the gods, any children of the couple were anticipated as treasures by both families.

But, one morning, Callisto was getting ready to bathe in a spring, and—unbeknownst to her— Zeus was watching her, as he'd been lusting after Callisto for some time.

Which isn't a shocker, considering the guy's history with women.

Seeing she was alone and about to undress, Zeus knew he couldn't pass up this opportunity. He disguised himself as Alonzo, approached Callisto, and attempted to seduce her. But Callisto loved Alonzo too well to be fooled; something felt wrong about this kiss, so she quickly pushed Zeus away.

Zeus, angered that she saw through his trick, took away her wolf spirit and transformed her into a bear. The change was permanent, and she could neither transform back into a human nor speak. She could only look and sound like a bear. Zeus knew his curse would eventually cause of her death. If she wasn't hunted down, she'd be isolated and helpless— forced to watch her beloved Alonzo, family, and friends from a distance. Should she ever try to communicate with them, he knew they would kill her. If, by some miracle, humans didn't kill her, Zeus knew she would die of a broken heart. Either way, he saw the result as a fitting punishment for her rejection.

Callisto, panicking and not knowing what else to do, immediately ran back to Arcadia seeking help. On his way to meet Callisto, Alonzo had witnessed the entire interaction but was too far away to intervene. Distraught, he watched his beloved—now forever a bear—run away, and was unable to catch her. He tried calling after her, but to no avail.

Alonzo confronted Zeus, demanding he change Callisto

back. Zeus, of course, had no intention of doing so. Alonzo threatened to tell King Lycaon of this betrayal, since Zeus had been the one to bless King Lycaon and his people with the spirt of wolves and the ability to transform into their physical form. Unwilling to face the consequences of his hasty actions, Zeus struck Alonzo down, killing him instantly, for he was too proud to admit he had once again allowed lust to cloud his judgement.

It wasn't long after Alonzo's death before Callisto, too, was dead. As Zeus predicted, Arcadians slew her, fearing the bear that had seemingly come to attack their families.

The aftermath was a nightmare; words and stories got twisted as emotions ran high. Unaware his daughter was dead, King Lycaon blamed Ambrogio, saying Alonzo caused her disappearance and swearing vengeance on every vampire on Earth. Ambrogio blamed Callisto for being a temptress who led his son to his death. He vowed to slay any werewolf who came near him. Because of this, the two species have been at war ever since, though some like to believe Alonzo and Callisto finally found peace with each other in the afterlife.

I close the book and take off my glasses. Rubbing my dry eyes, I prop my chin on my hand, processing this new information as I begin to make connections with other stories, all of which claim to convey the true cause of the ancient feud.

Other events in history supposedly added to the species' dislike for each other. Numerous records from all over the world point to completely different causes for turf wars and battles and some particularly petty reasons for the feud. I can't help feeling they could all originate from this story, especially considering the oldest records we have on vampire and werewolf origins also come from Greek mythology.

Eventually, vampires and werewolves began warning

their offspring about the other species, passing down false information and stereotypes.

Like Lila …

Crystal and Conan were terrified they'd created some abomination thanks to rumors they'd heard passed down from other vampires and werewolves. While I haven't been privileged to meet any hybrids yet, since they're pretty rare, I figured "abomination" was a load of bullshit. I've read about hybrids being special, unique, and powerful beings. No two ever seem to be alike as far as what they inherit from each side of their parentage.

Lila's case is especially rare, considering her mother is a dhampir who also happens to be an Elemental witch's descendant. dhampirs are known for having low birth rates, as they're supposed to only be able to reproduce with a pure-blooded vampire who's also their Blood Fated mate.

Perhaps Crystal's Elemental blood had something to do with it. Or perhaps it was because Conan is a pure-blooded werewolf. I've heard hybrids can only be born to mated vampires and werewolves, but others argue members of the two species could never be true mates. Could Conan's wolf think Crystal's human half is his mate? So many questions and so few answers. My only hope is that more progressive vampires and werewolves will outweigh those who still harbor hatred and prejudice for each other because of an old war started by a misunderstanding.

Luckily, in our modern era, some vampires and werewolves don't seem to care about the feud. Although it's still a very small percentage of the overall population, progress is progress. It only makes sense during this age of technology, stocks, companies, and schools that some would find it more beneficial to coexist instead of risking unnecessary setbacks or humans finding out things they're better off not knowing.

I wish I could find some hybrids to question and observe.

I know The Ravens will definitely have records of hybrids on file somewhere, but they never stay in one place for long. Since their existence is still pretty taboo to the majority of the vampire and werewolf population, the few who *are* out there, stay in hiding and make themselves hard to find by living a nomadic life.

Maybe since Lila is so special, she can help break the stereotypes. I don't doubt she'll grow up to be someone great in this world, and will make a difference. For Cici's sake, I can only hope.

An alarm on my phone begins to sound, and I lift the screen to see what notifications I've missed. I blink in surprise at the time, and quickly rise to my feet.

If I don't leave now, I'll be late to Cici's birthday dinner!

I tuck the book under my arm, not quite ready to return it to the stacks just yet, and quickly make my way toward the nearest exit.

CRYSTAL

I quietly make my way inside the dark nursery and look down at my still-sleeping baby in her crib. Out of habit, I gently place a hand over her chest to make sure she's still breathing. I don't care if it makes me paranoid—since, as far as we know, she's the first of her kind, there's no way to be sure what to look out for while she's an infant. I feel her tiny chest rise and fall several times before I'm reassured enough to remove my hand.

I'll let her nap for just a bit longer.

I exit the room, leaving the door cracked just enough to let me hear her, and nearly bump into Dad as I turn down the hallway.

"Whoa!" He gently grabs my arms to stop me from smacking into his chest.

"Sorry," I say sheepishly, "I have like, a bazillion things on my brain at once."

"Well, first off, happy birthday," he says with a chuckle, "and-" he stops mid sentence and just stares at me, his lips parted in surprise. His brain seems to have just … glitched.

"Uh, Dad?"

"Your hair!" he finally blurts out, extending a hand to ruffle it.

"Do you like it?" I ask, nervously, "I know it's a big change …"

"Like it? I *love* it!"

I feel my shoulders sag in relief as he scoops me into a hug.

"You do?"

"Yes! You look so much like my Mum. It's absolutely beautiful on you, Cici."

I hug him back in silence for a moment, debating whether or not to ask the question that's been nagging at my brain.

"Do you think she'd be proud of me, Daddy?" I ask softly into his jacket.

"Are you joking?" Dad pulls back and holds me by my elbows as he looks me in the eye, "She'd be the proudest Nan around."

"Even though Lila …?"

"Oh, Cici," Dad's eyes soften in understanding, "Yes, I'd like to think so. She was very open-minded for her time, and such a loving person. I'd like to think she'd love Lila to bits as the rest of us do."

"Really?"

"Crystal, we're all so proud of you. You've handled everything that's been thrown at you with such grace I sometimes wonder how it's even possible you're related to me. Chuckle all you want, Cici! It's the truth. However, your Nan was like that. She was a good mother, just as you are."

"Thanks, Daddy." Smiling, I blink away tears before pulling him into another hug.

"I've never been more proud to be your father. I've also never been more proud to be a grandfather, even though I quite despise referring to myself as one out loud."

I can't help but chuckle again, and Dad ruffles my hair then plants a kiss on my forehead.

"Yeah, yeah. Laugh it up at your old man. Are you ready to go eat dinner, birthday girl?"

"I am."

***

"Yes?" Victor asks, raising a pierced brow down at a scowling Ruby.

"Are you going to hog her all night or are you actually gonna let me hold her any time soon?" Ruby grumbles, clearly annoyed.

Victor feigns offense as he cuddles Lila closer to his chest.

"Tell your Auntie Ruby she lives with you and gets you all the time, Lila," he coos down at the baby, wiggling a tattooed finger in front of her face. With a gurgled laugh, Lila happily grabs the finger and promptly pulls it into her mouth.

Ruby's brow furrows in annoyance as she crosses her arms and taps her foot in impatience. Victor glances in her direction, smirking, before looking back down at Lila.

"Your Auntie Ruby is also *almost* as cute as you when she's mad."

"You've basically lived here off and on since you were a kid *and* you've been hogging her since she woke up!"

"No one likes a hater, Ruby."

"You're so lucky you're holding my niece, or I'd smack you!"

Victor's smirk spreads into a grin as he makes a point of not looking up at Ruby glaring a hole into his head.

"I swear, Vic," Mom chuckles, tapping excess sauce off a spoon before resting it on a plate next to the large pot, "other than the twins, you're the only one who can rile Ruby like that." She casts a glance over her shoulder as she wipes her hands with a dish towel, "I'm not sure who's worse, to be honest."

"It's a gift." Victor replies matter-of-factly as he lightly bounces Lila. Ruby looks ready to knock his lights out when he finally hands Lila over, chuckling.

"Okay, okay. I'll let you have a turn."

"Finally!" Ruby's entire expression morphs into genuine happiness as she cuddles Lila, who has now decided to grab a fistful of her hair. "Ow! Easy there, cutie!"

"She's got an iron grip, dude," Victor laughs.

"Right?!"

"Are you two going to behave now, or do I need to separate you?" I ask with a laugh. They both proceed to stick their tongues out at me at the same time. "Real mature, guys."

"Knock, knock!" Baylor calls out as he enters the kitchen through the back door.

We all greet him as he makes his way over to the table to set down a pink gift bag, then walks over to hug me.

"I told you not to get me anything," I say, hugging him back.

"It's just a little something." He pulls away to smile at me, his eyes widening in surprise. "Your hair! It looks awesome!"

"Thanks, Bay."

"Smells good, Mrs. Alice. Gumbo?" Baylor says as he turns to face Mom.

"You know it," she replies with a smile.

"Birthday girl goes first!" I call out as I begin to fill a bowl with rice.

"Ugh. I ate way too much," Uncle Silas, my godfather and Dad's best friend, says as he leans back in his chair and rubs his stomach.

"Maybe you should learn how to pace yourself instead of eating like a rabid beast," Dad teases.

"But, it's Alice's cooking! You know I have zero self-control when it comes to her gumbo!"

"You're so dramatic."

"My stomach is gonna explode …"

"You'd better make room for some birthday cake," Mom chuckles as she wags a finger in his direction.

"Oh, God," Uncle Silas moans, still rubbing his stomach, which earns him an eyeroll from Dad. This, in turn, earns Dad a grunted, "Shut up," from Uncle Silas

"Oh, yes. Before I forget …" Dad reaches into his pocket, "I've been meaning to mail this to you."

"Uh, you know it's Cici's birthday and not mine, right?" Uncle Silas raises a brow in confusion.

"Of course, you idiot, I'm just giving it to you while you're here. Plus, seeing your reactions in person is better, anyway." Dad says as he hands Uncle Silas a small, laminated card.

"What the hell is this?"

"I found an artist to remake your first driver's license."

Uncle Silas looks down at the card, then looks back at Dad, frowning.

"Are you fucking kidding me, Draken?" He flips the card around to show a photoshopped picture of himself riding a dinosaur, causing the entire table to erupt into laughter.

Uncle Silas is not only Dad's best friend, but his oldest. He also happens to be quite a lot older than my Dad, who was born in the 1800s. So, Dad loves to make jokes about Uncle Silas being ancient. He travels a lot, thanks to his work, but he always tries to visit when he can. He's also one of the very few people outside our family who know the truth about Lila.

Uncle Silas's scowl quickly melts into a grin of his own, and he takes out his wallet to shove the card inside, making a point to slide it in front of his actual driver's license.

"Their bromance is so fucking weird," I mumble to Baylor between bites. Stifling more laughter, he just nods.

"Don't talk about your father that way, young lady," Uncle Silas scolds.

"Don't speak about your godfather that way, Crystal," Dad says at the same time, wagging his finger in front of my face as though he's chastising Lila.

Baylor and Victor try to hide their laughter with obvious fake coughs as I pinch the bridge of my nose.

"What even is my life …"

"Who's ready for cookie cake?" Mom asks as she begins to cut the large cookie cake sandwich with hot pink icing in the middle.

"You got the double-doozie one?!" I ask, my mouth watering with excitement.

"I got the double-doozie one," she nods as she hands me the piece with my name in pink icing that matches the middle. I asked if we could skip the whole singing and blowing out candles tradition, since I hadn't really felt like celebrating to begin with.

Mom's home cooked food and a double-doozie cookie cake are sure brightening my spirits a bit, though ...

"Hell yeah, give me that corner slice!" Uncle Silas says, extending an empty plate out to Mom.

"I thought you were too full for cake?" Dad's tone is skeptical.

"Blasphemy! There's always room for cake!" Uncle Silas replies with a dismissive wave of his hand.

Everyone is gone or asleep, now.

I shut my bedroom door, then walk over to my bed and sit down. I bite my lip, feeling butterflies flutter around in my stomach as I slowly grab my phone from my nightstand. I unplug it from its charger, and let out a slow, shaky breath as I unlock the screen.

Let's check out this playlist.

1. NO MATTER WHAT – PAPA ROACH
2. MIRACLES – STONE SOUR
3. FOLLOW YOU – BRING ME THE HORIZON
4. I AM BROKEN TOO – KILLSWITCH ENGAGE
5. BASIC NEEDS – JONATHON DAVIS
6. EVERLONG – FOO FIGHTERS
7. ANGEL – THEORY OF A DEADMAN
8. SORRY – BUCKCHERRY
9. CLOSER – KINGS OF LEON
10. IT'S BEEN AWHILE – STAIND
11. ZOE JANE – STAIND

There's another message from him that I missed ...

Paws

The last song is for Pup.

He has a song for Lila, too?

My hand trembling, I open the link to the playlist and begin listening to the first song. The fact that Conan listened to every one of these songs to choose for me hits me hard in the chest. He's not the best when it comes to expressing emotions, so it makes sense he'd let lyrics do the talking for him. I'm just surprised he went through the effort to do it at all.

Certain lines from each track tug on my heartstrings as tears begin to slide down my cheeks. I feel my phone slip through my fingers as a hundred emotions slam into me all at once. My heart feels so very full, but aches so very badly at the same time.

He loves me, and he loves our little girl. He's only met her once, and already has a song for her!

A sob escapes my throat as I bring my knees to my chest and just allow myself to cry. Worried that someone will hear my sobs, I grab a pillow and prop it up against my knees, then reach for my phone. I press the button to replay the playlist from the beginning, then bury my face in the pillow as sobs of heartache, relief, and confusion rattle my chest.

I definitely have some thinking to do and some decisions to make.

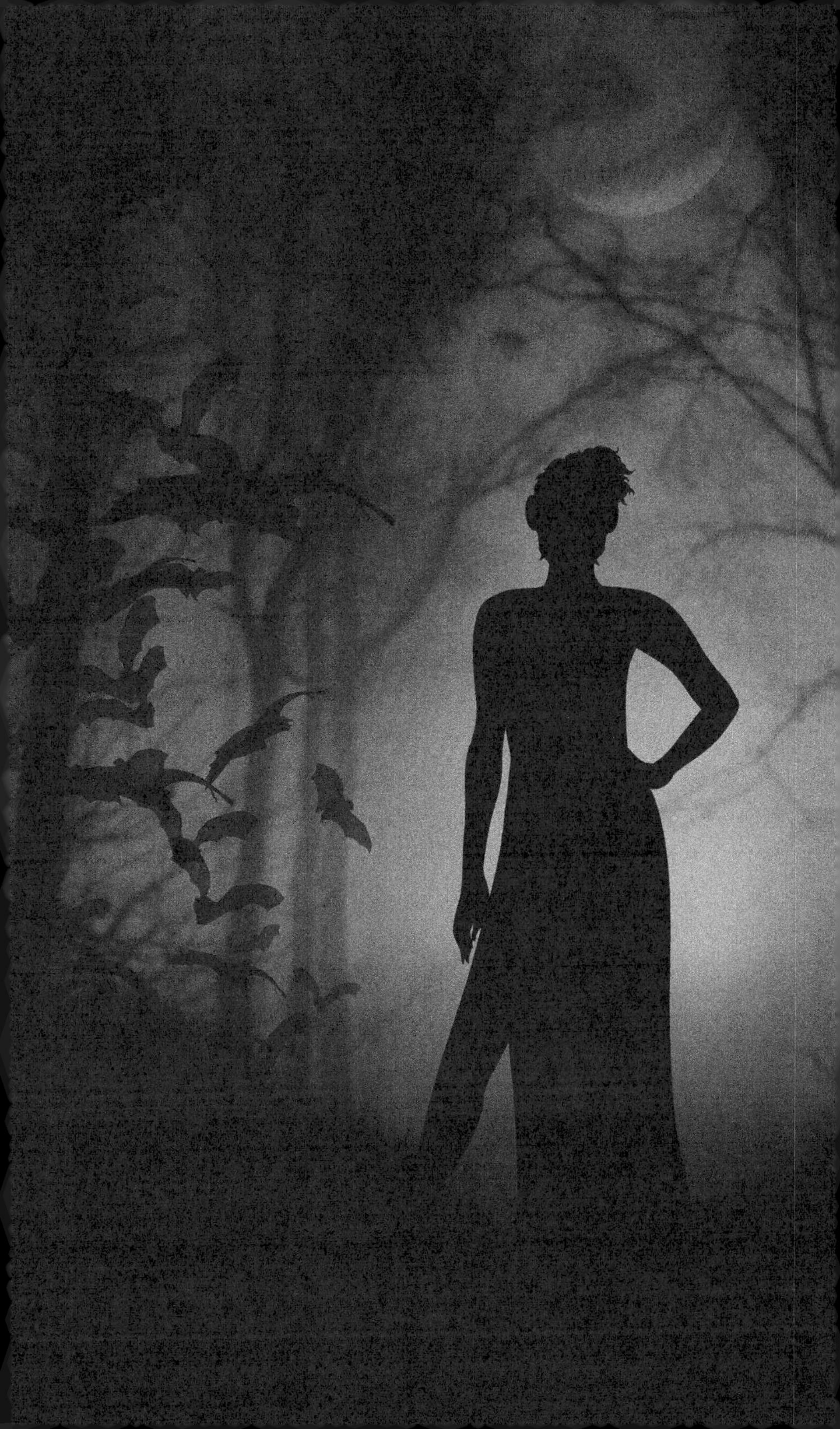

Four

CRYSTAL

"Cici?" The sound of Ruby's soft voice nearly makes me jump out of my skin. I was snot-crying so hard I didn't even notice her scent, much less hear her open my door.

I want to reply but, instead, a hiccup escapes my throat as I look up at her and wipe away tears with the back of my hand.

"What's wrong?" she asks, quietly shutting the door behind her.

"Nothing," I croak.

I can tell she isn't going to accept that answer—no one's ever accused Ruby of being stupid. Sitting on the bed beside me, she touches my shoulder and chews her bottom lip. I can practically see the gears turning inside her head as she calculates the best way to respond, and I move my gaze to my feet, my sniffling the only sound breaking the awkward silence.

"I heard some of those songs," she finally says. "They seemed pretty, ah, *personalized.*"

I freeze, too embarrassed to formulate a reply.

She heard those? How many did she hear? Does she know?

"Are you sad because they made you think of Conan?"

Yep. She knows.

"You could say that," I mutter.

We sit in silence for a few more minutes, and I continue to stare at my feet, unable to face her. A soft gasp of surprise finally has me looking at her.

"Did … did Conan *send* those to you?" she asks, realization lighting up her eyes.

I close my eyes and release a shaky breath before turning to face her.

"Please don't tell anyone." I whisper.

Ruby chews on her bottom lip again, eyes clouding with thought as she processes this information. She opens her mouth as if to say something, then closes it. After a few seconds I feel her hand grip my shoulder a little tighter. I look up to meet her gaze, readying myself for whatever disapproval or warning she's about to throw my way.

"He sounds like he's *really* sorry. I know I don't know him that well, but … I dunno. Maybe you two need to talk some more …" she mumbles, giving my shoulder another reassuring squeeze.

I blink in surprise.

That's definitely not *what I was expecting her to say.*

"You think so?" I can't keep the surprise—or unexpected hope—out of my voice.

"Well, I know we didn't discuss it much, but how did your other talk with him go?"

"He said he was sorry and wanted me back ... And to see Lila." Tears begin to fill my eyes, and I bury my face back in the pillow propped against my knees.

"Cici ..." Ruby murmurs as she begins to rub my back.

"I just don't know what to do," I admit sadly, my voice muffled by the pillow. "I'm so confused and scared."

"Do whatever you think is right," Ruby says as she pulls me into a hug, "I'll support you either way."

"Thank you, Ru." I twist my body to hug her back, letting the pillow fall to the floor. "I don't know what I'd do without you. Sometimes I think *you* should be the big sister."

"You've always taken care of me, now it's my turn to take care of you," she replies with a light chuckle as she squeezes me tighter. "It's what sisters do."

I squeeze her back, and just allow myself to sit there as I wait for my crying to subside again. When we finally break our embrace, Ruby darts to the bathroom and retrieves a small handful of tissues for me. I gratefully accept them to blow my nose and finish drying my eyes.

"Are Mom and Dad asleep?" I ask, throwing the tissues into my nearby trashcan.

Ruby rolls her eyes. "No, but they're *distracted*," she says in disgust.

"Whatcha mean?"

"They're in their room and I can hear *their* song playing."

"The Marilyn Manson one?"

"The Marilyn Manson one."

"Oh God, they'll be distracted for a while, then," I say with a shudder, and Ruby nods before pointing a finger at her open mouth and making a dramatic gagging noise for emphasis.

We've learned over the years to avoid their bedroom at all costs if we hear Marilyn Manson's Kill4Me playing from inside. For some ungodly reason they get *"frisky"* to that song and have ruined it for the rest of us. Mom says something about it makes her reminisce about when they became Blood Fated mates or whatever. Either way, it's freaking gross.

"They're nauseating," I cringe. "On the other hand, I guess now would be as good a time as any to sneak out."

"I gotcha covered," Ruby agrees. "I'll watch Lila. Unless you wanted to take her with you?"

"No, not yet. I'm not sure when or if I'm ever going to be ready for that …" I mumble as I look down to pick at a loose thread on my shirt.

"That's understandable."

"Thank you for everything you do, Ru," I say as I look up to meet her gaze, hoping she sees the genuine gratitude in my eyes.

"Just be safe."

"I will."

"Remember our code."

"Yes, I'll text you the word, 'red' if anything goes wrong."

"Promise?"

"Promise."

After a quick change of clothes, I make my way into Dad's home office and start with his computer, looking for any information he has on Conan. He definitely has the sources, and there's no way he hasn't been keeping tabs on him since he found out I was pregnant.

It doesn't take long to find the file Dad saved in a folder specifically for Conan. After scrolling through his school and hospital records, I see two addresses saved under his contact information. The first is his childhood home, Pack House in Riverstone; the second indicates a recent move to a rental house on the outskirts of Riverstone. The information for the address includes the move-in date—he rented the little place right after graduation—and has him listed as living alone.

Ensuring I've covered any evidence that'd tip off Dad I was digging around in his computer, I return to the home screen and leave the office. Then I sneak out to my SUV, the address ready in my phone's GPS.

The drive takes just over an hour and, as I get close to the small cabin, I see Conan's truck in the tiny attached carport.

I guess this is the place.

I turn off my lights as I slowly edge the car closer to the house, not wanting to give myself away just yet. There's always a chance he'll hear my car anyway, but I'd rather be safe than sorry. Parking a good distance from the front door, I crack the windows and turn off the engine so I can listen to my surroundings. I sniff the night air for scents of other wolves, but only pick up Conan's smell; I can tell he's spent a lot of time in wolf form. From what I can see—thanks to my excellent night vision—he does appear to be living alone. I don't see any other vehicles, and there are no other houses for miles. He seems to have completely isolated himself in the forest. A single light illuminates the window closest to the front door. It's faint, and keeps flashing, so I assume it's a TV.

Okay. Time to do this.

I climb out of my car and close the door as quietly as possible, freezing to scan the area and listen for sounds of unexpected guests, using every one of my heightened senses.

But nothing appears to be close by other than the expected wildlife.

This is probably really stupid. I could totally get back in the car and drive home without being detected, but ... I know I'll regret it if I tuck my tail and run home. I need closure—not only for me, but for Lila, too.

With one last scan of the area, I release a shaky breath and use every bit of stealth I possess to silently make my way to the front door. A million questions run through my mind as my heart begins to race with anxious anticipation.

Why did he move so far out of Riverstone's city limits?

Was he distancing himself from his pack?

Was he even still in a pack?

Is this still part of his pack territory?

How is he going to respond to me just popping up here unannounced?

As I approach the front door, I can hear the muffled sounds of an action movie coming from inside.

Is this nerd watching Iron Man right now?

Shaking off the random thought, I give one final sniff to make sure I don't scent any other wolves, but I still only smell Conan. I listen for any other voices and only hear Robert Downy Jr. After a few minutes, a commercial replaces the movie.

It's now or never.

I bite my lip and raise my hand to softly knock on the door.

CONAN

I'm just starting to doze off to the sound of some infomercial about a fancy blender when I could swear I heard a knock on the door. I startle fully awake, sitting up straight on the couch as I wait to see if I hear it again.

Was that really a knock?

Or a stupid tree branch smacking against the house again?

I do live in the middle of nowhere...

My little bachelor pad is on the border of my dad's pack territory, smack dab in the middle of the wooded mountains, so it's not normal for me to have a random visitor unless it's got something to do with pack business. I look at my phone to check the time—it's almost half-past two in the morning, and I've got no messages from Dad or the pack, so I shouldn't be expecting company ... But there it is again, louder this time.

Definitely a person and not a tree.

"I'm coming, I'm coming ..." I grunt as I stand up to stretch a bit before walking towards the front door.

I swear to fuck if Dad's pack is dropping by to give me some last-minute bullshit assignment I'll rip someone a new asshole.

I undo the locks, then swing open the door with a scowl.

"This had better be really fucking imp-" My voice cuts off and I freeze as the scent of green apples and vanilla envelopes me, and I'm met with two very nervous, very purple eyes staring up at me.

Crystal is standing on my fucking porch.

I try to speak, but nothing comes out, so all I can do is gape at her as if she's a ghost.

"We need to talk," she says, her voice barely above a whisper, and I glance down to see she's spinning her trademark opal ring around her finger.

The sound of her voice breaks whatever spell's been paralyzing me, and I don't even think, I just move. As if on autopilot, my arms reach out and snatch her up. A startled squeak escapes her throat as I hold her tightly to my chest, burying my nose in her hair. Her scent is a soothing balm to the ache that's been haunting my chest for too long.

"Conan-!" She gasps as she places her palms against my chest out of what seems to be reflex more than anything.

"You're really here …" I mutter into her hair, clutching her so tightly I hear a startled breath escape her lungs. "This time I can actually feel you …"

Ever since our last encounter in the woods, I've dreamed about her constantly, only to wake to a cold and empty bed. Just holding her, feeling her warmth, is a fix to the withdrawals every part of me has been going through without her.

But now it's her turn to freeze, She doesn't speak for a moment, allowing me to soak up every precious second of having her in my arms again. Then it ends all too soon when she gives a hard shove, forcing me to release her.

"Get off!" she shouts, and I swear it feels like she takes a chunk of my heart with her as she puts several inches between us.

We're a little over a foot apart in height, so her feet hadn't been fully on the ground while I held her, and she stumbles backward a bit. Her eyes are wide and fearful, and her heart is beating at an inhumanly fast rate, reminding me of a cornered rabbit.

"Sorry, sorry! It's just that Nero and I are so happy to see you and-" I pause, taking a few seconds to really look at her. "Your hair!"

Her waist-long curtain of silver locks is gone, replaced with a pixie cut. It's quite a drastic change from the last time I saw her.

"What about it?" she snaps defensively.

"It looks good ..." I murmur, sweeping my eyes over her face ... her bare neck ... "*Really* good."

Don't get me wrong, I adored her long hair, but damn does her uncovered neck look more appetizing than ever.

She blinks in surprise, obviously caught off guard by my answer. I suppose she was mentally preparing herself for my disapproval. Granted, I'm such an outspoken and opinionated dick, I can't really blame her.

"Whatever," she grumbles, "can you go put on a damn shirt?"

Her eyes bouncing around, looking everywhere but at me. I frown and glance down at myself. I'm only wearing a pair of sweatpants, but it's not like I'm completely naked or anything. And, let's be honest, she's already seen everything there is to see on my body, hence why we have a daughter.

"Why?" I ask, raising an eyebrow at her in confusion.

"Because it's really fucking distracting!" she snaps as she stares down at her black combat boots.

"Really?" I can't help but smirk, then lean against the front door to close it behind her, lingering there to look down at her.

Crystal grumbles something so incoherent even my wolf's ears can't pick it up.

"What was that?" I ask, tilting my head as I continue to stare at her.

She presses her perfect pouty mouth into a firm line and continues to glare down at her boots but, thanks the shorter hair, I can still see her cheeks as they begin to turn pink.

"Are you seriously blushing right now?" I can't help but chuckle.

She puffs her cheeks in her irritation, finally looking up to glare purple daggers at me.

"No!" she says a little too defensively, and we both know she's lying.

"Why am I not surprised?" I shake my head, letting out a light chuckle. She's still the same little flustered firecracker, I'm happy to see.

"Shut up, Conan!" she says, lifting her hands. "Don't think I won't use my powers to freeze your smug ass!" she warns as her hands begin to glow a soft, icy blue, and I notice the faintest bit of frost beginning to form in the middle of her palms.

Nero is absolutely loving how much of a little badass she's trying to be. I feel him rising closer and closer to the surface as an amused growl leaves my throat, causing her brow to furrow as she takes a step back, now fully pressed against my front door. I notice her left hand reaching behind her for the knob, and Nero begins to completely lose his mind.

"Fine then, freeze my ass if you want. I can't take it anymore." I grunt, not needing a mirror to know my eyes have gone gold.

"Conan–" She gasps before I cut her off by pinning her to the door.

In one swift motion, I have her lifted by her bottom, my mouth immediately crushing hers as she instinctively wraps her legs around my waist for balance. She stiffens at first, then —much to my and Nero's delight—she allows her body to relax and melt into mine. My tongue begins to trace her lower lip between nips of my now-elongated canines, and she parts her lips to allow me to deepen the kiss. Something between a growl and a purr rumbles out of my chest as my tongue begins to explore every inch of her mouth.

I couldn't stop myself even if I wanted to. What I feel right now is primal, and Nero quickly begins to take control. He and I both share the same thought: that we never want to let her escape our grasp, ever again.

I grip her short hair with one hand, grinding against her, which causes her to let out the softest sigh of contentment. My heart immediately swells with relief as I began to lift her black shirt over her head.

"I need your skin against mine. Now," I growl against her lips.

We break the kiss just long enough for her to help me pull off the shirt, then my lips are back on hers as I begin to unclasp her lacy, hot-pink bra. Once it's on the floor, I kick both articles of clothing away with my foot, and shove myself into her, chest to chest, revelling in how complete her bare skin against mine makes me feel.

It's not long before I feel desire pooling in my abdomen and, out of reflex, I grind my hips against hers. She's wearing a thin pair of black leggings, so I know she can feel every bit of me through my sweats. A soft moan escapes her throat, and I smell her arousal, causing Nero to nearly go into a full-blown frenzy. With an impatient growl, I move with lightning speed toward my bedroom, feeling her surprised gasp against my mouth.

Laying her down on my mattress, I frame her with my arms as her legs slowly fall away from my waist. Breaking the kiss in short intervals, I reach down to pull off her boots and toss them across the room before I start pulling at her leggings.

To my surprise, she doesn't fight me, not even once. It's like we're both in a frenzy of tension from the hormones so obviously crackling through the air between us. After removing my own pants, I lean back over her. Her face turns a brighter shade of red, and she looks away from me.

"Hey," gripping her chin, I force her to face me. "Don't

hide those pretty eyes from me," I say, unable to suppress a cocky grin.

She looks up at me, scowling. She's trying her best to look annoyed and dominant, but her eyes betray her. I can see the lust in them, the confusion, and most importantly … the fear.

And that breaks my fucking heart.

I bend down to kiss her softly, cupping her face with the hand I had on her chin. Her eyes flutter closed, and she hesitates for just a moment before kissing me back. After a few minutes, I slowly break the kiss to begin nuzzling her neck. Her breath catches in her throat, and she tenses for a moment before relaxing as I begin to trail kisses down to her breasts. The air she sucks in through her teeth as she grabs a fistful of my hair is music to my ears.

Slowly, I raise myself back up and look down at her; she's staring back at me, her eyelids heavy, and playing with my hair.

"Let me show you how much I missed you," I murmur softly before I begin to trail more kisses down her body and spread her legs. She doesn't fight me at all. If anything, she's trembling with what I assume to be excitement.

Once I've settled myself between her thighs, I kiss the inside of each, and she bucks her hips in surprise as she lets out a startled moan. I grip her hips with my hands, forcing her to stay still as my tongue begins to explore the rest of her. She tastes so fucking good. Soon, her legs begin to shake, and I push one finger inside her to begin stroking her sweet spot as my tongue continues to do sinful things. In seconds, she begins to moan, and her body convulses with pleasure. I take this opportunity to remove my finger, and sit up on my knees to ready myself between her legs, teasing her.

She lets out an annoyed noise, and I push myself inside her before she can make any other complaints. With a gasp, she starts to move her body in sync with mine. I bend down to nibble her earlobe as I savor the glorious feeling of every stroke, taking my time to revel in this body I missed so badly.

"I fucking missed you, baby," I whisper into her ear as I begin to pick up the pace.

She gasps in surprise, then begins to moan louder, her nails digging into my back. Nero is absolutely loving any mark she leaves on him and keeps pushing closer and closer to the surface. He reaches that thin line of control just this side of shifting and, as he looks at her through my eyes, I can see their brilliant gold glowing reflected in Crystal's heavy-lidded gaze. She notices, and her eyes widen in a mixture of surprise and wonder.

"I'm never letting you go again. You hear me? You're *mine*," my voice is full of gravel as I try to keep a hold on Nero and not shift.

The scent of her arousal thickens the air around us as she closes her eyes and tightens her grip to pull me closer. I can't help but smirk at how my words are affecting her.

"Mine," I repeat into her ear, and I feel her shudder in pleasure beneath me. "Say it," I demand, dominance dripping from my voice.

"Conan ..." she tries to argue, but another moan cuts off any protest she wanted to make.

I lick and nip her ear with the impatience building inside me.

"I wanna hear you say it," I say as I move my lips back down her neck. "Admit you're mine, baby," I growl between nips.

"Yours," she pants, "I'm yours."

Her words fuel me into a full-blown frenzy and, with canines fully extended, Nero takes the opportunity to clamp down on her neck to mark her as ours … and I don't stop him.

Crystal lets out a shocked gasp mixed with a whimper. She winces, then I feel her body begin to relax and she's letting out soft sounds of pleasure again. A shiver runs down my spine, followed by tingling from my scalp down to my toes; then I feel Crystal begin to shiver in the same way under me.

Canines still deep in her neck, I feel her pulse quicken and start to taste her sweet blood beginning to pool around the bite as I feel my body reaching the ultimate high. Another growl escapes my throat as I shudder in pleasure before collapsing on top of her.

We lie there for a few minutes, my canines still buried in the crook of her neck as we both breathe heavily. After our hearts begin to slow and the lustful fog dissipates from my brain, I slowly retract my canines from her flesh and clean the punctures with my tongue. She plays with my hair as I do, and we stay like that until the bleeding has almost completely stopped.

I raise my head and look down at her face. Her eyes are closed, and her short hair is sticking to her forehead with sweat. I gently grasp her chin and move her head to the side so I can examine my mark.

She's mine. That mark isn't going anywhere. She's mine, forever.

After releasing her chin, I slowly roll over to pull her into my side. Nero is practically purring with satisfaction. I can feel how much he's enjoying covering her with his scent.

"That was a hell of a love bite," Crystal says between pants, lifting her hand to gingerly circle the small holes with her fingers. "Although it should be healing up by now …"

"That's more than a love bite, C," I murmur, burying my nose in her hair.

"Huh?"

"I just marked you. Well, Nero did. And I didn't stop him."

"I'm sorry, what?!" She pushes me away so she can look up at me, confusion and disbelief painted all over her face.

"You're my mate, C. It's you. It's always been you. That's why I could never stay away and kept finding myself craving your presence no matter how hard I fought it." I gently cup her face, rubbing my thumb back and forth against her cheek.

Her eyes widen in shock and she stutters for a few seconds before shaking her head and sitting up straight.

"Are you sure?! How do you know?!"

I sit up as well, taking hold of her arms as I look into her eyes. "I'm very, very sure. Nero has made that quite clear." In my mind's eye, I can see the bastard puffing his chest with pride.

"But," Crystal shakes her head, "I thought only a Pure Blood vampire could ..."

This time I grab her face with both hands, lowering myself as far as I can comfortably go to stare into her eyes. "Apparently, a Pure Blood werewolf can too."

Her eyes begin to shine with emotion as she begins to shake her head back and forth. "There's ... There's no way ..."

I gently but firmly hold her head still and, although she can no longer shake her head, she keeps her eyes tightly closed.

"Crystal," I begin to softly massage her temples with my thumbs, "I know you can feel it." She slowly opens her eyes, worrying her lip with one tiny fang peeking out. "Tell me the truth, C. You can feel the mate bond, can't you?"

She doesn't say anything, instead she just continues to worry her lip. Eventually, the dam inside her shining eyes breaks and several tears make their way down her cheeks. I smooth them away with my thumbs, never taking my eyes from hers. I can feel they're back to their normal green, so she knows it's all me and not Nero's animalistic influence. Finally, she nods once, then wraps her arms around my neck as a sob escapes her throat.

"I … I feel it. I feel you. I feel this connection, it's …" her voice breaks.

I wrap my arms around her and turn us to lie on our sides, her arms still wrapped around my neck as she cries into my shoulder.

"I know, it feels foreign to you since you're not a wolf … It's gotta be really weird," I chuckle softly as I rub the back of her head.

The short tufts at the base of her neck feel so strange against my hands. I comb my fingers through it, wrapping my other arm around her back to hug her to me. I try my best not to crush her and have to force myself to make the embrace firm but not so tight so she can't breathe.

"You love me so much," she says, barely above a whisper, "I … I can feel you're not lying. You really, *really* love me. I can feel how protective you are, and how much it pains you to have hurt me, and … and just … everything! I feel everything!"

I feel her tears as they seep down the crook of my neck, all the way down my shoulder. Soon, even part of my chest begins to feel wet.

"I do, I am, and it does." I continue to just hold her as she cries. "Do you believe me, now? You're my mate. We're each other's mates," I whisper into her hair.

For some reason, that makes her cry even harder, but I feel

her nod her head between sobs. I kiss the top of her head, and just hold her as she processes it all. I know, after everything she's been through, it has to be a lot. She's mine, and now she knows she has a mate after thinking there was no one for her. She can't hate herself for being a dhampir anymore, I just claimed her for who she is.

Even though the mating bond isn't complete yet—she still has to bite me back—it doesn't take a genius to guess what's going on in her head. After I completely shattered her heart, she can feel how desperate I am to do anything to pick up the pieces and put us back together. After probably hating my guts for months, she's now overwhelmed by my love for her, and knows it's true and sincere.

"I love you." It's the only thing I can think to say.

"I love you, too," she whimpers into my neck, and I feel her squeeze my neck for emphasis before she goes back to sniffling.

"Bite me back."

"What?"

"Mark me as yours. Bite me back."

She finally lifts her head, her puffy, purple eyes filled with confusion. I begin to wipe away more tears with my thumbs, feeling my lips curve up into a small smile.

"I know you're not a wolf, but surely you can feel it's the right thing to do. You have fangs, use them to complete the mating bond."

"It'll work? Like … My bite will stay as your mark, too?" Her voice is a hoarse whisper, her brow furrowed in deep thought.

I nod. "Yes. I have zero evidence to back it up, since I don't know any other wolves with dhampir mates, but my instinct's telling me I'm right. What's your gut telling you?"

She pauses to chew on her lip for a couple seconds. "It's

telling me you're right. But … what if this is a mistake or fluke? What if my bite doesn't serve the same purpose as a wolf's? What if-" I silence her with a kiss, rolling over so that she's on top of me.

"Just bite me, Fangs," I say with a chuckle when I finally break the kiss.

She scrunches up her nose, then sighs. Slowly, she moves her head toward the left side of my neck to the same spot where I marked her. My heart begins to speed up with anticipation, my hand moving to the back of her neck to guide her. She kisses the spot, and another pleasurable shiver makes its way down my spine. She snakes her arms behind each of my shoulders, kissing the spot again, and I have to stop myself from moaning. I'm just beginning to wonder how long she's going to torture me when I finally feel the sharp sting of her little fangs piercing my flesh, and the air leaves my lungs.

All at once her emotions slam into me as if they're my own. I'd already been highly attuned to them before, but now it's amplified. I feel her love for me. I feel her pain because of me. I feel her nervousness that we're wrong about being mates. I feel as that nervousness melts away when she feels the bond complete. I feel her relief, her happiness, her … not knowing exactly what to feel as a bunch of emotions tackle her at once.

She lifts her head, then begins to lick the bite, and I feel her surprise.

"Your blood …" She laps up more, "it tastes … good."

"Is that bad?" I say with a lighthearted laugh.

"No, no. It's just, wolves are supposed to taste wrong to us. You … You really *are* my mate. You taste like, like …"

"Like …?" I prompt her, eager to hear the rest of that sentence.

"Like you're made for me. Like I can't get enough of you,"

she whispers before licking the two punctures again, and this time I can't stop the moan from escaping my throat.

To my disappointment, she lifts her head, wiping the corners of her mouth with the back of her hand.

"You can drink from me as much as you want." I tell her, tempted to guide her mouth back down to my neck.

"No," she shakes her head, "I could risk actually feeding from you and having my body go into recharge mode. I need to be able to stay awake and drive back home before anyone starts asking questions. Staying here for a whole day unable to answer anyone would be a horrible idea."

"I could answer for you," I reply quickly, "I could text whatever you want me to say to make it a legit excuse. You could recharge here, and-"

"Conan," she places one finger to my lips, silencing me. "I have to get back to Lila." Her smile is sad, and I can feel how badly she wants to stay with me. But I know she's right, and my heart sinks at the thought of her leaving me to go back home.

"Right. Of course." I nod in agreement.

Her sad smile lingers for a moment, then she begins to roll off me, and I have to fight the urge to pull her back. I want her skin against mine forever. The absence of her warmth leaves a cold, empty feeling inside me. I can feel Nero's displeasure as I watch her reach down to fish her phone out of her leggings pocket.

"I've already been here too long. I need to go." She sighs, and I can feel her sadness match my own. She surprises me by crawling back onto my chest to hug me.

"Five more minutes, and I have to leave," she mumbles into my chest.

"Five more minutes," I echo, and rest my chin on top of her head, holding her as close as possible, savoring every precious second. "Can you ever forgive me?" I whisper into her hair.

"Of course I can, you idiot," she says before planting a kiss on my chest. "Would be kinda hard not to forgive your soulmate now, wouldn't it?"

"I love you. I love you so much," I say before kissing the top of her head.

"I love you, too," she whispers back.

"Happy birthday, C." I smile as I tilt her chin up to plant a kiss on her lips, then rest my cheek on top of her head as we both allow the other to feel the mating bond snapping into place.

"I need to get back," she whispers all too soon.

"I don't want to let you go," I grunt as I squeeze her closer to me.

"I don't want to either, but my family …"

"I know," I begrudgingly release her from my embrace. "I guess we need to keep this a secret for now." I feel Nero's hackles rise in displeasure at the thought of not being able to show off his mate.

"Yeah," Crystal nods. "Until we can figure out what to do."

I fold my arms behind my head as I watch her slowly sit up, her fingers lightly rubbing over my mark on her neck. My eyes trail up to her face, then slowly down the rest of her body.

"What is it?" Crystal asks, lifting a blonde brow at my staring.

"Just taking in how different you look."

"Good different?"

"Very."

She smiles, biting her lip as she looks down to fidget with her opal ring.

"Don't get me wrong, I absolutely adored your long hair." I prop myself up on my elbow to face her better. "But that cut looks great on you ... And it shows off my mark better," I say with a wink, earning an eyeroll from her.

"Yeah, thank God it's fall, so I can hide it with scarves and turtlenecks for a while ... I'll have to experiment with makeup, too," she thinks out loud as she absentmindedly continues to rub her fingers over the bite mark.

My eyes flash wolf as I feel Nero rise to the surface, and a whiny growl escapes my throat before I can stop it. Crystal immediately jerks her head in my direction, eyes widened in surprise.

"Oh, stop it! You know it's just until we figure out what to do." She gives my shoulder a playful shove.

"*I* know that. Tell Nero, not me," I say, forcing my eyes back to their normal green and Nero back toward my subconscious.

"I'm just glad he likes me now," Crystal chuckles.

"Oh, he much more than *likes* you. He's especially happy to see you wearing that necklace," I say as I reach up to touch the wolf-shaped quartz on the chain around her neck.

Her cheeks turn a bright shade of pink as she looks down at it, smiling sheepishly. I'm honestly surprised she still has it. I figured she would've thrown it away after I broke her heart. I can feel through our mating bond how much that silly little birthday gift from what feels like forever ago means to her, which only makes my heart overflow with more relief and joy.

"Looks like both of us got a couple of new piercings, too." She points to the silver stud in her nose then reaches to touch the tiny piercings in my ears.

"And some new tattoos ..." I mutter as I rub my thumb

along on her forearm, where a purple flower with Lila's name inside its stem decorates her skin.

"It's an Aster, her birth flower," she explains with a smile before pointing to the blue center, "with her birth stone, a sapphire, in the center."

I smirk, then guide her hand to my upper arm. Her eyes widen with surprise as she notices the tiny paw print blended into my half sleeve of random designs.

"Pup," she whispers, eyes misting with emotion as her fingers trace the small letters underneath the paw print.

It's not immediately obvious, but if you're looking for it, it's there. I nod and feel the happiness swelling up inside her chest as if it were my own.

"You got a tattoo for her?" Her eyes shining with more tears, she continues to trace the design.

"Hidden in plain sight. I know where it is, but no one else is going to notice it, so it won't grab unnecessary attention. Plus, I'll lie my ass off if by chance someone does ask."

"What about the artist? Didn't they ask?"

"I went to a human tattoo artist out of town. He didn't ask, and just seemed to care about making money."

She bites her lip, smiling as she continues to stare at it while rubbing her own tattoo for Lila. With a sigh, she finally stands up and begins to reach for her clothes.

"I guess you've really got to go now, huh?"

"Yeah ..."

I roll out of bed and slip into my sweatpants.

"I'll walk you out," I say once she's dressed.

With a nod, she heads out of my room, and I place a hand on the small of her back as we make our way back toward the living room. Just as we reach the couch, Crystal skids to a halt and covers her mouth in surprise. Thanks to the mating bond, I can tell it's a pleasant surprise, but I'm still confused until I look in the same direction. Embarrassment flushes my cheeks when I realize she's staring at the opened Amazon boxes full of random baby things.

"Did you buy all of this for Lila?" she asks, turning to look up at me.

"Yeah." I clear my throat. "I don't know much about babies, but ..." She cuts me off with a tight hug.

"That's so sweet!" she exclaims with a sniffle.

"Hey, hey! I don't want you crying when you have to drive!"

"I'll be fine." She pulls away and begins to rummage through the boxes.

"Conan, this is all perfect! She's growing so fast; all these different sizes will come in handy."

"I, ah, figured. I wasn't sure, but I know werewolf pups grow pretty quick, so ..."

"You did so good! I won't bring anything now, because of your scent, but ..."

"I understand."

"I'm also going to have to scrub myself in the shower, and immediately wash my clothes," she sighs.

"Okay," I answer before Nero can start pouting again. "Be safe going home. Please let me know when you make it back."

I feel Nero huff in disapproval. He wants his mate here with us or, failing that, would much rather she stay covered in his scent if she has to go.

Trust me, I want that, too.

"I'll try my best to swing by tomorrow. I think I'll be able to sneak away again," Crystal says as she retrieves her keys from her pocket.

"Don't get into any more trouble on my account. I know

the mating bond is going to try to push you to be around me as much as possible, but…"

"It should be fine. I'll text you and let you know for sure."

"Until tomorrow, then," I say, hugging her one last time.

"Until tomorrow," she murmurs into my chest.

And, with a heavy heart, I walk her outside, help her into her car, and watch her drive away.

CRYSTAL

I arrive home unnoticed. After texting Conan to let him know I arrived safe and sound, I fill Ruby in on what happened. She seems honestly happy for me and promises to keep my secrets. Not only is she super-supportive, she insists on keeping Lila in her room while I shower and change into clothes that don't reek of Conan. I'm careful to wash myself with the strongest smelling soap and shampoos I have.

Twice.

As I stand under the hot spray, my head pounds at the thought of everything that just happened and how permanently my life changed in a single night. A million questions, scenarios, and fears play through my mind as I watch the water swirl down the drain.

There's still so much to figure out.

Soon. But not tonight.

CONAN

THE NEXT DAY
HALLOWEEN

"Are you sure you don't wanna come out? The party is all people you know," Rider's voice pleads in my ear as I balance my cellphone between my cheek and shoulder, my hands busy preparing dinner.

"Sorry, dude. I've gotta get all these files ready to email to Dad. Rain check?" I apologize as I begin to drain noodles through a colander in the sink. I hear him sigh in exasperation, and I feel guilty. But only for a second.

"I'm worried about you, dude. You don't leave that house for anything lately. Want me to come over after I leave here?" he asks, sounding genuinely concerned.

"No!" I blurt out, then quickly clear my throat, trying my best to calm my tone before continuing, "Ah, I mean, no thanks. I appreciate the offer, but I'm really okay. How about we shoot some pool next weekend? You can punch me square in the forehead if I try to get out of it," I chuckle.

"I'm gonna hold you to that. I'll pick you up if I have to," Rider replies with a laugh of his own.

"You got it. I gotta go, but you have fun tonight. Tell Mikayla I said hello."

"Is he seriously not coming? Conan! Your bestie misses you! Quit being a hermit!" I hear Mikayla yell in the background.

"Catch you later," Rider says with a chuckle, then the line goes dead.

I let out a slow exhale as I place my phone back down on the counter with my free hand, stirring the sauce with the other.

That was way too close.

I trust Rider. He's one of my oldest friends. But, I'm not quite sure how he'd react to a dhampir coming over to my house if he showed up.

A dhampir that also happens to be my mate.

Speaking of mates, ever since Rider marked Mikayla, they've been inseparable when she's not busy with her duties as her pack's Beta. I have zero idea how she'd respond to Crystal, either. She seems nice enough, but I'm not even ready to tell my best friend I'm mated and a father, much less his mate. Or anyone else, for that matter.

I hear my phone chime to alert me of a new text message, and I look down to see that Crystal is letting me know she's here. I quickly type a reply letting her know that I'm finishing up dinner, and to let herself in, before setting my phone back on the counter. My heart warms at the idea of her already coming back to see me so soon, even though the night without her felt like a lifetime of emptiness. Nero was restless, too, not liking the idea of his mate and pup being anywhere other than under his protection.

I hear the front door open, and feel a smile spread across my lips.

"Conan?" Crystal calls from the living room.

"Hey!" I call over my shoulder. "Come on in! Feel free to help yourself if you haven't eaten dinner yet!"

I hear her footsteps enter the kitchen behind me, and I grab a nearby dishtowel to wipe my hands as I turn to face her.

"I'm so glad you were able to–" My heart skips a beat and I freeze when I notice the little tuft of dark hair, *my* dark hair, peeking out from the bundled black blanket she's carrying.

Oh my God.

"We're both happy to be here," Crystal says sheepishly.

I dart over with inhuman speed to stand in front of her, my heartbeat pounding in my ears as I look down at the bright purple eyes—*her* purple eyes—staring up at me from within that blanket.

"You brought her with you," I whisper, gently grabbing her arms as I lean down closer to look at my daughter's face.

"Tell your daddy Happy Halloween!" Crystal says with a grin as she wiggles a finger in front of Lila's face.

"Oh my God. Her first holiday," I watch Lila grab Crystal's finger with a firm grip.

"Her Auntie Ruby had fun using her to get candy earlier," Crystal chuckles, looking up to meet my gaze.

I glance up at her and laugh, then can't help looking back down at Lila.

"Of course she did." It's then I notice Lila appears to be in some sort of pumpkin onesie, and the black blanket is decorated with tiny pumpkins and candy corn. I crouch down to get a better look at her, smiling.

"I've missed you so much, Pup," I gently rub my palm over her head. My hand looks huge compared to her tiny face. "Every day," I add, feeling my throat tighten.

"Here, take her," Crystal says, surprising me when she places Lila's small body in my arms, which seem to swallow her up. "Just watch her head."

I slowly straighten my spine to stand up as I look down at my beautiful little baby. I purse my lips together and clear my throat as she blinks up at me, making soft little cooing noises.

"Thank you," I say, glancing at Crystal. "You have no idea how much this-" My voices cracks, and I swallow hard. My heart has never felt so full. I never knew it was possible to love someone—someone I've only met twice—this much. I already know without a doubt that I would die for her. Anything and everything I do will revolve around this tiny little pumpkin in my arms.

"I know." Crystal lays a hand on my arm. She can undoubtedly feel the emotions bubbling through me.

I'm not sure how long I stare at our baby girl, memorizing every little detail, before I clear my throat again and look up.

"You're not risking anything by bringing her here, are you?" I ask, unable to hide the concern in my tone.

"No, we're fine. I take her for drives when she can't sleep, so it's nothing out of the ordinary." Crystal replies with a shrug, and I feel my shoulders sag in relief.

"We just can't stay for very long just in case ... I'm sorry."

"I'll take any time with her over nothing," I reply honestly.

"Also, there's something else I wanted to talk to you about while I'm here ..." Crystal says. I can feel that she's got butterflies in her stomach. She's not scared, but she's nervous about whatever it is.

"Anything, what is it?"

"It can wait a few minutes. Enjoy your time with your daughter for now."

"Gladly."

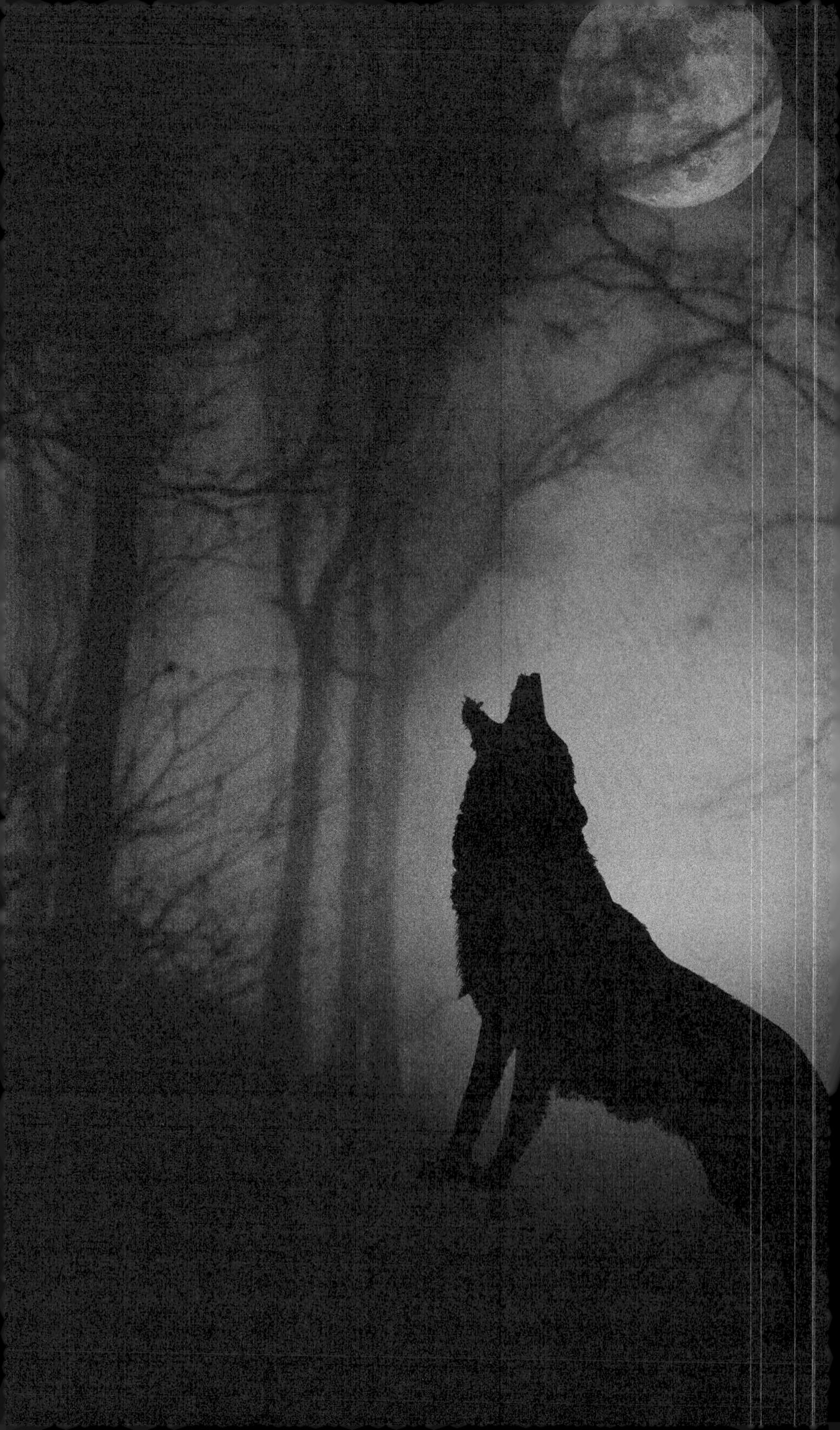

Five

CONAN

As pups, we're always told how hard it is for a werewolf to be away from his mate. A lot of wolves dream about finding their mates, a lot of them are scared they'll never find them. And—if you're like me—you roll your eyes at the adults and care less whether you even have one or not.

Now, here I am, eating my own words.

These past few days without Crystal have been torture. I honestly can't decide which is worse; her being away from me, unmarked, when I only suspected she was my mate, or her being away from me after claiming each other as true mates. Her scent lingering on my sheets was a comfort at first, but now it's slowly starting to fade and they only smell like me again.

Even though we've been in near-constant contact by phone, it still feels like the other half of me is missing. I'm just as restless as Nero, and the fact that she doesn't know when she'll be able to sneak away again has been pouring gas on the fire growing inside me. I want her and my pup here where I can see them, protect them, hold them.

I surprised Dad by volunteering to cover more patrol shifts around pack territory just to keep myself busy. When I'm home alone, in that bed alone, my mind tends to wander too much and all I do is torture myself thinking about the moments I'm missing in Lila's life, when I've missed out on so much already. I'm forever grateful that Crystal brought her here to let me hold her for the first and—so far, at least—only time. Getting pictures and videos of her daily is better than nothing, but every instinct inside me is shouting to go to her.

I've been extra careful to keep my mark covered any time I'm in my human form around Mom, Dad, and the rest of the pack. Either I show up in wolf form to perform my patrols or other pack duties, or I've been careful to wear shirts or jackets that cover it. It drives Nero insane, because his instinct demands we show it off, brag about our mate, brag about our pup … But, instead, I have to pretend like neither of them exist—for their own safety. Luckily, Crystal's little fangs only left two small, round scars and they're easy to hide. A human may not notice at first glance, but a wolf would.

A wolf would also notice it isn't a wolf's bite.

As I finish my run in wolf form, I allow Nero to navigate while I think over all the recent, drastic changes in my life. Any plan I try to come up with to have Crystal and Lila here—or anywhere—with me always comes to a dead end.

If only I could tell Mom. I know she'd be shocked at first, but I feel like she'd fall in love with Lila as soon as she met her in person.

But, telling her and not having Dad find out ...

Is impossible.

He's a hard-ass, always putting the pack first, and won't budge on his prejudice towards vampires. He's always had unrealistic and unfair expectations of me, and lets his temper get the best of him. Despite all that, as his son, I've let most of that shit go. I know there's no changing him, and I'll never live up to his standards. At least he's a good leader, has always been faithful to Ma, and made sure we were sheltered and fed ... I guess.

But, now that I'm a father, I'll never understand his lack of paternal instinct. I've only seen Lila twice in person, and I already know I would burn the world to the ground for her. I only want her to be happy, safe, and never doubt how much I love her. She will *never* have to question how much she means to me as long as I live.

After arriving back at my cabin, I shift back and head inside to shower. Once I'm dried and dressed for the night, I check my phone for any missed notifications from Crystal.

FANGS

> I'm still not sure when I'll be able to sneak away.
>
> I'm sorry.

I can feel through our mating bond anytime she's severely upset, angry or distressed. I know she wants to be with me as much as I want to be with her, and that provides a small comfort.

> I know, it's okay.
> We're figuring things out as we go.

I heat up some leftover pizza, then park my tired body in my recliner to hopefully numb my brain on TV.

FANGS

I love you.

> I love you too.

CRYSTAL

"How long do you think you'll be able to keep hiding it?" Ruby asks from behind me.

    I glance up at her reflection in the mirror, the hand dabbing make up on my neck pausing in mid-air. Her worried eyes are fixed on my mark as she leans against the bathroom door.

"I have no idea," I sigh.

Vampires and werewolves have been using make up, clothing, and magickal glamors to cover bite marks for centuries. The Ravens even helped develop a waterproof concealer designed specifically to fill in any healed bites and make the flesh appear even and undamaged ... which I had Ruby grab from my mom's vanity for me to borrow without her noticing. Thankfully, we have the same golden skin tone, so it's perfectly color-matched; I could only wear scarves and turtlenecks for so long. But I have to be careful not to use so much she notices someone else has been using it.

Wolf bites are a lot harder to conceal than vampire bites, that's for sure. Dad marked Mom the night he changed her into a vampire with the Blood Fate, and she marked him in return. But vampire bites are subtler than wolf bites. I've known few vampires who were true Blood Fated mates, but even a regular bite when a vampire drinks from a human is a lot less obvious than what I've seen of wolf bites.

Mom and Dad's permanent marks are just two white circles of scar tissue, and I noticed that's how mine appears to have healed on Conan's neck, too. It stands out against his dark tan skin, so he still has to hide it, but *his* mark on the other hand ...

"Doesn't help that wolves have four canines instead of two," Ruby mutters behind me.

"Yeah ..." I grumble as I continue to dab the liquid on my neck.

I only have Conan's bite for reference, but I imagine all wolves mark their mates with the bigger four-pointed punctures that leave a deeper mark. Each fang left a shrivelled scar similar to what I've seen humans refer to as chicken pox scars, only a tad deeper. But their symmetry made it clear they were caused by a bite.

Once my neck appears smooth, I close the concealer's lid and hand the tube back to Ruby. A thousand thoughts begin to race through my mind as I lightly fan the area, willing it to dry faster.

"If you have any ideas on how to explain to our parents that Conan is my mate, and how I was able to find out he was, I'm open to suggestions."

"Mom will take it better than D-Dad."

"No shit, Sherlock."

"Hey!"

"Ow!" I chuckle after Ruby pinches me hard on the arm. "I was just teasing, Ru!"

"I know this entire family uses humor as a coping mechanism, but this is serious. You really need to figure out what to do," she says quietly as she slides the concealer into her back pocket.

"I know, I know." I release a slow sigh through my nose before checking one last time to make sure my mark is fully covered. "We're ... We're working on it."

"What does that mean?"

"We've been in constant contact with each other and have been trying to brainstorm."

"Any ideas that seem promising yet?"

"No."

"Cici ..."

"We talk about it every day, Ruby," I say as I turn to face her, "I swear. It's a priority for both of us. We both hate covering our marks around our family. I don't see how mated couples do it so easily just to be around humans. This sucks."

"Really?" she asks, face softening once she realizes I'm being genuine.

I nod.

"It's like an instinct, I guess. It just feels …wrong. Like I'm defacing it."

Not to mention how my body physically aches at being away from him ever since he marked me.

"It makes sense."

"Yeah?"

"I could go into detail of my hypothesis behind it being tied to a natural instinct, if you'd like."

"I'm good."

"That's what I thought," she chuckles.

"I like to read for fun and all, but you're a whole new level of bookworm. You like to *learn* for fun." I scrunch my nose in mock disgust.

"You learned how to play guitar for fun!"

"Guitar." I hold up one hand, "Scientific research articles." I lift the other. "Apples to oranges, Ru."

"I'm going to try and slip this back before Mom notices," Ruby says with an eye roll before turning on her heel.

"Thanks," I say, waiting for her to walk away a few steps before I reach out and pinch her hard on her left butt cheek.

"Hey! Cici, what the hell?!" Ruby gasps, covering her butt with her hands as she spins around to glare at me.

"Revenge."

"Face me next time, coward!"

I laugh as I watch her stomp out of my room, then glance at my phone for the time.

It's about time to feed Lila.

I notice I have a text message from Victor, and tap to open it.

Vic

> Metal Blog's live in thirty min.

I glance at the timestamp to see when he sent the text, and realize I have about nine minutes left.

> Me and Lila will be watching.

Vic
> Kiss her for me.

> Will do.

I smile as I slip the phone back into my pocket and make my way toward Lila's room. Once she's been fed, I begin to rock her in the rocking chair, making sure we're both comfortable before I pick up my phone and go to Metal Blog's website. I've only missed a few seconds of footage when I tap on the notification alerting me that they're currently live-streaming.

"Look Lila, see Vic?" I ask softly, angling the phone so we can both watch.

She doesn't seem interested in the slightest at first, but I notice her head jerk to follow the sound of Victor's voice on the phone as he answers a question about growing up in Romania.

She recognizes his voice.

"See? Vic's right there." I lightly tap a fingernail over

Victor's face on the screen, and her eyes widen as she listens to him.

Victor has kept true to his word about stepping up to play the father role for her, and the bond between them grows each time he visits. I feel a pang of guilt twist in my gut as I think about how he's going to react to my not telling him about Conan. Vic is my best friend, but I'm still not ready to tell him just yet. It was hard enough telling Ruby, but when it comes to Victor …

How do I explain to him that we're mates without him and Conan trying to kill each other? They didn't get along before our breakup, but now it'll be worse than ever.

Keeping any secret from Victor isn't fun, anyway. As soon as I figure out a way to tell him without bloodshed, I will. It hurts me every time he's over and loving on Lila to fill the role of her absent father, knowing that Conan is indeed very present and involved in her life now.

Lila and I watch Victor answer a few questions about his latest songs before the host plays a few snippets of Vic's music video, giving the viewers a sneak peek. I'm an extra in the video, and tap the screen with my nail again when I see myself come into view, dancing behind Victor as he sings.

"Look, there's Mommy," I say as I cuddle Lila closer and rest my cheek atop her head.

She quietly watches the screen while chewing on her fist, not showing any signs of recognizing me. I think she's more fascinated by all the different faces and colors flashing in and out of view, so it makes sense she perked up when she heard Victor's familiar voice.

The song's titled, "The Best Damn Day," and there's a scene where we're all in a limousine while Victor's singing. The extras and I were instructed to act as if we were celebrating or headed toward the best party of our lives. I smirk as Metal Blog's host pauses the video right when I shake a bottle of champagne and spray it directly into Victor's face.

"See that? Mommy got him good," I mumble against Lila's head. She stretches and grabs my necklace, probably wanting to place the crystal wolf in her mouth. "You'll appreciate it when you're older," I say with a chuckle, making sure the pendant stays in her hand.

"That's your best friend, Crystal Fox, right?" The host asks, pointing at the screen behind them.

"Yes. See how she treats me?"

I roll my eyes as the host laughs, and turn off the comments popping up under the live. The last thing I want is to see what millions of strangers have to say about me.

"She's sung with you for two of your songs and is now in your first music video, that's exciting!"

"She'll definitely be featured in more to come."

"She has a beautiful voice."

"She does."

"Social media has been referring to Crystal's voice as, 'hauntingly beautiful,' and often compares her to singers like Amy Lee and Sarah McLachlan."

"You know Sarah's song, Angel? The one that played for all the sad dog commercials."

"Yes?"

"You should hear Cici sing it."

"I imagine it's lovely."

"Not when she only sings it because she's eaten the last chicken wing, or taken my last cigarette."

"Ah, so she makes you feel like one of those dogs!" The host chuckles.

"That's putting it mildly," Victor scoffs.

I quickly exit the live to send Victor an angel emoji accompanied by the middle finger emoji.

I see his response at the top of my screen when I pull the live back up. He glances at his smartwatch and chews on his lip ring to hide a smirk.

He definitely saw my message.

"Crystal's made it clear she has no desire to pursue her own path in the music industry, do you know why that is?"

"She never makes any sense," Victor says with a shrug.

Asshat.

I giggle to myself and notice Lila perks back up as if she just noticed his voice again. I take advantage of her being distracted to tuck the wolf pendant into my shirt while she watches the screen.

"Your fans were happy to see a video on your channel of her covering "Toxic," by Britney Spears. That seemed to fuel the fire of speculation as to why she doesn't drop her own album."

The host pulls up a video of me performing the aforementioned song in my own rock version. It's weird seeing myself sing, I don't know how Vic does it. I got a little too into the song and ended up deepening my voice to add a few guttural screams. I'm not as talented as Victor, as screaming in the metal genre seems to be easier for men, but I'm not bad, either.

The host pauses the screen on an image of me playing the guitar, hair tumbling over my face. Victor recorded it right before I cut my hair.

"Now, a woman who can do a proper growl or scream in rock is always hot. I never knew a Britney Spears song could sound so badass." The host wags his eyebrows at Victor.

"She learned from the best," Victor says with a cocky grin, and I swear he turns to wink at the camera.

"I know you've repeatedly cleared the air about you two being only friends, but fans still seem to be 'shipping' you two. The hashtag #Victal has become pretty popular in the comments of any of your work she's featured in."

"They can ship all they want, but *Victal* ain't happening." Victor shakes his head.

"You heard it here, Victor Thorne is still denying any romantic involvement with billionaire Draken Fox's daughter," the host says directly into the camera, and I can tell Victor has to stop himself from cringing.

I full on cringe and crinkle my nose in disgust.

Really?

"Just had to throw out her family in some way for publicity, eh?" Victor asks, a finger tapping on the arm of his seat in annoyance.

"The Fox family has always been shy of the limelight, and Crystal not wanting to pursue music just fuels the speculation," the host replies with a shrug.

"I'm aware." Victor's tone conveys his boredom with the topic.

Dad always tries to keep us out of the media as much as possible. It's natural for famous vampires to not feel like answering the inevitable questions, such as what plastic surgeon they see to keep them looking so young. But Dad hates the idea of us being under a magnifying glass, with people watching our every move, anyway.

Thankfully, we never were on the same level of fame as lots of actors and musicians, no one at Riverstone Academy seemed to recognize me or care to mention it if they did. The times I have been recognized because of my father have been minimal compared to what other celebrity children have had to deal with, that's for sure. As a billionaire entrepreneur, Dad knows media attention is inevitable, but he's always been pretty slick when it comes to things about us he does and doesn't want out in the world. Keeping my pregnancy a secret was one of his biggest challenges.

I kiss Lila's temple as we continue to watch the interview and think to her, *I hope for the day I don't have to hide you from nosy humans or from vampires and wolves that wouldn't take the time to understand you.*

"Well, is there anyone special you're currently seeing? Might take some of the suspicion off Crystal if we have a name," the host asks in a voice that I'm sure he believes is smooth.

"My career doesn't allow time for a relationship right now."

"Didn't hesitate a bit, I guess you're telling the truth!"

"Always do."

"Well, you've promised our viewers a first listen of your new song. Shall we get to it?"

Victor nods and stands, then walks off to prepare.

"Smash that Like button and don't forget to subscribe and share to catch more exclusive sneak peeks like this!" The host practically gushes, beaming at the camera.

"Ready to hear Vic sing?" I whisper to Lila.

CONAN

"All right, I'm out," I grunt, setting the pool stick on the table.

"Sore loser!" Rider calls out, with Mikayla giggling in his lap.

I only came to keep Rider from getting worried enough to come by my cabin unannounced, and was barely paying attention to the game. I pocketed the eight ball on purpose to end the game early, but tried to be subtle about it.

This was our third match and I let Rider win two out of three. My dad had built this little "man cave," as he calls it, for the pack to have fun when they aren't on duty. Since it's basically in my parents' backyard, I'm able to drop by for a quick visit to keep them both off my ass for being antisocial. Two birds, one stone.

"Ready for me to whip your ass?" Mikayla asks Rider as she stands to retrieve the pool stick I just set down.

Mikayla and a few of her pack mates dropped by to mingle with ours, so I guess it's technically just a "wolf cave" for tonight.

"You can hope all you want, and I'll be glad to actually whip your ass later after I whip your ass in pool, if you ask nicely," Rider replies with a wink, and I watch as her cheeks redden.

"Get bent," she retorts as she turns away to hide her blush.

"Like I said, that'll be you later … *if* you ask nicely."

"Shut up," she snorts as she begins to set up for the next game.

"See you later, dude," Rider says as he makes his way over to me, bumping his fist against mine.

"Bye, Conan. Don't worry, I'll avenge you," Mikayla adds with a wave.

"Thanks," I chuckle. "Show no mercy."

The two begin to playfully argue as I walk out the door. I'm happy for Rider but, God, do I wish I could have my mate sit on my lap in front of the pack. I wish I could show her off as mine. I wish I could show off my daughter. I'm so thankful for every picture and video Crystal sends me, but it pains me to keep her a secret. I can't even have either of their pictures as my phone's wallpaper like every other mated father does.

I unzip my hoodie and turn the air on full blast once I'm inside my truck. I was burning up in there, and walking out into the cool night wasn't enough.

I can't wait until I don't have to hide my mark anymore … How am I going to survive the fucking summer?

I cringe slightly at the thought as I begin to drive back to my cabin.

We've got to find a way before then. I'm not sure if I can take another fucking week of this, much less a few months.

Every night I stare up at the ceiling trying to come up with some way for us to be together without any fucking drama. I swear I must've thought of every possible scenario, but nothing seems like it'll work out well for either of us.

When I arrive home, I kick off my boots and plop down into my recliner. I lean back and begin to mindlessly scroll through my phone, trying to distract myself. My thumb freezes when I notice Crystal's name in a headline attached to a video.

Metal Blog.

Victor.

I instantly feel myself growing agitated, even though I know I have no reason to be. I already believed Crystal before when she told me their relationship was platonic and, now that we're mated, I have all the more reason to not question it.

He still pisses me off.

I find myself watching a recorded live stream uploaded earlier today, even though I know it's just going to irritate me more. It sucks watching him, able to talk about her so openly to a large audience, when I have to keep her a secret.

I wonder if he knows.

Victor is Crystal's best friend, but something tells me I

would've received a visit from him by now if he knew. He's too protective of her and mad at me to stand by and not do *something*. At first, I'm jealous as I watch her in a clip of his stupid music video.

Her hair was still down to her waist. I wonder how long ago she filmed this?

I find myself smirking when she sprays him with a bottle of champagne.

Okay. That was satisfying.

I watch in awe as she sings some Britney Spears song, throwing her own her metal twist on it. I'll never get tired of her voice. I've missed the sound of it so much, I replay pieces of the video just to hear the parts that send a delightful shiver up my spine. My eyebrows shoot up in surprise when I allow the video to reach the end and see the mother of my child using her voice to growl and scream into the microphone.

Fuck, that was hot.

I replay that part a few times, too, before finally allowing the video to continue.

"Now, a woman who can do a proper growl or scream in rock is always hot. I never knew a Britney Spears song could sound so badass," the host says with an obvious lustful look in his eye.

Nero's hackles immediately rise and my jaw hurts as I grind my teeth in anger. I feel my canines threatening to elongate, and I know my eyes have to be flashing gold.

"She learned from the best," Victor's wink makes me roll my eyes, but Nero isn't threatened by him.

His personality in general still irritates the both of us, though. The dude's existence is just always going to be annoying, probably.

I hear a low, rumbling as the host goes on to pester Victor about the fans wanting him and Crystal to be together. After a second, I realize the sound is coming from me, and I'm not sure if Nero started growling or if I did. I have to restrain myself from gripping my phone hard enough to smash it.

This is your only form of communication with your mate and your daughter, I remind myself.

I'm still growling as they stop talking about Crystal and move on to a new topic. When I finally close the video, I notice I have a couple missed texts from Crystal, and force myself to take a few deep breaths and open them once I finally quit snarling.

A picture of Lila sleeping in Crystal's arms immediately turns my anger into sadness.

I can't take this anymore.

I scroll back to find the message where she sent me her address. Since we were both unsure when I'd see her again, I sent her a few things for Lila and made sure to put her name on the return address so it looked like she ordered them for herself.

100 Foxtrot Lane,

Twin Leaves, Colorado

Of course she lives on a street named after her family.

I knew Draken Fox was loaded, but was unaware exactly how famous he was until I heard that dipshit discuss how Crystal and her family have been kept out of the limelight by their dad.

God, I hope he was able to keep her pregnancy a secret.

I frantically type Crystal's name in the internet search bar, but see nothing about a baby. I see a few old pictures and videos of her, and a few articles mentioning her when the spotlight was on Draken, and that's it.

I never knew I could just look her up on Google. Her dad has his own freaking Wikipedia page.

The whole time she was in Riverstone, I never knew.

Then again, I never really stayed up to date with any news or trends. Hell, I barely get on social media. I prefer what's in front of me, instead of worrying about what other people are doing. But everyone at Riverstone Academy came from wealth, so it wouldn't have been much of a hot topic for people to talk about. Plus, Crystal's father is known for his wealth rather than acting, singing, or any shit like that. No one would really care to talk about her unless some scandal in her family was released to the press.

Like a teenage pregnancy.

I breathe a shaky sigh of relief, happy that Draken seems to know how to keep his personal life personal; then reopen Crystal's messages to look at my sleeping daughter's face again. I'm not sure how long I sit there before I finally stand up. The same instinct that forced me to go to the hospital the night she was born has me copying and pasting Crystal's address in my GPS. As if on autopilot, my feet slip themselves back into my boots, my hand picks up my keys, and I'm out the door.

CRYSTAL

"You okay?" Victor's voice interrupts my thoughts.

I've been staring at the screen for I don't know how long, hoping Conan will respond to the picture I sent him of Lila sleeping. I can feel through our mate bond he's upset. At one point, I could feel his anger so strongly I thought I might explode, then he settled back to irritated and sad. I can't feel every emotion he experiences throughout the day, but anytime something seriously distresses him, I feel it. And he's currently *very* distressed.

"Yeah, sorry. Spaced out." I force smile.

I type Conan a quick message asking if he's okay before placing my phone back into my pocket. Seconds seem like hours as I wait to feel it vibrate with his response.

Lila's been fussy all evening, and Victor has been trying his best to help me soothe her since he arrived after dinner. Mother's intuition is telling me she senses how upset I am, and I feel so guilty. Each day I'm unable to be near Conan is taking its toll, thanks to the mate bond. Right now, I can't tell who's feeling so antsy, me or him.

Both.

Once I started feeling Conan's distress, Lila started to become unsettled. The more I tried to calm her, the more I wound myself up. She was full-on crying when Victor showed up, and I was *this* close to crying along with her.

"Do you need a hug, too?" he asks with a smirk as he bounces Lila, unsuccessfully trying to distract her.

"Shit, maybe." My laugh is brittle, even to my ears.

I'm grateful for his company, since I'm all alone tonight. The twins are still out of state, and Mom and Dad took Ruby to some science museum she's been itching to visit in the next city over. I think they feel guilty about giving so much attention to me and Lila, so they set aside a night just for her. Which she absolutely deserves, so I'm not upset in the slightest. But boy does this big old house feel extra empty with no one inside it but me and Lila. When Victor texted me that he was going to stop by, I could've jumped for joy.

"Aren't you hot in that thing?" Victor asks.

"Huh?" I tilt my head in confusion.

"You're wearing a thick scarf indoors. How are you not dying? I know you've got an affinity for ice, but you're making me sweat just looking at you." He raises a pierced eyebrow.

"Oh, ah ... hormones. One minute I'm sweating, the next I'm freezing."

Its only partially a lie. Postpartum hormones did do strange things to my body, but I was actually unable to use any more of Mom's concealer. I'm uncomfortable, but a scarf was the only clean thing I had that would cover my mark. Since everyone was gone for the evening, I hadn't worried about it much and just threw it on when I found out Victor was on his way.

"Weirdo," Victor grunts.

"Shut up."

After what must be an hour, my phone finally vibrates and I have to force myself to look neutral as I retrieve it. Luckily, Victor is distracted, singing a song in Romanian to Lila. Her cries turn into whimpers. I swipe my thumb across the screen to open my messages, my heart fluttering when I see Conan's name.

Paws

> I'm outside.

What?!

I jerk my head toward the window and scan my eyes over the front yard, and sure enough I see a tall figure exiting a familiar truck parked in the driveway. My heart skips a beat as dread creeps over me. My stomach feels as if it's doing somersaults.

No, no, no, no! This cannot *be happening right now!*

"I'll be right back," I say in as calm a tone as I can muster as I quickly leave the room.

"Wha- Uh, okay?" I hear Victor say behind me before he resumes his song.

As soon as I'm out of the nursery, I all but fly down the stairs as I race to the front door, heart pounding in my ears. With a shaking hand, I fling open the door and feel the blood drain from my face as I see Conan inches away from me. As soon as his earthy scent hits my nose, my stomach fills with butterflies at the euphoria of having my mate at arm's length. But I just shake my head, and blink up at him.

"What are you doing here?" I ask, wondering if I look as frantic as I sound.

He nervously scratches at the small beard that's grown out on his chin, his eyes scanning behind me.

"I can't take it anymore, Crystal," he admits as his hazel-green eyes settle back to meet mine. There are bags under them, making him look like he hasn't slept in weeks.

CONAN

"Have you lost your mind?!" Crystal all but screeches at me as she grabs one of my arms and squeezes tightly.

Had I not been such a nervous wreck scanning for any signs of her parents every five seconds, Nero would've purred at finally feeling her touch.

"I'm tired of living in hiding. I want to talk to your parents." I gently remove her death grip on my arm, and then hold her hand between my own.

"I told you to wait!"

I brush my thumb over her knuckles, unsuccessfully trying to calm her. I open my mouth to speak, but she cuts me off.

"Do you have a death wish?!" she snaps as she jerks her hand away from mine.

She looks ready to push me toward my truck and I instinctively catch her wrist in my hand.

"I'd rather die than be away from you or our daughter any longer," I say truthfully.

Her brow furrows for a moment before panic and anger take over her features again.

"Conan, you know that since we-"

"Where are they, Crystal?" I ask, cutting her off.

"They're not here right now, but-"

"Then take me to see Lila. I want to see her before shit hits the fan." I use my size to force myself inside, causing her to step backward.

"Conan, listen to me! Y-"

Once I'm fully inside and close the door behind me, I try to scent Lila to find her myself. Another scent hits my nose just as I hear her cry.

"You've got to be fucking kidding me," I growl as I make my way to a set of stairs and begin to march up them.

"Wait, don't!" Crystal tries to grab my arm, but I use my superior speed to escape her grasp.

I hear her curse under her breath as she tries to catch up with me. I stop outside the open door of a pink room, and see Victor holding my baby, his back turned to me. Lila is still crying, and now I can see her little face showing how upset she is. Nero is absolutely nerve wracked and wants to jerk her out of his arms.

"What's the matter? Tell Dad all about it, da?" Victor coos

in a soft voice and I feel my canines lengthen as I process what I just heard him say to Pup.

My pup.

His head jerks in my direction when he hears the loud growl rumbling from my chest.

"What the *fuck* did you just say?"

Six

CONAN

"Stop it!" Crystal yells as my fist slams into Victor's jaw. I'm not sure exactly when Lila went from Victor's arms to hers, but I *do* know as soon as my Pup was out of harm's way, Nero nearly took over completely, and Victor and I have been in the hallway, beating the shit out of each other ever since.

Victor wipes at a bit of blood pooled in the corner of his mouth then gives me an icy-cold smile as his red eyes narrow on me. Before I can so much as blink, his fist pops me in the left eye.

Motherfucker, that hurt!

Guess Pretty Boy can actually fight.

"How *dare* you show your sorry face around here!" Victor says before shoving me so hard my back connects with the wall behind me, sending two large, framed pictures crashing to the floor.

He's strong, I'll give him that. Then again, I shouldn't expect anything less from Dracula's grandson with a pure vampire bloodline.

But not stronger than me.

Before I have the chance to snarl a retort, he pulls his fist back and appears to be aiming for my other eye.

The bastard wants to give me a matching set!

He's fast, but I block his punch and quickly hurl my own fist at his nose. He turns his face in the nick of time, and my knuckles collide with his pasty ass cheek instead.

"How dare *you* call yourself my kid's dad?!" I half yell, half growl, pulling my fist back to aim for his eye next.

An eye for an eye, dickhead.

With an almost feline speed and grace, Victor ducks and avoids the punch, then proceeds to hit me as hard as he can in the stomach. I feel the air leave my lungs, and backtrack a few steps to regain my composure.

"Because I've been here, where the hell have *you* been?" Victor sneers as he darts forward to catch up with me.

I feel his fist connect with my left cheek bone three times before I'm finally able to grab his arm with my right hand, then swing back at him with my left. The sound of his teeth clacking together as I uppercut his jaw is music to my ears.

"Why don't you mind your own fucking business for once?!" I snarl as I pull my fist back to deliver another blow, but the sneaky vamp blocks that one, ripping his arm out of my grasp and jumping backwards.

I'm ready to just charge at him like a damn bull when he starts to laugh, and it takes me off guard. He wipes more blood from his face, shaking his long black hair as he laughs even louder.

I always suspected Victor was insane, but what the hell?

"That's really rich coming from you," he says coldly, with that creepy grin still smeared across his face.

I immediately bristle at the comment, a low growl rumbling from my chest as he dashes forward again, making another attempt at my right eye. I step out of the way just in time, and his fist collides with the wall behind me punching through it, as large cracks splinter up towards the ceiling.

Before he has the chance to yank his fist out of the wall, I extend my claws and grab him by the shoulder as hard as I can. He hisses in pain as my claws pierce through his clothes and into his shoulder, and I pull him downward, punching him in the nose twice. Before my hand can make contact a third time, he delivers a swift knee jab to my rib cage and jumps backwards, freeing his skin of my claws. I'm pretty sure he cracked a rib or two, but adrenaline and instinct are dulling my pain at the moment.

"Stay the fuck away from my Pup and my mate!" I say through gritted teeth as I force myself to straighten, feeling Nero threatening to take over completely as my chest begins to expand abnormally. I'm on the verge of shifting as I try to rein in control.

Victor blinks once in surprise.

"Your *what?*" he sputters as I begin to charge at him, closing the distance between us.

"THAT'S ENOUGH!" Crystal shrieks as she places her body in the small space left between us, holding her palms out and I immediately lower the fist I'd raised.

Victor's nostrils flare with irritation, but he doesn't move either. I see frost beginning to form in the middle of her palm as she glares back and forth between us.

"If I have to freeze you two in order to force you to quit fighting, I fucking will!" she snaps, eyes red.

Both of us open our mouths to argue, but Lila's cry makes us shut up and we immediately snap our heads in the direction of her room. Crystal rubs her hands together, dusting off the small ice crystals. Her breathing is heavy with rage and fear and, now that I can focus on her feelings through our mate bond, I absolutely hate that she's so upset.

"See what y'all did?!" she snaps, sounding almost exactly like her mother in that moment, "You're upsetting her!"

A pang of guilt hits my gut harder than Victor's previous blows, and I try to force myself to calm down, willing my heart and breathing to slow.

Don't shift.

Control yourself.

I repeat the words in my head like a mantra, and I notice Victor's eyes are no longer red, but back to their dark blue as he looks just as guilty at the doorway to Lila's room. His chest is also heaving, and I can tell he's trying to calm himself, too.

After a few seconds of a very tense silence, Victor's eyes make their way to meet mine.

"This isn't over," he says in annoyed tone before walking toward Lila's room.

"Where the hell do you think you're going?!" I snap, Crystal's sudden death grip on my arm preventing me from charging at him.

"Stop it, Conan!" she says through clenched teeth as I feel the prick of her sharp nails digging into my arm.

Victor doesn't stop until he's at the doorway.

"To go check on *my* kid," he calls over his shoulder in a disdainful tone before he walks inside.

Crystal grips my arm even harder, and puts her body in front of mine as I lunge after him.

"Knock it off!" she yells, slapping my chest with her hands.

"I'm going to rip his-"

"You'll do *nothing!*" she shouts even louder, pointing at my nose with a sharp nail coated in my blood.

I'm just about to grab her by the shoulders to gently move her out of the way, when my head suddenly snaps to the side as another fist connects with my face. I hear Crystal shriek in surprise right before two hands grip the front of my shirt and lift me off the ground. As I blink away the stars, I see Draken giving me a death glare, his eyes a scorching-hot red and his fangs bared as he curls his lips in disgust. He's shorter than me by a few inches, and I know I'm much heavier than he is, but he actually has my feet off the ground. All I can do is stare as, at lightning speed, he has me pinned to the wall Victor just punched a hole through, and my entire body sinks through the hard surface as if it's made of cardboard.

Shit.

"Daddy, stop!" Crystal cries, her eyes wide with fear as she grabs one of his arms with both hands.

"No, let him. I deserve it." My voice is a raspy whisper from the wind being knocked out of my lungs.

"What the bloody hell is this dog doing in my house, Crystal?" Draken asks, his cool tone belied by his red glare, which never leaves my face.

"Daddy, please! Don't kill him!" Crystal begs, still tugging on his arm in vain. I can feel her fear. She's not overreacting, she's actually scared for my life.

"Too late," he responds as he raises a hand, looking as if he's about to use his own sharp nails to tear open my throat.

"We did the Blood Fate!" Crystal cries out.

His hand stops barely a centimeter from my throat and he finally jerks his head in her direction to face her.

"Did I hear that correctly?" he asks, his voice growing louder with each word.

"If you kill him, I'll die too!" Tears begin to spill from her own red eyes.

Draken's hand hovers in the air at my throat, his other still tangled in my shirt as he seems frozen in place, processing what she just said.

Victor darts out of Lila's room, his eyes wide with shock as he stares at Crystal in disbelief. Lila is still crying, making every inch of me want to wriggle out of Draken's grasp to go to her. But I stay still.

"Are you bluffing right now?" Victor asks in disbelief.

"What the hell is goin' on?!" Alice shouts as she hurries up the stairs.

Victor asks a question in Romanian, and Crystal quickly nods her head in confirmation. Draken blinks once, his face still frozen in an icy glare as he glances towards Victor then back at Crystal. He asks her a question in Romanian, as well. Through the pounding in my head, I suddenly remember what Crystal told me about all the pure-blooded vampires using Romanian as a universal language, whether or not they're Romanian. They clearly don't want me to understand something, which just irritates me further, but I grind my teeth and wait.

"Of course I'm not joking!" Crystal snaps back in English, her hands beginning to tug at her short hair in frustration.

Draken tenses, then asks her another question in Romanian.

"No! No one's making me say anything! Conan didn't know what the hell a Blood Fate even was until I told him!"

she replies, looking as if she's one small step away from full-blown hysterics.

Between Lila's cries and Crystal's despair, my chest is aching, but all I can do is try to stay still and not make things worse, which isn't hard considering my entire body is throbbing.

Victor mumbles something in Romanian, then quickly begins to descend the stairs. I'm not sure what his facial expression means, but it isn't anger. He seems ... lost. Alice casts him a nervous look, then looks back towards Draken.

"Everyone just calm the hell down! Let's sit down and talk this out." Her tone dares anyone to argue.

Draken glances towards her once, then his eyes are back on mine, filled with absolute loathing. I know if he could kill me without putting his daughter in danger, I'd already be dead.

"Now." Alice snaps her fingers, then points down the stairs. "We clearly have a lot to discuss!"

"Yes," Draken grumbles as he slowly lets me go. "Yes, we do."

I hear Crystal let out something between a sob and a sigh of relief.

"Downstairs. Kitchen. Now." Draken orders, and uses inhuman speed to disappear down the stairs in a blur.

"Dad?" a tiny voice squeaks in surprise from below.

Ruby cautiously makes her way up the stairs. Her big doe eyes grow even larger as she they land on me. I give her what I hope is an apologetic look as I pull myself out of the wall and nearly sag onto the floor.

"What's g-going on-?" Ruby starts to stutter, but Alice cuts her off and points towards Lila's room.

"Go watch Lila while we talk downstairs."

"B-but-"

"*Now.*"

CRYSTAL

Even though Mom said we needed to, "sit down and talk things over," no one was sitting. We're all in the kitchen just looking at each other. The air is so thick with tension, I swear I feel like I'm choking on it. Mom taps her high-heeled shoe impatiently, arms crossed as she glances back and forth between Conan and me, her scarlet lips pursed into a thin line as if she's deciding where to start. Dad's standing next to her, facing Conan. His hands are balled into tight fists at his sides as he continues to glare, and I know he's fighting every urge and instinct within him telling him to kill Conan. His eyes are back to their normal stormy gray color, and it's a small relief he's managed to calm himself even that much.

Conan is standing beside me, looking as if he just got out of a bar fight… one where it was him against the entire bar. His face is expressionless, but I can feel how nervous and on edge he is. Both of us have stayed quiet, having come to the unspoken mutual agreement to let my parents start whatever conversation is about to ensue.

"I just have one question to start out with," Dad finally says after several more awkward seconds of silence.

Conan shifts uncomfortably, and clears his throat.

"Uh, yes sir?" he mumbles, raising an eyebrow in question.

"Why weren't you fighting back?" Dad asks, eyes narrowed in suspicion.

Mom and I both let out the same impatient sound of disbelief as Conan just blinks in confusion.

"Uh …" He clears his throat again, "Come again?"

Dad is directly in front of Conan in seconds, but Conan doesn't show any sign of alarm or surprise.

"You and Victor were just beating the hell out of each other. Why weren't you putting up a fight with me?" Dad coolly asks, causing Conan to only furrow his brow in further confusion.

"Seriously, Dad?!" I say in disbelief, throwing out my hands in exasperation.

"Draken, that is hardly the point-" Mom begins before Dad raises a hand to cut her off, earning himself a now red-eyed glare from her.

"It's just a question," he states, his icy glower still locked on Conan.

"Uh, all right. I just …" Conan shifts uncomfortably again, scratching at his neck nervously as he tries to find the right words to say.

Dad shoots him an impatient look and he sighs in defeat, shoulders sagging.

"I know I deserved it from you," he finally admits, his hazel-green eyes showing nothing but honest regret, and my chest aches. "I actually came here to talk to you and your wife."

Dad lets out a humorless laugh. "Did you now?"

Now scratching at the scruff on his chin, Conan nods. Dad tilts his head in amusement, encouraging him to go on.

"You have absolutely every right to be angry with me. Please don't be angry at Crystal. She didn't know how to tell you." Conan's words tumble out in a rush.

Dad raises a blond brow, then looks back toward me, his eyes flashing red again.

"How long have you two been seeing each other again?" he demands.

"Not long!" Conan blurts out before I can reply. "I only just figured out that she's my mate and-"

Dad's head snaps back to Conan, eyes blazing and fangs bared, causing Conan to clamp his mouth shut.

"Did you *mark* her, on top of the Blood Fate?" He jabs a finger in Conan's face. Conan opens his mouth to confirm, but Dad spins to face me instead, eyeing my neck. "Take off that scarf right now, Crystal Celine!" he barks, and I flinch.

I let out a shaky breath, glaring back at him for a moment. *Damn it, Conan! Way to dig this hole even deeper!*

"Fine," I mumble as I raise my shaky hands to unwind the scarf from around my neck.

I toss it to the nearest counter, and cross my arms as I expose Conan's mark. I glare at Dad in silence as his eyes widen with shock, and I hear Mom let out a soft gasp.

"Yes, she's my mate," Conan continues, "she always has been. I'm sorry it took me so long to figure it out. I apologize for everything." He said in defeat.

Conan has never been much of a talker, so I know this has to be hard for him. Dad turns to face him again, his chest heaving with anger as he curls his hands into fists again.

"I'll spend the rest of my life making it up to her and Lila if you'll let me," Conan says softly, and Dad scoffs, curling his lip in rage as Mom reaches out to grab one of his wrists. "But, I won't live in hiding." Conan raises his hands in surrender, "I'd rather risk getting my ass kicked by you than never see my daughter or Crystal again."

He glances over at me, his eyes soft and hopeful that I know every word is true, and my heart aches even more.

"For fuck's sake!" Dad snaps, throwing his hands up in exasperation, before smoothing his hair back.

"I'll do anything in the world for either of them," Conan adds quickly, moving his gaze back to meet Dad's. "You have to believe me. I'll protect them with everything I have. I love them both with all my heart."

I have to stop myself from crying as Conan lays bare his heart for everyone to see, knowing how hard and scary this is for him. But Dad just grinds his teeth in frustration as if every word is causing him to come close to boiling over.

"Conan ..." Mom says softly as she continues to hold Dad's wrist, "Why don't you tell us what happened and how things got so ugly?"

"It was his family, Mom!" I blurt. "He was raised-"

She raises her free hand to silence me, and my lips close in frustration as I glance at Conan to give him an apologetic look. His eyes soften in understanding before shifting back to Mom.

"I want to hear it from *him*, Cici," Mom states as she looks at Conan, then nods for him to answer. Dad is practically shaking with rage as his nostrils flare, but he doesn't move.

"I had no idea it was even possible for us to be mates. My family had me so brainwashed with prejudice, I just couldn't see it at first." He shoots me a sad look before continuing. "So, I pushed her away to protect her, because I never stopped caring about her, even if I tried to fight my feelings."

He's still talking to Mom, but his gaze still hasn't left mine. I feel his sadness and regret, and I wish I could hug him or comfort him in some way without Dad blowing a gasket. All I can do is try to tell him with my eyes how much I love him, that I forgive him, and hope he can feel it through the mate bond.

"There's no way you were able to do the Blood Fate with her," Dad finally spits out.

"Well we did!" I snap. "The blood stayed red! He's my

true mate, but if you wanna test the theory out and see if we both die, then go ahead!"

"Crystal Celine!" Mom says in a horrified voice.

"You watch that bloody mouth of yours, Crystal-" Dad roars, a mixture of pain and anger in his eyes as he looks completely repulsed by my challenge. Of course, I didn't mean it, but it certainly got his attention and, hopefully, he'll take us both more seriously now.

"Mr. Fox, please," Conan says softly. "We're true mates. She brought over this really old cup and made me slice my hand. Our blood mixed together and stayed red, then we drank and she bit me. You can look at my neck if you wa-"

"Yes, I see it! Shut up!" Dad says sharply.

Conan shuts his mouth and awkwardly scratches at his scruff again.

Dad doesn't blink as he glares at Conan for what feels like forever, even though it's probably only a few seconds. Finally, he exhales sharply through his nose. His shoulders drop and he lets out a pained sigh.

"What exactly do you want, Conan?" He sounds defeated and tired as he runs a hand through his hair.

"To see my kid and to be with your daughter. It would mean a lot to both of us to have you and your wife's blessing," Conan answers without hesitation.

Dad bristles. "You can bless my shoe right up your-"

"That's enough, Draken!" Mom cuts him off before swatting at his chest.

Dad casts her an annoyed look as Conan clears his throat, drawing his attention back to him.

"I'm begging you, Mr. Fox," Conan says quietly.

"Bloody hell," Dad sighs with a frown. "Well, it's not like I can kill you. So what other damn choice do I have?"

"Thank you!" Conan stammers, eyes widening with hope, "I swear that-"

"Hold it right there!" Dad jabs a finger at Conan's nose, silencing him. "Do not mistake my mercy for weakness. I am only stomaching the sight of you because it would result in my daughter's death if I killed you. If it weren't for the damned Blood Fate, there would be nothing left of you but a stain on my rug. Understood?"

"Yes, sir." Conan grunts, shoulders slumped.

We're making some kind of progress, I guess.

"Draken ..." Mom groans, raising a hand to her brow in frustration, but Dad ignores her.

"You and I will be having a little chat later. But, for now I need a damn drink and a cigar. You are to stay out of my sight unless I summon you. Got it?" Dad asks, straightening to his full height, which is still a few inches below Conan's, his expression daring him to argue.

"Loud and clear," Conan replies with a sigh.

"Good," Dad grunts before stomping off towards his office.

As soon as he's out of sight, I throw my arms around Conan, feeling guilty as he winces in pain.

"Sorry!" My voice is muffled in his chest, and I loosen my grip.

"It's okay." He wraps an arm around my waist to hug me back, then kisses the top of my head.

I hear the click of Mom's heels across the tiled floor as she makes her way over to us. I tense for a moment, then feel her warm hand lightly rub my back. I could cry with relief.

"I know you're trying, Conan," she says, "but you might have to give Draken a while."

"I completely understand," Conan responds before resting

his chin atop my head. "I honestly can't believe you're as calm as you are."

Mom lets out a slow breath behind me.

"I can see you're serious. It's just ..." Her hand grabs my shoulder and gives it a squeeze, "Cici was *so* upset. It killed us to see her that way when you broke her heart."

I feel Conan's pain and regret through our bond as he pulls me closer into his chest.

I'm so sorry. You've proven already how sorry you are. Everyone just keeps beating the dead horse ... I want to say, but instead I just stay quiet, inhaling his scent to comfort me.

"I know," Conan sighs, the remorse clear in his tone. "Believe me, I know."

"You should also know you're not one hundred percent in my circle of trust, either. You're definitely gonna have to earn it," Mom replies.

"I understand," Conan says before burying his nose in my hair. I'm willing to bet he's using my scent to comfort himself, too.

"But," Mom continues, "between the beatings you got from Vic *and* Draken, I think you're good on punishment for the time being."

"I'm so glad you're okay," I whisper into his shirt, feeling a couple tears begin to dampen it.

"I'm just a little banged up. I'll heal fast," he responds with a light chuckle.

I finally raise my head to look up at him, and he kisses my forehead before looking back at Mom.

"Where is Victor, anyway?" he asks in an annoyed grunt.

"He left." Mom replies.

"Good."

"Conan!" I warn, not wanting to deal with any more testosterone-fuelled drama.

"We're *hoooome!*" An all too familiar voice calls out from the living room and I tense.

Please, no ...

Conan's eyes dart toward the sound, his brow furrowed.

"Boys?" Mom asks, excitement in her voice, "Is that you?"

Not them. Anyone but them.

"Who-" Conan starts, but Heath is immediately at his side, standing only an inch or two shorter than Conan.

"Well, well, well ..." Heath says as he grins at Conan, looking at him like a cat that's cornered a rat.

Conan tenses as Reese pops up on his other side. They're both using their vampire speed to their full advantage, trying to spook him.

"What do we have here?" Reese says, his grin matching Heath's.

Conan blinks in surprise as he looks back and forth at the identical twins.

"Looks like someone got to him before we did."

"Was it Dad or Vic?"

"Looks like both to me."

"Oooh, was it both? That would have been wickedly cool. He-"

"SHUT UP!" I snap, throwing my hands up as Conan looks so uncomfortable sandwiched between the two idiots.

"It was both." *I could strangle them.*

"Uh, I guess these are your brothers?" he asks, his eyes still ping-ponging between them.

Before I can respond, Reese makes his way between us, shoving me behind him. Conan's eyes flash gold and he immediately begins to growl.

"We are-" Reese starts.

"Your worst nightmare." Heath finishes as he stands directly behind Conan, basically sandwiching him.

"Ever hear of personal space?" Conan grunts.

"Don't you two start. We just got this house calmed down," Mom warns, once again tapping her foot in agitation as she places her hands on her hips.

"Start what?" Reese asks, his gaze never leaving Conan's as he tilts his head in amusement. "We haven't even done anything. Yet."

"Isn't this dear old dead-beat Dad we've heard so much about?" Heath claps a hand on Conan's shoulder, causing him to tense as his growl grows louder. The twins have never met Conan, but it isn't hard to tell the werewolf in the house is my baby daddy.

Plus, I'm sure they went through whatever information Dad dug up to keep an eye out for him.

"Back off." I snap, elbowing Reese out of the way to stand in front of Conan.

"We heard you stirred up quite a bit of trouble for our sweet little Cici," Heath says as he prowls around to stand beside Reese, the last three words coated with sarcasm making me tut.

"You two are both still way too close for comfort," Conan growls, placing a hand on my waist. I can tell my presence has calmed him a tad since Reese separated us, but he's still pissed.

"Well, *you* got a little too close for comfort with our sister." Reese retorts with a sneer.

"Excuse me?!" Conan's clearly taken off guard.

Oh my God he did NOT just say that in front of Mom.

"Reese!" I shout, giving him the best *what the fuck* look I can muster.

"That's enough!" Mom snaps, stomping one foot and causing the twins to flinch and their smiles to falter. "You two come with me. *Now.*"

Mom walks towards the living room, not bothering to look back to see if they're following her. She knows if they want to stay alive, they will.

"This isn't over," Heath grumbles.

"Not by a long shot," Reese agrees.

"I'll keep that in mind," Conan replies through gritted teeth.

"Would you two fuck off already?!" I shout, shooing them away with my hands.

They roll their eyes, the red turning back to their normal icy blue.

"Sleep with one eye open, *cause we'll be adding to your bruises later.*" Heath whispers into Conan's ear before following Reese into the living room to face Mom's wrath.

I release a slow, shaky breath once we're alone in the kitchen.

"I'm sorry about them," I say softly as I look up at him.

"No problem." He's still watching the door to the living room. "I understand they're protective of you."

"That's an understatement," I snort.

"I just wish they'd stay about three feet away from me at all times."

I can't help but laugh at that and, although he wasn't trying to be funny, he smirks down at me.

"Well, you didn't get us killed," I say, reaching up to softly touch the bruises and cuts on his face. "And world war three hasn't started yet."

Conan gently removes my hand and closes both of his large ones around it.

"I'm sorry for all this, I just felt like it was the right thing to do," he murmurs.

"Truth be told, I'm glad it's over." I sigh. "So, uh …" I chew on my lip a moment as he furrows his brow, waiting for me to continue. "Do you wanna tell your family anything yet, or …?"

His eyes widen and he immediately shakes his head. "For the time being, no."

"Let's cross that path another day then. How about we go relieve Ruby of Lila and let her know we're still alive?"

"Nothing would make me happier." The grin on his face leaves no doubt as to the truth of his statement.

Seven

CONAN

The past couple of hours have been peaceful without any other incident. I know I have to go soon, but there's no way I'd even dare to ask if I could stay here at the Foxes' home even though the idea of going back to my cabin that's over an hour away gnaws at every instinct to stay as close as possible to my mate and pup. I even considered a hotel, but I've got pack duties expected of me tomorrow and I don't want to raise any eyebrows or prompt any unwanted questions until… or rather *if* I ever get to the point where Lila and Crystal are no longer secrets in my life. So, I decided to soak up every second with Lila I'm allowed, and have been holding her while sitting on the corner of Crystal's bed ever since. She told me I could rock her in the nursery, but I'm honestly afraid that little wooden chair would snap under my weight and I know it'd be uncomfortable as hell to sit in anyways.

I glance up to look at Crystal while Lila grabs one of my fingers.

Strong grip for something so freaking tiny.

I can sense Crystal's stressed. Even though Ruby seemed to be confused, she didn't give Crystal any trouble when we relieved her of babysitting, so I know it's not that. What just happened downstairs would stress anyone out, but even Crystal said she was relieved to have everything out in the open with her family now and I could feel her honesty. Of course, she'd still be on edge afterwards, but there's something else. I just can't quite put my finger on it.

"What's up?" I ask, watching as Crystal's thumbs work away at what I'm assuming is a text message. She's been checking her phone and typing frantically ever since we got to her room.

She looks up at me, brows furrowed with one fang peeking out. The fang and her ring spinning are her tells when it comes to her being upset or nervous. I raise both eyebrows and shoot her a look that I will know she's lying if she tries to shrug it off. She glances back down at her phone, then sets it down on her desk. She's also been standing this entire time she's been glued to her phone.

She looks back up at me and pauses, as if trying to find the right words as she begins to spin that opal ring around her finger in thought.

What have I missed?

Is one of the Foxes texting her that I need to leave?

"It's just ... I know I hurt Vic." She finally says after a few seconds of silence.

I resist the urge to roll my eyes, but can't help the grunt that escapes my throat as I look back down at Lila.

"Conan ..." She sighs in exasperation.

I don't look up at her. Instead, I wave a glittery pink rattle Lila seems to be fond of in front of her face. I know Victor is her best friend, but I don't want to hurt her feelings by not showing any sympathy to the dude I just fist fought when I caught him trying to play daddy to my kid. So, I decide to go with the, *'If you have nothing nice to say, don't say anything at all'* route.

They'll make up.

I'll put up with him as much as I have to.

CRYSTAL

I feel my heart sink as I watch Conan's truck leave the driveway. I know better than to ask if he could stay, but it doesn't make his absence any less difficult. He had promised to be back day after tomorrow if he can slip away without suspicion after fulfilling pack duties. He looks back and waves at me one more time before driving away out of view. I wave back with my right hand, hold Lila with my left as I force a smile. My shoulders slump as I turn back to walk inside.

Well, today was an absolute shit show.

My family now knows I'm mated to the guy they all hate for knocking me up with a borderline illegal baby, my best friend is hurt that I kept him out of the loop along with aforementioned family (except Ruby), and I had to watch aforementioned best friend and mate beat the shit out of each other before my psychopath of a father jumped on him next.

At least it's over with now, I guess.

I nervously look around before heading back upstairs. I have this dreadful feeling in my gut that my parents or the twins are going to corner me now that Conan's gone, but no one appears to be waiting to pounce on me ... for now.

"Let's go get you fed and bathed, hm?" I say softly to a sleeping Lila, kissing her little head before walking up the stairs before entering my room.

I nearly jump out of my skin when I feel my phone vibrate as I lay Lila down in her crib. Victor has been giving me the silent treatment after some very heated messages were sent.

Calm down. It might not even be Vic.

Don't wake up Lila over nothing.

I quietly rush back to my room and sit down on my bed before looking at my phone.

My hand shakes a bit as I realize it is indeed Victor. I'm both relieved and nervous that he's finally responded to me.

V<small>IC</small>

>   How long?

>>   How long what exactly?

V<small>IC</small>

>   How long has she had her dad back in her life while you let me believe otherwise and continue to take on the role?

Ouch.

I bite my lip as I try to find the words to explain. Nothing that comes to mind doesn't make me sound like less of a bad friend.

> It's very recent. I decided to talk things out with him after my birthday. I was never expecting us to be mates, vampire or wolf way. It was a lot for me to take in and believe for myself before I could bring myself to tell anyone else.

Except for Ruby, but I'm not gonna bring that up.

He hasn't responded yet, so I continue to add onto my last message.

> I was already shocked when he marked me the wolf way, and I felt all of these new and weird things inside me down to my core. Even though he proved I was his, I still didn't want to get my hopes up that the Blood Fate would work on us. You can imagine my shock when it did. Ever since, my entire body has been... rewired? I don't know how to describe it. I only know of what I watched between my parents and other Blood Fated vampires, but I feel that the wolf way is more... intense? Keep in mind that this is all after I'm dealing with all of the bodily changes of being a new mother to an unheard of species of kid.

I wait for a few minutes but he still doesn't respond.

I kinda did give him a couple of essays to read ...

I can't help myself and decide to continue my spew of word vomit.

> I promise I never meant to mislead you or hurt you. I am thankful for everything you've done for me and Lila. Up until my birthday you have been her dad, and I still want you in her life. I was going to tell you, I was just trying to find a way how. I'm sorry, Vic. I really, really am. I love you, and I know I've been a shitty best friend. I'll quit spamming you now.

I force myself to set my phone down then flop backwards onto my bed, my feet still dangling off the side as I stare up at the ceiling. I'm not sure how many minutes pass before I hear my phone vibrate again. I slowly pat around for it and then bring it to my face.

V<small>IC</small>

> That wasn't a bluff to keep your dad from killing him? You're truly Blood Fated mates?

> I swear.

A few minutes of silence pass, but I continue to hold my phone above my face and stare at the screen. My gut clenches as soon as I see the three dots pop up that indicate Victor is responding, then they stop. They start again, then stop. This goes on for a few more minutes before a message is finally delivered.

Vic

> If what you say is true, I understand. Just the idea of you taking that asshole back and letting him all of a sudden into Lila's life after everything he's done was like a slap to the face. I wanted to throttle you for being so stupid.

> You can still throttle me, tbh. I still probably deserve it.

Vic

> Don't tempt me. Did mating all of a sudden give him a pair of balls to man up and be a father or what?

I sigh in relief.

Victor is a cool-headed person that doesn't hold a grudge or stay mad for very long. I thought I had really done it this time, but he's acting like his usual self, and I can tell he still genuinely cares and just wants to be updated. I spend the rest of the night updating him about how I confronted Conan, then realized we were mates, how he showed genuine remorse and guilt, bought things for Lila, and his reasoning of pushing me away to protect me. He's still not happy at the situation, but he accepts it none-the-less.

VIC

> Well, this solves the problem of figuring out how to hide her scent or any other wolf traits she inherited later on while trying to front I'm her dad I guess, huh? Just call me Uncle Vic.

>> It really was a plan that probably wasn't going to do well, long term. I'll still always be in debt to you for it, tho. And Uncle Vic it is.

VIC

> Go to bed. It's almost sunrise. We can talk more later.

>> Good night, Vic.

VIC

> Night.

BAYLOR

Despite all the jokes about red-heads having a temper, I'm really not an easy to anger guy. But, I have to say, Conan Knight tends to bring out that side of me. My knuckles are white as I grip the steering wheel pulling into the Foxes' driveway. Victor had asked for me to use my DJ skills to compose a beat for one of his new songs and when I invited him over to have a listen, he told me everything I've missed. The fact that I'm a *Raven* and all of this happened without my knowing really irritates me, but Conan having the audacity to so much as think about Crystal after our last conversation floors me. Victor tells me they're Blood Fated, so I'm here to see that for myself.

I glance over at Conan's parked truck as I kill the engine. I had Victor find out the next time he would be over here, and I'd rather confront him here on Fox territory than stupidly make a scene on his pack's territory and risk Luther finding out how I know him. Crystal understands the fact that Victor doesn't care to be around Conan when he wants to visit with Lila, so she gives him a heads up when he does come.

Draken and Alice both have told me on multiple occasions that I am welcome to walk right on in their home anytime, but I ring the doorbell anyway.

"I'll get it!" I hear what sounds like Ruby calling out. A few moments later, she opens the door and blinks up at me in surprise.

"Oh, hey, B-baylor." She says with a small smile. She doesn't stutter around people she knows well and trusts unless she's nervous. I'm assuming she's anxious at the fact that I'm here while Conan is. I give her a forced smile back, then clear my throat.

"Where's Conan?" I ask flatly.

Her already large doe eyes widen in panic and she glances nervously over her shoulder.

"Uh, um, h-he-"

"I know he's here. I just need to talk to him."

"Oh, o-okay. He's in L-Lila's n-n-nursery, but-"

"Thank you." I say before stepping around her.

"B-but-!" She sounds like she wants to stop me but

doesn't follow me. Despite her petite size, Ruby is a full-blooded vampire and could drag me back if she really wanted to, but she doesn't. I hear an exasperated sigh behind me as I make my way up the stairs.

The door to Lila's nursery is open, and I see Conan cuddling Lila to his chest beside her crib. Even though she appeared to be a healthy, full term baby, Lila looks ridiculously small in Conan's giant arms. His eyes dart to me before I finish walking through the threshold. He scowls and raises an eyebrow in silent question at me. Crystal and the rest of the Foxes' aren't anywhere I can see or hear.

"Having fun playing Daddy, are we?" I ask, crossing my arms.

His eyes flash gold for a moment and his lip curls up into a snarl. I don't even blink as I continue to stare at him. I know this is very stupid. Staring down a dominant wolf like Conan after provoking him on purpose is basically asking for an ass kicking, but I don't care and stay glued to my spot.

He glances down at Lila, whom I can now see is sleeping, then glares back up at me.

"I *am* her Daddy." He whispers through gritted teeth. "And lower your damn voice. If you wake her up I'll rip your throat out with my teeth."

I roll my eyes, and hear a quiet but deadly sounding growl begin to rumble through Conan's chest. "Fine," I whisper back, "Can you please speak to me out here then?" I ask, taking a couple of steps back into the hall.

Conan looks like he'd rather eat glass, but he grunts then nods with a scowl. He sets Lila down into the crib, and it's so strange seeing his big, hulking form move with such a gentle grace. He pauses, as if waiting to see if she wakes up, then prowls toward me with a murderous look. He softly closes the door behind him, despite looking as if he's angry enough to rip it off the hinges.

"Well?" he grunts.

"I'm sure she's inherited good hearing from her parents, where's the best place we could chat?" I ask softly, forcing my face to keep a neutral expression.

Still scowling, he nods his head toward Crystal's bedroom. I silently follow him, closing the door behind me after we both enter.

"Where is Crystal?" I ask, giving a quick glance around her empty room.

"Showering." Conan says, crossing his arms. "I'm guessing you're wanting to know why I'm here and how I'm still alive?"

"Not exactly."

"Well, I know from our last conversation you're not happy to see me here. So, what is it?" Conan asks defensively, as if daring me to try kick him out of the house or tell him he shouldn't be here.

Pfft. As if anyone in their right mind would try to make rules for Draken Fox's house ...

Other than Alice, that is.

"You need to back off of Vic's case." I reply in as neutral of a tone I can muster.

Conan blinks once, then his eyes change to gold permanently as his frown deepens.

"Excuse me?" he asks incredulously, and I notice his canines have lengthened as well.

"Just hear me out," I say as I hold up my hands in a placating gesture, "that's all I'm asking."

He growls again but doesn't reply, so I take that as my green light to continue.

"Surely, Crystal and Victor's platonic relationship doesn't

need to be explained again, especially if you're mated to her and feel what she feels for yourself, right?"

"Yeah, yeah." Conan grunts, waving a hand to indicate that he wants me to get to the point.

"Well, in that case," I continue, "you need to understand this loud and clear. You need to back off because I'm sure you're now also aware that while you were gone, Victor was there to fill your shoes."

Conan opens his mouth to argue, but I hold up a hand and continue before he can interrupt.

"Save whatever excuse you have, I've heard the story. You did what you did to protect Cici, blah blah blah. But, next time you get pissy at Victor, keep in mind that when he wasn't doing shows or interviews, he went to every doctor appointment that he could make it to while Cici was pregnant. He knew that Cici *and* Lila's lives were in danger due to Lila's ... unique bloodline. But he risked his own neck to lie and say that *he* was Lila's father, that way no one would question Crystal if anyone discovered she was pregnant. Don't you understand? He risked his entire family name, *Dracula's* family name, knowing that any of the Elders or Pure Bloods could have his head for covering for your ass if they found out. He risked it *all* to save *your* daughter's life."

Conan's mouth thins into a firm line, and I can tell he's gnashing his teeth together, but he says nothing.

"He stepped up while you stepped down," I continue, "not every guy can do that. Hell, it's hard to find a step dad to do that, much less just a friend taking on the role as a father that has zero intentions of being romantically involved with the mother! Diapers, feedings, late nights, he did everything!"

Conan's eyes fade back to green, and he scratches at the five o'clock shadow growing on his face.

"He really did all that stuff, huh?" he grumbles, face softening a bit.

"Damn straight! That's just the type of guy Vic is. He will always put his friends that he considers to be family above anything else. You basically swooped on in and made him feel as though all of that meant nothing, even though he'll never admit it. The guy that broke his best friend's heart and abandoned her child just decides to clock back in, and it's bullshit how you went about treating him. Keep all of *that* in mind next time you feel like having a pissing contest with him."

Conan appears to be too stunned to speak, but I've said everything I have to say. I slip past him and leave without another word. Victor will not be happy about this, Cici might not be happy about this, but I don't care.

It needed to be said.

CONAN

I don't bother to stop Baylor when he leaves. I'm not sure how long I stand there staring into nothing as I process everything he said. Mental images of Victor caring for a depressed, pregnant Crystal flash through my mind. More scenarios of Victor caring for a newborn while Crystal dealt with the pain and depression I caused while also juggling the tasks of being a new mother, as well as the pressure of keeping everything a secret play through my head, and I feel sick to my stomach. He didn't just take on the title, he took on the job, too.

Well, shit.

I run a hand through my hair, releasing a slow breath. I

didn't know it was possible for me to be more disappointed in myself than I already am, but here we are.

"I can't exactly hate him now without being a huge jerk, can I?" I grumble to myself, rubbing my face with both hands.

"N-no, you can't." A tiny voice says behind me, and I tense in surprise. I whip around to see Ruby, shyly leaning against the doorway. Ruby's scent is all over the house, so I didn't smell or hear her tiny feet approach. Although, with how much of a storm cloud is brewing in my mind, she could've probably doused herself in perfume and came in banging pots and pans without me noticing.

"S-sorry, I didn't mean to st-startle you." She says with an apologetic smile.

"It's fine, ah …" I clear my throat awkwardly, "What's up?"

She rubs her arm, looking nervous as she makes her way fully into the room. I always am amazed at how tiny she is. I'm used to everyone being shorter than me, and I thought Crystal was short since she barely comes up to my shoulder. When Ruby stands directly in front of me, she barely comes up to my chest on her bare feet. She looks as if she's twelve instead of seventeen.

"Well, I c-couldn't help but overhear and um …" She starts fidgeting with her hands as she avoids eye contact with me.

"Go on, I'm sure I deserve whatever it is. You have every right to hate me too." I say with a sigh, shoulders slumping as I ready myself for whatever it is Ruby wants to tell me.

"W-whoa now!" She jerks her head up and holds up both of her hands as her large gray eyes meet mine, "I don't hate you!" She begins to fidget with her hands nervously again, but remains holding eye contact with me. "N-not at all!"

I blink in surprise.

"Uh, you don't?" I ask in confusion.

"No!" she replies, eyes saddening as she begins to rub her arm again. "I actually told Cici to go f-find you." She adds barely above a whisper.

I blink once, twice, then shake my head in disbelief.

"You … you did?"

She nods with a nervous half smile.

"Uh, go on …" I say after it appears she isn't going to say more. I don't know how to respond to that if she was waiting on a reply from me.

"S-sorry. This st-stupid stutter …" she grumbles before taking a deep breath.

"Hey," I reply softly, "take your time. No pressure."

I remember what Crystal told me about her having a stutter thanks to severe social anxiety. I know I'm not the most pleasant person to be around regardless of species, and I will myself to look as unthreatening as possible. I've been told my entire life that my resting face is usually a scowl or that I just appear intimidating in general, so I try my best to soften my expression to match my heart. I can tell this is hard for her.

"Well, like I said, I overheard you and Baylor talking, and …" She takes another deep breath, her face full of concentration. I'm assuming she's doing whatever she can to speak clearly, but I don't care. She can stutter every word and I'll listen to what this tiny vamp has to say without interrupting.

"Please don't be angry at Victor anymore," she continues, and I force myself to keep my face neutral and not groan, "he r-really is a g-great guy that just loves our f-family a lot …"

How much longer am I going to have to talk about freaking Victor today?!

"I know," I reply calmly, "I'm … I'm trying to come to terms with that."

"If you really are Cici's mate, that means you're b-basically my brother-in-law, right?" she asks with a small smile.

"Yeah, I-" I stammer a bit in surprise, "I guess so. If you want to even bother to claim me as such."

I don't know what I was expecting her to say, but that *was not it.*

"Of course, I do! You make Cici so happy." Ruby says matter-of-factly.

I swear my brain stops working for a minute. It's as if this unexpected kindness caused my mind to glitch.

"You think so?" I finally blurt out and she nods.

"I do. I know you love her. Th-those songs you sent her really said it all."

Ah, she knows about Crystal's birthday present.

I guess I shouldn't be surprised.

I scratch at my neck awkwardly unsure of what to say. She offers me a knowing smile and gently places her tiny hand on my arm.

"I think you really feel bad about how everything went down."

Yeah, that's an understatement.

"I also think a lot of it had to do with your upbringing."

Hey, she's not stuttering as much. That means she's not as nervous around me, right?

"I mean, Dad w-wasn't exactly thrilled when he found out Crystal was carrying a w-wolf's child considering we've been taught to be enemies …"

My gut clenches at the thought, and all I can do is stare down at my feet. I don't even want to know how Draken responded to the news.

I'm such a piece of shit.

"But," Ruby continues, "I think you sh-should use this opportunity to start over. Everyone deserves a second chance, right?"

My gaze looks up to meet hers at that, and she places her hands behind her back and shrugs one shoulder, still giving me that small smile.

"Besides, you're mates in more ways than one, right? It's not like there's any way to go back now. All we can do is try to move forward with both of you."

I stare at her silently for a few seconds, then bend down to envelope her into a hug without a second thought. I probably should've asked if touching her was okay first considering how anxious she is, but if she's uncomfortable, she doesn't show it. Instead, she just lets out a small gasp of surprise, unmoving.

"Thank you, Ruby." I want to say so much more, but that's all my aching chest will allow me to say. She continues to surprise me by hugging me back.

"Y-yeah, sure!"

💋💋💋

I've been coming by every single day I can. Driving back and forth isn't fun or cheap, but it's so worth it. I know Crystal appreciates it. Ruby and Alice have been nothing but kind to me, although I'm still not convinced I deserve it. Draken is mostly gone for work, but when he is here he just mainly ignores me. The twins have been doing their own thing, as it appears they both work for Draken and are just as busy, but still like to try and give me a hard time. Nothing too over the top, just annoying the piss out of me. I ignore and just endure it. Plus, I've seen they both adore Lila, and despite being Crystal's biological cousins, they clearly love her as a sister. I can't really stay too frustrated at them after witnessing that firsthand. They annoy Crystal and Ruby too, but overall they're good brothers and uncles.

Any work for the pack I can do from home, I do. I've even brought my laptop here with me a few times to do some things while Lila sleeps. My parents aren't happy with the fact that I don't see them outside of mandatory work I have to do on the property, but I have to hide my mark until I figure out what else I can do. I also know I can't keep Lila a secret forever, but no other plan seems to sound like it'd end well, so I just will myself to be patient and take things day by day. Now that her family knows about me, my priority for now is repairing the damage I caused among them.

I turn off the water and reach for the towel Alice had fetched for me. My thoughts had run wild with me as I showered and I almost have the urge to shake my head to return to the present. After drying myself the best I can, I wrap the towel around my waist and walk into Crystal's room to find her seated at her desk, slumped over with her head buried in her arms.

"C? You okay?" I ask, lightly tapping her shoulder.

"Mmwake!" She darts up, eyes half open.

There's a faint red ring around her pupils ...

She pushes her chair back away from her desk and stretches before looking up at me. I notice her pupils dilate when she eyes me in my towel.

"Did you just shower?" she asks, eyeing me as if I'm a piece of steak on a silver platter.

"Yeah, after I bathed Lila, she decided I needed a bath too." I grunt.

"She puked on you again?"

"Like that scene from *The Exorcist*, but milk instead of green goo."

At that she crinkles her nose and begins to giggle.

"It didn't even just get on my chest like normal. *Noooo.* This time it got in my hair, and my beard, so Alice all but demanded I use your shower. My pants are still clean, but she's washing my shirt despite me telling her I could wash it at home." I say, before shaking my head back and forth, causing Crystal to laugh and flinch away from the falling water droplets.

This reminds me of her laughing at me doing this after the first time we showered together ...

"Watch it, Paws!" she playfully scolds before swatting at my arm.

"That's your karma for laughing at me."

"Wuss."

"Rude."

I feel her eyes follow me as I walk over to my boxers and sweatpants that are waiting for me on her bed. I had just reached for them when I feel her breath on the back of my neck.

Damn, she moved quick.

Sometimes I wonder if Crystal can fucking teleport with how fast and silent she is. Probably another superpower I don't know about.

"Can I help you?" I ask, giving her a casual glance over my shoulder.

"You don't need those."

"I don't?"

"No."

Before I can reply, her lips are on my neck and I nearly melt in her arms as she begins to kiss and suck at her claiming mark. Her hands around my torso tighten as she softly runs her tongue over the two puncture marks and I immediately feel myself growing hot with lust.

I stand and she hisses in agitation while reluctantly letting go of me. I turn around and sit on her bed, chuckling as I pull her down onto my lap.

"C … Your family wants to kill me enough as it is …" I warn, even though Nero is doing everything in his power to try and persuade me to immediately claim her right here on her bed.

She glances at her bedroom door, then repositions herself into a more comfortable position to straddle me. The towel has now slid down, and I know she can feel everything through her leggings. I swear the little vixen grinds on me a little longer on purpose before settling her hands on my shoulders.

"Is the door locked?"

"Yes, but-"

"Lila's asleep?"

"Yes, but Cry-"

She places a finger onto my lips to shush me, and tilts her head as if she's listening for something.

"No one is moving around nearby, I think we'll be safe for a few minutes …" She purrs into the crook of my neck, kissing at her mark again.

Fuck. I'm doomed. I'm powerless.

"I'll turn this up, just to be safe …" she mumbles against my skin before reaching over to her nightstand to pick up her phone. I hadn't even noticed music playing but she has a random rock playlist on. She turns up the volume quite a bit, then places it back on her nightstand.

"Crystal, are you sure?" I ask one more time, feeling every ounce of self-control leaving my body as I watch her shrug off her sweater.

"Yes. I also need to feed." She replies, standing to remove her leggings. She kicks her clothes and my discarded towel off to the side before straddling me again.

I figured that's why her eyes have a tinge of red …

"Wait, you wanna try feeding *from* me?" I ask, blinking in confusion.

"M'hmm."

"You still think it'll work? I know we talked about it after you marked me but …"

"I'm very sure it will. You smell and taste like you're made for me." She smirks and glances down at the twitching reaction those words just sent down below my abdomen as heat begins to pool in my stomach.

"Well, then by all means …" I grumble back as I grip both of her hips in my hands.

"This is my first time feeding since before I got pregnant and couldn't keep the blood down. You remember I'll be out for most of the day?"

I nod once, licking my lips.

"I'll need you to tell my family I've fed so that someone can care for Lila when you can't."

"Consider it done."

She bites her lip, chuckling darkly as she begins to rake her black and pink painted nails up and down my chest.

"You seem so eager …"

"Just bite me already, Fangs."

Before I bite you. Again.

"I like to play with my food." She says with a grin before shoving me hard so that I'm now laying beneath her on the bed.

I want to be mad; I really do, I'd even settle for frustrated … but damn if this isn't turning me on more.

She's still grinning as she settles herself between my legs

and I'm aching for her touch me at this point. I have to stop myself from bucking my hips, clenching her blankets so tightly in my fists I might just rip them.

Oh well, I'll buy her a whole new fucking bed if needed.

She knows she's torturing me, that smirk never leaves her lips as she trails her tongue slowly down my stomach until she reaches exactly what she was aiming for.

"Crystal …" I warn.

"Mm?" she hums before taking me into that perfect pouty mouth, careful not to scratch my most sensitive area with her elongated fangs.

"Oh, *fuck* …" I hiss through clenched teeth.

I really, *really* missed that mouth of hers.

Those red rings around her pupils are beginning to bleed more into her purple irises as she locks her eyes with mine and continues to do the most sinful things to me with her mouth. I love how her short hair shows off my claiming mark, but damn do I wish it were long enough to pull right about now …

All too soon, she releases me and sets a firm hand on my abdomen to keep me from jolting up and pouncing on her. I raise an eyebrow at her in irritation, but any words I was ready to spew out escape me as she perches herself to sit right on top of me. She doesn't let me enter her, no, the little minx is grinding herself against me instead. I know my eyes flash gold as a warning growl vibrates from my throat, which only makes her grin wider.

"Aren't we impatient?" she teases.

I bare my now elongated canines at her in response. If she doesn't stop torturing me I'm going to snatch her little ass up and claim her until the whole house hears her screaming my name. I don't give a shit about the consequences at this point.

She winks at me, then slowly, painfully slowly, lifts up

and angles my length to line up at her entrance. She slowly slides down on me, and once she's fully down, I jerk up and grab her throat with one hand and wrap my other around her hips. She lets out a startled gasp, but other than her eyes widening in surprise she doesn't move.

"My turn." I growl into her ear before I begin to slam into her, forcing her up and down.

She's riding me but has zero control as I move and guide her. A shocked moan escapes her lips as I bite down on my claiming mark, continuing to pound into her relentlessly. She digs her nails into my shoulders and throws her head back, little noises of ecstasy escaping her throat as I feel her entire body begin to tighten. Sweat mixes in with the blood trickling down my shoulders and makes the fresh scratches sting. I don't care, if anything, it's even more of a turn on and I just bite down harder on her neck as I quicken my pace. She chokes out my name between thrusts. I growl in response and feel her come undone on top of me. I have to hold onto her even tighter as her body grows limp. I slow down a bit, releasing her neck as I pull my canines out of her flesh. Her eyes are almost completely red now, half lidded as she's still high from her release. I slow down a bit more so that I can lick the blood from her reopened mark. She trembles with every stroke of my tongue. Once the bleeding has mostly stopped, I lift my head and lick her blood from my lips.

"Looks like I got to bite you first."

She smirks.

Suddenly she's grinding her hips, riding me roughly to pick the pace back up. I slack off and let her take the lead as I grip her ass with each hand. She's sucking, licking, kissing and nipping at her own claiming mark on my neck and I feel myself twitch inside of her each time.

A sound that is a mix of a moan and a growl escapes my

throat as she rides me faster and harder using her dhampir speed and strength. I can't fucking take it anymore so I flip us over to where we're both completely on the bed. She doesn't pause once as she continues to nip and suck at my neck while I push her knees up to her chest to continue slamming into her. Two sharp little pricks on my neck cause me to jerk once and pause as my brain registers the euphoria consuming all of my senses.

I've always heard that a wolf's mate biting your mate mark feels like pure bliss, and I've heard that a vampire bite is supposed to be comparative to any drug resembling ecstasy when they feed from a human; but experiencing my mate biting and feeding from my mark is a pleasure I can't even begin to put into words.

I'm not sure how many seconds passed when my body froze after malfunctioning from feeling too good, but I'm slowly brought back down to earth as Crystal begins to rock her hips and move at a steady pace beneath me. My hips soon find rhythm with hers and I don't even bother to stifle my moans as she continues to drink from me.

She begins to suck a little harder and it's not long before I explode inside of her. She hums with pleasure as she continues to drink from me and I have to force myself to prop myself up on my elbows to keep from going deadweight on top of her. She gently guides me to roll over and I happily let her.

Once I'm propped up against her headboard, I allow my body to completely relax as I try to catch my breath. My arms loosely wrap around her waist as I lean my neck to the side, allowing her easier access. I hear a pleased grunt come from her throat between gulps, as she tangles her fingers into my hair. Having her drink from me is as good as claiming her body over and over again. I completely understand why humans get caught up in being bloodwhores, now.

And Crystal's only half ... I wonder if I'd simply melt into a puddle if she were a full-blooded vamp.

Crystal was right about werewolf blood not supposed to be appealing to vampires, and vampire venom is supposed to make us sick ... But, I suppose us being mates cancels that out ... Because this, fuck, *nothing* feels better than this.

I'm starting to feel a little lightheaded when I finally feel her fangs release me. She laps up the pool of blood that follows, then begins to lick the wounds to aid them in healing. I've read somewhere before that vampire venom can make wounds bleed more, or heal up quicker depending on some sort of pheromones they release? I have no idea of how the science behind that works, but I really don't care. If anything, I'm disappointed she's stopped.

"Did you get enough?" I ask, my voice a little gravelly.

"More than enough."

"You can keep going if you want ..."

I feel her tongue give my neck one final lick, and I feel my shoulders sag with disappointment.

"I'd rather keep you alive, Conan."

"I'm fine."

"Your face says otherwise."

I want to raise an eyebrow at her, but all I can do is blink my heavily lidded eyes instead.

"Shit, I took way too much." She finally separates our bodies by standing up and leans over me to cup my face into her little hands. I can't help but chuckle at the image of her red eyed, blood-stained face looking at me with worry.

"What the hell are you laughing at, weirdo?!" she asks, shaking me by the shoulders.

"You look like a cute, little, worried ... demon."

She blinks in surprise then shakes her head and swats my chest.

"Conan!"

"What? You do."

She wipes at the blood on her chin with the back of her hand then furrows her brow in worry.

"I'm fine, C."

"Are you sure?" she asks, cupping my face in her hands again to inspect me closer.

I close my eyes and nod.

"You look pale. You never look pale."

"Just lemme rest up. Probably the same as donating blood … Just gonna feel a little weird for a while."

She rolls her eyes then exhales sharply through her nose.

"I'm fine, baby. I promise." I try to assure her, slowly forcing my eyes to open as I place my hands over hers.

"Promise me if you feel worse, you'll have my mom take care of you."

"Say what now?"

"I mean it. She's a witch, Conan. She can probably whip you something up to help."

I feel my lips turn up into a half smile.

Her worrying about me is so cute.

"Conan!"

"Alright, alright," I lift my hands in surrender, "I promise."

"Thank you." She mutters before slowly sliding off the bed and heading into her bathroom.

I hear the sink turn on and off, then hear her clattering around in some drawers or cabinets for a few seconds until she makes her way back into the bedroom.

I open one eye to see she's cleaned up her face and tamed her hair. She quickly slips on an oversized band t-shirt and a pair of pajama pants before making her way back to me.

"Can you stand?"

"Five more minutes."

I don't hear a reply, but I can feel her concern through our mate bond. I open my eyes and take in her worried expression through heavy lids. Her left fang is peeking out as she bites her lip while spinning her opal ring.

"For the last time, I'm fine. I'm just ... overwhelmed."

"Overwhelmed?" Her head jerks up as she narrows her eyes in confusion.

"I have never felt something ... like that."

"Oh, yeah. Vampire bites are supposed to be fun ... I guess dhampir bites are too." She says as she shyly runs a hand through her hair.

"Fun? Are you fucking kidding me? That was phenomenal. Absolute bliss." I say as I reach for one of her hands and squeeze it for emphasis.

"You're dramatic." She chuckles.

"You know a werewolf is never supposed to feel that. I swear my soul left my body."

"Well, glad you enjoyed yourself at least ..."

"Oh, baby ..." I feel some strength returning to me, and I use it to pull her on top of me. "You're never drinking from an animal or a blood bag ever again. Just me."

"Conan ..."

"I mean it. Plus, you could feel when to stop, I know you could. You'd never let yourself hurt me."

"Yeah, but I couldn't feel how weak you really were underneath all that pleasure you were experiencing ..."

"Blame the mate bond. Definitely the Blood Fate's fault, not the wolf's way."

"Shut up."

I chuckle and kiss her forehead.

"I'm already feeling better. Promise."

"That smart mouth of yours never stopped working, that's for damn sure."

At that I laugh, a little harder than I intended to. She scowls, but I see the hints of a smile underneath. I cuddle her to my chest and smooth her hair, hoping to soothe her worries.

"So," she says, then drags her tongue across her teeth in thought, "O positive, huh?"

"You can tell that?!"

She just laughs in response.

When I trust myself enough to stand up and not fall over, I finally go clean myself up in the bathroom then put back on my boxers and sweatpants.

Crystal's eyes are getting heavy, and I know she's fighting that weird coma vampires go into after feeding.

"You're really okay?" she asks as I pick her up to tuck her into bed.

"Yes, Fangs."

"Ass."

"You're the sweetest, really." I smirk as I cuddle her, allowing her to settle herself under my arm to place her head upon my chest. Once she seems comfortable, I reach over to turn down the music that helped muffle our sounds. I freeze when I hear Victor's voice begin to sing, and I quickly skip the song, causing Crystal to laugh hysterically.

"Thank God that didn't play while we were in the middle of …" I shake my head and shudder in disgust.

"You're extra as fuck, Conan."

"What does that even mean?"

"Nothing, I love you. Weirdo."

"I love you too, even when you're rude."

She smiles up at me, then lays her head back against my chest. I circle patterns on her lower back until I hear her breathing change and her body fall limp. I carefully move her arms, which remind me of a lifeless doll, and slowly slide out of the bed.

She's completely still. The slight rise and fall of her chest is the only indication that she's alive. I'm not sure if I'll ever get used to seeing her like this, it makes me so uneasy that she's completely vulnerable and defenseless like this for a day.

I roll her onto her back and place her arms at what I hope is a comfortable position at her sides, making sure her head is on the pillow just right. When I'm satisfied with her placement, I cover her up with a blanket and turn her lamp on before turning the lights off.

Seeing her so still in the glow of the lamplight reminds me of Sleeping Beauty, if only a stupid kiss would wake her up. Didn't Snow White go into a coma and have to be woken up by a kiss, too? What is up with Disney Princesses and comas? Did a vampire help write those fairy tales?

... *Meh. I wouldn't be surprised.*

I gently run my fingers through her hair, wishing she would scrunch up her nose, or stir in the slightest. I'm not sure how many minutes pass when my phone vibrates. I retrieve it to see the app connected to Lila's baby monitor is going off, and I unmute it to hear a fussy little baby making noises and see her stirring on the camera. I pocket my phone, kiss Crystal on the forehead, then head out to take care of our daughter while her mother rests.

Since Crystal couldn't keep blood down while she was pregnant, and this is her first time drinking it postpartum, there's a chance her body might need a little extra time to "recharge" after the lack of blood during her entire pregnancy, so I've told her I'll watch her for the day until she wakes up or her family kicks me out.

I've just laid Lila down for a nap after giving her a bottle, and I stare at her tiny face for a few moments. She's growing a little more every day and I wish I could stop time and make up for all the time with her I've missed.

She's perfect.

I'll do whatever I can to be the best Dad, Pup.

Even when you barf on me, you're still perfect.

I smile softly to myself as I continue to watch her, when my phone begins to ring. I quickly fish it out of my pocket and dart out of the room before it wakes her up. Once I'm in the hallway, I growl in irritation when I see it's my father calling.

"Yeah?" I grunt, making my way toward the staircase.

The last thing I want to do is wake up Lila or have him hear a baby crying in the background in case she wakes up on her own. I pause at the landing, and lean on the handrail that overlooks the entrance to the house. No one appears to be downstairs, and I'm relieved that there's less noise I need to worry about.

"Oh, so you're alive?" Dad asks sarcastically.

"Uh, yeah?" I roll my eyes. "In case you haven't noticed, I've been on top of all my duties for the pack. I literally sent you an email less than an hour ago, if you'd like more proof of life."

"Don't be a smartass."

Then don't ask me stupid questions.

"I need you to attend a mandatory pack meeting tomorrow night. Usual time and place."

So much for taking over for Crystal.

"Yeah, okay." I want to protest, but I don't want him to come looking for me to wonder too much about what I'm doing. Even though I want to fulfil my promise to take care of Lila by myself while Crystal sleeps, I know it'd be safer for her and Lila both to just go and not cause a fuss.

I bet whatever it is could be sent to me in an email instead of forcing me to go stand around a fire and listen to the same old topics.

"Make sure you stick around to visit your mother afterward," he grunts. "Your mother says she's almost forgotten what you look like."

"Will do."

"Good." He hangs up without saying goodbye.

I make sure my phone is silenced before making my way back to Lila's room. I'll have to make sure to give myself enough time to shower the scent of being in a vampire household off of me as well as make sure I have an outfit that will cover my mark.

I lean over the crib and am relieved to see Lila hasn't budged.

I won't ever let him meet you, Pup.

He doesn't deserve to.

It's thanks to his old, ignorant teachings that I missed your birth. I think as I frown bitterly.

Plus, he's just a jerk.

My chest aches at the thought of my mother being upset.

I wish Ma could meet you, though.

If she could just get past that prejudice, I know she would love you just as much as Alice does.

I shake my head. It doesn't help anything by focusing on the what if's and maybe's.

Oh well, so many people love you here already.

Speaking of ... I sigh.

There's someone else that loves you very much that I need make things right with.

I exit the nursery, each step feeling heavier than the last as I approach Ruby's door and lightly knock.

"Come in!" she calls out.

I open the door and walk in to find her curled up in her little reading nook that appears custom made for her beside her window. She sets her book down in her lap and looks up at me in mild surprise.

"Hey …" I rub the back of my neck, "got a minute?"

"Yeah …" she looks me up and down, "Did you come in to ask if you could borrow a shirt?"

I blink in confusion, then look down and remember I'm bare chested.

Aw, shit. This is probably awkward.

Wolves are so used to running around mostly naked in front of each other between shifting back and forth that I didn't even think about it.

"Ah, you guessed it." I feel my ears turn hot as I spread my arms with a half smile. "Your niece barfed on me. Got anything that'll go well with my eyes?"

She giggles into her palm, and I can't help but let out a chuckle, too.

"Sorry, I think that might be a smidge too small." She replies, placing her hand in front of her eye while bringing her forefinger and thumb close together.

"Damn it." I snap my fingers in mock disappointment.

"What else can I help you with?" she asks, and it makes my heart happy to hear her stutter around me less and less the more I come over.

"I was just wondering if …" I sigh, resisting the urge to groan. I must be making a face because she furrows her brow in confusion.

Just spit it out already.

"As much as this physically pains me, could you please give me Victor's address?" I ask in defeat.

"S-sorry?" Ruby asks as if she's heard me wrong. I don't blame her.

"I wanna go talk to him." I grunt.

"Good talk or b-bad talk?" she asks, narrowing her eyes in suspicion.

"Good, I swear." I sigh, rubbing a hand down my face in annoyance.

I look up at the sound of her clapping her hands. I raise an eyebrow at the smile she has as she stands up.

Did she seriously just clap her hands with glee?

"Yeah, sure! I'll text you his address right now!" she replies happily as she picks up her phone.

"Thanks."

Better go and get this over with while I have time.

"Crystal is still ah, recharging. Could you please keep an eye on Lila? I just laid her down for a nap."

"Of course!" Ruby nods.

"Thank you. I appreciate it. I wanted to stay the whole time, but- why are you grinning at me like that?"

"Oh come on!" She throws her hands up in the air, "This has been long overdue!"

I grunt and she laughs again.

"I'm sure you two will grow to be great friends if you play nice!" she adds with a smirk.

"Don't hold your breath." I scoff.

I turn on my heel and exit her bedroom to the sound of her laughing even louder behind me.

"I'm proud of you!" she calls out, and I freeze mid-step. "You're being the bigger person here!"

"You're like, three feet tall." I reply over my shoulder. "Everyone to you is the bigger person."

"Hey!"

I can't help but smirk when I turn around to see her glaring daggers at me. Her normally kind gray eyes now have the stormy color of her father when he's pissed.

She still looks adorable when she's mad though.

"I'm five feet tall, thank you v-very much!" she snaps, placing her hands on her hips. "And you're like, seven feet tall so shut your face! Your opinion d-doesn't count!"

"I'm six foot, five inches *thank you very much.*" She scrunches her nose into a scowl, reminding me so much of Crystal that I can't help but chuckle.

"Were you seriously just mocking me?!"

"It's what big brothers do."

She blinks in surprised silence and I wink at her.

"Get outta my room and go see Vic!" she stammers, pointing at the door.

I laugh the entire way to the stairs, and swear I saw the hint of a smile before I left.

Eight

CONAN

I can hear the sound of an electric guitar, plugged into an amp, over the music I have playing in my truck from down the road.

Guess I didn't need to worry about finding the right house.

I pull into the driveway of a building, that I can only describe as … *black.*

It's what appears to be a two story apartment, but I can tell Victor lives on both floors. Its bricks were painted black, along with the door, the shutters, and the motorcycle parked out front. I glance up at the car in front of me, also black, and blink.

Is that a freaking Firebird?!

Of course Pretty Boy has one. She *is* a beauty, though. I cut off the engine then step out, only to have the noise of the guitar amplified times ten. He's definitely playing outside. I walk around toward the gate on the side, noticing several plants around the house.

He even has black flowers. Really?

All it needs is a splash of pink, and this would be Crystal's dream home. It makes more and more sense why they're best friends the more time I am forced to spend with Victor. I shake my head, and resist the urge to roll my eyes as I hop over the locked gate. I could've easily broken the chain, but I'm here to make peace, not piss Victor off ... unfortunately. As I make my way toward the back of the building, I see Victor rocking his body in tune with the melody he's playing, his long, dark hair flying around his head. His back is to me, but I'm not sure if he could see me through all of that head-banging, even if he was facing towards me. He appears so caught up in his playing, that he doesn't show any sign of noticing my presence. I notice he has a lit cigarette hanging from his mouth, so that might be helping cover my scent, along with him being very distracted. I come to stand about a foot behind him, and cross my arms awkwardly across my chest as I clear my throat.

"Uh, Victor?" I say in a loud voice. He doesn't notice.

"Victor!" I call out, cupping my hands around my mouth. Still nothing.

I know better than to sneak up behind a vampire and touch him, so I yell his name even louder. He jumps about a foot in the air, causing the guitar to let out a pained whine as he spins on his heel to face me with startled, red eyes. His hand catches the guitar from hitting the concrete porch just in time, and I can't help but raise my eyebrows impressed.

"Nice save." I grunt.

"What the hell, dude?!" Victor yells, his Romanian accent sounding a little thicker due to him being flustered, I'm assuming.

"Your face was priceless just now." I can't help but smirk, chuckling a bit.

He runs a hand through his hair, pushing it out of his face, as he grumbles what sounds like a curse in Romanian.

"The *fuck* are you doing at my house?" he demands in clear English, eyes still red. I can see the pointy tips of his fangs peeking from behind his lips, letting me know how very unwelcome I am.

Great. This should go well.

"I come in peace." I say, holding up my hands placatingly.

Victor flicks the ash from his cigarette, and I can see indentions on the filter from his teeth before he takes another long drag.

"You've got ten seconds to explain yourself, then get the fuck off my property."

"All right, I hear you." I reach into my back pocket to pull out a cigarette of my own. "I just want you to know how much this is literally killing me to do this. I would rather drink bleach right now, but ... got a light?"

He rolls his eyes, and I notice they're back to their normal dark blue as he digs in his pocket, glaring at me. In the blink of an eye, he throws a lighter as if it's a dart directly at my forehead, and I catch it right before it makes contact.

"Thanks," I grunt, then light my cigarette, "Ioweyouanapology." I cough out.

"Was that even English?" Victor asks, raising a pierced brow in confusion.

I take a long pull from my cigarette, then sigh in a slow exhale. I throw the lighter back at his own head, to which he also catches effortlessly.

"I'm ... sorry." I grumble. "I'm sorry, okay? For everything." I grunt, a little louder this time.

Victor blinks at me once, twice, then erupts into laughter. I scowl as he clutches at his stomach, waiting for him to let it all out while fighting the urge to leave right then and there. I impatiently smoke, glaring at him as his laughter finally dies down into a chuckle. He wipes a tear from his eye before pulling his own cigarette toward his lips.

"Are you quite done yet?" I ask flatly.

"Sorry," he exhales a puff of smoke, still grinning, "it's just ... I-" And he begins to laugh again. I roll my eyes, and he holds up both hands in surrender. "Okay, okay!" He catches his breath, then lets out one more chuckle. I know my eyes must be flashing gold, because his grin widens. "I just know how much that bruised that big ego of yours, and it brings me *such* joy."

"Can we be serious, now?" I grunt.

"Da, I suppose." Victor nods, wiping another tear from his eye, much to my chagrin.

"Look," I say, hoping to cut him off from erupting into another fit of giggles, "I just ..." I sigh impatiently, trying to find the words and feeling as though I'm failing miserably. "I know how much you've done for Crystal and Pup, and I genuinely appreciate it."

"Pup?"

"Oh uh," I feel my ears growing hot with embarrassment as I clear my throat, "it's just a nickname. I called her that before I learned what her name was and it's just stuck."

"Ah, I see."

"Anyway, I know we haven't always gotten along, but I love Crystal with all of my heart. I want you to know that I would die for her and Lila. I know you probably already guessed this from the fact that we're mates, but I still wanted you to hear it from my own mouth. And well, with that being said …" I take another drag of my cigarette, "I also know you genuinely care for my kid, I now understand how much you put on the line for her safety, and I thank you."

I feel like crawling out of my own skin, but thankfully Victor appears to be listening, his expression now neutral.

"I also understand how much your friendship means to Crystal, so I know you're not going anywhere. So, I might as well stop being an ass and try to make peace with you." I grunt with a shrug.

Victor appears to be digesting everything I've said, his expression thoughtful and void of any of the earlier jesting. He strokes his goatee for a moment, as if deciding how to respond. I'm just about to tell him that he doesn't need to say anything and offer to leave, when he finally speaks.

"Well, considering you're obviously the reason why our Blood Fate didn't work, and are her true soul mate, I suppose you're not going anywhere either." He says with a smirk, and I blink in surprise.

"I ah, I never really put it into that perspective."

"It's just facts, da?" He takes another drag of his cigarette, "I'm just happy to know that it wasn't because she's a dhampir, and that she found her other half so that she could quit blaming herself. I've been very blessed to stay as a part of that family after everything was said and done. I'll also be nice to you as long as you are to me."

"So, truce?"

"Truce." He extends a hand, and I take it.

"Glad we're able to handle this like adults." I say, shaking his hand.

"Cool," he nods in agreement, then looks down as he starts strumming his guitar again, "now get the hell off my property."

"No arguments there." I grunt in agreement, wincing from the noise as his fingers begin to speed up and down the strings as the tune grows louder with each second, and I immediately walk away without a second glance.

CRYSTAL

THE NEXT DAY

My eyes flutter open, and I sit up to stretch. I always feel on top of the world post feeding, but this is the absolute best I've ever felt. I'm not sure if it's due to the fact I haven't fed since before Lila, or if it's thanks to feeding from my mate. Either way, I'm not going to question it.

When I enter the bathroom to brush my teeth, I spot some dried blood on my chin, as well as the swollen claiming mark Conan had reopened yesterday, and watch as my cheeks turn bright pink.

Hormones and being newly mated has turned me into an insatiable monster.

Oh well, it's not like Conan seems to mind.

I can't help but smirk at my reflection as I turn on the tap and begin to wipe my mouth.

Once my face is clean and my teeth are brushed, I poke my head into Lila's nursery and find her crib empty. I walk toward Ruby's closed door, pressing my ear to it, and smile once I hear her softly cooing at my baby from inside. I knock once, then slowly open her door to peek inside.

"Want me to relieve you?" I ask with a smile.

"Nah, we're doing some aunt and niece bonding. Go grab some breakfast." Ruby replies as she lightly bounces Lila in her arms.

"Are you sure?"

"Yes. Conan's here, by the way."

I raise my eyebrows in surprise before glancing at my phone.

"This early?" I ask.

"He said he's off today and wants to spend as much time with you as possible. I almost had to throw hands with him to get Lila."

"Is that right?" I chuckle at the mental image.

"Yeah, Mom helped me win that battle."

"She found out he hadn't eaten yet?"

Ruby nods triumphantly and I laugh a little harder this time. Mom refuses to allow any empty stomachs into her house, and if Ruby had already eaten then she definitely forced Conan to let her take over Lila duty and eat.

I make my way toward the stairs and spot Reese and Heath making their way up. As soon as I open my mouth to greet them, Heath immediately thumps me on the forehead.

"Ow! What the hell!" I snap.

"You're bloody disgusting." Heath says with a scowl.

"What did I- *Ow!* Reese!" I rub my arm on the sore spot Reese just pinched.

"Absolutely revolting." Reese adds with a glare.

"Did you both wake up on the wrong side of the bed this morning?!" I snarl as I throw a fist at them both, and much to my displeasure they both dodge each swing.

"We were *trying* to eat!" Reese says as he goes to thump my nose, but I slap his hand away in time.

"And *someone* bit their mutt for all the world to see. It's gross enough you were both marked already, did you seriously have to reopen them?" Heath scolds, sounding like a disappointed father.

I stammer, feeling my cheeks turn pink with embarrassment as I try to slap them both. Reese grabs my arm and yanks me closer as he inspects my neck.

"*Ew!*" he says, pointing a finger at my mark as he wrinkles his nose in disgust.

"He reopened yours too? Have you two no shame?" Heath asks with a mock gag.

"Would you two mind your own business?!" I shout, flustered as I yank my arm back.

They look at each other then nod.

"Let's teach him another lesson." They say in unison as they turn back toward the stairs.

"If you touch a hair on his head, I'll tell Dad about that *special* shipment from Jamaica that you put on the company's credit card." I warn and they both freeze, feet hovering over the first step.

"How do you–" begins Reese as he turns to face me.

"–know about that?" Heath finishes as he gives me an incredulous look.

I give them a triumphant smile, ignoring them as I shove through the gap between them, making sure to elbow them each in the ribs as I make my way down the stairs smirking. I hear them both whispering furiously to each other as I descend toward the kitchen. If growing up with two annoying older brothers has taught me anything, it's to always have blackmail.

CONAN

Bastards.

I scowl as I rub my sore shins.

The twins gave a horrified look at my neck, and at first I was worried they were going to announce to the entire household that my mark has been reopened ... then I saw them nod at each other as if they were speaking telepathically and I realized that was the least of my concerns.

Throughout breakfast, they each took turns kicking my shins and smirking at how I tried my best not to react. I've been rolling with their metaphorical punches ever since I've been coming over since I know they're just being overprotective of Crystal, but I'm *not* rolling with their kicks. After the third time, I delivered a swift kick back to one of them and watched as he hissed in surprise. The rest of the morning entailed of the three of us both going back and forth as I tried my best to keep a neutral tone and expression as I answered each of Alice's questions. Thank God Draken decided to eat at his office this morning.

Ruby had my back, though. She pinched one and tugged on the other's ear as she made her way toward the stairs with Lila once she had finished her plate. Watching the twins both try to silence their pain behind Alice's back was very rewarding. After they finally had enough, they made sure to give me one last glare before placing their dishes in the sink and leaving.

"I'm surprised you don't have a maid." I admit, as I look around the mansion. I grew up in a large home thanks to my dad being an alpha, but this mansion has me looking for staff.

"Hm? Oh no," Alice says with a shrug as she begins to load the dishwasher. "I prefer to do my own cleanin' *and* cookin'. I'll hire a cleanin' service to help give the whole house a deep clean once a month, but the dailies I do what the kids don't do for themselves."

"No nannies either?"

"God no. Ain't no one watchin' my kids but me and their dad."

Huh. I was not expecting that. Draken appears the type of man to send the kids off with a nanny and have someone tie his shoes for him. I guess I misjudged him a bit. It actually makes me kinda proud that my mate … (and in-laws?) aren't the snobby hands off parenting stereotype.

"That would be the twins' sperm donor that acts the way you're thinkin' of." Alice continues, shutting the dishwasher with a little more force than necessary.

"Draken's brother, right?"

"Unfortunately." She nods with an eye roll. "He probably wouldn't know how to wipe his own ass, thankfully their previous nanny had the boys potty trained before we got custody of them."

"How long have you had them again?"

"Since they were five. Crystal was about two years old when they came to live with us and I got pregnant with Ruby shortly after."

"Do they ever see their 'sperm donor'? Or is he out of the picture completely?"

"Oh, he tries to reach out whenever he wants somethin', but they shut him down quick. I always told them if they wanted to try and pursue a relationship with him I wouldn't stop them, but they never have been interested. At five years old they could tell he wasn't exactly father of the year. That's why we're Mom and Dad and he's just 'Weston'."

Weston Fox … That name sounds familiar. Other wolves might've talked about him if he's a troublemaker.

Crystal makes her way into the kitchen, rubbing her eyes.

"Just wakin' up, Cici? You fed okay?" Alice asks as she hands her a plate.

"Yeah, everything is back to normal." Crystal replies as

her eyes meet mine and a soft smile spreads across her lips. I see her cheeks pinken as she turns to the stove to begin loading up her plate.

"Good. You hungry for some real food?" Alice asks as she begins to wipe down the kitchen counters.

"Uh, is the Pope Catholic?" Crystal shoots back as she makes her way to sit next to me as Alice just laughs in response.

I lean over and press a kiss to her temple, watching her cheeks darken as her grin widens.

"Good morning, sunshine." I say with a smirk.

"Mornin' ..." Crystal mumbles shyly between bites of scrambled eggs.

Hm ... I wonder if she's feeling frisky after feeding and just doesn't wanna show it around Alice ...

It's been awhile since I've been around post feeding Crystal, but I remember very well how 'feisty' she'd get the day after. As if reading my mind, Crystal's eyes meet mine and the red tinged eyes flash a brilliant red that devours all of her purple as she licks her fork suggestively.

Oh, she totally is horny.

I smirk with satisfaction and give her a wink in response.

"Can y'all like *not* undress each other with your eyes while I'm in the room?" Alice says casually with her back turned to us.

I cough and Crystal nearly drops her fork in flustered embarrassment.

How did she even know?! Does Alice have eyes on the back of her head?!

Awkward.

"I mean," Alice continues, "I love the idea of havin' lots of grandkids, but damn. Give it a rest, yeah?" She finally glances at us over her shoulder to let us see her roll her eyes.

"*Anyway-*" Crystal clears her throat, "How did everything go yesterday while I was out? Was Lila good for you?"

"I actually left earlier than I wanted to, but she was fine until I left her with Ruby." I reply before taking a swig of my now lukewarm coffee.

"Oh?" Crystal tilts her head in confusion. "Did you get called in for work?"

"Nah," I shake my head, "I went to see Victor."

"You did what now?!" Crystal asks, nearly choking on the strip of bacon she had been chewing on.

"I apologized and asked for a truce." I grunt with a half shrug.

"Oh, Conan! That's …" Crystal's voice broke as she begins to sniffle.

"Hey, now! Don't cry!" I say confused as I begin to rub her back, unsure of what the hell just happened.

"She's just happy, baby." Alice calls over her shoulder .

"Well, ah … It's the least I could do?" I say sheepishly as Crystal gives me a watery smile.

"What's wrong, Ru?" I look up to see Alice wiping her hands on a dish towel as a very exhausted looking Ruby begins to pour herself a mug of coffee.

"Is Lila being cranky?" Crystal asks, head jerking toward her.

"No, not at all. I actually just laid her down for a nap so that I could try and knock out some homework." Ruby says as she begins to stir some creamer into her mug. "This last Calculus problem is kicking my butt, so I came down to get more brain fuel." She says as she holds up her mug then takes a sip.

"I could help you with it, if you'd like." I say with a shrug.

"Conan is more of a math wiz than you are," Crystal nods

in agreement, "he actually helped me out a lot with my problems I struggled with at Riverstone Academy."

My stomach gives a little flutter at her compliment, and I feel my ears begin to redden as Ruby and Alice both give me appreciative looks.

"If you w-wouldn't mind ..." Ruby says shyly.

"Not at all. Let me put away my dishes and I'll see what I can do."

DRAKEN

"I can't believe I forgot this bloody file *again*." I grumble to myself as I slam the bedroom door a little harder than necessary. I tuck the wretched thing that's caused me to come home two days in a row now, under my arm, and begin to make my way towards the stairs.

"All right. So what's got you stuck?" I hear that mutt's voice ask from Ruby's room.

What the hell is he doing in there?

I scowl as I creep towards her open bedroom door, making sure I'm out of sight and my steps are silent.

"Here ya go." Ruby replies and I hear the crinkling of paper.

It's quiet for a few moments, and I hold my breath as I wait.

"This is an easy fix. You were just over thinking it. Here, I'll show you." Conan replies.

I hear Ruby hum thoughtfully as the sound of a pencil scratching on paper fills the rest of the silence for the next few minutes.

"There, that should do it." Conan says as I hear the sound of him setting down the pencil onto a hard surface. Her desk or nightstand, probably.

"Lemme see." Ruby says, and I hear the sound of the paper being passed again.

It's quiet for a moment, then I hear Ruby let out an annoyed noise, causing my shoulders to stiffen.

"Oh my gosh, that's it! Thank you!" she chirps happily, and I hear the mutt chuckle in response.

"Not a problem. That was a pretty tricky one, but judging from the rest of your flawless work you're pretty smart, Ru."

"Oh, w-well, yeah I guess ..."

"There's no guessing needed. There's not even any eraser marks on this page other than that one I just helped you with."

"Well, I take pride in my work." Ruby lets out a soft chuckle. "I'm really hoping to graduate valedictorian."

"I can definitely see that, I'm sure you will. I was the salutatorian for Riverstone Academy."

"Really? That's amazing!"

Hmm. Helping her with homework?

And she's not stuttering much around him.

I feel my shoulders relax and linger for a bit longer as they exchange school memories before I finally feel comfortable enough to leave

He gets a few points for that today.

I'll just never let him know that.

Nine

CONAN

Now to see what could've been sent to me via email.

I roll my eyes as I park my truck in front of my parents' house. I don't want to be here, but I do feel a pang of guilt over the fact that my mother has been missing me. I don't particularly want to be distant from her specifically, mainly it's just *Luther*. However, it's also hard for me to look my mother in the eyes knowing that I'm keeping a mate and grandchild from her.

I'll just eat whatever she's cooked for after the meeting, then mention how exhausted I am.

I double check that my mark is covered before exiting my truck. Nero still hates me for covering it, but it's not like I have any other choice.

I wish we could show off our mate too, bud. Let's just get this over with so we can get back to her and Pup as soon as possible, hm?

He huffs in response, clearly still agitated as he paces in my mind's eye. He's not pushing to come out or for any sort of control, though. With a sigh, I light a cigarette as I make my way toward the bonfire.

I'm clearly the last one to arrive, so I'm sure I'll get my ass chewed by Dad about that even though I'm not late. I see Rider waving me over, his arms draped around Mikayla who is sitting on a log in front of him. It's not surprising to see her here, but I am caught off guard to see Marisol sitting beside her.

I wonder if they're here to discuss Mikayla joining our pack ...
Would Marisol give up her Beta so willingly, though?

After giving the ladies a respectful greeting, I go to stand beside Rider and listen as he catches me up on whatever small talk I've missed before my arrival. I'm super distracted by my thoughts of my mate and pup, and grunt here or there when I feel it's necessary to give a response. Luckily Rider has never minded that I'm mostly a listener instead of a talker, and to be honest he talks enough for the both of us anyway.

"There's my son!" I hear my mother exclaim happily before enveloping me into a bear hug.

I lift an arm to hug her back, moving my cigarette away from her face with my other. She frowns in disapproval and shakes her head.

"Haven't I told you to cut back on those things?" she says, nose wrinkling.

"Uh huh." I grunt, taking one last drag before flicking the butt into the fire.

She starts to fuss at me in Italian, but Dad's booming voice quickly cuts her off as he announces it's time for the meeting to begin. She gives me a look that heavily implies that this conversation isn't over before she heads over to stand beside him. I half shrug with an apologetic smile, and she only rolls her eyes in response.

"So, I'm sure you all have noticed that we have Alpha Gonzalez joining us tonight." Dad says as he gestures toward Marisol. Everyone nods in agreement and shoots her a glance as she stands up.

"Marisol has been updating me about evidence of a rogue bouncing between our territories that's been covering their scent." Dad continues. A few start to mutter amongst themselves, but he quickly silences them all with a raise of his hand.

"My girls have been trying to track this one down every day, but no luck. Whoever this is has done this before." Marisol adds.

"It appears that the rogue has moved on somewhere else, whoever they were, but I still would like our pack to work with hers and come up with a schedule to patrol every inch of our territories. Red will be updating you after he and Mikayla discuss their plans." Dad says. Everyone nods or voices approval in response.

A rogue, huh?

I doubt it's another teenager if they're able to cover their scent like that and have been clever enough to avoid Marisol's pack.

BAYLOR

I knew it was going to be on a bad side of town, but damn!

I slowly exit my mustang, checking out my surroundings. This part of Riverstone is mostly deserted. Several boarded up buildings that have been abandoned and neglected by time have been here for as long as I can remember. The Ravens have had to bust quite a few crime rings in them, or shoo away rogue wolves and vampires that have made one their home and cause trouble for the surrounding humans. There's more graffiti, garbage and abandoned bits of broken furniture dotting the road since last time I was here. I didn't know it could get worse than it already was, but here we are. The only inhabited areas are a few shabby rent houses that are in desperate need of some TLC, and barely appear livable next to a run down convenience store that I'm pretty sure has had more robberies than sales.

I glance down at my phone, making sure I have the correct address before looking up at the rent house I'm here for. I have to stop myself from hesitating before forcing my feet forward to the front door.

I always feel like I'm being watched out here.

I repress a shudder as I step over several pieces of cardboard boxes and other trash strewn about the sidewalk. I nearly jump out of my skin when I hear a cat yowl in the distance, and two strays proceed to fight each other beside a tipped over dumpster. I quicken my pace until I make my way to the rotting wooden steps, careful of each step I take until I'm in front of the door. I glance one more time at the numbers, then knock. I hear angry footsteps approach, then the sound of several locks coming undone before the door swings open to reveal my target.

"I already told ya, I'll have your stupid rent by the fifteenth and-"

The raven haired hybrid standing before me pauses as she

takes in that I'm not her landlord. Her aqua blue eyes narrow in suspicion as she scrunches her black painted lips into a scowl.

"Who the fuck are you?" she barks in a heavy New York accent. She's from Queens if I remember right.

"Sorry, I didn't mean to alarm you," I say with a polite smile as I extend my hand towards her, "I don't know who you were expecting, but I'm Baylor-"

"Get out of here before I kick your ass." She cuts me off, ignoring my hand as she crosses her arms across her chest.

"Look," I raise my hands in a placating gesture, "I'm not of any threat-"

"You?" She snorts, "A threat?"

I have to force the agitation from my face as she laughs humorlessly.

"Get out of my face." She says with a straight face.

"I didn't mean-"

"What part of 'get out' do you not understa-"

"Would you *please* let me finish one sentence for the love of God?!" I snap.

Her eyebrows raise in surprise, and I notice one has two piercings in it. She scrunches her nose, which is also pierced, in irritation but doesn't say anything else at the moment.

"Thank you." I sigh as I try to calm myself.

"You've got five minutes." She snaps, placing a hand on each hip as she prompts me to continue.

"That's all I need. Look, I have a friend that could really use your help. Considering what you are, I figured you could talk to her and-"

"Oh?" Her eyes flash red, a smudge of gold around her pupils. "And what exactly am I?"

"Aren't you a hy-" Before I can finish my sentence, she has me picked up by the collar of my shirt and I yelp in surprise.

She's my height, and built like an Amazon, but I know that even if she was Ruby sized picking me up would be nothing for her.

"I will *not* be a part of any experiment side show or whatever the fuck you're planning." She snarls through gritted teeth, a low growl rumbling through her chest as her eyes begin to be consumed by more of the gold.

"You don't under-" She holds me out, and drops me at the base of the steps. I stumble, stopping myself from landing on my hands and knees.

"If I catch you around here again, I'll rip you to shreds. Got it?" she barks before stomping back inside and slamming her door. I hear the click of the many locks again followed by her retreating footsteps.

That went over really well.

I dust myself off with a sigh, and turn back toward my car in defeat. I could have used my self defense training, but I didn't want to intimidate her anymore than I already have. Hybrids are paranoid creatures and it would've accomplished nothing more than a hospital visit for me. Despite whatever training or weapons I could've had on me, hybrids are a ridiculous level of strong and I didn't feel like finding out how it'd feel to be her chew toy.

I'll have to try and reason with her another way ...
She could really help us.

CONAN

I didn't sleep at all last night, irritated at the fact Red will have me running random patrols that will mess up the schedule I've tried to balance out with spending time with Crystal and Lila. Once the sun rose, I decided to go ahead and head over there while I have the first half of the day free.

I pull up to the quiet mansion a couple of hours later, and look to see if any signs of life are happening. I see a light on in Crystal's room so I assume she must up tending to Lila. I use the key Alice gave me to let myself in, and pause when I notice the kitchen light is on as well as various sounds coming from it. Even though I'd rather just sneak up the stairs to Crystal's room, I want to continue making a good impression to the Foxes and force myself to walk in to greet whoever is in there.

I'm relieved to see it's just Alice, who's still in her pajamas as she pours herself a cup of coffee.

"You're here earlier than usual." Alice says, her sleepy eyes widening in surprise.

"Good morning, Mrs Alice." I greet shyly and begin to awkwardly scratch at my neck. "Sorry, should I have waited until at least lunchtime or …"

"Nah, it's fine." She says, waving a hand dismissively. "And I've told you to just call me Alice, hun." She says as she hands me a mug with a sleepy smile.

"Uh, yeah. Right." I mumble awkwardly as I take the mug and begin to pour myself some coffee.

"Really, Conan. You're provin' yourself." Alice says as she gently places a hand on my shoulder and gives it a reassuring squeeze. "Plus, we're practically family now, huh?"

My stomach flutters at that, and I feel my ears begin to grow hot as I clear my throat.

"What's wrong, baby?" Alice asks, her brow furrowing with concern as she searches my eyes.

"I just …" I sigh. "I know you've forgiven me but I haven't really forgiven myself yet."

"Aw, Conan ..." She surprises me by hugging me, her head barely coming to my shoulder just like Crystal's does, only I think she's an inch or so shorter. I freeze, because I genuinely don't know how to respond to a vampire mom hugging me. "What's in the past is in the past, okay?" She pulls away to look up at me. "Let's just move forward. I know you love my Cici and my grandbaby."

"I ..." I have to clear my throat again, and she gives my arm another assuring squeeze as she smiles up at me, "I'm glad you're able to see that. You and Ruby both." I say quietly.

"Well, I mean it's kinda sealed in blood." Alice says with a chuckle as she places her hands on her hips.

"Er, yeah ..."

She laughs harder at my awkwardness before turning to pick her mug back up. I had forgotten I was holding mine and am so glad I didn't scald her while she was trying to have a nice moment with me.

"You can just go ahead and start stayin' over here sometimes, too. It's gotta be exhaustin' to drive almost an hour every day." She says as she begins to stir creamer in her coffee.

"That's ... very kind of you to offer." I say, blinking in surprise. "But I'm not sure how your husband would like that ..."

"He'll live." She says, rolling her eyes before offering the creamer to me. "Believe it or not, he's seen how hard you're tryin', too. He just won't admit it." She says with a sly smile before turning to add a few spoonfuls of sugar into her mug.

"Really?" I blurt out in surprise.

She nods, then slides the sugar toward me before continuing to stir her mug.

"That's great, I'm glad. But, uh ..." I search for the words to say as I begin to pour creamer into my mug. "I still don't wanna push any boundaries. Ya know?"

"You leave that old grump to me." She sniffs before taking a sip of her coffee.

"As sweet as this is, you should still sleep with one eye open." One of the twins calls from the entryway and I have to resist the urge to groan.

Why are they awake so early?

"Especially if you plan on stayin' here." The other twin adds. I still can't tell them apart and don't understand how Crystal can. Alice and Ruby appear to be able to as well, but Draken has a tendency to shout, "Whichever one you are!" when he's speaking to them, so at least I don't feel alone.

"Knock it off, you two." Alice warns as she points her spoon at them. They scowl, and she looks thoughtful for a moment before smiling. "Actually, I have a few errands you two could start on for me since you're up."

"Aw, come on!" they protest in unison.

"It wasn't a request, now move it!" Alice snaps, her eyes flashing red. The boys widen their eyes and immediately dart back up the stairs.

"Just text us what you need!" one calls behind him.

I can't help but chuckle while Alice shakes her head then turns back to face me.

"Sorry about them."

"It's fine. Seeing them run in fear of you made it totally worth it."

"Nobody messes with Mama Alice around here." She says with a wink.

"You remind me a lot of my mom, actually." I admit with a pang of sadness forming in my gut.

I wish Crystal was able to talk to my mother casually like this
…

My face must betray my sadness, because Alice softens her eyes before rubbing my arm.

"Don't be too sad, hun. I'm sure she'll come around when it's safe to tell her about everythin'."

"I hope so."

"Well, if she's anythin' like me, she'll always put her babies first in the end." She says with a wink. "What about your dad?"

"I'd rather not talk about him." I sigh, pinching the bridge of my nose.

"That's okay. I understand." She says softly before turning to face the stove.

"Crystal up yet?" I ask, hoping to change the subject.

"I'm not sure. Probably so with Lila, but why don't you go check on her? I'll have breakfast made in a bit if you want some."

"I would love that." I reply with a half-smile before heading toward the stairs.

Thankfully I don't run into the twins on my way to Crystal's room. Her door is open and I walk in to find her scrolling on her phone. She doesn't appear to have noticed me yet, and I go into full stealth mode as I creep silently in front of her. Whatever she's reading has her full attention.

"I feel ignored." I say once I stand directly in front of her and she squeaks in surprise and jumps a little.

I chuckle, and she smacks my chest with an irritated sound escaping her throat.

"Wow. Rude."

"How many times have I told you not to scare me?!"

"Remember when I would slam your locker door closed and you'd nearly pee your- OW!" I rub my chest in the throbbing spot she's just punched me.

"I hate you."

"Uh huh. Keep telling yourself that."

"Why are you here so early, weirdo?" she asks, trying and failing miserably to stifle the smile spreading across her face.

"I was just in a hurry to get to you and Lila." I admit sheepishly.

Her face softens as she pulls me into a hug, reminding me a lot of her mother. She nuzzles her face into my chest and I feel my chest rumble with pleasure.

"You've got Nero all excited now." I mumble into her hair as I hug her back.

"Aw, really?" she asks as she smiles up at me.

I nod, and have to force the bastard to stay back in my subconscious. He's like an eager puppy when he realizes she's giving him an ounce of attention.

"Does … does he want to come out?" she asks after a few minutes of probably watching my facial expression implying that I'm holding him at bay.

"Very much." I grunt. "He's dying to get to you."

"Why not let him?"

"Oh, uh … I suppose I could." I feel my cheeks warm with embarrassment as I scratch at my neck. "I just know he can be a bit … much."

"Well, I know our first meeting wasn't um, the greatest first impression." She says with a light chuckle, and my gut twists at the memory of Nero chasing her through the woods before he realized she was our mate. "I just really would like to see him again now that I know he likes me …" she adds with a small smile.

"Yeah, sorry about that. I was still learning to control him and you were underage back then, so he didn't recognize you as his mate. Now the bastard wants to be around you all the time and fight me for your attention."

"Really?" Her smile widens.

I nod, and she clasps her hands together with excitement, her purple eyes sparkling.

"Please let him out so I can meet him properly as his mate this time." She pleads, standing on her tiptoes to plant a kiss on my mouth.

"He's super excited to hear you say that." I reply honestly, and Nero immediately begins to claw for the surface. "Sorry to strip, but I would prefer not to rip my clothes." I add with a chuckle as I begin to pull my shirt over my head.

"Hey, I'm not complaining." Crystal says, wagging her eyebrows before walking over to lock her bedroom door.

CRYSTAL

I thought watching Conan shift would be weird or uncomfortable, but surprisingly it only fascinates me. Maybe because we're mates? I'm not sure how I would've reacted to watching his body morph as his bones crack a year ago. Now? I'm on the edge of my bed, kicking my feet with excited impatience as I wait for him to finish.

The large black wolf gives his entire body a shake, then looks up at me. His golden eyes are staring at me so intently, but I can feel it's with adoration instead of aggression.

He's beautiful.

I slowly slide down onto the floor, then raise my hands slowly toward him. His tail wags, and I hear a whine escape his throat as he quickly trots over to close the distance between us.

Now that I can see him in broad daylight instead of dark woods ...

Now that I can gaze at him for as long as I want rather than fleeing for my life ...

Now that I can take him all in ...

I can really take in just how majestic of a creature Nero is! He's *huge!*

He dips his large head to where we're eye level, standing just out of my reach and his tail continues to slowly wag. He tilts his head as if to say, "Is this okay?"

"Come here, handsome." I mumble, reaching my hands to gently scratch behind both of his ears.

His tail begins to wag faster before gently nudging his forehead against mine. We lock eyes again as I slowly begin to stroke the fur of his neck. He lets out another whine, and I hear his tail wagging so fast it's beginning to make a loud *thump thump thump* on my bedroom floor. I softly smile at him and we just stay as we are for a moment, no words needed. He gently licks my cheek and I can't help but giggle.

"It's good to see you again too, Nero." I whisper and a soft, rumbling noise begins to vibrate from his chest.

Is this his version of purring?

"I love you so, so very much." I say, as I gently wrap my arms around his neck and begin to rub my cheek against his, causing the rumbling to grow louder. "Tell Conan to let you out to see me more often, okay?" He answers me with another lick on my cheek and I bury my face into his soft neck. I can feel without a doubt how much he loves me and how strong his urge is to protect me.

There's no other feeling like it in the world.

Ten

BAYLOR

"What're you working so hard on?" I hear Ella ask from behind me. I straighten in my seat to stretch my sore back, my eyes grateful for the break from the computer monitor.

"Trying to find more information on that hybrid I found, but she's pretty damn good at keeping a clean slate." I say as I swivel around in my chair to face her.

"Understandable. She's probably been on the run a lot. More than likely used a few aliases, too."

"Yeah, I can tell she has. She hasn't been in Riverstone for long, but ..."

"But what?"

"It looks like someone tried to log info about her a few years ago, but when I click on it …" I turn back to face the desk, and move the mouse over the file that has only a few dates as a name. I double click it to show Ella that it's empty.

"That's weird." Ella muses.

"Yeah, I've tried looking through the edit history and nada. Only thing I can think of is that it was a mistake? I don't know." I sigh, pinching the bridge of my nose.

"Want some coffee to give your brain a boost?"

"Nah. Thank you, though."

"Ella Zavala?" We both turn toward the entrance to see one of the receptionists holding a very expensive looking vase of roses.

There must be about two dozen!

"What on earth?" Ella stammers, her eyes widening in surprise.

"Ooh, do we have a secret admirer?" I tease as I rise from my seat.

"Shut up, Bay- Hey!" she squeals after me as I quickly cross the room to take the roses from the receptionist.

"I'll take these, thank you." I say as I turn them over to look for a card.

The receptionist gives me a questioning look, then shrugs before walking away. Ella stomps up to me, scowling.

"It's made out to, 'Cupcake'." I say as I lower the vase onto the nearest table, dangling the card just out of her reach.

"Are you serious?! Give it-" Ella shrieks, her eyes wide and … is she blushing?!

I place my other hand on her forehead, holding her back as I open the card and clear my throat.

"Cupcake, I just felt like letting you know that when I get arrested by The Ravens again, I'd prefer to have you frisk me. Best,

Reese Fox." I can't help but roar into laughter as she delivers a swift kick to one of my shins. "Ow!"

"Give me that!" she snarls as she snatches the card from my hand. She turns it over, her cheeks growing a darker shade of red as she glances back and forth between it and the roses. "That idiot." She grumbles.

"I told you he has a crush on you." I tease, rubbing my shin.

"The Fox Twins have a crush on any female with a pulse." She scoffs.

"Oh, shall I throw them away then?" I ask, jabbing a thumb toward the bouquet.

She glares at me for a moment, then without a word picks them up and scampers back toward her office.

"So you do like them, then? I'll be sure to let Reese know!" I call out after her with a grin.

"Shut up!" she yells over her shoulder.

I laugh as I make my way back over to the computer.

Reese you've got a death wish.

CRYSTAL

"Everything okay?" I look up to see Dad placing an arm on Mom's shoulder.

I continue to pat Lila's back to burp her, and study Mom's face. Her brow is furrowed in the way that shows she's extremely anxious about something as she listens to her phone for a few seconds, then sighs in exasperation when she pulls it away from her ear to look at the screen.

"Draken, I don't like this. Somethin' is wrong." Mom says, voice shaking.

"What's going on?" Dad asks.

"Ruby has been gone since early this mornin' and won't pick up her phone. Cici, has she answered any of your texts, yet?"

"Not yet." I reply, shaking my head.

"What?" Dad snaps as he looks back and forth between us.

"She said she was going shoppin', but it's unlike her to be out for so long without letting us know somethin'." Mom says as she begins to wring her hands.

"Yeah, it's unlike her to ignore both of us this long." I mutter, feeling my stomach begin to knot with worry. At first I thought Mom was just being her usual worrying self, but now I'm starting to feel nervous about the whole situation, too.

"If she forgot to keep that bloody phone charged while out on her own again that phone and her car are mine for a month!" Dad shouts, practically foaming at the mouth. I can't help but flinch in response, and Lila grunts in protest.

"Draken, please. Somethin' isn't right. I can feel it." Mom says softly, her voice breaking at the end.

"I'm sure she's okay, Mama." I say as I cuddle Lila closer to me.

I hope she is.

Mom nods as her lips tremble, before a few tears roll down her face. Dad's expression immediately softens as he pulls her into a hug.

"Calm down, love. Cici's right, I'm sure everything is fine. I'm going to talk to the boys and try to figure something out, okay?"

Mom nods, sniffling.

"I'll call Victor and see if he's heard from her. She might've gone to visit him while he's recording today." I add as I fish my phone back out of my pocket.

"Good plan." Dad nods before taking his own phone out.

BAYLOR

"And that's why they call it bloodlust, baby ..." Victor finishes singing into the microphone, strumming his guitar until the song reaches an end.

That one is definitely going to be another hit.

"And that's a wrap!" his producer Dante announces as he claps his hands with excitement.

Victor grins, giving him a thumbs up before setting down his guitar and removing his headphones. As he exits the recording studio, he smiles to me in greeting.

"Baylor, to what do I owe this pleasure?"

"I wanted to chat with you over lunch if you had time for a break." I reply, fist bumping him.

"It's about time for a break. Just don't talk too much. Rest those vocals, Thorne." Dante says, nodding in agreement.

"Yes, Mommy." Victor replies, batting his eyes innocently at him.

Dante rolls his eyes and shakes his head.

"I'm going to order us some Chinese. Sound good to you, Baylor?" he asks as he looks up at me while taking out his phone.

"Chinese would be great, thanks." I reply with a nod.

"I've got to return a few calls for smartass over there," Dante says as he nods in Victor's direction, "I'll let you two visit while I catch up on the many rounds of phone tag I'm behind on."

"Your words wound me." Victor says, a mock frown on his face as he clutches at his heart dramatically.

Dante waves him off dismissively as he walks out of the room, phone to his ear. I can only shake my head, grinning at this goofball of a friend of mine that just so happens to be Dracula's grandson.

"So, what's up?" Victor asks, taking a seat.

"Think I might've found us a hybrid." I reply, taking the seat across from him.

"You serious?"

"Yeah. She's not exactly cooperative, though. I'm gonna keep trying."

"If I can help, let me know."

"Leave this one to me for now. I don't wanna piss her off more than I have and scare her away."

"Sounds like she gave you a run for your money, da?" Victor asks with a chuckle.

"You have no idea. She picked me up like I was made out of feathers and DANGLED me over her steps. She's terrifying." I groan.

Victor blinks in surprise before erupting into laughter.

"Rub it in, Vic." I scowl.

"Sorry." He says, as he pretends to wipe tears from his eyes.

"No, you're not." I grunt.

"No, I'm not." He agrees, chuckling again.

Before I can retort, his phone begins to ring.

"It's Crystal." He says as he looks at the screen before tapping the screen to answer. "Cici? What's up?"

He furrows his brow in confusion as he listens.

"Ruby? No, she's not with me. I haven't seen or heard

from her today, actually. Why?"

That doesn't sound good.

"Hm. One sec, Baylor is here." His eyes lock with mine. "You haven't heard from Ru today, have you?"

I shake my head.

"I haven't, sorry."

He frowns then lets out a sigh.

"Oh, well. You know how she gets when she shops. I'm sure everything is fine, I'll let you know if I hear from her, though." Victor says before ending the call.

"Everything okay with Ru?" I ask.

"Apparently she's been gone for awhile to go shopping and no one can get in touch with her."

"Hm. Draken *has* lost his top on her before about not keeping her phone charged when she's out for a while."

"True. Like I said, I'm sure it's fine."

"Yeah, she's probably going to be grounded until she's thirty, though."

He chuckles and nods in agreement.

"So, I heard you and Conan kissed and made up?" I add.

"Apparently I have *you* to thank for that," he says as he rolls his eyes, "He was actually, dare I say, polite?"

"Oh, really?"

Victor nods.

"Well, you're welcome." I reply with a wink.

Victor shakes his head and chuckles as his phone vibrates again. He glances at the new message that's popped up on his screen then rolls his eyes.

"What is it?" I ask.

"I just ah, have to be the bad guy again." He grunts as he shoves his phone back into his pocket.

"Ah, girl problems again?" I tease.

"Dude, I try to be as clear as possible that I have no time

for serious relationships with all the traveling my music is about to have me doing!" he groans.

"And they already have wedding bells playing in their heads as they completely ignore that."

"Yes," he rubs his temples, "I've even got screen shots to prove I've said it more than once. But they still cry or act like I'm an asshole."

"Well, you are an asshole."

"This time I'm not trying to be on purpose!"

"I know, I know. The price of fame, eh?" I chuckle as I clap a hand on his back.

"I guess. Wanna go see if the food is here yet?"

"Yes, let's go drown your sorrows in soy sauce and fortune cookies."

CRYSTAL

"Victor didn't hear anything?" Conan asks, rubbing my back as I stare down at my black phone screen, chewing on my lip.

"No. She's not with him and he hasn't heard from her today." I sigh.

"Baylor?"

"He was there with Vic, he said the same thing."

"Has your Dad heard anything back from the twins?"

"That would be a no." Dad says as he enters the kitchen, his eyes filled with worry.

"Damn." Conan mutters with a frown.

"I'm starting to get scared, Dad." I admit as I begin to fidget with my ring. Conan squeezes my shoulder, and I can feel how my stress is making *him* stress.

"I just got off the phone with Reese, nothing from him or Heath." Dad sighs as he takes a seat at the kitchen table.

"Where the hell could she be?" I breathe as I look up at Conan.

"Hopefully she just forgot to charge her phone." He responds before his vibrates. My heart flutters with hope for a second, even though I know Ruby has no reason to text Conan.

"Ugh." He scowls as he rolls his eyes before shoving his phone back into his pocket a little too aggressively.

"What is it?" I ask. Dad looks up at him in question as well.

"My father." He grunts. "I'm really sorry, I wasn't supposed to have to go back over there today, but he's calling some sort of emergency pack meeting that is probably some bullshit that he could've just texted me as usual."

"Go on, then. We don't want you raising any suspicions." Dad says with a wave of his hand.

Conan nods before pulling me into a hug.

"Text me if you get an update on Ru?"

"I will."

"It's going to be okay, I promise. I can come back tonight if you want me to." He says softly before kissing my forehead. I hear Dad snort in disgust.

"Please do." I whisper.

"I'll be back as soon as I can then." He pecks a kiss to my lips then hugs me tighter. "Love you."

"Love you, too."

"Can you two wrap this up please?" Dad grumbles.

Conan clears his throat as he releases me awkwardly.

"Seriously Dad?! Now is hardly the time!" I snap as I turn to face him, only to be met by his glare.

"Right, uh, well I'll be leaving." Conan says before picking up his truck keys and exiting the kitchen.

Dad looks down to tap at his phone screen a few times before standing up.

"I'm going to go to my office and see if I can trace her car or her phone."

I blink in surprise.

"The phones I knew about, but you have a tracker on her car?!"

"Yes. Yours, too."

"*Seriously?*"

"Times like this are exactly why." He replies coldly before strutting out of the kitchen.

I roll my eyes then glance down at my phone, disheartened to see no new notifications.

Where are you Ru?

BAYLOR

"I can smell you, human." Cadence's voice calls out in a warning tone from behind her closed door. I nearly jump out of my skin in surprise. "You have five seconds to leave or I'll open this door and knock your teeth out of your head."

"You don't even have to open the door!" I reply quickly. "I'm just here to leave you my information. I'm placing an envelope on your doormat. What you choose to do with it is up to you." I bend down, making as much noise as possible so that she can hear I'm doing exactly what I'm saying I'm going to do. "I'm leaving now. I hope to hear from you." I say before cautiously backing down her steps.

She doesn't reply or open the door, so I take this opportunity to hustle back to my car before she changes her mind and kicks my ass anyway.

DRAKEN

"Dad?" Reese says, his voice filled with concern on the other line. "We have an issue."

The knot in my gut clenches as a wave a nausea passes through me at the thousands of horrible scenarios that play through my mind at his words.

"What is it?" I snap. "Is her car where I told you to look?"

"It is, but it's empty. We talked to a security guard and he said Ruby was there before lunch this morning, but he hasn't seen her since."

I feel my blood turn to ice in my veins.

"Are you fucking with me right now?" is all I manage to spit out.

"I'm afraid not." He replies quietly. "Heath is asking around at other stores nearby, but so far nothing ..."

"Well, keep looking!" I stammer, resisting the urge to pull my hair out. "I'm going to try to make a few phone calls and see if I can get more eyes looking for her."

"That's not all." Reese sighs.

"Well? Spit it out!" I feel as though my heart is going to beat out of my chest. "What is it?!"

"I don't know if it's related to her being missing or not, and I hope to God it's not, but ..." He releases a shaky breath and I have to force myself not to rush him. "There's a faint scent of wolf nearby where her scent ends."

"*What?!*" My hearts skips a beat, and I feel as if the world is crumbling beneath my feet. I have to slam my hand onto my desk for support. "I'm on my way. Do not, I repeat, *do not* tell your mother anything about this." I say before hanging up.

Within seconds my keys are in my hand and I'm peeling out of the driveway.

I'm coming, Ruby.

Eleven

DRAKEN

The poor kid behind the counter at the last store Ruby was seen must be twenty at the most. I can smell his fear as well as hear the thumping of his heart in his chest. He reminds me of a rabbit cornered by a fox as I take a step to close the distance between us.

"I'm really not supposed to let anyone behind the counter, sir. I'm … I'm going to have to ask you to leave!" he sputters nervously, one word tumbling over the other.

"Any demands will be made by me." I reply coolly.

I watch the poor lad reach for the button under the counter that is undoubtedly a silent alarm to alert the police, not that it would help him, and raise a hand to gesture to the twins. In seconds they each have one of his arms, and he is momentarily startled by how fast they moved. They didn't hide their super speed, and I don't care. This can be a problem for The Ravens if I don't put the fear of God into him from speaking out first … if I allow him to live.

"H-hey! How did you-" I cut off him off by snapping my fingers in front of his face.

"You will be silent unless spoken to, if you wish to keep your tongue inside your head."

He nervously glances longingly at the button that was just out of his reach under the counter, then slowly looks back at me, lips pursed into a firm line. Sweat is beginning to pool everywhere on his body, and the stench of his raw fear is growing stronger by the second.

"I want to have a look at your security tapes." I say firmly.

"I-I'm not allowed to do that!" he says as he begins to squirm, which only causes the twins to tighten their grips on his arms and causing him to let out a yelp from pain.

"Does it look like I give a shit?!" I snap, and allow my eyes to flash red for a moment.

The terrified look on his face confirms that he indeed saw them, and his brain seems to glitch as he stares at me in open-mouthed silent horror. I see the twins smirk in unison before they give him a shake.

"Answer him." They say sharply in unison.

The kid swallows hard, then slowly nods.

"What I meant to say was …" He clears his throat smartly. "Right this way?" He nods toward a door in the back of the shop.

"That's more like it. Walk." I grunt.

The boys let go of him, and one of them, Heath I think?

Shoves him towards the door he gestured to. My sharp hearing picks up that he mumbles something like, *"I don't get paid enough for this shit,"* under his breath. Under normal circumstances I would probably laugh at that, but for now my nerves are forming tight knots of anxiety in my gut. Without another word, the boys and I follow him to see if we can find any clue at all of where Ruby went.

CRYSTAL

Once Lila is down for her nap, I make my way downstairs and hear the sound of Mom softly sobbing in the kitchen. My stomach flips with worry as I head toward her. I see her leaning over the counter, still in her pajamas as she cries into her hands, an untouched mug of more than likely cold coffee, next to her.

"Any news?" I ask quietly as I gently place a hand on her shoulder.

She shakes her head and continues to cry, not even looking up at me.

Shit.

I have to force myself to not let my imagination run wild with the endless scenarios that could currently be happening to my sister. I blink away a few tears of my own, and release a slow and shaky breath before pulling Mom into a tight hug. She hugs me back, her cries growing louder as she squeezes me back as tight as she can.

"We'll find her, Mama." I whisper. I'm not sure if I'm trying to convince myself or her, but I have to stay positive.

Surely this is all a big scare for nothing, and Dad will be lecturing her for it as they walk through the door any minute. *Right?*

CONAN

I flip down the visor mirror one more time to make sure my mark is covered before facing Dad's pack house. Once satisfied, I kill the engine and stare at the abandoned house. Dad wanted it to look uninteresting so that it would make the perfect place to interrogate any enemies, or store away anything that might be of use or dangerous later. Although the house isn't taken care of, the pack keeps the basement maintained since that's the main part we use.

What the hell could be here that's so important for an impromptu meeting?

I decide it's useless to try and flip through the endless list of things it could be in my mind, and finally step out of my truck to go see for myself. I hear Louis laughing inside and walk in to see Collin glaring back at him with a huge bruise on his face, along with a few scratch marks that look as if a very pissed off cat went to town on his cheeks.

What the fuck?

"Well, well, look who decided to finally show their face around the pack again." Louis snorts, as he looks up to meet my gaze when I walk through the threshold, ducking under spiderwebs as I go. Collin turns to fully face me and scowls.

"Decided to finally grace us with your presence, young prince?" he sneers as he rubs at one of the fresher scratches and winces slightly.

"Dude, I know you're not talking shit to me when you look like *that*." I scoff. "The fuck happened to your face?"

Collin just frowns with a frustrated sigh and Louis cackles again.

"Marcus caught a little vamp earlier, and she showed Collin that she wasn't completely defenseless when he got too cocky as we were interrogating her." Louis says, as he jabs Collin with his elbow. Collin elbows him back, a low growl rumbling from his chest which only makes Louis chuckle again.

"Little shit is much stronger than she looks." Collin grumbles as he tenderly rubs his face again.

Oh, that's just fucking wonderful.

"Vamp?" I ask raising a brow, trying to appear as neutral as possible.

Wait …

Every hair on my body stands on end once a familiar scent hits my nose. I glance down to see blood stains on Collins hands and sleeves and take a step closer, taking a deeper breath.

That scent …

Nero begins to claw his way toward the front of my mind as my canines begin to elongate, and I have no doubt my eyes are now violent gold.

"What's the vamp's name?" I growl, forcing myself to use my words instead of just roaring at them both.

"Pain In The Ass? Why?" Collin asks, clearly irritated as he is confused by my sudden shift in mood. I can feel his wolf straightening to full alert in alarm at Nero's behavior.

This time a loud growl rips from my throat as I grab him by the shirt and pull him up to my eye level.

"WHAT'S HER FUCKING NAME?!"

"I don't remember! What the hell is your problem?!" Collin stammers as his own eyes flash gold in warning.

"Whoa, whoa! Her driver's license said Ruby. What's it to you?!" Louis sputters as he tries to come between us, but a quick snap of my teeth in his direction makes him back away with his hands raised in surrender.

"Conan, wh—" I don't even know who asked.

My anger boiled over to the point I wasn't sure who was more pissed between Nero and me. I think we took turns taking control as I began to punch Collin's face repeatedly until I heard his nose crack, the scent of his blood almost covering Ruby's. I might've heard Louis shouting, but I have no idea what he said as I dropped Collin to the ground and kicked him in the ribs as hard as I possibly could, feeling bone crunch as his body went sliding across the dirty floor leaving a streak of blood behind him. Either he was unconscious, or the wind was knocked out of him because he didn't move. Louis began to shift out of fear, but I scruffed him by the neck mid-change and began to repeatedly slam his face against the wall until his screams and yelps turned into low, weak groans. The only small sliver of sanity left in my brain, stopped me from beating him unconscious as I gripped a fistful of his blood caked hair to hold his head up.

"WHERE IS SHE?!" I snarled.

He coughed, spitting blood before mustering up the strength to try to kick my legs out from under me, his claws biting into my forearm with a firm grip. I didn't even flinch, the primal rage and adrenaline made me barely feel it even though I'm sure his claws probably were close to bone deep. Before he could make another move, I balled my other hand into a fist and punched him as hard as I could under the ribs, causing him to double over with more pain, then kneed him in the groin. It was playing dirty, but I didn't give a shit. With a rattling cough that sprayed blood everywhere, he fell to his knees as his hands flew to protect his crotch a little too late.

"Where." I growled as I dug my own claws into his throat, careful not to crush it to the point where he couldn't answer me.

"Fuck you." Louis spat out more blood, not raising his head.

"Is she downstairs?" I asked, placing my boot directly over his hands to let him know that I'll break them along with his pelvis if I have to.

"Yes! Shit!" he groans begrudgingly.

I released his throat and heard him try to talk more shit that I didn't catch as I kicked him once more to move him out of my way. His body curled up into a fetal position as I began to dash toward the basement door at full speed. Luckily no one else got in my way as I flew down the creaking steps.

"HAVE YOU LOST YOUR FUCKING MIND?!" I hear Dad bellow, causing me to freeze. The door is open to the interrogation room, but at this angle I can only see the back of one of his shoulders. Marcus appears to be cowering in front of him.

"Alpha, wh—"

"Tell me we don't have Draken Fox's daughter held hostage!" Dad yells as he begins to shake Marcus by the shoulders. I don't have to see his face to know he must be foaming at the mouth.

Dad knows who Draken is?

"That little baby doll is sired by *The Ripper*?!" I hear Rider mumble in shock.

My stomach twists with pain and betrayal. The idea of my best friend being involved with ... whatever they've done to Ruby makes me physically ill.

"W-who?" Marcus stammers.

"Draken 'THE RIPPER' Fox! Ring any bells?!" Dad snaps.

I see Marcus's eyes widen in horror as something seems to click.

"I-I swear I didn't know, Alpha!" he says in a tone that sounds as if he's pleading for his life ... which he very well may be.

Does Draken have an alter ego I don't know about? Why do they keep calling him The Ripper?

"Now what're we going to do, you idiot?!" Dad groans, rubbing his face anxiously as Marcus continues to stare at him wide-eyed.

"I'll drop her off, and—"

A loud smack echoes through the basement as Dad's backhand nearly sends Marcus flying backwards. I hear Rider let out a quiet gasp, but I still can't see him.

"So she can bring him straight to us?!" Dad yells.

"S-sorry, Alpha." Marcus says quietly as he rubs his face.

Dad's breathing is as heavy as mine and with how loudly my heart is pounding in my ears, I begin to wonder if I just can't hear them over the sound until Marcus finally speaks again.

"Alpha, I—"

"Shut the hell up and let me think." Dad snaps, as he begins to pace. He still hasn't looked this way to notice me. Marcus drops his head in shame, staring at his shoes, so I know I'm still in the clear from him as well.

"Well, we can't keep her here." Rider finally chimes in, and I notice both Dad and Marcus snap their heads in his direction.

"And what do you propose we do?" Dad asks impatiently through gritted teeth.

"I don't know! But whatever *this* is," his voice pauses and

I can imagine him gesturing to something ... maybe Ruby? "I want no part of!"

Maybe Rider wasn't in on it after all?

"Rider ..." Dad warns.

"No." I blink in surprise at Rider's quick reply. He's never talked back to my dad.

Ever.

"This is fucked up, whatever it is. Vamp or not, this is *disgusting*." Rider continues, and at that point I can't wait any longer. I need to see whatever they've done to her. My entire body trembles with anger as I quickly stride inside, causing everyone to pause mid argument to look at me.

"Conan?" Dad blinks in surprise. "It's about time you showed up! We've got quite a mess."

"Tell me ..." I stalk closer to him. "You had ..." I'm only inches away from his nose as I grip my hands into tight fists, my claws lengthening to prick my palms. "No part in this, Dad." I finish, my voice too calm even to me.

"What're you on about, boy?" Dad says with a confused frown.

"Where is she? What did you d—" My heart stops and feels as though it's dropped to the pit of my stomach as I look past him to see a tiny, crumpled form on the floor. Her back is to me, and I see blood.

So much blood ...

Oh my God! No!

"Ru?!" I abandon every other thought as I rush over to her. There are claw marks all over her back, her shirt ripped to shreds. My hands shake with fear and rage as I gently turn her over to look at her front. Her body is limp and so, *so* cold.

"Ruby?! God, please no!" My voice shakes as I gently place a hand on her clawed chest to see if she's alive.

I could nearly fall over in relief at the feel of her heart

beating and her chest rising in a shaky breath. She's unconscious, but she's *alive*. I feel my eyes sting as I look over her. Her little face is drained of color, her normally pale complexion now a sickening shade of white. Her lips are also too colorless and covered in a huge scab. I force my shaking hand to be steady enough to push her hair out of her face and see it's covered in bruises. She's got the telltale signs of a black eye beginning to form, and a long gash from a werewolf claw from her temple to her chin. The front of her shirt is just as shredded as the back. Even her jeans are torn and caked with blood, and one tiny foot is missing a shoe. I glance at her arms to see bruises from where fingers gripped her too tightly, and I feel my entire body pulse as Nero threatens to shift. I force myself to stay in my human form so I can safely carry her the hell out of here.

"Conan, what the hell are you *doing?*" I hear Dad ask, bewildered.

I look over my shoulders, growling loudly. All three of the wolves stare at me in shock.

"What the hell did you sons of bitches do?" I spit out. "Ruby is the most loving and innocent person I know! What the hell possibly caused you fucking monsters to do this?!" I yell as I angrily wave in Ruby's direction.

"Did you just refer to that *leech* as a person?" Marcus asks in disgust.

"How the hell does my son know The Ripper's daughter?" Dad snaps, his eyes widening as he looks me up and down, as if he hopes to find the answer by scanning me all over.

"I'm no son of yours!" I snap back, and his mouth parts in shock as his face turns an angrier shade of red. "I'm taking her with me and *none of you* will get in my way. I will not hesitate to kill any of you." I growl through clenched teeth as

I turn back to Ruby and begin to pick her up as gently as I can.

"Conan!" Dad finally sputters. I can't tell if he's more angry or confused.

"That includes *you*, Luther!" I bark over my shoulder before turning back to Ruby. Once she's cradled securely in my arms, I slowly stand. "Come on, Ru. Big Brother's gotcha now." I whisper into her hair, my voice threatening to crack at how absolutely lifeless she feels in my arms.

"Conan, you better drop her or else-!" Marcus starts, but I don't care.

I dash out of there as quickly as I can, hoping I'm not hurting Ruby more than she already is. I swear I hear Rider snap back at him behind me, but I can't understand what he's saying. Ruby still feels so cold against me, and I silently pray that my body heat helps warm her up on our way to the truck. It's pretty chilly outside, so after I carefully lay her down in the back seat, I quickly shrug off my jacket and drape it over her. She's so tiny that it nearly covers her perfectly as a blanket. Once I feel she's safely secured to not roll around, I jump in the front seat and crank my truck to life, turning up the heat at full blast.

"Wait up!" I hear Rider yell, as he runs at full speed toward my truck. I blink in surprise, debating if I should just gun it and peel out of the driveway, but he's already in the passenger seat before I can make up my mind.

"What the–Rider, what the hell are you doing?!"

"Take me with you!" he says as he slams the passenger door.

"The fuck did you just say?"

"There's no time! Just go!"

I stare at him, wondering if I should trust him. This has been my best friend for years, and he seemed totally against all of this. I just hope he knows what he's doing. We'll both be rogues and blacklisted from the pack once we leave the property. I exhale through my nose as I shift the gear in reverse and began to back up as fast as I can, glancing in the rearview mirror at Ruby to make sure she's alright.

"Fine. Just keep in mind there's no going back." I tell him as I speed toward the highway, surprised to not find Dad or any of his men following me.

ALICE

"You're gunna be okay, baby. You're gunna be okay." I chant out loud as a mantra more to myself than anyone else, considering my baby girl is a mangled, unconscious mess in my arms.

When Conan brought her in, I nearly fainted at the sight of the blood covering him, until I looked down to see that he was carrying my equally blood-stained baby. Once I found myself strong enough to not burst into tears or vomit on the spot, I took her from him and began to bark orders to him and Crystal both, to gather my medical supplies. She has cuts, scratches, bites, broken bones… all from werewolves that basically used her as a chew toy.

I keep whispering promises to her as I lay her on her bed, checking her wounds and bandages for what must be the hundredth time. Once I've done every mundane thing I can do, I begin to siphon every bit of healing magick I hold within my core, to flow down to my finger tips and begin to softly caress the air above her body. Ruby's not a fully matured vampire just yet, so I feel like magick is the faster way to heal her than if I were to give her my blood. Once she's conscious enough to swallow, I'll feed her some to help if I feel the medicine and magick isn't enough.

And she will wake up. Don't even think like that, Alice.

She will wake up. She's still breathing, her heart is still beating, she will be okay.

I brush my fingers through her bangs, feeling myself begin to grow dizzy. I know I gave her too much of my energy too quickly, but I don't care.

She has to be okay. Or I ...

My eyes begin to well up with tears as I take in every single bruise, cut, scratch, bite mark and just ... everything. Everything my poor Ruby has been through. She wasn't just beat up by some thugs, she was full on *tortured*.

"My baby ..." I hear Draken choke out behind me.

I look over my shoulder to see his already pale skin a sickly white, his eyes wide and wild with both rage and pain.

"Draken ..."

I see his eyes taking in every detail of our daughter's broken little body and his breaths begin to come out in quick, ragged huffs as his eyes flash a bright, murderous red.

"I'll ..." his voice is so hoarse he has to swallow and clear his throat before he can continue, "I'LL KILL WHOEVER HAS DONE THIS!" he roars, his fists shaking.

"Hush! Don't you dare wake her up!" I hiss through clenched teeth. To be honest, I doubt she will be able to be woken up for quite some time, but I still don't think him yelling like a barbarian is any good for her, conscious or not.

He huffs a sharp breath through his nostrils as he begins to pace, his eyes never leaving Ruby. He's grinding his teeth as he runs his hands through his hair, looking as though he's ready to rip it out.

"I know, I'm sorry, it's just ... she ... seeing her ..." He pauses and begins to run his hands over his face.

"I know," I slowly stand to face him, "I want to torch whoever did this, to a crisp. Believe me."

Draken clenches his jaw as his eyes move from me back to Ruby, his nostrils still flaring as his entire body is still trembling with anger. He opens his mouth to reply, then quickly snaps it closed. He blinks once, twice, then to my shock he begins to sob.

"Draken!" I immediately wrap my arms around him and hug him to me as tight as possible.

"I wasn't there to protect her, Alice!" Draken chokes out as he continues to stand there, looking at our daughter helplessly.

"This isn't your fault, Draken!" I blurt out, my throat burning as tears begin to slide down my cheeks.

He doesn't say anything, he only gently removes my arms as he walks over to the bed and sinks down to grab one of Ruby's tiny, bruised hands, holding it to his chest. I place a hand on each of his shoulders, my heart breaking at the sight as he continues to sob. In the nineteen years we've been married, I've *never* seen Draken cry. I've seen him sad before, but nothing like this. Seeing our baby so broken and maimed has destroyed him. All I can do is continue to hold him as we cry together.

Whoever did this will pay.
No doubt about it.

CONAN

"Thank you for bringing her home!" Crystal sobs into my chest for what must be the millionth time.

"Shh, of course I did." I run my fingers through her hair, wincing at how disgusting I am with all the blood still coating my skin. "She's home now, and that's all that matters."

Crystal nods with a sniffle, then slowly peaks behind my shoulder. "Who ... who is that with you?"

I blink in confusion before realization smacks me in the face like a brick as I remember Rider followed me here. He stood off awkwardly to the side in the hallway as Crystal and I hurried to bring Alice everything she requested to clean and care for Ruby's wounds, before she shooed us away to give her space to work.

"Oh, uh," I clear my throat awkwardly as I gesture Rider to come closer, "this is Rider."

"Uh, hi." Rider says in a very strained, polite voice. He looks as though he's a mouse surrounded by cats, and since he's a wolf in a vampire home, I can't really say I blame him.

"Um, hello." Crystal replies just as awkwardly, glancing up to me as if asking what to do now.

"Apparently Rider was tired of the pack's shit as well." I say.

"It's true." Rider nods, rubbing the back of his neck awkwardly. "I just couldn't stomach watching what they did to that poor little thing. It was barbaric." He adds as his face twists with disgust.

"I'm ... I'm glad to see Conan isn't the only wolf that sees things that way." Crystal replies.

"Speaking of," Rider says as he turns to face me, "Conan, you haven't exactly told me how you've come to be allies with the Foxes ..."

"Oh, uh, well ..." I glance toward Crystal, silently asking if she's comfortable with me telling Rider the truth. She only gives me a half shrug as a response before looking back at Rider nervously, one of her fangs peeking out as she begins to fidget with her ring. I nod and turn to face Rider fully, putting myself between him and Crystal out of instinct before continuing, "Crystal here is my mate."

"What?!" Rider gapes.

"Gotta problem with that?" I ask, bristling. My eyes are now gold as my canines begin to lengthen, Nero creeping further to the surface of my subconscious as back up.

"N-no! I just … I just wasn't expecting …" He pauses, tilting his head thoughtfully for a moment. "Actually, this makes so much more sense now."

I raise an eyebrow at him.

"And it *definitely* explains why you've been wearing so many scarves and high collared stuff lately." Rider continues with a smirk.

"You're taking this rather well." I grunt.

"Well, I suppose it's safe to tell you one of my childhood friends was a hybrid." Rider shrugs.

Crystal and I exchange a shocked glance.

"You know a hybrid?!" Crystal blurts.

"Are you serious?! You never told me that!" I add.

"Knew. I *knew*, a hybrid." Rider corrects. "I haven't seen her in years. She was like a sister to me. No idea where she is now."

"Oh, I see." Crystal mutters, shoulders dropping with disappointment.

"At least we know one is out there." I say, gently taking one of her hands. We've been toying with the idea of tracking one down to see how they are in person so we can know what to possibly expect for Lila's future.

"Maybe she's still close by." Crystal agrees.

"Why are you guys worried about that?" Rider asks suspiciously as he eyes the mark on Crystal's neck. I was just about to growl at him to mind his own business when Lila decides to announce her presence by wailing angrily from down the hall.

"Don't worry about it." I answer quickly as Rider's eyes widen in shock.

"Conan! Are you a *father*?!"

"I-"

"Not only are you mated to The Ripper's daughter, but you had a *baby* with her too?!" Rider exclaims, still clearly in shock.

"Why does everyone keep calling Draken that?" I ask, glancing at Crystal who's extra fidgety all of a sudden.

"You don't know your own father in law?!" Rider shouts, looking at me as if I've suddenly grown another head.

"What's he talking about, C?" I ask, raising an eyebrow at Crystal.

"Yeah. Uh, I'm not gonna answer that right now. Bye." Before I can open my mouth to respond, she's gone down the hall to Lila's room in a flash.

"This conversation isn't over!" I yell after her.

"You seriously haven't the slightest idea whose house you're in?! What family you're apart of?!" Rider asks in disbelief.

"Uh, you mean Draken? Her dad?"

"Conan! Remember we had to learn about dangerous vampires throughout history? You were a straight A student!"

"Yeah?"

"Does *Jack the Ripper* ring any bells?!"

Every thought in my brain comes to a screeching halt as I process what he just said.

"Wait ... *What*?"

"Now are you on the same page?!"

I remember learning all about the serial killer called Jack the Ripper, but I don't recall us ever going over his real name.

"Crystal and I obviously have a lot to talk about." I grunt as I pinch the bridge of my nose.

"I'd say so!" Rider says sarcastically as he continues to stare at me as if I'm a freak of nature.

How the hell does he know all about the Foxes anyway? Much less who one of them used to be back in the 1800s? Wait, how old is Draken? For fuck's sake, never mind that for now.

"Anyway, you do realize you're technically a rogue wolf now, right? There's no turning back." I say, deciding to talk about more pressing matters.

"I've been thinking about leaving for a while now. This just was the straw that broke the camel's back."

"Does Mikayla know yet?"

"No, I haven't touched my phone at all since I jumped in the truck with you. I'll just find the right time to tell her later ..." he replies nervously.

"Well, I suppose I'd better fill you in on a couple of other things and–what's with you?" I ask, as I watch Rider's eyes grow bigger and bigger until I realize he's staring at something, or someone, behind me.

"Conan." I hear Draken's voice before I can scent him. I can't tell if it's all the blood caked to me or if he's hiding his scent.

"You're freaking out because he's behind me, aren't you?" I grunt at Rider, not hiding the judgment from my glare. Rider just continues to stare behind me in stunned silence. I roll my eyes before turning to face Draken fully. "Yes, sir? How's Ruby?"

"Alive because of you." He says before releasing a sigh. For the first time, Draken looks *old*. I've never seen him out of proper businessman attire, and now he looks as if he hasn't slept in years. He just seems so defeated. Which is *very* unlike him.

"Conan," he continues as he claps a hand on my shoulder and I have to stop myself from flinching, "I owe you everything for what you did. From now on, consider yourself welcomed into this family. You have my blessing and forgiveness for everything. Whatever you need or ask for, is yours."

"Mr. Fox I ... I don't know what to say. I was just doing the right thing. Ruby is like a little sister to me." I ramble out as I still try to wrap my head around everything he just said.

"Please, Draken is fine." Draken says as he raises a hand dismissively.

"Oh, uh ..." I stammer. He just keeps adding onto my shock. "Okay, but really ... I would do it all over again. I've officially turned my back on my pack," I gesture to Rider behind me, "we both have."

"Yes, who is that you have with you? He looks as though he's seen a ghost." Draken says as he steps aside to get a good, clear look at Rider, who is still standing there like a stunned mannequin.

"This is Rider. He left the pack with me and is against everything they've done to Ru."

"Well, in that case, an ally of yours is an ally of mine. Welcome to my home, Rider."

After a few minutes of awkward silence I elbow Rider in the ribs, causing him to jump in surprise.

"You might wanna say something, dude." I grunt through gritted teeth.

"Yes, sir." Rider clears his throat, careful not to make direct eye contact with Draken as if he were an Alpha. "Thank you. It's ah ..." He clears his throat again, "It's an honor to meet you, Mr. Fox."

"Ah, I'm assuming you've heard of me." Draken says in an amused tone.

"Yes, sir."

"That explains the look on your face." Draken chuckles, "Relax, boy. If I wanted you dead I would've already killed you a long time ago."

"He's not wrong." I shrug.

"Eh heh ... right." Rider says through a strained smile before shooting me a look that lets me know neither of us made him feel any better.

"So, tell me what you know about who is responsible for this." Draken says, his face now void of all humor.

"My now ex-pack mate Marcus and his two cronies Collin and Louis. I can tell you *everything* you need to know about them." Rider responds.

"I knew they weren't the greatest people, but I never expected *this* from them. I wonder what Dad's next move will be ..." I sigh, my whole body now feeling ten times heavier now that the adrenaline and rage has fully worn off as reality begins to sink in.

"Alpha Knight actually didn't order this. He had no idea until he arrived to the interrogation room. He freaked when he found out she was The Ripper's daughter."

"So, he didn't lay a hand on her?" I ask, as relief floods me from the inside out. I still can't stand my father, but I'm so glad this isn't his dirty work.

"No. Don't get me wrong, he still hates vamps obviously, but he didn't even know they had her. He flipped his shit on Marcus when he heard the name, 'Fox'." Rider says. For once, I'm actually proud of my dad. Still disowning the old bigot, but that's one less reason to hate him.

"So, this Marcus is the ring leader in all this? Is he Beta?" Draken asks, and I snort.

"He wishes." Rider and I say in unison.

"Does your father know why you saved Ruby, Conan?" Draken continues.

"He doesn't. He just knows that I know you and saved Ruby because I know you. He has no idea about me and Crystal, and I've made sure *no one* knows about Lila."

"That's the truth. I only learned Conan was mated and had a child today. Is Lila your pup's name?"

Every instinct wants me to hide her from the world, but I know I can trust my best friend.

"Yes." Is the only thing I reply with.

"Well, for now why don't we all get some rest?" Draken interrupts, "I plan on hunting down those fools that got Ruby one by one after I learn everything about them." Draken says in a voice so cold it sends chills down my spine.

"I'm surprised you didn't go on a bloody rampage tonight." I say honestly.

"As tempting as that is, I need a level head to plan out what exactly I want to do and how I want to do it. Taking care of my little girl is my top priority right now." Rider and I both nod silently in understanding. "Rider, you're more than welcome to stay in one of our guest rooms. I'll be having a conversation with you about your ex-pack mates first thing in the morning."

"Yes, sir." Rider nods.

"I'm going to check on Ruby again, good night boys." Draken says before heading back toward Ruby's room.

"Well," I turn to face Rider, "I'm glad you didn't faint."

"I seriously can't believe that just happened. I just met *The Ripper*." Rider replies sounding both terrified and starstruck.

I can only roll my eyes in response.

"I have to say, I'm pretty shocked, though." He continues.

"At what?"

"He seems ... he seems like a really good dad."

"He is." The scent of Alice behind me causes me to turn. "Hey, how is sh-" I'm cut off by a bone crushing hug from such a tiny woman and am rendered speechless for a moment.

"Thank you, thank you, *thank you*, Conan!" she exclaims, her voice muffled by my shirt before she releases me just enough to look up at me. "I can't thank you enough for bringin' my baby home!" Her eyes look so tired and heavy as she blinks away fresh tears. I awkwardly stand there for a moment, then find myself scooping her back up into a hug.

"Of course, Alice." I reply quietly.

"That must've been hard on you to walk away from your father and your pack like that. I'm so sorry it's come to this." She says softly as she squeezes my arm.

"Don't apologize. As far as I'm concerned, he's not my father." I reply coolly. I can hear Rider shift uncomfortably behind me.

"Whoever did this is goin' to pay big time." Alice says, her glittering eyes aflame with revenge. I swear for a moment the air around her feels scorching hot but it's already feeling back to normal before I can comment on it.

"Don't worry, ma'am. I'll be giving your husband their info and anything else that might be helpful in the morning." Rider quietly chimes in.

"Goodness, I'm so sorry, hun. I've been so preoccupied I forgot you were here." Alice says, clearly a little startled.

"That's okay ..." Rider says with a shrug and a half smile.

"Alice, this is Rider. He's left the pack with me." I explain.

"Oh my ..." Alice gasps, her eyes widening as she looks Rider up and down.

"It's been a long time coming, to be honest." Rider assures her.

"Well, we appreciate any allies we can get at this point. Please, let me show you to a guest room." Alice says, jabbing a thumb over her shoulder.

"Uh, yes ma'am. Thank you," Rider replies sheepishly.

"Talk more in the morning?" I say, clapping a hand on his back.

"We obviously have a lot to catch up on." He says with a nod.

"Don't you hesitate to ask me for anythin', now. Come on, this way." Alice says as she begins to walk down the hallway.

I see Rider rub his arm awkwardly as he lets out a shaky breath. Hospitable or not, he's still around a species he has been raised to be weary of, and I'm sure the reality of leaving everything behind is beginning to weigh down heavily on him.

"She's the sweetest, you're safe. I promise." I reassure him as I gently nudge him to follow her. He nods, then quickens his pace to catch up with her. Another angry cry from Lila grabs my attention, and I snap my head toward her nursery.

"Are you still giving your Mom trouble, Pup?" I mumble to myself as I quickly make my way over to the open door to see Crystal pacing as she bounces Lila. "Someone's still awake, I hear?" I say as I close the gap between us to look down at Lila's very displeased and scrunched up face that reminds me a little too eerily of myself when I'm pissed off.

"Yeah …" Crystal sighs, "I think she feels all the tension in the house."

"Let me take a quick shower to get all of this shit off me and then I'll take over so you can go to bed." I say as I examined the caked-on blood all over my arms and under my finger nails.

"Conan, look at you. You look as if you've just left a battle scene. You *must* be tired. I'm fine." Crystal insists as she continues to bounce Lila.

"No. I mean it, you and your family have had a nightmare of a day. I'll be fine. Besides, I've missed her all day." I say with a small smile. "I'll explain every detail of what happened today tomorrow, I promise. I'm sure there's a lot you have to tell me, too."

Crystal hesitates for a moment, then finally sits down in the rocking chair and nods. "Okay, if you're sure …" she says, still sounding very unsure herself.

I bend down to kiss the top of her head. "I'll be quick." I promise, as I jog toward her shower. I can hear her humming as a last attempt to soothe Lila the entire way to the bathroom.

Once I'm in the shower and only have the running water as noise, the reality of what happened today begins to fill my mind with unwelcomed flashbacks. Once most of the blood is washed off my hands and arms, I begin to scrub at my fingernails. As I watch the blood tinted water circle the drain, my stomach flips at holding my daughter with such filthy hands, and I scrub harder. Finally, all traces of today seem to be erased and I begin my usual shower routine. Ruby's little crumpled body flashes in my mind's eye when I close my eyes to rinse the shampoo out of my hair, and I have to steady myself. The Foxes faces of both relief and horror appear next, and I feel my stomach begin to flip again.

She's safe.
She's back here at home with her family.
My mate and pup are safe.
I'm finally out of that pack.
It's going to be okay.
It has *to be okay.*

I spent a little longer than intended to compose myself, but I finally forced myself out of the shower to go keep my promise to Crystal. Once dried, I quickly change into a pair of sweatpants and peek my head into Crystal's room. The lamp is still on, but she's passed out on her bed, her body on top of the blankets as if she meant to only rest for a moment. Knowing her, she probably was trying to wait up for me even though I specifically told her to go to bed.

Good, Lila must've finally gone to sleep.

I had just turned to go check on her when she decided to let me know she was awake by letting out an angry cry.

Well, shit.

I hear Crystal stir, and look over to see she's starting to sit up. I dash over to her bedside and gently push her to lay back down.

"Don't get up. I'll go check on her. Go back to sleep." I say softly.

Crystal is so exhausted she lays back down without argument, much to my relief. I quickly lift her body to tuck her in under the covers before making my way to go soothe Lila.

"Hey, hey, why are you awake again? Hm?" I mutter as I lift Lila's tiny body into my arms. After a few minutes of bouncing her, she finally settles down again, but it's clear she's still fighting her sleep even though she's not crying anymore. She just looks cranky and inconvenienced, and if I had any doubts before that she was my child, that face alone would've cleared that right up for me. I can't help but chuckle a bit as I kiss the top of her head then continue to lightly bounce her.

Even though I'm beyond exhausted, seeing her little face (no matter how displeased) makes it all worth it. I hope when she grows up, she knows just how loved she is, and how we'll always continue to fight for her. I don't care how big she gets; I don't care if her unique bloodline makes her super strong and powerful. She'll always be my baby to keep safe. She'll always be my Pup to protect.

Forever.

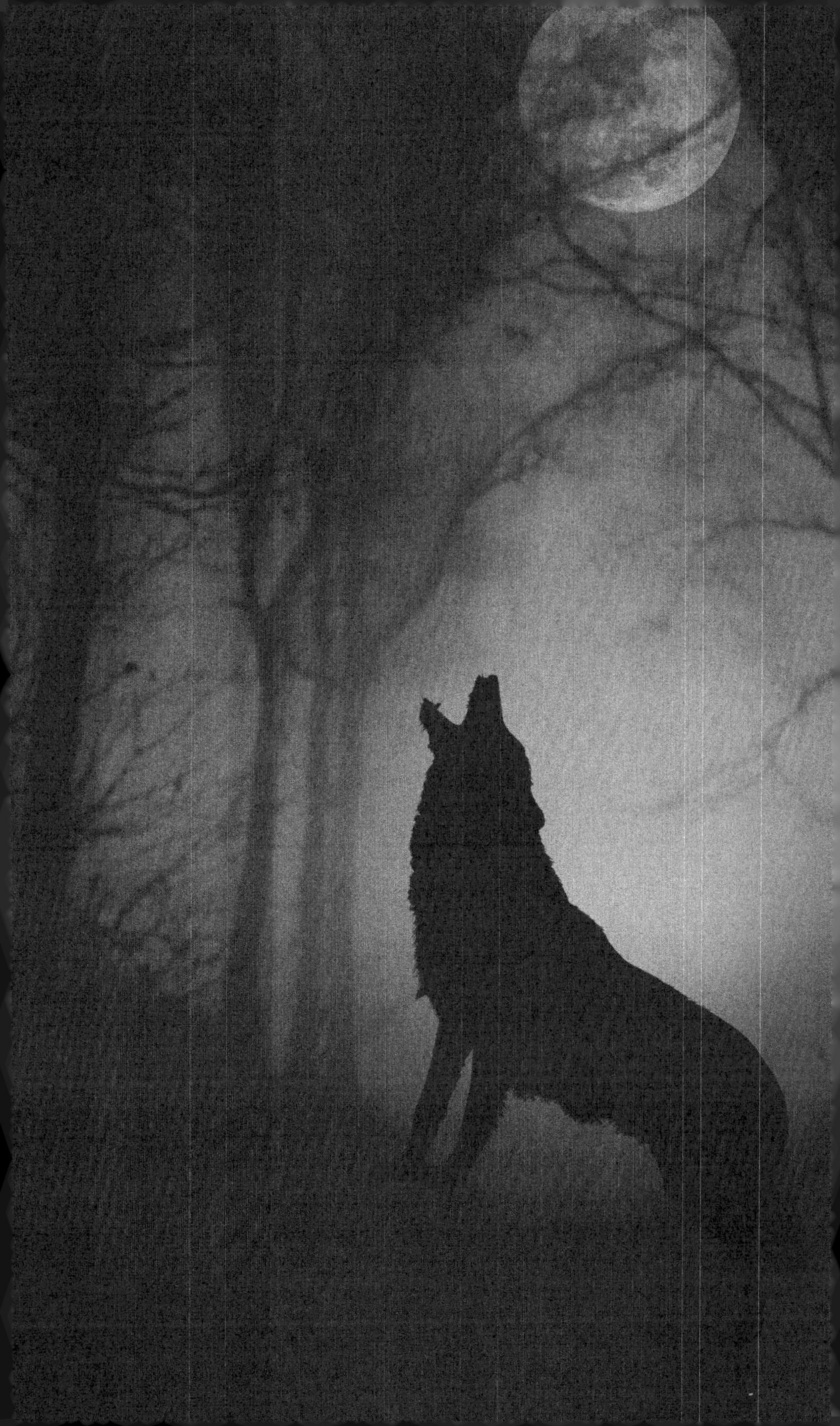

Twelve

CONAN

"Quit hogging her!"

"Shh! You're going to wake the whole bloody house up!"

I let out an irritated combination of both a groan and a growl as I sit up in bed, my mind still *very* foggy from sleep.

What the hell is all that noise?

I glance over to see Crystal still sleeping, then raise a hand to rub my face. I hiss as a surprising pain shoots up my arm, and memories of the horrors from yesterday come crashing down on me like a wave of ice cold water.

"See? She obviously likes her Uncle Heath better."

The twins must be in Lila's room.

I rotate each sore shoulder before slowly sliding out of bed, careful not to wake Crystal. She must be so used to those two loud mouths that it doesn't phase her. Or maybe the stress and trauma from yesterday have taken such a toll on her mentally she's just exhausted. Perhaps a combination of both. I glance at her repeatedly as I slip on a pair of sweat pants and hoodie, but she never stirs.

I feel every muscle I used to beat the shit out of Louis and Collin ache as I head toward the nursery. I can definitely feel some bruising, but luckily they should fade pretty soon thanks to werewolves' advanced healing.

Upon walking in, I see one of them lightly bouncing Lila as she coos, while the other has his arms crossed and is clearly pouting. Neither of them acknowledges me until I close the distance between us.

"What're you two doing?" I grunt, my voice still gravelly from sleep.

The one holding Lila turns to face me.

"We heard her fussing so we decided to come check on her so you and Cici could sleep in." He says as the other nods in agreement. I believe this is the first time both of them are talking to me in a normal tone without a glare or a scowl plastered on their faces.

"By 'we' he means himself," the other scoffs, "considering he won't let me have a bloody turn."

"I keep telling him she likes her Uncle Heath better, but he's clearly in denial."

Ah. The one holding her is Heath.

"Uh, thanks. Here, I can take over." I say, extending my arms toward Heath as he gently hands her over. "She looks ready to go back to sleep, I'll let her sleep in a bit more before breakfast." They nod as I walk over to her crib, gently setting her inside.

"Oi, Heath."

"Yeah?"

I hear behind me as I make sure Lila is comfortable.

"You forgot something."

"What's that?"

"This,"

Curiosity has me looking over my shoulder, as I see Reese holding his pointer finger and thumb to make a circle, leaving the other three fingers free as he holds his hand against his thigh in order to make Heath look down.

Is that-

"Damn it." Heath snaps.

"You looked." Reese grins impishly before punching Heath square in the shoulder, causing him to flinch and swear under his breath.

They're playing the fucking Circle Game.

I remember in elementary school all of the boys enjoyed playing it because the rules were simple. Get someone to look unexpectedly at the hand gesture, then have an excuse to hit them. I remember everyone became paranoid to the point where if anyone tried to point out they dropped a pencil or tried to point anything out to help, no one would look and made it a point to quickly avert their eyes in the other direction. It was a very stupid game, but of course we loved any excuse to hit each other. Needless to say, the teacher quickly put an end to that in class; but that didn't stop us from playing it during recess or away from school. I hadn't thought about the Circle Game in years, and these two grown ass men, that are older than I am, are currently playing it.

"Piss off!" Heath snarls as Reese continues to laugh at him.

"She's gone back to sleep guys," I say as I straighten myself and turn to face them both. "Don't wake her up."

"Yeah, Heath. Quiet down." Reese whispers with a light chuckle as Heath rolls his eyes.

"So uh," I clear my throat as I take a step toward them. "Thanks for checking on her this morning."

"It's no problem at all, mate." Heath says with a shrug.

"We love spending time with her." Reese agrees.

"If anything, we should be thanking you, yeah?" Heath says, his eyes looking genuinely grateful as Reese nods.

"Me?" I blink in surprise. They were being much too nice this morning and it had me feeling quite suspicious.

The twins look at each other, some sort of unspoken agreement being passed between them telepathically before turning back to face me.

"We know we've been giving you hell since you've first arrived." Heath starts.

"Not that you can really blame us." Reese adds.

"But, without you we might not have gotten our baby sister back alive." Heath says somberly, all traces of sarcasm and humor void of his expression.

"You're family now," Reese says, his expression mirroring his brother's, "you've more than proved your loyalty."

"Oh," is all I can manage to say as flashbacks of my escape with Ruby's broken little body in my arms quickly flip like the pages of a book through my mind. I close my eyes tightly and clear my throat. "Of course. She's practically my little sister, too."

The twins share a glance then zero in on me, making me nervous again.

"Although, now that you're one of us you must know what that means." Heath says as his impish grin returns to his face, quickly jerking his arm down causing me to immediately glance down out of reflex.

Shit.

I furrow my brow and scowl at the stupid circle of his fingers before feeling a quick punch to the sorest spot on my arm.

"Welcome to the family, brother!" Heath chirps happily as I wince.

"Damn it! Ow!" I hiss through my teeth as I begin to rub the now throbbing spot on my arm.

"Shh! Didn't you *just* say not to be too loud?" Heath chastises.

"Yeah! You'll wake Lila!" Reese clicks his tongue in disappointment.

I roll my eyes, resisting the urge to grab them each by the neck and bash their skulls together.

"I still hate you both." I grunt, before turning on my heel to check on Lila one more time, then leave the room, hearing their quiet chuckling behind me.

I find the bed empty when I arrive back in Crystal's room. I take a quick peek in the adjoining bathroom to find it also empty, then walk back out into the hall.

She must be checking on Ruby.

Ruby's door is open, the lights are still off but the morning sun is illuminating the room through the window. Crystal is standing a few steps inside, nervously chewing on her thumbnail as she stares at her sister. Ruby hasn't moved an inch, the only sign of life being the slow rise and fall of her chest. The bruises that I can see between all the bandages are much move visible against her pale skin. Alice is lying beside her, looking old for the very first time as she strokes Ruby's hair without casting a glance in our direction. Draken seems to be asleep, his arms folded on the side of the bed with the rest of his body on the floor.

"How is she?" I whisper, while placing a hand on Crystal's shoulder.

"It doesn't look like she's moved since you brought her home." Crystal replies softly, her eyes never leaving Ruby.

I let out a grunt of acknowledgment, giving her shoulder a light squeeze.

I bet Draken and Alice stayed here all night with her.
That's good.

After a moment, Crystal finally turns to face me.

"Was Lila okay?"

I nod.

"Reese and Heath were tending to her so that we could rest."

"That's good …"

I look up to see Alice quietly approaching us. I hadn't even noticed her move.

"Alice, is there anything we can do?" I ask.

"Did she ever wake up?" Crystal adds.

"No, Conan. Thanks for askin'," she turns her haunted eyes toward Crystal, "and no, she probably just needs more rest. A lot of it."

Crystal nods and begins to fidget with her ring.

"I'm going to get dressed and start breakfast, we all need to keep our strength up after yesterday." Alice says, her voice cracking at the end. She turns to look at Ruby one more time before leaving the room, her hand gently squeezing my arm as she passes.

Crystal nods and turns to look back up at me.

"I'm going to shower then feed Lila." I nod, kissing her forehead before she leaves the room.

I turn back to face Ruby, my heart breaking as I take in the sight of her. My eyes wander down to Draken. His eyes are still closed, but his brow is furrowed, and his jaw is clenched so tightly I can see the cords of his neck muscles in detail.

He's probably the cockiest and scariest vamp there is …

And he's sleeping on the floor to make sure his baby girl is okay.

Fatherhood has already enlightened me to know without a doubt, that I would do the same for Lila. I stare at him for a few more minutes, then decide I should probably leave before my gawking is the first thing he sees when he wakes.

I want to learn more about "The Ripper."

I decided to check on Lila once more to see she was very much awake and brought her with me back to Crystal's room. Sitting on the bed, I find myself just staring at her as I wait for Crystal to get done showering.

She's very active this morning, making all sorts of adorable cooing noises and gurgling sounds as she quickly moves her arms and legs. It saddens me to notice she looks as if she's grown a bit overnight.

Crystal emerges from the shower as she dries her hair with a towel. Her eyes still look so very tired, but her lips turn up into a small smile when she sees us. She's quiet as she dresses, her eyes glazed over as she seems to be somewhere very far away in her mind. She wordlessly reaches for Lila, then begins to feed her as she sits beside me.

I look down at my hands to see how my scuffed up knuckles are healing, then flex my hands and fingers to see exactly how sore they are.

"Do they hurt?" Crystal softly asks, finally breaking the silence.

"Nothing unbearable. They seem to be healing normally. Should be back to normal in a day or so."

"Are ... are you hurting elsewhere? What did they do to you?"

I look up at her to meet her worried eyes glancing all over me as if she could see through my clothes.

"I'll be just fine. They're a lot worse off than I am, I can promise you that." I say as I gently squeeze her knee.

She nods, and looks down at Lila for a minutes in silence.

"Then, what's on your mind? You seem to be concentrating very had on something." She finally asks.

"Tell me about The Ripper." I say without hesitation. She blinks for a moment in surprise.

"Oh ..." She looks back down at Lila, "Well ... that used to be who he was."

"So, he like, I don't know just stopped randomly being a serial killer or ...?"

She chews on her lip a moment, seeming to weigh her words carefully before speaking again.

"He doesn't talk about it much with us." She finally says with a half shrug, still not looking at me.

I know she can feel me staring at her, silently willing her to continue. She glances back up at me, looking a bit uncomfortable.

"Um, from my understanding, he basically chilled out the older he got, was a playboy for a while until he met Mom." She forces an awkward half smile and shrugs again, "Then apparently he really mellowed out when I was born." I continue to stare at her, and she quickly looks back down at Lila. "That's really all there is to know."

"None of it bothers you?" I ask.

"I mean, he's my dad no matter what." She looks back up to meet my gaze. "And a damn good one at that. We all have our demons. He just ah, has quite a few more than most ..." she trails off.

"From my understanding, he's one of the most feared vampires in history."

"Meh."

"The fuck do you mean, 'meh'?!"

"The Ripper isn't my father." She says flatly, her eyes piercing into mine without any discomfort this time. I shut my mouth, allowing her to speak even though I still have a million questions.

"The Ripper might've *used* to have been who my dad was, but the dad I know and grew up with just worried about making sure his family was well taken care of and safe. I mean, he threatens to kill people all the time, sure ..." she smiles a little sheepishly. "But, he always tried to shield us from as much violence as he could. The man had tea parties with us, it's hard to picture him any other way than just my dad."

Now I would kill to see Draken Fox attending a little girl's tea party ...

"Anything else?" Crystal asks with Lila now against her shoulder as she pats her back to burp her.

"I suppose not. It's not really my business anyway."

"Right. Now then," Crystal clears her throat and goes back to looking uncomfortable, "tell me everything. I want to hear what happened to my sister and how you rescued her."

My gut feels as though it's doing somersaults, but I did promise to tell her today. Despite how awful it is, she deserves to know.

"All right ..."

CRYSTAL

Horrible images of what Conan told me continue to flash through my brain as I lean over to vomit into the toilet again. Poor Conan rubs my back with one hand while holding Lila in his other arm. My stomach feels empty, so after flushing I close the toilet lid then rest my face on it as I softly cry.

"I shouldn't have told you. Or, or, I should've waited." Conan says, clearly distressed as I he continues to rub my back.

"No," my voice cracks and I clear my throat while trying not to wince at the taste of bile still present in my mouth, "I needed to know, or my mind would've come up with worse. Not sure how it can be much worse, but …"

Conan's expression softens as he places a warm hand on my cheek, his thumb stroking the tears still running down my face.

"I'm going to see if the twins will watch her and be right back." He kisses my forehead then stands, carrying Lila out of the room.

My sister was tortured and maimed just for being a vampire. They did it for fun. Like she was an animal they hunted for sport.

I shut my eyes and take several deep breaths so that I won't begin to dry heave. There wasn't much in my stomach to begin with, but now it's for sure empty.

She's safe now.
Conan got her.
She's safe now.
She's home, not with them.
She's home, not with them.
She's home not with them.

In the middle of my mantra I feel a cold wash cloth press against my face as Conan begins to softly clean it.

"I'm fine. I just need a few." I say as he helps me up.

"I know you definitely don't want breakfast, but please at

least drink some water or something." He says, his eyes pleading with me not to say no. I can feel his worry and guilt through our mating bond.

I nod, then turn on the tap to begin washing my mouth out.

"Do you want me to bring you a bottle of water? Or tea? Or whatever other shit your Mom probably has down there?"

I shake my head as I reach for my toothbrush, "I'll come down. You go ahead before she starts to worry about us."

He hesitates then nods. He kisses the top of my head then exits the bathroom.

One highlight of this depressing morning was watching Mom practically threaten Rider's life that he had better eat after he had tried to be polite and decline. Conan said he hadn't meant it as an insult because he's so worried about being an added on burden after what our family just went through, but Mom will not ever accept someone not being fed in her home. I wasn't hungry, but she made me some tea that was supposed to help with my nausea, and added a few other ingredients from her potions cabinet that were supposed to help provide some sort of nourishment. After breakfast Dad wanted to interrogate Rider for everything he knew about Ruby's attackers, so Conan and I decided it was best to leave. Conan was worried about some of his things and stuff he had gotten for Lila that were still at his home. I told him I would accompany him to go pick up whatever he needed to fully move in with us after asking the twins to keep an eye on Lila. He didn't seem fond of the idea, but he let me come nonetheless. I think he knew I needed to get out of the house and focus on something else.

"Do you think your pack will be waiting for you there?" I asked once we were in the truck.

"Ex-pack, and no." He shook his head, "They know I wouldn't be stupid enough to stay there after the betrayal I committed."

"Ah." Is all I could think of to respond with as I twirled my opal ring repeatedly around my finger.

"I just hope they haven't ransacked the place. I don't have Lila's stuff out in the open, but …" His voice trailed off as his fingers tightened around the steering wheel.

"Whatever has happened or will happen, we'll get through it together." I say in the most reassuring voice I can muster as I reach over to gently grab his knee.

He lets out a sigh through his nose and nods, his eyes never leaving the road.

"Is that everything?" I ask, as I watch Conan pick up a brand new car seat he must've ordered to have his own for his truck.

He nods.

"Should be all I need for now. I was more worried about erasing all and any evidence of Pup's existence. I only had a few things I needed for myself." He says as we exit the front door out onto the front porch. I took his keys to lock up as he made his way down the steps.

"Conan?" I hear an unfamiliar female voice say, causing me to freeze.

I hear Conan slam the truck door, then immediately dash back up the steps to stand in front of me.

I look over to see a man and a woman emerging from the woods, instantly feeling Conan's panic through our mating bond. The woman has auburn hair, her face full of worry, and the man is tan with a dark buzzcut, looking as if he wants to murder Conan. Their scents hit me, alerting me they are *very* pureblooded werewolves.

"Who is that?" I whisper as I slowly place his truck keys into his hand. He grips them tightly behind his back, using his other hand to grip my forearm from behind him, clearly wanting me to stay in place.

Before he can answer, the man has clearly noticed me and looks feral at the realization.

"You want to explain what the hell you're doing with a dhampir?!" the man shouts, jabbing a finger in my direction even though my body is mostly obscured by Conan's large frame. This man is pretty large too, even the woman is tall with broad shoulders and hips.

"Conan, why did you just have a car seat in your hand?" the woman asks, sounding frantic.

"Don't you dare tell me that's Draken Fox's other daughter!" the man spits with rage.

"Wait," the woman looks from the man back to Conan, eyes wide, "Is that the dhampir that was at your school?!"

"How do they know who I am?" I ask as my heart begins to pound against my chest, "Conan, what the hell is going on?!" Conan only squeezes my arm tighter as he pulls me closer to his back in a protective stance.

"None of your fucking business, Luther!" Conan shouts, finally speaking. "Get in the truck, now." He says as he begins nudging me toward the truck, but I stay planted to the spot, now gripping his arm back.

ALLIES AND OUTCASTS

"Conan, what's going on, *figlio*? You're scaring me!" the woman shouts back, wringing her hands as she continues to glance back and forth from Conan to the man beside her.

"It's all adding up now," the man says as his face twists into a disgusted sneer, "Tell me you didn't." He says a little too calmly as his eyes flash gold.

"*Now*, Crystal!" Conan says as he begins to shove me harder.

"I won't leave you!" I hiss through my teeth, digging my nails into his arm.

Conan growls in irritation, then starts slowly sidestepping with me in tow down the steps.

"What I do is none of your fucking business, Luther. And Mom," he hesitates as we make it down the final step and he stops for a moment, "I'm sorry, but I can't explain right now."

It feels as though my heart has dropped into my stomach as I gasp with realization. The man could be an older, more scarred and battle worn version of Conan, and the woman's eyes are the exact same shade of hazel green as his.

Mom?!

Is that his mother?! Are those his parents?!

"Explain what?!" the woman shrieks, running her hands through her hair the exact same way Conan does when he's stressed. "You've been MIA for weeks! And now I see you loading up a car seat with a dhampir woman at your side?! What have you been doing, son?!"

"Isn't it obvious?" the man spits on the ground, "He's bred with that ... that ... that blood sucking demon!" he snarls as he jabs a finger in my direction again.

The woman, his mother, gasps then whirls back around to face Conan.

"Is this true, Conan?!"

"It must be!" His father interrupts before Conan can

answer, "Just look at his damn neck! I can see the little leech's mark from here!"

A loud growl rips from Conan's throat, causing me to flinch.

"Don't you *dare* talk about her like that you miserable, old jackass!" Conan roars.

"Calm down, Paws." I say quietly, voice trembling as I begin to rub his arm.

"I'm sorry I didn't tell you, Mom." Conan says, his voice still hard but his volume a little more under control, "But that reaction from your husband is exactly why!" he snaps, then begins to pull me toward the truck again. "These are the facts, Crystal is my mate and the mother of my child, like it or not." My skin prickles as my stomach twists at the sound of Conan telling everything we've fought so hard to keep a secret. He opens the passenger door and begins to all but shove me inside.

"Disown me, whatever, I don't give a flying fuck." He slams the door then makes his way over to the driver's side, his eyes never leaving his father's as if daring him to stop him. "You'll be the ones missing out on seeing your grandchild for old, petty reasons." He snaps before slamming the driver door closed and cranking the engine to life.

"Conan! Wait!" his mother calls out as Conan quickly throws the truck in reverse and begins to peel out of the driveway.

"GET BACK HERE BOY!" I can hear his father bellow from behind us, and I wince.

I turn around and watch them grow smaller and smaller until trees obscure them from my vision. They didn't appear to move an inch, so I don't think they're going to follow us, but I keep watching the roads behind us just in case.

I hear Conan's heavy breathing and feel so many

conflicted emotions rolling off of him at once through the bond. I finally allow myself to turn back around, then grip one of his hands and pull it into my lap.

"Are you okay?" A stupid question, but I have to ask.

He doesn't answer for several heartbeats, and for a moment I don't think he will.

"As long as you're safe, I'll be fine." He finally snaps. I rub my thumb over his knuckles wishing I knew something useful to say. Wishing I knew what I could do.

"We're about to have a lot more problems, though." He says flatly, as we continue to speed down the road.

I already knew that, but hearing him say it makes it all the more terrifying.

Thirteen

BAYLOR

I can hear the sound of my cell phone vibrating from … somewhere.

I force my eyes to open and immediately regret it thanks to the ray of sunshine that happens to be shining directly onto my face through the smallest opening between the hotel curtains.

That's right.

I didn't go home last night.

My phone grows silent for a moment and I happily shut my eyes and turn with my back facing the window. A warm body snuggles up to me, and memories of last night have me growing a little too … excited.

Well.

That woke me up.

Jillian, a very hot woman I've been seeing for a little over a month now, and I had quite a few drinks last night and booked a room at the Fox Den. Okay, maybe more than a few. Everything has been going great, but it's been quite intense.

Jillian has given me multiple reasons to suspect that she is a werewolf. A normal human may not have noticed or shrugged off the little things I've noticed, but thanks to my training as a Raven I picked up on them pretty quickly. She loves to wear anything of mine, not to be cute or romantic but to be covered in my scent. She buries her face in my neck to inhale it a little not so discreetly. She grew *very* possessive over me a lot quicker than the usual relationship timeframe; not in an unhealthy abusive partner way, but more of a primal way. The way she walks, looks at her surroundings, reacts to certain things, all scream primal. When things are heating up between us she always nips and bites at a particular area on my neck, but so far she's been careful to conceal her fangs.

Last night my suspicions were confirmed by catching a glimpse of her smokey blue eyes flash gold for a split second when a random drunk woman nearly spilled her drink on me. I don't want to assume, but looking back, it appears that she's getting ready to claim me as hers. I have no idea if she thinks that I'm her mate, or if she's just being the usual territorial she-wolf.

My phone begins to vibrate again and Jillian grunts in annoyance before nudging me with her foot.

"Sorry." I chuckle before kissing the top of her warm brown hair, then slide out of bed to hunt down my phone. The room is still mostly dark, and I spot the lit-up screen on the floor next to my disregarded pants. I see Victor's name flash on the screen before I answer.

"What's up?" I yawn.

"They found Ruby." Victor's voice replies flatly.

"Really? Is she okay?" I ask as I feel my heart begin to quicken its pace.

"From what I understand, it's not good, Bay. I'm going over there to check on her and the rest of the Foxes. Want me to pick you up?"

"Yeah, sure. I'm at the Fox Den, just text me when you're here and I'll meet you in the lobby." My stomach begins to churn at the endless scenarios I picture Ruby could've gotten herself into.

"Be there in ten." Victor replies before hanging up. He didn't crack one joke about me being at a hotel to get laid, so that's how I know things must be bad.

Really bad.

"Work?" Jillian calls over her shoulder, voice still thick from sleep.

"No, a bit of a family friend emergency."

💋💋💋

"How bad is it, Alice?" I ask, feeling my heart sink at the sight of her. She wrings her hands and glances back at Ruby's bedroom door behind her before turning back to face me.

"She still won't wake up all the way. She comes in and out of it. And she … she just looks so …" Alice chokes back a sob as she raises her hands to cover her face. Victor immediately envelopes her into a bear hug, and she pats his back lightly as she clears her throat. "I'm fine. I'm fine." Victor reluctantly releases her as she takes a deep breath, wiping away the few stray tears from her cheeks. "I'm going to try to make somethin' for her to eat along with breakfast, if y'all are hungry please stay and help yourselves."

"Thank you." I reply as Victor solemnly nods. I don't think either of us have an appetite at the moment.

"I'm just warnin' you both, she looks rough. If it hadn't been for Conan ..." Her voice cracks as she closes her eyes, seeming to try to ground herself before opening them again. "Anyway, I'll be downstairs, holler at me if she wakes up or needs me." She casts one more glance at Ruby's room, then makes her way down the stairs. Victor and I glance at each other before making our way inside.

It's horrific.

The bite and claw marks that are taking too long to heal, have me nauseated at first glance. They're pretty ugly, and normally werewolf bites take longer to heal on a vampire and Ruby is an underage one. From the marks to seeing her pitiful, little body covered in bandages, my heart is broken.

"Oh, Ru ..." I breathe out. "This can't be real."

Victor is stunned and wide eyed. I'm not sure if he's moved since he first laid eyes on her, as if he's gone into shock. I clap a hand on his shoulder, and he still doesn't move for a moment. Finally, he blinks as he slowly makes his way toward the bed. He crouches down and gently lays a hand on her forehead.

"Oh, Ru ... Who did this to you?" he asks just below a whisper. "We'll get them back for this. I *promise*, little one." His voice cracks at the end. I walk up behind him and place a hand on his back, my eyes never leaving Ruby. Other than her chest slowly rising and falling, she's eerily still.

"I know everyone said it was bad, but *this* ..." I trail off, unable to finish the sentence.

We watch her in silence for I'm not sure how long. What else was there *to* say?

"Ru?" Victor asks quietly, and I dart my eyes to her face to see that her brow is furrowed and she's began to pant.

"Ruby, are you awake?" Victor asks as he gently lays a hand on one of her shoulders, she's borderline hyperventilating as she begins to whimper. Before Victor or I can say another word, she shoots up to a sitting position and begins to scream her head off.

"Ruby! Are you in pain?! What's wrong?!" I ask, frantically. She doesn't reply, instead her unfocussed, glazed eyes dart around the room, seeing things we cannot as she begins to cry.

"Hey, hey! It's okay!" Victor says in a soothing voice that is clearly trying to hide his panic. Ruby's entire body is shaking as she begins to sob between rapid breaths. "I think you're still dreaming ..." Victor murmurs as he looks down at her eyes.

"St-stop! M-make them st-stop!" Ruby cries in a hoarse voice, still not fully conscious.

"Ruby, it's just me and Baylor, you're safe now." Victor says as he scoops her up into a hug, careful not to hurt her. He's handling her as though she's made of glass as he rubs her back. "You're safe." He repeats.

"Hurts ... st-stop ... I don't know! I don't know! I don't kn-kn-know! Please!" she cries out, still shaking all over, panting as if she can't catch her breath.

Victor sits on the bed, her head tucked under his chin as he pulls her onto his lap against his chest.

"Little one, they're not here. You're safe. You're safe. You're safe," he whispers into her hair as I pick up her comforter that had gotten kicked to the foot of the bed. I lay it over her as Victor lightly rocks her, continuously rubbing her back.

"It's us, Ru. Can you hear us?" I ask, gently placing a hand on one of her knees after I make sure she's properly bundled up. "It's Baylor. Can you hear me?"

Ruby's eyes are closed again, her cries and shaky breaths are her only reply.

"It's just a bad dream, little one. Just a bad dream," Victor whispers into her hair, "You're here with us, not there. You're never going back there."

"P-please, p-please …" Ruby whispers, "I d-d-didn't do anything, I d-didn't!" She whips her head back and screams again.

"Hey, hey, hey, I've got you!" Victor says as he holds onto her to keep her from thrashing, "I've got you."

"I'm going to get Alice." As I turn to face the door, I see her there already, looking frantic.

"What happened?!" Alice all but shrieks as she darts over to the bed.

"She's not fully awake, it's like she's reliving through night terrors." Victor replies, sounding defeated. Ruby whimpers as she buries her face in his chest.

"Baby, it's Mama. Can you hear me?" Alice asks, her voice loud but gentle as she gently shakes Ruby's shoulder. Ruby doesn't respond, she's still violently shivering, but she seems to be back into a deep sleep. I think we all collectively hold our breath as we watch her and wait. Several minutes must have passed by before Alice looks up at Victor.

"I can take her." She offers, but Victor shakes his head.

"Let's not move her. You go finish trying to make her something to put in her stomach, I've got her." He whispers as he leans back against the headboard, still holding her to his chest.

"Are you sure?" Alice asks sounding exhausted, to which Victor nods.

"I'll stay with her and try to comfort her if she starts up again, do whatever you need to do." He replies. Alice nods, but doesn't stand as she strokes Ruby's hair.

"What can I help with, Alice?" I ask.

CONAN

"Draken!" I shout, gripping the doorframe to his home office as I pant. He looks up from his laptop and stares at me, wide-eyed.

"What is it?" he asks as he quickly gets to his feet.

"I need ... to talk ... to you!" I say between breaths.

Draken looks me up and down, as if trying to assess if I'm injured before swiftly walking around the desk to close the gap between us.

"My parents know everything. We just ran into them." I admit in defeat, unable to look him in the eye.

"What?" He grabs my shoulder, causing me to glance back up at his face, "What do you mean by 'everything'?"

CRYSTAL

"Mom!" I call out as I scoot to a skidding halt in the kitchen. She nearly drops the potion bottle in her hand, but quickly catches it and sets it on the counter before turning to face me.

"What? What's wrong?" she asks, grabbing a nearby dishcloth to wipe her hands, her face lined with worry.

I swallow a deep breath before continuing, "I … I just got to meet Conan's parents."

"What? When?" She gasps, rushing over to me.

"What happened?" Rider asks quietly from the doorway.

I wait for him to enter the kitchen fully and stand next to us as I try to slow my pounding heart.

"We went to Conan's to grab a few of his and Lila's things and they were there." I explain, nervously wringing my hands as I look between them.

"Oh shit." Rider whispers.

"They caught us with Lila's car seat and now they know we have a baby together!" I say as I begin to pace, still very much full of adrenaline. We had tried our best to remain calm on the drive back, but the more we talked about the situation and what threats it could bring into the future for Lila, we were practically chomping at the bit to get to my parents and make some sort of plan.

"What did they do?" Mom asks quietly, her hand reaching out to gently grab my arm to stop my pacing.

"Conan made me get out of there, we didn't stick around to find out but they weren't exactly thrilled to be grandparents." I groan as I begin to rub my eyes with the heels of my hands.

Mom and Rider are silent as they process everything I've just said, probably both imagining all the scenarios that brought me and Conan both into a panic. I hear Mom let out a shaky sigh, her face looking as if she's trying to find the right words to say.

"I'll talk to your dad," she finally says, "everything's going to be okay." She assures me before pulling me into a hug.

"Conan is filling him in on everything right now." I reply as I return the hug.

A hesitating hand lightly grabs my shoulder.

"I'll help in anyway I can, of course." Rider offers with a sad smile.

Fourteen

BAYLOR

When Cadence finally agreed to meet with me, I thought I had dreamed it. I must've reread her text reply a dozen times before our arranged meeting time finally rolled around. She had agreed on a little coffee shop, mentioning that I would be treating her. I didn't even care, I agreed immediately. She could buy out the entire menu for all it mattered to me. Upon parking, I could see her sitting at an outdoor table in the front, smoking a cigarette as she scrolled through her phone. Luckily any other customers seem to be inside to get away from the nipping wind.

"You're late." She says without looking up once I take the seat across from her.

"By like, two minutes!" I say, exasperated after double checking the time on my phone.

She smirks up at me, her aqua-blue eyes looking me up and down before crinkling her nose.

"You reek of a she-wolf. Decided to become a willing chew toy?"

"I'm not here to discuss my love life." I say, feeling my cheeks warm.

She rolls her eyes, waving her hand dismissively.

"Let me get some coffee in me before you start interrogating me, yeah?"

"I can do that." I nod, trying my best not to smirk at the way her New York accent makes her pronounce coffee like, "kawf-ee."

After a waitress takes our orders, I fold my hands in front of me on the chilly iron table. She snuffs out her cigarette and looks at me expectantly.

"First off, I want you to note that me asking you questions because you're a hybrid is not for any sort of malicious motive. So please don't punch me this time for bringing up the subject." I say gently as she rolls her eyes again.

"Yeah, yeah. I wouldn't be here if I hadn't thought over that. Get on with it, will ya?" she snaps, crossing her arms tightly across her body. Something in me knows it's more of a defense mechanism than the chilly temperature outside.

"My friend has a daughter that's like you except ..." I pause, choosing my words carefully, "A different kind of hybrid."

"Define what you mean by, 'different'." She says, eyeing me warily.

I pause when the waitress returns with our coffees, and wait until she's back inside before continuing.

"Her mother is a dhampir, and her father is a wolf." I reply quietly.

Cadence pauses mid sip of her steaming black coffee, then slowly sets it down.

"That's possible?"

ALICE

"Now to just let that brew for a couple of hours …" I murmur to myself. After lots of research in our library, I had found what I thought would be a good dreamless sleep potion for Ruby. The entire kitchen smelled of lavender, and I paused to rest my forehead in my hands, breathing it in to try and soothe myself. Tired steps trudged into the kitchen, and I looked up to see Draken looking as if he hadn't slept in years, approach. Honestly, I think this horrific experience has aged us by centuries.

"What's wrong, honey? Couldn't sleep?" I ask, wiping my hands on a nearby dish towel as I turn to face him.

"No," he rubs his face with his hands. His normally clean shaved face was now covered in stubble, and his bedhead indicated he had tossed and turned before giving up on sleep. "I know you said you'd stay up to check on her but I just can't sleep until I know she's okay."

"Draken …" I feel my heart cracking as I wrap my hands around his waist, nuzzling my face into his bare chest. "Has anyone ever told you that you're the world's best dad?"

"You do every day." He replies quietly as he slips his arms around me, pulling me closer to bury his nose into my hair.

"It's because you are!"

"I don't feel like it lately, though." He sounds so defeated; my heart can't take it.

"Draken, we talked about this," I raise my head to look at him, taking his face into my hands as I stare into his bloodshot eyes, "it's not your fault."

He closes his eyes for a moment, his grip on me tightening.

"I know, love. I just can't help it." He whispers.

"And that's exactly why you're the world's best Dad." I reply before planting a gentle kiss upon his lips. "Can I make you some tea or somethin'?"

"Sure, why not?" He rubs at his eyes with the heels of hands. "It's not like I'll be getting any sleep soon."

I walk over to the sink and begin filling our electric kettle with water.

"You talked to Silas earlier?" I ask over my shoulder.

"Yeah, he said he'll help us out with anything we need. He also wants to come see her soon."

I had figured as much, being as Silas was the girls' godfather. It only made sense he wanted to come check on Ruby in person.

"Maybe that'll cheer her up." I say hopefully, placing the electric kettle on its base to begin heating.

Before Draken could reply, Ruby's shrill shriek of terror rang throughout the house. Draken and I made it up the stairs and into her room in seconds, using every ounce of supernatural speed we had in us.

Ruby was sitting straight up in her bed, letting out blood curdling screams as she gripped the covers tightly with shaking fists. Her glazed eyes were wide with terror as she relived whatever horrible nightmare was taking place.

I pulled her toward me, and begin to shake her. "Ruby! Ruby, baby, wake up!" I plead.

"They're here …" Ruby panted, her eyes glancing around the room as if she were in a totally different place. "Th-they're gonna g-get me! I don't wanna g-g-go back!" Her voice cracked in panic as she began to curl into herself, shaking violently. "I don't wanna go b-back!"

Draken sat on the bed, pulling her into a tight embrace.

"No, they're not, babydoll. Daddy's here." He said softly as he rubbed her back, "You're safe. You're here with me and Mum."

"We're here, baby." I say, my voice catching in my throat as I reach for her trembling hands. They're cold as ice. "You're home, you're in your room with us." I add as I begin to warm her hands with mine.

Ruby's entire face drops, her eyes never focusing on either of us. Her body now limp as she tries to catch her breath.

"Princess?" Draken asks, but he gets no reply.

"She's gone mute again." I sigh. Ruby hasn't spoken a word other than when she has a night terror. She blinks a few times and looks at me rubbing her hands. I know she's fully awake now, but she still doesn't move or say a word.

Draken lets out a pained sigh as he continues to hold her, rubbing his hand in soothing circles on her back as I continue to hold her hands long after they're warmed. His phone begins to vibrate, causing us both to jump. Ruby seems unbothered as she continues to blankly stare at her hands in mine, while Draken fishes the phone out of his pocket then raises it to his ear.

"Who on earth is callin' you at this hour?" I ask.

"This had better be bloody important to call me this late." Draken growls into the phone, icy venom coating his words as he gently hands Ruby off to me. I hold her close as I watch his face harden, his eyes flashing red as he listens. Ruby's labored breathing and pounding heart make it hard to tune in on what the person on the receiver is saying.

"You're absolutely positive?" Draken says flatly, his entire back stiffening as he awaits a reply. "Text me the address right now." He says before hanging up. He swiftly gets to his feet while pocketing his phone.

"What is it?" I ask.

"I'll be back." Is all he says as he stalks toward the hall.

"Where on earth are you goin'?!" I call after him.

"Something that's been long overdue." Is his only reply before he disappears.

"Draken Alistair Fox, where are you goin'?!" I call after him, debating on if I should follow him or not. Ruby flinches, and I instantly regret raising my voice. "I'm sorry, baby." I say, lowering my voice to just above a whisper. "Come on, let's get back in bed. I'll lay with you, okay?" I offer only to unsurprisingly get no response as I turn down her blankets to slide into bed next to her.

Something that's been long overdue ...

I replay Draken's response in my mind. It could only mean one thing.

He must have found one of the wolves that did this to her.

DRAKEN

Conan and Rider had provided us with Marcus's address, but he had apparently been staying at a relative's after angering Conan's father one too many times and was momentarily unwelcome on pack territory. Which was better in the long run to get to him without risk of a pack coming to his aid, but it had been a little trickier for my resources to sniff him out.

Marcus was relaxed enough to sleep with the doors unlocked. I'm not sure if it was due to him being forgetful, cocky, or drunk, perhaps all three, but I strolled into his uncle's small one bedroom home without issue. A typical bachelor pad his uncle had put up for rent after recently buying a bigger home for his new mate, now turned into a shelter for his slob of a nephew. Clothes, pizza boxes, fast food bags and beer cans littered the floor as I made my way to the bedroom. His loud snores led me right to him so I didn't have to guess or try to scent him out amongst the filth.

Watching him drool on himself, I contemplate how I want to do this. I've had the entire drive to Riverstone and still can't seem to pick a favourite. So I slam his bedroom door shut and stand right out of his view from his bed. He wakes up with a start, coughing a bit as he scans his room. I've masked my scent so he can't scent me, and after glancing back and forth he rubs his eyes.

"What the hell?" he grumbles to himself.

He yawns and stretches, then heads to the adjoining bathroom. After relieving himself, I stand just right to show half of my face in his mirror as he looks down to wash his hands. I move out of sight as he nearly jumps out of his skin, cursing as he spins around, scanning where I stood. Then he frowns, turning back to the mirror.

"Am I going crazy?" he asks his own reflection.

I dart over to stand just over his shoulder as he rubs his face vigorously.

"No, I just felt like fucking with you." I reply coolly into his ear.

He freezes, and from this close I can see every hair on his pathetic body standing on end. He swiftly turns to face me, eyes wide with fear as his heart begins to pound inside his chest.

"Ripper?!" he chokes out, looking at me as if he wonders if this is a nightmare or if I'm really here. Time to let him know I am very much here, and he's about to feel for himself that I'm very much real.

"The one and only." I reply with a smirk, feeling my fangs elongate as my red eyes reflect in his.

In seconds I have him pinned to the bathroom wall by his throat, the sorry bastard tried his best to use whatever futile combat training he knew to block me and failed miserably, as he now claws at my hands, choking for breath.

"I'm going to make you pay for every second of pain you inflicted upon my daughter." My guttural voice sounds foreign to my own ears as I feel my face break out into a wicked grin. "You'll be begging for death by the time I'm done with you."

"I-I-I had …" he chokes out and goes back to gasping. I decide to humour him by lifting the pressure of my thumb on his throat, just enough for him to speak. He coughs violently for a few seconds before continuing. "I had no idea th-that she was your d-daughter, I swear!" he rasps. The sour smell of his fear is so potent in the air I can practically taste it on my tongue. All I can do in response to that is laugh, and he eyes me as if I'm a mad man.

"Because her not being my daughter would've made it all better, right?" I chuckle, shaking my head.

"Please, I-"

I tighten my grip on his throat again, my face and tone now completely void of any humour.

"Did she plead with you while you tortured her?" I hiss through my teeth as I push him farther into the wall, the tile now beginning to crack behind his head. "Prepare for the longest night of your life, you mangy mutt."

I slam his head into the wall once, then throw him to the ground. His claws are now out as he tries his best to fight me off while scrambling away. I jerk his foot toward me, causing him to fall backwards as his head makes a satisfying crack on the tile floor as blood begins to pool where it landed. He's momentarily dazed, and I take the opportunity to grab him by the shoulders before ripping off an ear with my teeth. He howls with pain, and I catch the hand that instinctively reaches for his head and bite down on his wrist until I feel bones crack, then use my free hand to swiftly break each finger, one by one, in a matter of seconds. He lets out a roar of pain, his wolf now threatening to come out as he kicks at my stomach, only to have me grab him by the leg and swing him across the bathroom until he collides with his bathroom sink. Water and blood now begin to flood the bathroom floor, and he slips while trying to get back up in a panic.

I jump on top of him, pressing all my weight onto his chest as I repeatedly bite at his face, his neck, his arms that try to shield his face. He's clawing at my head, but the rage and adrenaline inside me doesn't care. I had made sure to break what I saw was his dominant wrist so that his punches and slashes were clumsy. I jump off him as he lands a kick to my ribs, it momentarily knocked the wind out of me, but I just stand over him and chuckle as I wipe the blood from my mouth.

"Vampire bites bloody hurt don't they, boy?" I ask as I watch his entire body shake with pain as he tries and fails to get up. "That's what your fucking bites felt like to my kid. My kid, that's not even a fully matured vampire yet. My kid, that couldn't heal like you or I."

Our bites have always been slow to heal and a lot of pain

to each other in the history of forever. I know he and his cronies fucking knew that based on how many *precise* bite marks I found all over Ruby. Thanks to her being a juvenile, everything was ten times worse for her.

"Fuck you!" He spits out a bloody tooth, cradling his broken wrist to his chest. "You all deserve to fucking rot, you savage bloodsuckers!"

I can't help but laugh again as I deliver a kick to his stomach, causing him to curl into a ball as his scream echoes off the walls. Thanks to him only being in his underwear, I was able to place several more bites all over his legs as he thrashed. His body began trying to change as bones started to crack and fur began to sprout all over his body as a clawed paw swiped at my face again. I grabbed it and broke his left wrist next, hearing a cross between a human scream and a wolf's yelp. I stood over the half-turned creature, sneering at how pathetic he looked as he still eyed me with feral rage. His strange screams continued to fill my ears as I stomped on his feet, breaking every bone in them I could. His body slowly shifted back to human as he stayed a broken, crumpled mess on the wet floor. Another stomp and his ribs cracked, and from the sounds of his wheezing, laboured breaths I knew a lung collapsed.

With a satisfied smile I carefully step through the puddles of water and blood over to the bathtub and sit on the edge, getting into a comfortable position as I fold my hands.

"Now to let you slowly bleed out and hopefully your body tries to heal a bit before we do it all over again." I promise, feeling my face split into a grin from ear to ear.

CONAN

Lila was refusing to sleep after hearing Ruby's screams. I walked her downstairs to try and soothe her with a bottle in the kitchen. I begin to walk with her, lightly rocking her and patting her back as I wait for it to heat up, and she finally stops fussing. Her little purple eyes are still wide and alert as she looks up at me, chewing on her tiny fist.

"You are so squirmy tonight; can you please stop trying to kick me in the chest?" I mumble with a smirk. She only responds by continuing to kick her feet rapidly. "I'm going to have to sign you up for kick boxing, hm?"

The sound of the sliding glass door in the kitchen causes me to freeze and jerk my head in that direction, but I relax when I see it's Draken. Once he fully emerges under the kitchen light I stiffen again as the stench of Marcus's blood fills the room, and I see he's completely drenched in it.

"Lovely sunrise this morning." Draken says casually as he pushes his sticky, red tinged hair out of his face resulting in a smear of blood across his forehead.

"I see you paid Marcus a little visit." I say as I turn to where Lila can't see the current state of her grandfather.

"Certainly helped that he wasn't on your father's pack territory any longer." Draken agrees as he kicks his shoes off and tosses them out the door into the back yard.

"I hadn't even realized he wasn't on the property. He must've been trying to suck up to Dad by catching a vampire." I say, my lip curling with disgust. Draken only gives me a bone chilling grin, his teeth stained with blood.

"Didn't work out so well for him now, did it? Definitely

don't have to worry about him snatching up any other vampires in the future."

"So, he's dead then?" I ask, a lot calmer than I probably should be.

"Very." Draken replies nonchalantly as he begins to undress all except his pants then reaches under the kitchen sink for a garbage bag to throw them in. "Pity, I loved this shirt. I don't imagine Alice would want the trouble to try and get these stains out, though."

It should bother me that one of my old pack mates is dead. It should bother me that Draken is speaking about his most recent murder as if he had simply gone on a trip to the grocery store. It should make me feel some sort of discomfort being around him with my daughter after seeing a full glimpse of Draken's reputation as The Ripper. At least, I think it should.

But, it doesn't. Not in the slightest. If anything, it only makes me respect him as my father-in-law even more. Plus, Ruby deserves every bit of their suffering as justice. After seeing firsthand what they did to her, I feel no sympathy for them.

"I'm assuming Collin and Louis are next?" I ask, picking up the now heated bottle so that it won't get bloody from Draken now washing his hands up to his elbows at the kitchen sink.

"The twins are on it, and Victor is volunteering to help I believe." Draken replies casually before splashing his face with water. I blink in surprise.

"The twins I expected, but Victor?"

Draken gargles some of the water then spits into the sink. "Bloody hell, no offense but werewolf blood is the most disgusting thing I've ever tasted." I simply shrug in response as he wipes his mouth with the back of his hand and turns to face me fully. "What you must understand, is that Victor has known Ruby since she was eight years old, and after seeing her he was deeply disturbed. Plus, you can't very well expect the grandson of Dracula to sit and do nothing, can you?"

"Okay, that's valid." I nod. I'll deny it until my dying breath, but it made me respect Victor a little more as well.

"Right, well then," Draken offers a small smile at Lila whom I still have positioned away from facing him, "Lila darling, Grandpa would love a cuddle and kiss goodnight, but I'm afraid it'll have to wait until a shower washes away the rest of my sins."

I can't help but snort at that, my lips threatening to curve into a smile at the absurdity of this entire situation.

"What?"

"Sorry, it's just you're speaking as though you're dirty from yard work, not murder."

"It's all work, innit?"

"Sure, ah, by the way ... before you go," Draken pauses at the bottom of the stairs to look at me and raise an eyebrow, "Rider received some information from his mate. It can wait until you're cleaned up and rested, but I definitely think you'll want to hear." Draken nods once in acknowledgement and continues up the stairs.

I look down at Lila as I offer her the bottle, "What kind of family did we bring you into, Pup?"

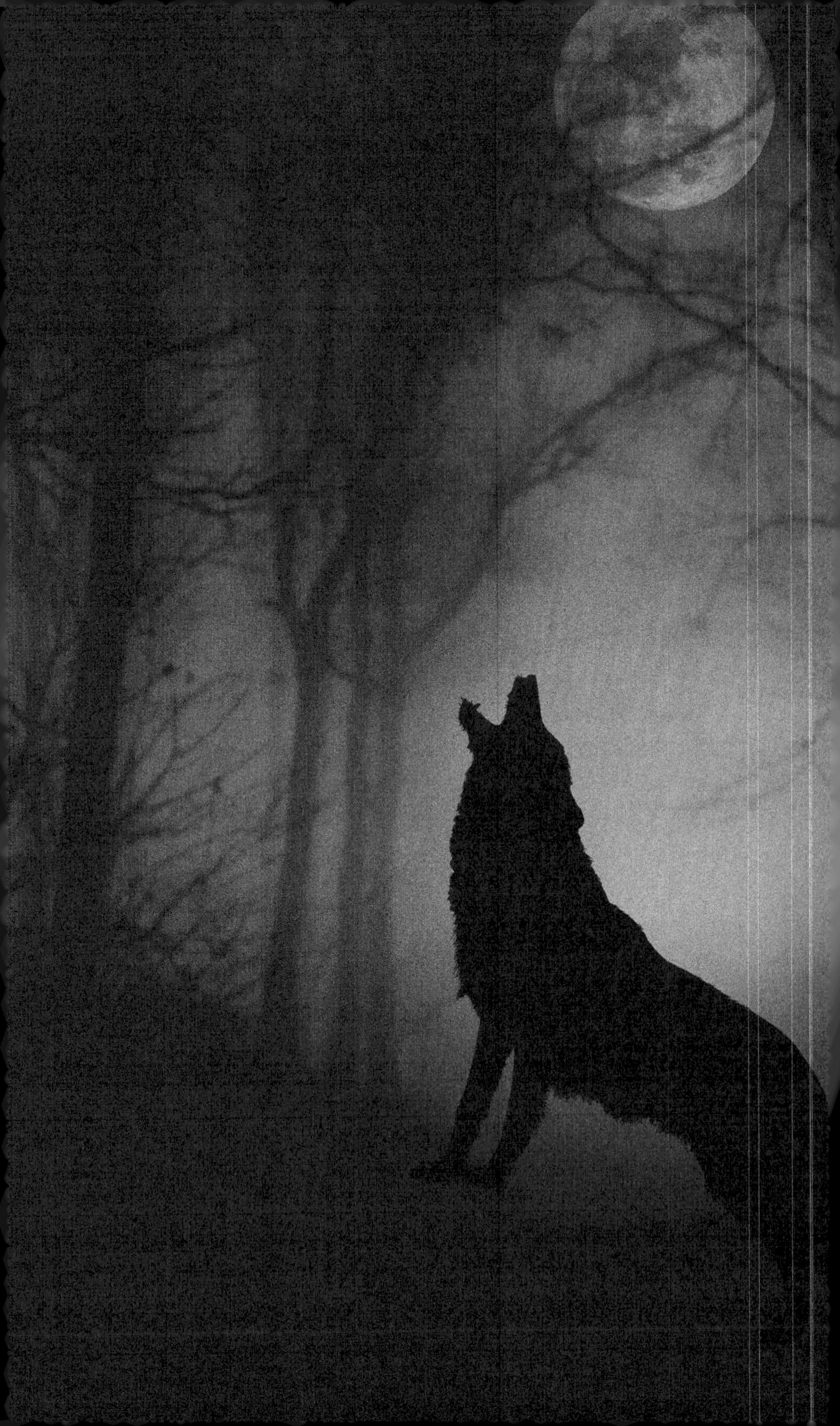

Fifteen

CONAN

"Did you hear that Louis and Collin are both dead now, too?" Rider asks as he takes a seat beside me at the kitchen island.

"No, I've deactivated all of my social media and barely use my phone since we left the pack." I reply in between sips of coffee.

Good.

All of them that were in on torturing Ruby deserve it.

"Do you think Draken killed them too?" Rider asks as he continues to scroll through his phone.

"Probably." I answer with a shrug. I hadn't seen him make a bloody grand entrance again since he got ahold of Marcus, but that doesn't mean he didn't find the time to pick off the other two in between his work meetings. Crystal hasn't told me anything about it either.

"It wasn't Draken." Alice replies as she makes her way over to the stove. Rider's cheeks flush in embarrassment but Alice doesn't even turn to look our way as she begins to heat up a skillet; as if we were simply discussing the weather.

"Surely they didn't kill themselves after all this?" I ask. I just can't picture the two goons having any such remorse.

"Reese and Heath got a hold of one, Victor took care of the other." Alice replies coolly as she begins to toss pieces of bacon into the skillet.

Rider chokes on his orange juice and I blink in surprise. The twins I could absolutely see taking after their father and killing anyone who hurt their sisters without any hesitation, but *Victor?*

"Victor killed one of them?" I blurt out in disbelief.

"He's the grandson of Dracula, you're really surprised?" Rider replies, more in shock of the normal tones everyone is using for this conversation than the knowledge of who committed the murders.

"Well, he just doesn't seem the type to get his hands dirty." Hell, I've been in more scraps than I can count, and some got very, *very* bloody, but even I haven't killed anyone yet.

"You didn't see the look on his face when he saw her." Alice says quietly over her shoulder. "Victor is very level-headed and good at diffusin' situations when he's not being a smartass, but if you mess with the people he cares about there's nothin' he is opposed to doing."

I lean back on my bar stool and sip my coffee again in thought as she returns to cooking. I suppose I could see that. Victor loves all of the Foxes as if they're his own family. He's more than just a pretty boy shithead after all, I suppose.

"I'm surprised you didn't burn them to a crisp, to be honest." I find myself saying aloud.

Alice wipes her hand on a nearby dish towel and turns to face me. "I wanted to, believe me. But, my desire to stay here with Ruby overrides that. Plus I knew they wouldn't be breathing for much longer whether I did it or not."

"Fair point." I nod.

Rider lets out a cough, then clears his throat.

"Will Draken be coming down soon? There's something I'd like to tell him, something I think he should know about." Rider asks as he sets his phone down on the counter.

"Everything okay?" Alice asks over her shoulder as she begins to flip the bacon.

"More of a precaution than anything." Rider replies.

"Is it that stuff Mikayla texted you about last night?"

"Yeah."

"Speaking of your mate, how is she feeling about your new living situation?" Alice asks.

"I'm truly lucky, to be honest," Rider replies sheepishly as be begins to rub the back of his neck. "She's supportive of my decision and would like to meet all of you soon providing that you're all comfortable with that in the future."

"I'm sure that won't be a problem once Draken hears whatever it is you have to say to him." Alice nods as she places a large plate of bacon for us to share on the counter between us.

"I want you to know as well, I just figured it would be easier to tell you both at once, yeah?" Rider replies shyly as he reaches for a piece, "Ow! Hot!"

"Well, no shit I just took it off the dang stove!" Alice chides.

"Idiot." I grunt.

"Fuck off!" Rider grumbles as he sucks on his forefinger and thumb.

"You wolves act like y'all are always starvin', I swear!" Alice says, exasperated as she turns back to the stove and begins to crack eggs into the bacon grease, muttering something unintelligible under her breath.

"What language is that? Romanian? They all speak Romanian, right?" Rider asks, looking back and forth between me and Alice.

"She's from Louisiana, so she probably called you an idiot in Cajun French too."

"How many languages do you speak?!" Rider exclaims as he turns back to face Alice.

"Enough." She replies, turning to face him with her hands on her hips. "And I basically asked God to have mercy on you gluttonous wolves. If I called you a fool it'd be 'coullion', for future reference." She says before turning back to finish scrambling the eggs that are cooking.

"Coo-wha?" Rider says, and I can't help but chuckle.

"Ah, yes. I've been called that many a time over the years." Draken says coolly as he makes his way into the kitchen.

"Rightfully so." Alice replies in a mockingly sweet voice.

"Morning, boys." Draken says as he begins to fill an electric kettle full of water.

"Morning, er, I was hoping you could take a look at this ..." Rider says as he unlocks his phone then slides it toward Draken.

"What is it?" Draken asks, quirking a brow as he sets the kettle down on its base and turns it on before picking up the phone.

"Mikayla, my mate, is Beta to the Valkyrie Pack. Her

Alpha told her about a meeting all of the Alphas in our surrounding areas are attending soon. Conan's father is supposedly the reason behind it due to the most recent happenings. That's everything she knows about it so far."

"Valkyrie ... That's the all female pack led by a female Alpha, yes?" Draken asks as he scrolls through Rider's messages.

"Yes, sir." Rider replies with a nod.

"That pack sounds pretty cool." Alice says as she begins to scoop a large helping of scrambled eggs onto the same plate as the bacon. "Do not touch for a few minutes!" She scolds, holding a finger in front of Rider's face.

"Yes, ma'am." Rider grumbles, and I let out a snort earning myself a glare from him.

Draken leans over the counter as he continues to read, rubbing his chin with his free hand. After a few minutes he begins to hold the buttons to take screen shots. "I'll be sending copies of these to my phone." He announces. "I'll save my number to your contacts in case there's anything more you want to tell me. Tell your mate she's free to text me anytime as well."

Rider nods as he tentatively reaches for a piece of bacon again, testing its temperature before eating several pieces at once.

"Save some for the rest of us!" I snap, slapping him upside the head.

"She's making more!" Rider mumbles through a full mouth as he gestures over to Alice.

"That doesn't mean eat the entire first serving by yourself!"

"There's a couple of pieces left!"

"Bloody hell," Draken pinches the bridge of his nose as he slides Rider's phone back to him, "if I wanted to hear this shite I'd go find Reese and Heath!"

"It's fine. Everyone eat as much as you want, I don't allow any hungry bellies in this house." Alice chuckles as she waves a hand dismissively.

"See?" Rider smiles triumphantly.

"Glad you've finally started to become comfortable here, bro." I grunt, rolling my eyes.

"If you two ladies are finished with your cat fight," Draken drawls, "Rider, tell your mate I would absolutely be open to meeting with Marisol and I can send a copy of my schedule to see what day and time are best for her."

"Wha-?" Rider blinks, looking at his phone.

"She just sent you a message about it while I was reading." Draken explains as he turns to pour himself a cup of tea from the now boiling kettle.

"Oh! Well, that works. That's … This is a good thing, wouldn't you say?" Rider asks, swivelling in his bar stool to face me.

"I really don't think it would hurt. Marisol seems to be down to earth. If we get her on our side, the better." I reply with a shrug.

"Well, I would certainly love to meet a female Alpha." Alice adds as she scoops the second helping of bacon in front of us.

"Conan, it's good to see you again." Marisol says as she shakes my hand. I notice her eyes linger on Crystal's claiming mark for a second, but her cool expression never changes.

"You as well, Alpha Gonza—oof!" Mikayla cuts me off by surprising me with a hug.

"Thank you for taking such good care of my Rider!" she says in a muffled voice as her face is currently buried in my shirt.

"Uh, it's the Foxes you should be thanking really ..." I mumble as I awkwardly pat her back until she releases me.

"Yes, you're right!" she says happily before turning to face Draken and Alice, who have been silently standing by the front door ever since letting them in and exchanging pleasantries. "Thank you so much for allowing him to stay with you!"

"Of course," Alice says sweetly as Draken nods, "Rider has been no trouble at all. We enjoy having him."

"Speaking of your mate, where is he?" Marisol asks and Mikayla instantly begins to glance around.

"I just texted him that you've both arrived, so he should be down any—" I start to say when the sound of Rider's hurried steps down the stairs echo into the room, "—second."

Rider zooms past all of us before scooping Mikayla into a hug. She lets out a happy squeak as she hugs him back, burying her face into his neck as Rider gives a polite nod of respect toward Marisol.

"You're looking well, Rider." Marisol nods back, smirking.

"Can I get y'all somethin' to drink?" Alice asks, jabbing her thumb in the direction of the kitchen.

"She won't take no for an answer so just comply." Rider warns before either Mikayla or Marisol can open their mouths to reply. Mikayla tilts her head in confusion and Marisol just smiles while raising an eyebrow.

"Well, in that case, water would be lovely." Marisol replies to Alice.

"Same." Mikayla says with a nod as she laces her fingers with Rider's.

Alice rolls her eyes at Rider then gestures everyone to follow her to the kitchen. "Right this way, y'all sit down and make yourselves comfortable." She calls over her shoulder, Draken right at her heels. If Marisol or Mikayla are nervous being in a vampire's home, they don't show it. They both just take in their surroundings as they each find a seat at the kitchen island where Alice already has a pitcher of iced water prepared along with glasses and a plate of finger foods.

"I already had water out, but if either of y'all want anythin' else let me know." Alice says as she pours them each a glass.

"Thank you, but this is fine." Marisol replies with a polite smile, Mikayla nodding in agreement as they each take a seat in one of the barstools, Rider standing behind Mikayla's as he places his hands on her shoulders. I opt out of a seat and just lean over the counter to rest my elbows upon it as Alice and Draken stand on the other side to face the wolves. Not that I'm any good at talking anyway, but I decide to just keep quiet and let the Foxes start and just speak up if I feel that I'm needed.

"Well, welcome to my home." Draken says, placing his hands behind his back. "Gonzalez, it's a pleasure to meet the infamous female Alpha of the all female pack."

Marisol smiles as she swirls the ice cubes around in her glass. "I'm flattered The Ripper has heard of me. Thank you for having us."

Draken chuckles in response. "I hear just about everything. Mikayla, it's a pleasure to meet you in person."

"Rider has told us all about you." Alice adds with a grin.

"She's not joking, I don't think he's left a single detail out." Draken agrees with an eye roll.

"Aw!" Mikayla looks up to meet a blushing Rider's gaze as Marisol chuckles.

"Isn't that the truth." I scoff.

"Shut up, you're just as obsessed with Crystal!" Rider stammers.

"I suppose it's just a wolf thing to be clingy," Draken says before I can retort, and I feel the back of my neck grow hot, "I thought it was just usual male behaviour to annoy the father of the female they're after despite the species."

"*Draken!*" Alice scolds as Marisol tosses her head back and laughs.

"No, no. He's correct, wolves are very touchy with their mates. Animal instinct and all that, you could say." Marisol explains with a grin.

"Well, I suppose that gives you points then that it's a universal thing instead of just a reason to irk my nerves." Draken says as he raises a brow in my direction and my face has never felt hotter. I open and close my mouth a few times before deciding to just leave it closed and study the details of the marble counter instead.

After Marisol and Mikayla are done chuckling at my expense, Marisol clears her throat and faces Draken. "I suppose I should get right down to the point before any other distractions arise," she starts, her expression sobering. "As Mikayla relayed to you, I have been called to an emergency meeting among several other Alphas." Draken and Alice nod somberly as they wait for her to continue. "You see, a lot of times a few of these Alphas can jump the gun on a few topics, and thanks to Alpha Knight of the Crescent Falls pack, Conan's father, we have been made aware of his concern over Conan's mating of your daughter."

I sigh in annoyance. "Luther jumps the gun at every

opportunity he possibly can." I grumble as I begin to clench my hands into tight fists.

Marisol gives me a pitying look as she nods. "I know your father can be quite …"

"A dick?" Mikayla offers.

"I was going to say highly strung." Marisol replies as she gives her an annoyed look, causing Mikayla to look down in submission.

"No, she's right. He's a dick." I grunt with a shrug as Rider nods in agreement.

Mikayla perks up at that and Marisol only looks more heartbroken for me, which makes me bristle a bit. I don't need or want pity, I only want to be done with him.

"Moving on," Marisol says as she clasps her hands together on the table, "my next question was to see if you're truly mated to this Crystal, but judging by that claiming mark on your neck I would say there is zero doubt about it."

I don't miss the sneer that appears across Draken's face before Alice smacks his arm as I nod, showing my neck to Marisol so that she can see the mark in its entirety.

"Yes, we're true mates. Both the wolf and vampire way." I respond. Mikayla doesn't seem like she needed convincing at all as she smiles at me, but I watch Marisol's calculating brown eyes take in every detail.

"Your drenched in her scent, that's for sure." She says with a nod as Draken rolls his eyes, earning himself another smack from Alice, "You said the vampire way, you've done what is it, the Blood Fate?"

I nod.

Marisol rubs at her chin thoughtfully as she processes the information for a moment before speaking again. "No one can claim it's not a true mating, that's for sure. Some will still try to say you're delusional, but any wolf with half a brain can see for themselves that you're truly mated to her."

I nod again as Mikayla looks around. "Where is she? I've been wanting to meet this Crystal I've heard so much about." Marisol nods as she glances around as well.

"She's upstairs keeping our other daughter company." Draken replies coolly as I watch Alice's eyes sadden for a fraction of a second before clearing her expression back to normal.

"Of course, she is under absolutely no obligation to, but we would both love to meet her if she consents." Marisol replies as Mikayla adds her agreement.

Draken only nods without giving a reply. "So, what should we expect if every wolf around can see Conan is really mated to her?"

"Well, that brings me to another question," Marisol says as she begins to tap a nail against the counter, "Mikayla has told me that Conan and Crystal have a child together?"

Even though there is no threat in her words, my back instantly straightens and my shoulders tense. I catch myself holding my breath as I await to see how this conversation is going to go from here on out. Draken and Alice look calm and collected, Draken keeping his hands behind his back as he slightly tilts his head to the side.

"Indeed they do." Draken replies, his cool grey eyes peering into hers.

"And Crystal is only half vampire, yes?" Marisol asks, a slight look of confusion on her face as she glances between Draken and Alice who are both clearly full vampires.

"She is." Draken agrees.

"I was human before Draken claimed me as his mate and changed me with the Blood Fate." Alice explains.

Marisol's eyes widen in understanding, but Mikayla seems unfazed as I'm sure Rider had already filled her in.

"Ah, I see." Marisol nods, "That makes sense. So this child is …"

"Half wolf, a quarter vampire, and a quarter human." I supply for her.

"Has something like this ever been heard of? Hybrids are already rare as it is, but …" Marisol trails off as Draken shakes his head.

"I've been using every resource I have available to look into it and can find no other 'tribrid', as we've dubbed her." Draken replies with a sigh.

"I don't doubt that you have much more resources than most." Marisol says quietly as she begins to drum her fingers along the counter again, thinking. "This is quite a big deal, Conan." She faces me again. "Your child is a girl, yes? She was healthy? Anything that's raised concerns?"

"Not at all." I shake my head. "I'm sure we'll see what side of which genetic pool is going to be the most dominant when she reaches puberty and then perhaps we'll be able to answer more questions, but for now she's a normal baby as far as I or anyone else can tell."

"We have a few contacts with The Ravens that come to do regular check ups on her in place of a pediatrician." Alice adds.

"Very smart." Marisol replies.

"So, what sort of a bullshit is Luther feeding the rest of you about his grandchild?" I ask, readying myself for the pounding headache that will undoubtedly come after hearing her response.

"Knight has some very … *interesting* concerns." Marisol says, looking as though she's trying to choose her words carefully.

Oh, God.

"He seems to believe that The Ripper and his family are blinding you to the reality that this child can be used as a weapon in the future."

I blink once, replaying her words as I try to force them to make sense.

"What?" Is all I can blurt out.

"Excuse me?" Alice stammers in disbelief, but Draken doesn't appear shocked in the slightest.

"Hybrids have a history of being forced to use their special strengths as weapons in wars, territory fights, illegal fighting for gambling, etc. I'm assuming Conan's father believes that our grandchild is being raised to turn into a weapon of mass destruction against him?" he asks dryly.

Marisol shrugs. "I guess. He's all emotion and no logic right now, but is stirring an uproar of mass hysteria among other Alphas."

"Fucking idiot." I groan as I begin to rub my face in my hands.

"Then of course that on top of the usual old school thinking of how vampires and werewolves should be enemies not sleeping together sprinkled on top for emphasis, that his son needs an intervention of some sort." Marisol adds with a grimace.

"He's the one that needs to be shipped to the mental ward!" I snarl, slapping my hands on the counter.

"Conan, as much as I want to agree with you, you know that most vampires and werewolves are going to share that view with your father." Draken says calmly and I nod, trying to keep my temper in check.

"Yeah, just look at how *you* responded to Crystal being pregnant by a wolf." Alice mutters under her breath, earning a glare from Draken.

"Anyway," Draken grunts as Alice waves a hand dismissively at him, "I'm guessing you don't seem to mind them being mates?" he asks as he faces Marisol again.

"Not really." Marisol shrugs. "I have had years of practice of having a more open mind, though. I'm gay, so I'm for anyone being with anyone as long as both parties are of age and consent after receiving shit all my life by homophobes for my romantic choices, and sexists for my Alpha status and choice to only allow females in my pack. It's bad enough a lot of male Alphas don't take me seriously just because I'm a female, but once they find out I'm a lesbian that usually just pours gas on their fire of bigotry."

"You'd think in this day and age that wouldn't be such an issue anymore." Draken replies thoughtfully.

"You would think." Marisol agrees.

"It's usually dumb old men that can't mind their own business." Mikayla grumbles.

"A lot of older Alphas have the old school mentality on a lot of things." Rider agrees with an eye roll as he rubs Mikayla's shoulders.

"You're also not the first female Alpha I've heard of, so I don't know why that would be such a big deal." Draken says thoughtfully. "I mean it's not common, sure, but even in the wild actual wolves will submit to females."

"Sad when a vampire realizes that but your own kind doesn't." Marisol replies with a bitter smile.

"You literally just have to turn the TV onto Animal Planet once in a while. It's not rocket science."

"I like you already, Ripper." Marisol chuckles.

"I do tend to have that effect on most people." Draken smirks.

"You're ridiculous." Alice says with an eye roll.

"I like you even more, Mrs. Fox." Marisol says with a grin. "You'd make a fine Alpha."

"Why thank you," Alice beams, "And really, Alice is fine."

"With how Alice keeps everyone in line, she truly would be an intimidating Alpha." Rider says and I can't help but nod in agreement.

"You flatter me." Alice chuckles as Draken pinches the bridge of his nose.

"Um, Alpha …" Mikayla says quietly. Marisol turns to face her, raising an eyebrow for her to continue. "Didn't you also want to ask them about …" Mikayla nods her head in the direction of the stairs.

"Oh," Marisol's expression hardens, "yes, thank you." She takes a deep breath before facing Draken and Alice again. "It's also come to my attention that your other daughter was attacked by Knight's pack?"

"Yes." Draken replies icily as Alice's expression falls and she looks at the floor. I feel my own stomach form knots as I let out a breath.

"It was unprovoked? She was nowhere near the Crescent Falls pack's territory?" Marisol asks, all business now as her back straightens.

"Not at all. She was just out shopping and the bloody mutt snatched her up off the street, then he and a couple of his pack mates tortured her. For fun."

I have to force myself to stop the growl that begins to rumble in my chest. Marisol and Mikayla both wrinkle their noses in disgust.

"I'm proud of you for not standing for that and leaving." Mikayla says quietly to Rider.

"There was zero hesitation to stay after I witnessed what I did." Rider replies, his voice unnaturally cold.

"How is your daughter now?" Marisol asks softly.

Draken lets out a sigh, then looks over at Alice. Alice nods, blinking rapidly as she begins to busy herself by taking the pitcher to refill it. Draken nods back, understanding between them both from whatever silent conversation they just exchanged as he looks back to Marisol.

"Why don't you see for yourself?"

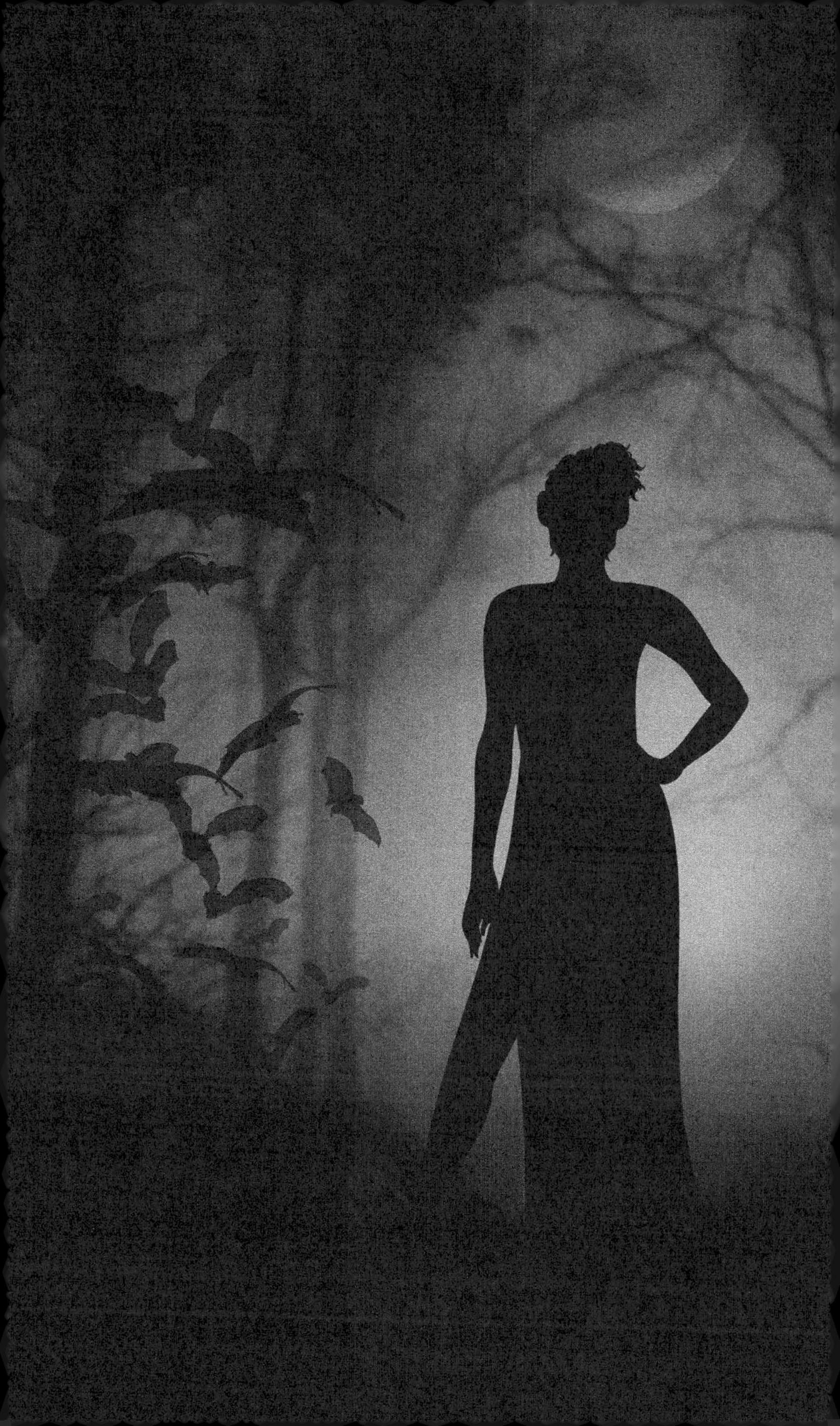

Sixteen

CRYSTAL

Even though Mom and Dad have told me in advance of Marisol and Mikayla coming, it still puts me at unease to see two strange wolves in the same room as my sister, whom is still recovering from an attack by wolves.

I grabbed her hand as soon as I heard them making their way into her room and continue to rub my thumb back and forth over her palm. I'm not sure if it's more to soothe her or myself, to be honest.

She's unresponsive as expected, just staring into nothingness propped up on her many pillows when I hear a gasp from someone. I glance up to see Marisol and Mikayla both staring in a mixture of horror and disgust as they take in the pitiful sight that is my sister. Rider has shown me plenty of pictures of his mate and her pack, so I already knew which was which, but the dominating vibes radiating from Marisol would've told me right away that she was the fearsome female Alpha I've heard so much about. It's only them and Dad, as I'm sure they don't want to crowd Ruby with everyone in the house in her bedroom. I'm sure he and Mom had a fierce debate over who would be escorting the two new strangers that we're supposed to trust in, but it makes sense he won if so.

"Believe it or not, she looked a lot worse than this when Conan first brought her back home." Dad says, finally breaking the silence.

Marisol swears under her breath in Spanish, then takes a deep breath as if trying to compose herself. "I've never been more disgusted in my entire life." She replies, her eyes never leaving Ruby.

"Rider warned me it was bad, but it's … It's totally a different level of shock to see this in person." Mikayla quietly adds, her eyes also glued to Ruby.

"I've heard you took care of the pendejo that did this to her?" Marisol finally flicks her eyes in Dad's direction.

"Let's say he and his other two pals that were in on this had a very long night and won't be bothering anyone ever again." Dad replies coolly, standing up straighter as he folds his hands behind his back.

"Good." Marisol nods. And she seems to truly mean it. Neither she nor Mikayla seem bothered in the slightest that my father just openly admitted to killing three of their kind.

"My wolf would love to piss on their graves." Mikayla says, further proving my observations.

"There wasn't enough left of them to bury," Dad shrugs then nods his head in my direction, "Anyway, that would be my other daughter, Crystal that's at her side."

"Is it okay with you if we come closer?" Marisol asks, glancing at both Dad and I for both our consent, it seems since they haven't moved from their spots at the doorway.

Dad raises an eyebrow at me, I nod, then he turns to nod at Marisol. Marisol shares a look with Mikayla before they make their way over to the bed, but still giving us a good bit of space.

"It's a pleasure to finally meet you in person," Marisol says with a soft smile.

"Same here," Mikayla adds. "Rider has told me so much about you. I only wish it were under better circumstances …"

I smile then shift from the bed to stand on my feet, extending a hand to Marisol first to shake it.

"Likewise for both of you," I say, turning to shake Mikayla's next, "I'm glad to see more wolves that understand we aren't monsters."

"My pack is all about being progressive, believe me." Marisol smirks before turning to face Ruby, her face falling again. "I understand she isn't responsive right now, but would it cause her stress if I talked to her?"

"I'm really not sure, considering you're a wolf … No offense." I reply sheepishly.

"None taken."

"However, it really doesn't seem to be affecting her in any way that you're in here." I shrug.

Marisol chews on her lip thoughtfully, nodding. After a moment she slowly lowers herself to a squat at Ruby's side. She moves a little closer to her, but doesn't touch her or the bed. She pauses, making sure Ruby doesn't seem to mind before deeming it safe to try and talk to her.

"Ruby, I know you don't know me, but I'm Marisol." She pauses again, and Ruby still stares at her lap, slowly blinking as if nothing was said. "I think you're very brave to have overcome the injustice that was done to you, and I want you to know that me and my pack are on you and your sister's side."

Still nothing from Ruby, but I find my eyes misting at Marisol's words.

"I also wanted to tell you …" Marisol continues, "That you and your sister are both far too pretty to be daughters of someone that goes by *The Ripper*." She says with a smirk, glancing back at Dad who blinks, then lets out a surprised laugh.

Ruby's lip twitches once, then any evidence of it happening is gone in an instant. Dad and I both make eye contact at the same time, mentally asking the other if they saw that just happen.

"I can't wait to properly meet you when you're up for it," Marisol says as she begins to rise to her feet. "I can feel Mikayla staring a hole into the back of my head impatiently waiting for her turn, so I suppose I'll back off now."

Mikayla sticks her tongue out at her Alpha, who chuckles quietly as she backs away to go and stand back next to Dad. As they quietly converse with each other, Mikayla squats in the same position and spot Marisol had just been in.

"Hello Ruby darling, you don't know me yet either, but I'm Mikayla. You and I are going to get to know each other well, and I can't wait for you to properly meet my mate, Rider. He's told me all the most embarrassing things we can tease your brother-in-law about, since they're besties and know all each other's dirty little secrets. So that just tells me that you and I are going to have to get as much dirt on the both of them as possible, I bet your sister would be willing to help …" she says, looking in my direction to give me a cheeky smile.

"Oh, I'm all about bullying Conan since he loves to tease me. He also loves to pick on Ruby as if she were his little sister, so I'm sure Ruby will be more than happy to assist getting back at him once she's up to it."

"That settles it, then." Mikayla announces confidently as she stands up straight. "We're going to make this happen. We're all friends now, no take-backsies."

Ruby may not have responded again, but the entire room feels lighter and happier.

CONAN

Nero is pacing back and forth, hackles raised the entire time Marisol and Mikayla have been in Lila's nursery. After gaining my consent, Crystal offered to let the two she-wolves meet our special pup that they had heard all about. Even though neither of them have done anything threatening, and I fully trust that they are indeed on our side, the primal instinct to be cautious of strangers around my pup is strong.

"She's absolutely precious!" Mikayla squeals.

"Gorgeous." Marisol agrees.

They're standing a foot away, but are absolutely soaking up all of our daughter's attention as she simply blinks at them and yawns in Crystal's arms.

"Thank you." Crystal responds with a soft smile as she bounces Lila.

"Sometimes I still find it hard to believe something that

beautiful came from me." I lightly chuckle, crossing my arms and bouncing on my heels to try and ease Nero's tension.

I hear a disgusted scoff from the other side of the crib, and imagine what I just said could not have painted a pretty picture for Draken. I hear Crystal snort, watching her bite her lip as she tries to suppress a laugh, but Marisol and Mikayla are both obvious about their amusement from it as I awkwardly scratch the back of my neck and clear my throat.

"Sorry, Draken."

He merely grunts in response, probably soothing himself by imagining my death for the millionth time I would presume.

"This pretty little doll just looks so dangerous; I'm shaking in my panties. I can see why everyone is terrified of hybrids." Mikayla says, breaking the awkward silence.

I roll my eyes and sigh, while Crystal chuckles.

"I don't even want to know the ways his old-fashioned imagination is conjuring up theories of what threats he believes Lila poses." I grumble as I pinch the bridge of my nose, my head aching at the mere attempt to process it.

"It's not just your Dad, a lot of both vampires and were-wolves still think that way." Crystal tries to console me with a half shrug.

"If anyone knows about the pains of old-fashioned thinking, it's me." Marisol says with a snort.

"I'm sorry," Crystal says quietly, true sincerity shining in her eyes. "You don't deserve that. No one does."

"No, no they do not," Marisol agrees while she stares at Lila a little longer, her expression a mixture of both curiosity and affection. She glances back up at Crystal and clears her throat, "Which is why I'd like you and your family to know that I'd like to offer my pack's alliance."

I blink.

Did I just hear that correctly?

"Oh," Crystal gasps, looking as if she's trying to process what exactly Marisol just told her.

"Is that right?" Draken inquires, stepping forward to stand right beside me.

Marisol nods as Mikayla smiles knowingly. "It's been quite a heavy discussion among my pack ever since Rider left Luther's to come stay here. Once we found out all of the details, I decided to come and meet the Fox family for myself and see what exactly was truly going on after hearing word of the shit storm Luther kicked up." She gestures to me and Crystal, "What I see is two true mates trying to raise their daughter, and vampires that are taking care of two wolves better than their previous pack did." Crystal and I glance at each other hopefully as Marisol threads her fingers together in front of her, tapping her thumbs. "Not much shocks me anymore after the life I've lived, but I must say; hearing that The Ripper took in Mikayla's mate and gave him sanctuary despite being a random wolf off the street even had me surprised. A wolf that has mated to your daughter, I understand, but …"

"It was a last minute decision for him to come here." I say.

To put it mildly, anyway.

"Yes, I heard the whole story from Mikayla once Rider was settled in for the night here." Marisol replies, and I feel my cheeks and neck burn from mild embarrassment.

Duh. Of course she did.

"To be fair, he wasn't a random wolf that Conan asked to come over for a sleepover," Draken interjects. "My main focus was making sure Ruby was okay, then I heard he left his pack behind because of my Ruby, despite her being a vampire. He also is someone Conan trusts."

Hearing that Draken actually considers my opinion of trust gives me a feeling of ... something I can't even describe. Happiness? Relief? Pride? All of the above? But, I absolutely make sure my face displays nothing so that it doesn't ruin the moment.

"His background check also came back clear to my liking." Draken adds.

Background check? Of course Draken Fox runs background checks on people and has the resources to do it that quickly.

Mikayla blinks in confusion but Marisol seems unsurprised.

"Well, either way, it's not something just any vampire would have done. I'm just happy to see you didn't throw your daughter and grandchild out, to be honest."

"As if. My children can commit nearly any crime known to man and be allowed back home. Just ask my two godless heathens of sons. Besides, it's not like I can exactly be too judgy with a nickname like 'Ripper' can I?"

"It's true." Crystal shrugs.

I really don't know whether to fear or admire my father in law. It's probably a mix of both, but still quite a gray area.

"No, I suppose you can't." Marisol replies with a smirk.

"Seriously, thank you all so much for taking care of my Rider." Mikayla says as she looks across the room at all of us. "Being a rogue wolf can be so dangerous, so seeing in person how safe and well taken care of he is here has put me and my wolf at ease."

"Of course, he's a good lad." Draken replies nonchalantly.

"He's my best friend. I'll always look out for him." I reply.

"I'm happy someone so close to Conan can be here to be around Lila since we've just been alienated to my family." Crystal adds with a small smile, and her words make my heart ache a bit at the realization that Rider truly is the only person on "my side" that has even met my daughter. I quickly shove that feeling into a box then push it far back into my mind.

"I would've been able to offer him temporary sanctuary, and was still planning to offer to, but it appears he wants to be here as long as the Foxes allow him." Marisol says as Mikayla nods, "I won't undo my vow to keep an all female pack, but any mate of my pack members is family. Even after any of my girls leave my pack to join a mate, they are always family and forever have my pack's support; so you have my alliance for helping protect one of my own, when it boils down to it."

"My father seriously needs to take notes from you when it comes to pack ethics." I say, half joking, half earnestly.

Marisol chuckles. "One must be willing to learn to be taught."

"And there lies our biggest problem with him." I grunt.

She chuckles again and I extend my hand to her, causing her to raise a pierced brow.

"I can't thank you enough for your alliance. I may not have fulfilled my Alpha training, but I know that's not something to be taken lightly."

She clasps my hand and gives it one surprisingly hard shake.

"Of course. It's what family is for."

I wish my dad could get that memo. Another thought and feeling to shove into another box to keep pushing deep, deep down.

Draken extends his hand next, "Anything your pack needs that I can provide, just ask."

"I certainly won't take that offer from *the* Draken Fox lightly," Marisol says with a cheeky grin as she shakes Draken's hand.

After exchanging contact information, Alice treated Mikayla and Marisol to dinner before their departure. All of me seemed to feel loads lighter long after they left, knowing that my family now has an army of one of the toughest wolves around behind them if my dad sends any trouble our way.

For the first time in what felt like forever, my shower tonight actually felt relaxing instead of a break to reflect on all of the fucked up shit that has been plaguing us back to back. I walked out of the bathroom, feeling like a whole new wolf to Crystal's empty bedroom. I can hear her singing to Lila in the nursery next door, as I get dressed and slip into her bed. Her and Lila's rooms are now covered in my scent, and that makes Nero feel both proud and at ease. I've even shifted a few times to allow him to mark his scent all over the Fox's property to help with how antsy he's been since our arrival.

I pick up my phone to check for any missed notifications while I was in the shower and notice one voicemail from my mom and my stomach drops. My mind races with questions and scenarios before I finally decide to rip the band aid off by just listening to it, my stomach now doing flips as I raise the phone to my ear.

"Conan, honey? Please, call me back. I want to talk to you about all this …" There's a long pause, and I almost thought that was the end of the voicemail before I hear her sniffle, and my heart breaks. "I …" She clears her throat. " I love you, son. We'll figure this out, somehow." I can hear her let out a small cry before hanging up.

Another thing to add to another box, and shove even deeper down.

Seventeen

ALICE

The sound of Ruby's screams has me racing up to her room, heart pounding. I make it there in seconds and see her sitting up in bed, sobbing hysterically. She's still half asleep, still trapped within the web of a memory turned nightmare.

"Ruby! Ruby, I'm here! Mama's here!" I say loudly as I sit down, pulling her close to me. I embrace her tightly, patting her back firmly to help bring her back to the present. "I'm right here, baby. It's okay."

She lets out a loud gasp then continues to cry a little quieter, but is still clearly shaken up. I switch from patting to rubbing circles onto her back, and I feel her relax her stiff frame the slightest bit.

"It was just another nasty dream," I whisper into her hair. "Deep breaths, that's it ..."

Ruby takes a few shuddering breaths, staring at nothing as she angles her head toward her lap.

"Feel a little better?" I ask.

No response, which isn't surprising, but still disheartening.

"Are you hungry?" I try one more time, giving one of her hands a tight squeeze. They're cold and clammy, which makes my heart ache even more.

After a few more minutes of silence, I feel my shoulders sag in defeat.

"N-no," comes a quiet, raspy response.

I feel my eyes widen in surprise as I look back at her while squeezing her hand again.

"You talked while you're awake!" I practically shout with glee.

She's still not looking at me, or anything really, as she continues to glance down at her lap. Her eyes aren't as fogged over as they once were.

"You've got a little more color in your cheeks today." I add, hoping to prompt more words out of her, but she doesn't say a word or move an inch. I pull her hair behind her shoulders and out of her face. "Are you sure you're not hungry? You need to keep your strength up, baby."

Nothing.

"That's okay, hun. Don't overdo it. I'm just so happy to hear that sweet, little voice answer me!" I say before giving her another hug.

My phone vibrates with a new text message, and I take it out of my pocket to glance at the screen before standing up.

"If you feel like stayin' up for a bit, I have a couple of surprises for you. If you don't, that's okay, they'll be waitin' for you when you wake up." I say as I start walking toward her door.

"Okay." I hear her reply in a small, tired voice.

I grin back over my shoulder at her.

"I'll be right back!" I promise as I race down the stairs.

After hurrying to grab everything from downstairs and race back up the stairs without dropping any of it, I drop everything onto the foot of Ruby's bed. She blinks, eyes widening in surprise as she sits up a little straighter to get a better look of the goodies now covering her lap.

"These are from Marisol and her pack," I say as I open a white box to reveal what must be two dozen cupcakes inside. "I know you don't have your appetite all the way back yet, but you can tell they're made from scratch! All of the wolves in Marisol's pack are women, and she told me they all worked together bakin' and decoratin' them for you." I say as I let her glance over the multicolored icing and sprinkle decorations, each of them very different to show they were made by multiple different pairs of hands that put care into every crumb.

Ruby's eyes soften, then glaze over in thought as she processes my words. Maybe she remembers the visit Marisol and Mikayla paid her? We weren't sure if she was conscious enough to register them in the same room as her. I shut the box and set it on her nightstand.

"You can try one whenever you're ready. There's a card inside the box too. Either you can read it, or I can read it to you." I say before reaching for a plastic bag, fishing out the two articles of clothing inside. "Two of Marisol's packmates know how to sew and knit, they each made you a sweater." I lay them each on Ruby's lap so she can get a better look at them, and she blinks rapidly before gently reaching to finger the material of one between her fingers. She still doesn't say anything, but I watch her look over them both, smoothing her hands over each. One is a deep crimson red, her favorite color, with white swirls of various patterns: and the other is a cool gray that I know would make her gray eyes she inherited from her dad really pop if she wears it.

After she withdraws her hand, I take each of the sweaters and quickly hang them in her closet. I turn to see her staring at a large stuffed unicorn that's leaning on the footboard of her bed. It's rainbow, with a large bow wrapped around its neck along with a tag that reads, "Get well soon, Little One."

"That's from Vic." I tell her, pushing it closer to her reach. She nods, pulling it to her chest. She probably could tell by his handwriting if she noticed the tag. Ruby still loves stuffed animals to this day, her collection growing larger each year, and unicorns have been her favorite animal since she was a toddler. She hugs it tight and closes her eyes for a few seconds, then looks back down at the final box resting between her ankles.

"Baylor knows you're a bookworm, so he and his friend Ella that works with him over at the Ravens, each got you a book from your favorite authors as well as some they just think you would like." I say happily as I take out nine books from the box. Ruby's eyes widen again, then grow soft as she glances over each cover.

"You want to pick one out to read and I can put the others on your shelf?" I ask. She nods then selects one from the pile and begins reading the back cover while I begin to place the rest on her shelves. I grin to myself, my heart swelling with joy. This is the most responsive she's been since she's been home. My phone buzzes in my pocket, and I quickly take it out to glance at the screen to the text I've been waiting for.

"You have one last surprise." I say as I turn to face her, clasping my hands together as I try to control my excitement. Ruby looks up at me, a question in her eyes as she sets her new book down in her lap.

"Did you miss me?" Silas calls out happily as he struts in her room, his hands behind his back. Ruby's eyes instantly brighten and she lifts the covers and turns in the bed to set her feet on the ground. "No, no! Don't get up!" Silas stops her as he walks over to sit next to her on the bed, placing a large cardboard box beside him. Ruby hugs him around his waist, burying her face in his chest and my eyes immediately fill with tears. She adores her godfather, and I just know this is a visit she needed.

"How are you feeling, sweet girl?" Silas murmurs as he hugs her back. She only hugs him back tighter in response.

"She's still not talkin' much." I say after clearing my throat.

"That's quite all right. You take your time, Ru." Silas replies, ruffling her hair as she sits up to look up at him. She bats his hand away, but a small smile spreads across her lips.

I can tell Silas is trying hard not to look at her remaining wounds that haven't healed yet. He's doing his best not to lose his shit more than he already has. He responded just as well as Draken when he found out what happened, and I know he's doing his best to bottle up that rage while in front of her.

"I come bearing a gift I heard you wanted." He says as she tilts her head. From within the cardboard box he pulls out a hamster cage, with a tiny white hamster with golden-orange and brown spots on his head.

A small gasp escapes from Ruby's throat as she takes the cage from him. She looks inside, poking her finger between two bars, the hamster cautiously sniffs the tip and she smiles. *Really* smiles.

"I think I got everything he needs to start out with, that's just a travel cage though. I've got a bigger one on the way– Oh, don't cry Ruby!" Silas says as he begins to rub her back. Tears streak down her cheeks, and she sniffles as she gently sets the cage down and turns to bear hug him.

"She's just really, *really* happy." I say, dabbing at my own eyes with a tissue. "She's been wanting one forever. Especially after she got into that anime about one."

"That's what I heard. Tell Draken to shove it about not having a pet rat in the house, yeah?" Silas chuckles as he hugs Ruby back, resting his cheek atop her head.

"I think he'll be fine with it to see her so happy." I reply.

"Hey, listen," Silas says as he pulls away, and Ruby looks up at him as she wipes at her cheeks. I hand her a tissue that she gladly accepts. "In order to take care of that little guy, you have to take care of yourself, right? You have to get stronger so you can provide the best home for him. So allow yourself to heal, but also make yourself get up and eat, shower, walk outside whenever you can. Okay?"

Ruby looks down at the cage, her eyes following the hamster explore the various little toys set inside. She blows her nose, then looks back up at Silas.

"Okay." She replies in a voice barely above a whisper.

"That's my girl." Silas says proudly. "Why don't you think of names while we find a place to set him up until his bigger cage comes in, hm?" he says as he reaches inside and takes out the hamster. "Don't bite me now, you little bugger …" He gently places the hamster inside Ruby's awaiting cupped hands. "Don't bite her either."

Ruby strokes his fur with her thumbs as she looks down at this little rodent like he's the most precious thing in the world. I swear it's similar to how she looks at Lila when she holds her. Silas begins moving things around so that he can place the travel cage on top of her dresser.

"Let me guess, you wanna name him Hamtaro? Or after one of the other little characters from that show?" I ask as I kneel down beside her, stroking the hamster's back with my forefinger. He really seems to be a patient and friendly little guy.

Ruby smiles, but shakes her head.

"No? Any other ideas then?"

She pauses, just watching him as a few seconds pass.

"Mr. Nibbles." She declares as she looks up at me.

Ruby might love that show, but she's always favored naming things "Mr." or "Miss" for some reason. It started about the time she was old enough to participate in tea parties with her sister.

"I think that's a perfect name." I smile, rubbing her back.

"Me too!" Silas agrees, gesturing toward the cage. "This seem an okay place for now?"

Ruby nods and goes back to looking at Mr. Nibbles. She holds him under her chin, closing her eyes as she cuddles him. Silas and I meet each other's gaze and I mouth a "thank you" to him. He nods, smiling. I could swear I see emotion shining in his his eyes as well, but he'll never admit it.

Draken's best friend helped bring my daughter back, and I don't think I'll ever be able to repay him.

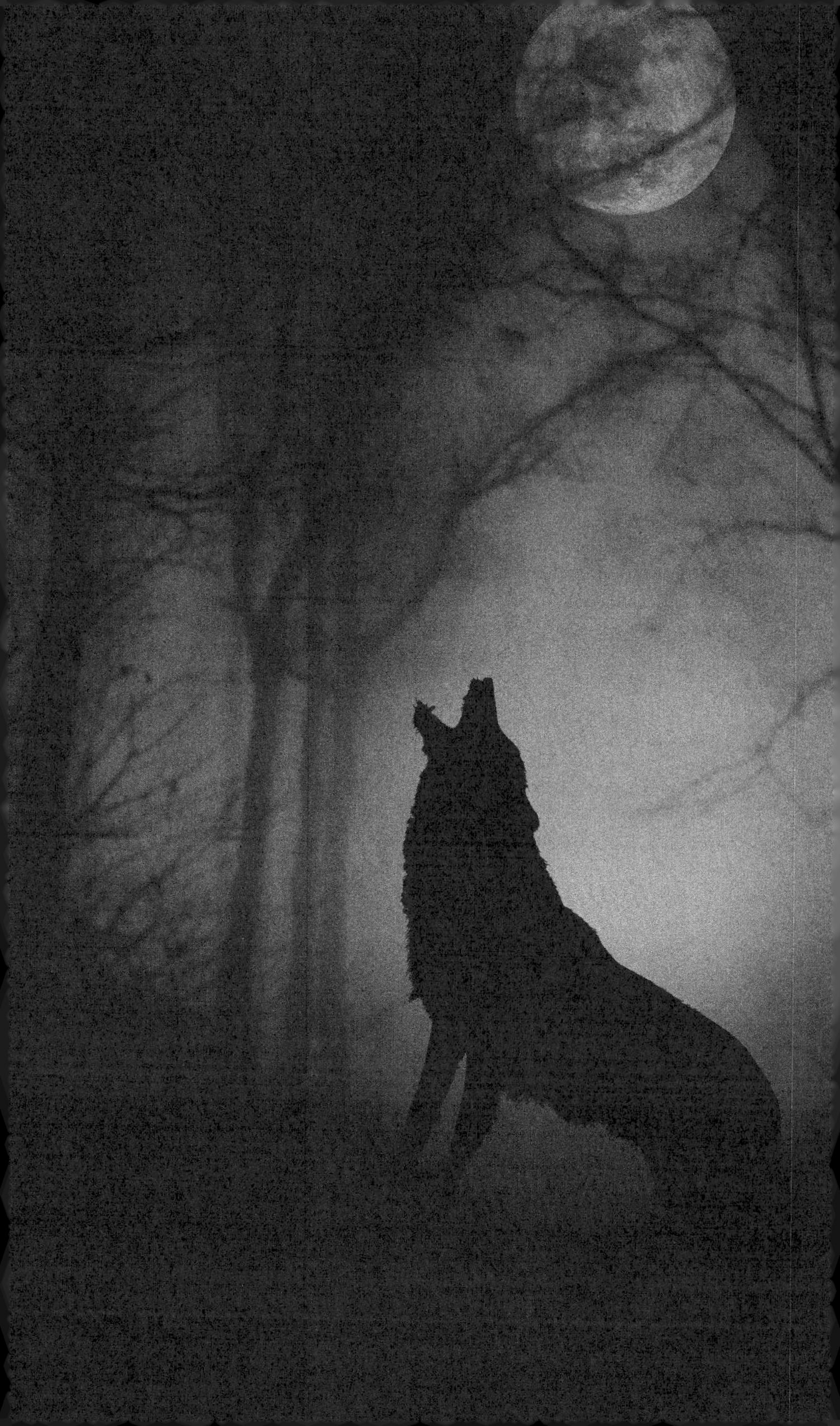

Eighteen

CONAN

There is a fine line between sending a message and potentially starting a war, apparently.

As the night of the meeting among all the Alphas approached, Marisol and her pack have been visiting the Fox Manor frequently for us to come up with a plan. Due to Baylor's position as a Raven, he absolutely has to stay neutral but he has come over to let us know what actions could lead to The Ravens having to step in or put a mark on us to be watched. His coworker and friend, Ella, has been over as well for some of the visits. It's painfully obvious that Reese has the hots for her, but I can't quite decide if she returns the feeling or hates him.

Might be both, to be honest. Draken wanted her presence because she also works for him at the Fox Den, and she could be helpful with watching out for any retaliation from wolves there. Their disgusting acts against Ruby help his case if he ever needs to execute self-defense in front of any of his human patrons.

Draken has been yelling at Reese to keep it in his pants. Reese does not seem to care. Marisol has found the Foxes to be quite amusing, and I must admit it lightens up a usually very serious and foreboding conversation.

"Baxter Jameson is the name of the bloke hosting this meeting?" Draken asks for confirmation.

"Yes," Marisol nods. "He has the largest pack in Colorado."

"Right, do you know if the meeting will be held indoors or outdoors?"

"Indoors. He has a large dining room used to host many pack events."

"Any way you can send me a layout of the house and property?"

"Easily."

"I did not hear that." Ella says, covering her ears.

"I can cover your ears and distract you with a kiss—OW!" Reese rubs at the area Ella slaps.

"You're a vampire, you're fine."

"You hit hard for such a tiny human!"

"Baby."

"Oh, is that your new pet name for me? Call me baby again. OUCH, what the fuck?!" Reese rubs at his head after receiving a backhand from Draken.

"Focus! With the head on your shoulders not the one in your pants!" Draken snaps while Ella chuckles.

"Grouchy old coffin dodger …" Reese grumbles.

"I'll also work on having a head count of who all will be attending." Marisol says with a smirk.

"Do we know exactly how many pack members Jameson has without guests?" I ask.

"I can give you *fifty-three* reasons why I can't tell you." Baylor states.

Draken lets out a low whistle in astonishment.

"That *is* a pretty damn big pack." I say, scratching at the scruff on my neck.

"I was expecting somewhere in the twenties, maybe even the thirties, but fifty three is … a lot." Draken grumbles to himself. He pulls out his phone and begins to type up what I assume is notes he feels the need to keep track of for later. "Right, well, either way we can handle that." He says after placing his phone back into the pocket of his black slacks.

"Usually it's only Alphas and their Betas that attend these meetings, so whatever the number is it'll be doubled for sure. Typically they don't bring their mates or other pack members." Marisol says.

I nod in confirmation.

"Dad and Red will be there for sure. So that's fifty-five right there."

"Right, okay." Draken says more to himself than anyone else, nodding. "I have a few phone calls to make and a few favours to call in, Marisol get me that number of guests as soon as you're able to." He says as he heads toward his office.

Marisol nods, then looks over at me.

"Nervous?" she asks, reaching up to clasp me on the shoulder.

"A bit, but this is all necessary." I admit.

"I agree. You're so young to worry about any of this, but you're handling it really well."

"You think so?"

"I know so. I can also say without a doubt that you're handling yourself ten times better than Luther ever would." She says with a small smirk.

I laugh humorlessly.

"Well, at least there's that."

I have to hand it to Draken, he calls in some pretty good favors. We can all hear and see what Marisol hears and sees thanks to the small hidden camera she wears. She's also equipped with an ear piece that she can hear us at a muted volume to where other sensitive ears can't pick up what we're saying to her. A few of us are all packed inside of a van that is far enough to not be on the property line, but close enough to receive reception.

Although the view is limited, the long dining table has every single seat filled with wolves. Marisol is the only female Alpha, but there seem to be several female Betas. A few might be mates to the Alphas attending, but I doubt it.

Only Alpha Jameson and his Beta I can't remember the name of, sit at the table from his pack, the rest I'm positive are scattered around the pack house and surrounding property for surveillance. The table must have around twenty people sitting, so there's definitely over seventy wolves around the Jameson property currently.

My heart feels as if it's in my throat as Jameson begins to clink one extended claw against a wine glass in order to get everyone's attention. Once the chatter dies down, he retracts the aforementioned claw and stands, clearing his throat.

"Thank you all for coming," he says, spreading his arms wide with welcome. "As eldest with the largest pack in Colorado, I took it upon myself to host this meeting therefore I will start us off."

"He looks like an uglier version of Mr. Clean." Heath whispers, and I can't help but chuckle at that. Marisol must've heard too, because we hear her clear her throat and cough a few times before she takes a sip of water.

Baxter Jameson is of average height and build with a bit of a beer belly beginning to form, and a clean-shaven face with a shiny bald head. His face is dotted with a few old scars, and his mouth is framed by deep set laugh lines that remind me of a ventriloquist puppet.

"I understand not every Alpha was able to make it on such short notice," Jameson continues, "so thank you to those of you that were able to come. And thank you to the Betas that also accompanied your Alphas. I don't believe we have any mates here, correct?" After some murmuring of agreement Jameson nods in understanding. "We'll try to make this as quick and painless as possible so all of you that are mated can get back to your mates and pups."

"Ow!" Reese hisses as Heath (I can only tell them apart because I memorized who was wearing which jacket) elbows him to get a better look at the monitor.

"Get off my nuts!" Heath snaps.

"Both of you shut up!" I hiss under my breath.

Rider rolls his eyes and leans back against the blacked out window of the van.

"Stealth is not our group's specialty." He grumbles.

I ignore whatever retort the twins spit back at him as I lean forward to catch what Jameson is saying.

"For those of you that have not been formally introduced, I am Alpha Baxter Jameson, and this is my Beta, Neil." Jameson gestures at the tall bearded male that towers over him at his side. He tucks a lock of brown hair behind his ear before nodding acknowledgment and offering everyone a polite smile before taking his seat again. "I understand some of you are frustrated and tired from your journeys here, so let's get straight to the point then, shall we?" Jameson says, cracking his knuckles as he finally takes a seat himself.

He picks up a stack of papers and begins to straighten them, then flips through a few pages. He seems to find the page he was looking for, then takes a sip of his wine before speaking again.

"As some of you are aware, there has been lots of vampire activity lately." He says with disgust as he passes a paper to Neil, who takes the paper and passes it down. "Here you will see the vampires we have for sure identified." Jameson clarifies as each wolf takes a look over at the paper before passing it around. "I can have Neil make anyone who wants a physical copy, but I already planned on emailing each of you a digital copy of it for your packs' records."

A few gasps and swears are heard, and I just know information about the Foxes is on that paper. I feel the twins tense beside me, and I assume they've come to the same realization. To my surprise, they stay quiet and watch the monitor with identical glowing red eyes.

"We have acquired a lot of new information regarding Jack the Ripper and his family. Some of you might know him by his government name, Draken Fox." Jameson's lips curl into a snarl as Draken's name leaves his lips. A few growls answer, and it never ceases to amaze me of how large of a reputation my father-in-law has built for himself, and how I had never heard of him before.

Although, Dad could've very well mentioned him in the past and I could've tuned him out, since I usually spaced out anytime he talked about any sort of pack business.

"Alpha Knight, would you like to share the information you've shared with me?" Jameson asks, and I freeze. Marisol's body turns to face my father and Red, and I swallow hard.

"I'm Luther Knight, Alpha of the Crescent Falls pack. This is my Beta, Red." Dad grunts as he gets to his feet. Red does the same and nods in acknowledgement. "The Ripper and his cronies have killed three of my pack mates in cold blood."

I scowl at the lie.

Cold blood? They were avenging Ruby!

Reese and Heath, who are responsible for one of the aforementioned deaths, simply chuckle. It's not their usually mischievous chuckle, but darker. Their eyes stay red as a sinister smile spreads across each of their faces.

Boy am I happy that I'm on their good side now.

"The Ripper has also brainwashed my son. He attacked the pack mates I mentioned shortly before their deaths, then turned his back on our pack. The Ripper has somehow tricked him into believing that my son and his daughter are mates." Dad all but spits out the last word. He has to pause in his speaking to allow the outrage from the other wolves to die down.

"Brainwashed?" I scoff. Rider sighs and shakes his head, and the twins chuckle darkly again.

"After his departure, those three of my pack mates he turned on slowly started dropping like flies. He is well aware of the laws surrounding vampires, and I do not condone his ac–"

"Now you hold the fuck up." Marisol cuts him off, slamming her hands on the table as she gets to her feet. Movement beside her shows Mikayla getting to her feet as well, and I notice Rider tense.

Dad scowls in her direction as Red raises an eyebrow at her. A few people whisper in confusion as Marisol slams her hands down on the table again, causing many of the wine glasses on the table to shake and slosh wine and water everywhere.

"Marcus, Louis and Collin deserved their fates after what they did to Draken's daughter." Marisol snaps. A few gasps and confused muttering amongst the wolves can be heard as Dad's face grows redder with rage by the second. Red simply looks confused along with several others.

"Are you seriously defending vamps right now?" An Alpha I don't recognize asks, venom coating every word.

Marisol whirls around to face him, and I can hear Mikayla growling in warning at him. Rider begins to growl too as he leans forward to get a better look at the monitor.

"I'm defending a father that was getting revenge for his daughter!" Marisol shouts, then proceeds to call the Alpha a series of Spanish words that I can only assume are insults.

"This is what Knight's pack did to Ruby Fox!" Mikayla says as she holds up a file then slams it on the table. Pictures of Ruby's injuries and medical reports are spread across the table. "Unprovoked I might add!" Mikayla says as she begins to shove one of the pictures at the Alpha that questioned Marisol.

"Tell me you wouldn't have done the same for your kids!" Marisol challenges.

The Alpha merely glances at it then rolls his eyes, shoving the paper away. An Alpha next to him, I believe his name is Zayn, snatches it up, frowning.

"Your men did this to Jack's daughter for no fucking reason?" Alpha Zayn asks Dad.

Red sighs as Dad stammers for a minute.

"Marcus was only trying to see what she was doing so close to our turf, but I quickly disciplined him once I learned who she was and–"

"So she wasn't even on your turf? Just close to it?!" Zayn asks, bewildered. His Beta, who I know for sure is named

Asher because I've had to talk with him before for pack business, grabs the paper from Zayn.

"She's The Ripper's *minor* daughter at that?" He looks over at Zayn, his nose wrinkled in disgust. "She looks like she might weigh eighty pounds soaking wet. Real threat there."

Zayn scoffs then looks back at Dad.

"I would've done the same fucking thing as Jack if anyone did this to my pups!"

"I have to agree with Zayn." Another Alpha chimes in. I've met him a handful of times, and after staring at his face a few more seconds I remember his name is Caspian.

"I'm surprised at you both!" Jameson blurts out, clearly shocked.

"I'm not!" Dad snaps. "We all know Zayn is buddy-buddy with Marisol, so it's no surprise he's trying to be more progressive." He says "progressive" as if it's a dirty word. "And to be quite frank I'm not shocked to see Caspian as a sympathizer with how much of a push-over he is."

Dad earns himself growls and snarls from Zayn, Caspian and their Betas as he plops back down in his chair and crosses his arms. Red looks embarrassed, and for a moment I feel bad for him.

"Your pack member attacked an underage girl that was unarmed and not a threat to you or your turf." Zayn says, enunciating each word slowly and clearly as if speaking to a toddler.

"Vampire or not, that's just freaking low." Caspian agrees.

"I can't believe anyone at this table is seriously sympathizing with those blood-suckers right now." Another Alpha pipes up, and the Alpha that received Marisol's wrath nods in agreement with him.

"The only good vamp is a dead one!" Another Alpha calls out from across the table.

After that, chaos ensues.

Everyone is shouting their agreements or disagreements, several fists pound the table, several wolves stand to get in another wolf's face, and Marisol sits, crossing her arms as she watches quietly. Her work is done.

"Who even invited *her*?" an Alpha named Dwayne asks, jabbing a thumb in Marisol's direction. "This is precisely why women don't belong in politics!"

"That is my Alpha and you will treat her with respect! She deserves to be here just as much as any of you!" Mikayla roars as she gets in Dwayne's face.

"It's all right, Mik. Stand down." Marisol says calmly.

Mikayla and Dwayne have a growling stand off for a few more minutes before she takes her seat back next to her Alpha, her eyes never dropping from his.

"You okay?" I ask Rider who is clearly bristling at his mate's expense.

"Fine." He snaps, his eyes flashing back and forth from gold to brown.

"You insult Alpha Gonzalez again and I will rip your damn throat out, got that?" Zayn says coldly as he points a finger in Dwayne's face.

"ENOUGH!" Jameson bellows, and the table slowly comes to a quiet hum of growls and hushed angry whispers.

"This is absolutely ridiculous!" he says incredulously as he looks around the table from wolf to wolf. "Why is this even up for debate? *All* vampires are nothing but trouble!"

Neil had looked like he was nodding along with agreement with him at first, then shakes his head as if to clear it then gives his Alpha a perplexed look, mouth agape, as if he can't believe what he's hearing.

"Draken Fox has kept to himself the past few decades until his daughter was attacked." Marisol says firmly.

"Sympathizer!" A random Alpha yells out.

"Draken Fox has taken my son from me!" Dad yells, getting to his feet again. His big hands crash onto the table, causing the wood to crack and several glasses fall and shatter. I widen my eyes in surprise.

I knew he was going to argue, I just wasn't expecting him to say ... *that*.

"And now he's forced my son to help create some sort of ... of ... weapon spawn!"

I feel my hackles rise as he refers to my daughter with such untrue malice. His own grandchild. A part of me is hurt and disappointed, the other part is not shocked in the slightest.

"Your own ignorance has taken your son from you!" Marisol counters.

"Shame on you for not getting to know your only grandchild!" Mikayla adds.

Dad only glares back at both of them, and I see Red whisper something I can't decipher into his ear.

"If there really is a hybrid sired from the Ripper's bloodline, that spawn needs to be taken care of before–"

Marisol cuts him off with a loud growl and stands on her chair. She walks onto the table, treating it as if it were her own cat walk, kicking over and smashing glasses toward Jameson and then crouches down in front of him.

"Alpha Gonzalez!" Jameson starts, but is shut up by a pointed, mint green fingernail.

"You touch a hair on that baby's head and it won't be Draken you have to worry about because I'll make sure you're six feet under long before he gets to you, *pendejo*." Marisol says, her voice low, cold as ice. Jameson's brain seems to glitch as he tries to process everything Marisol just said and did, and she takes the gap in conversation to hop down from the table. Mikayla meets her as they both stand against a wall, eyes darting from wolf to wolf.

"The Fox family is under the protection of my pack, too." Zayn announces after a moment, then goes over to stand next to Marisol, his Beta following him.

"Do you *really* want to start a war between packs?" Caspian asks, taking turns to eye both Dad and Jameson. "Because I know which side I'll be on." He finishes before rising to go stand next to Zayn, his Beta also following him.

Wolves begin to chatter amongst themselves when another Alpha stands up, his Beta rising to his feet beside him.

"Now wait just a damn minute." The Alpha states.

"Please help us talk some sense into these lunatics, Cairo." Jameson grunts as he begins to rub at his forehead.

The Alpha, Cairo, snorts in disgust.

"Talk some sense into *them?* You're messing with the mate bond! Marisol, has Knight's son claimed Fox's daughter?"

"Yes. Both the wolf way and the vampire way." Marisol confirms.

"They've done the Blood Fate?" Cairo asks, eyebrows raised, to which I assume Marisol nods. He turns back to face Dad. "If your son is mated to Fox's daughter, you should all back off and respect nature!"

"Respect nature?!" Dad stammers, his face reddening again at the audacity of Cairo's words.

"Yes! You do realize the Blood Fate means your son will die if his mate dies, right?"

At that, Dad presses his mouth into a firm line and says nothing.

"Plus, some of you are talking about harming an innocent child!" Cairo's Beta speaks up.

"Knight's son claiming to be mated to the little leech is what really goes against nature!" Jameson yells.

"Don't tell me you're a hybrid sympathizer, Cairo." Dwayne groans, pinching the bridge of his nose.

"Acting like a cave man doesn't mean you're for nature, Baxter!" Marisol snaps.

"Considering your ... lifestyle, you can't even have a proper mate bond. So don't you preach to me about nature!" Jameson snaps back.

Marisol barks out a surprised laugh.

"Are you seriously resorting to making jabs at me because I'm a lesbian?" she asks in mocking disbelief.

"And just what's wrong with being gay and mated?" Cairo's Beta asks.

"So you have a problem with my Beta and his mate, then?" Cairo asks in a warning tone.

Jameson rolls his eyes and shakes his head.

"Cairo, what your Beta does in his own free—"

"Jameson, I cannot support any of this." Neil says, cutting him off.

"That's *Alpha* Jameson to you! And Beta or not, you will treat me with respect and are either with me or against me!"

"Then I would rather be a rogue." Neil retaliates, walking over to stand next to Marisol and the others.

"Are you trying to say you're leaving my pack?" Jameson babbles, his eyes looking as if they're about to pop out of his head.

"Yes." Neil answers simply.

"We'll be happy to take you in until you're back on your feet." Zayn says, offering a hand to Neil. Neil nods and clasps his forearm in agreement.

"Neil! You dare betray me over a damn vampire?"

Jameson shouts, his face turning from red to purple with shocked rage and betrayal.

"I refuse to harm a child!" Neil snaps, stomping his foot with emphasis.

"Only a coward would." Marisol agrees.

"This is *exactly* why I would never allow a female Beta, much less take a female *Alpha* seriously. Letting maternal instinct cloud their judgment is clearly a problem for them!" Dwayne scoffs.

"And this is exactly why you're not mated. The universe knows you could never please a female and don't need to reproduce." Marisol claps back.

Dwayne turns red with both anger and embarrassment as several wolves either gasp or laugh.

"Luther, please reconsider," Red says to Dad so quietly I have to strain my ears to hear. "You really don't want a war between packs …"

"I'll never stop trying for my son!" Dad yells, and I scoff.

As if he gives a shit about me.

He only cares about using me and grooming me to be the perfect Alpha to take his place.

I look away from the monitor disgusted.

"Luther, please stop this!" I hear a familiar voice call out.

"Ma?!" I blurt out as I whip my head back to face the monitor.

Sure enough, my mother can be seen walking up to my dad.

Several wolves whisper and mutter to themselves as they seem to focus on her and Dad's interaction.

"Camilla?!" Dad stammers, clearly startled by her appearance. "I thought I told you to stay at home!"

Red looks relieved, I bet he and Mom were in on this together.

"I'm going in." I say, standing.

"Are you sure you want to start this *now*?" Reese asks warily.

I nod and open the door to the van and hop out.

"Let's get this show on the road!" Rider announces as he follows me out.

"Tell them to leave my mother out of everything." I say to the twins.

Heath nods and speaks into his smart watch, "Conan says to leave his mother out of it. Auburn hair, brown leather jacket, brown boots."

Satisfied, I slide the door to the van closed and watch it peel out towards the designated meeting spot Draken had picked. Rider and I begin to jog towards Jameson's pack house. The scent of blood and wolves is all around us.

Draken's handiwork probably.

I can't detect a scent, and I know Draken is able to cover his. Thanks to his handiwork, no wolves on patrol bother us. I have no idea if Draken had to kill any or not, but I'm also not worried enough to ask. I'm not sure if that makes me a bad person or not.

Rider doesn't say much about it either, but I know his main focus is getting to his mate's side. I know waiting in that van and watching her from a screen must have had him itching out of his skin to get to her.

With our speed and no interruptions, it doesn't take us long to get to the pack house. I'm surprised to not find any wolves guarding the entrance, but a smear of blood under my boot tells me all I need to know and I enter the building with Rider behind me.

We stalk silently down the entry hall toward the noise erupting from the dining room, and I hear my mother's voice.

"I refuse to sit at home while an entire discussion about

my son is taking place!" I hear her snap, a growl rumbling in her throat afterward.

A few wolves blink at me in shock as I strut into the dining room, head held high. Mom is in Dad's face, and neither of them have noticed me yet, but Red has. His eyes round in shock and his lips part as he glances between me and Rider.

"Since we're all talking about me," I say loud enough to have every head turn in my direction, "does anyone want to know what *I* think?"

Nineteen

CONAN

"Conan?!" Mom gasps as Dad jerks his head in my direction.

"C-" he stammers for a moment, "What're you doing here boy?!" he finally spits out, clearly caught off guard. My father isn't easily surprised, but my sudden appearance here definitely has given him quite a shock.

"Not like most of you would even listen to what I think, but …" I continue with a shrug before turning on my heel and walking out.

I smirk to myself as I hear the scooting of chairs, the rattling of the broken glass on the table, and a trample of feet scurrying behind me.

"Conan!" I hear Red call out.

"Get back here boy!" Dad shouts after him.

I ignore them and walk quickly out of the pack house and onto the snow covered lawn toward a line of trees.

"That's Luther's boy?!" someone asks.

"What's he doing here?!" another questions, sounding equally flabbergasted.

"Follow him! Don't let him get away!" I hear Jameson bellow and I snort. I'm not running away. I'm luring them all exactly where I want them.

I pull my hood over my head as fresh snow begins to fall, then turn to face the pack house as a sea of wolves flood out of its doors. I simply wait patiently, shoving my hands into my hoodie pocket as I debate lighting a cigarette.

Nah, Ma is being put through enough stress tonight.

She hates that I smoke, and I don't want to cause her anymore stress than I already have, even though a cigarette seems pretty insignificant compared to the rest of what's going on.

"Keep your distance, we can talk and hear each other just fine." I say loudly as all of the wolves come closer, maybe ten feet away from where I'm standing.

A few, especially my parents and Jameson, look as if I just asked the most ridiculous thing they've ever heard until growling from behind me stops them in their tracks.

Rider had shifted as soon as we made it back outside, and joined up with Marisol's pack members in the woods. All in wolf form, sixteen wolves fan around me. They growl loudly and bare their teeth in warning, causing all of the wolves attending the meeting to come to a halt.

"Decided to join the party early?" Marisol asks with a wink as she and Mikayla both come forward to stand at my side. I simply smirk at her in response, then nod my head at

Mikayla who is already stripping down to shift into a cream and gray colored wolf that joins her pack and mate behind me.

"What is this?!" Jameson demands.

"Conan, did you organize some sort of ambush or … or …" Dad can't even finish his sentence he is so mad and confused he can't seem to think straight, which I figured would happen.

"It's not an ambush, it's a conversation." I reply coolly. "I figured I'd help with all of the speculation about me so that you could just ask me yourselves."

I notice Marisol give Zayn a nod, and he and his Beta make their way over to stand beside her. Shortly after, Cairo and Caspian share a look before they and their Betas accompany us as well. I give a respectful nod to each of them, before returning to face the others.

"This is ridiculous. One of you grab him!" Jameson shouts, and I see my mother glare at him, her eyes flashing gold.

"He's my son, I'll handle it!" Dad says, his back straightening as if he dares Jameson to disagree with him.

"None of you will be touching him." Draken announces as he struts over to my side, hands in his pockets as if he hasn't a care in the world. I knew he was nearby, but I swear it's as if he appeared out of thin air.

The wolves in front of us gape, muttering curses or declarations of shock. Zayn was in on everything, but Cairo and Caspian both look him up and down, eyes wide. Neither of them moves or appears to want to switch sides, though.

"Ripper?!" Jameson asks, spitting out the word as if it were a dirty curse.

"Conan, what is the meaning of all this?!" Dad demands,

Mom clutches his arm, her eyes darting between Draken and me.

"How is he standing on my property right now, still alive?!" Jameson roars, looking around the tree line for his pack.

As if on cue, Reese and Heath drop from the trees to land in front of me, causing more of an uproar among the wolves facing us.

"We had a nice visit with your pack mates that were on patrol." Reese says with a grin.

"Pity they couldn't stay long." Heath adds as he picks at his fingernails, sounding bored.

"You ... how did you ... *What* did you do with my men?!" Jameson snarls as he takes a step forward, earning himself growls and snapping of teeth from the wolves still surrounding us.

"You're just going around killing wolves for sport?" Dad asks with a growl, lifting his chin to meet Draken's eyes.

"Only the ones that are a threat to my family." Draken replies with a shrug.

"We let *you* live because Conan and Rider assured us what happened to Ruby wasn't your fault or doing." Heath replies, pointing a finger at Dad.

"This is your last chance. You might be our new brother's father, but one wrong move and we won't hesitate to have you join your spineless pack members." Reese adds with a sneer.

"What about *my* men?" Jameson exclaims, his eyes scanning the trees around us as if he can't quite believe that we truly have the upper hand.

"The ones that played nice you can have back. Maybe." Draken replies with a shrug.

"I have the largest pack around here, there's no way—

How many more of you are there?!" Jameson stammers as one by one, Alice, Silas and Victor emerge from the trees.

"Enough." Draken grins. "My wife is particularly good with controlling numbers."

Alice smirks before raising her hand to snap her fingers, causing a flame to flicker.

"He brought his witch of a wife!" a random Alpha whispers.

"We'll back you up, Baxter." Another calls out to Jameson, moving to stand at his side with his Beta. "Just say the word."

"Or, hear me out, we could make an agreement for all of you to leave me and my family the hell alone and we'll do the same for you?" I say calmly, spreading my hands out in front of me. I want Jameson to make the first aggressive move against me in front of an audience.

Jameson drags his tongue across his teeth, his eyes narrowing. I swear for a moment that a fleck of snow sizzles when it makes contact with his boiling, angry bald head. He knows the other wolves are going to follow his lead. He doesn't want to appear weak but he also isn't stupid, either. He scans his eyes along the tree line once more, as if hoping his wolves will come riding in like the calvary to save the day, but none show. He opens his mouth to speak, then closes it, pauses and opens it again.

"This isn't over." He says with pure malice.

"I can make it over right now." Draken promises with a predatory smile. His fangs are fully extended and his eyes flash red.

Jameson is seething, giving Draken a look that could kill as his eyes flash gold in return.

"I would choose your next words very carefully, Jameson." Victor says, dragging a body out from behind a tree. He tosses the large male over to land in front of Jameson's feet as if he were a bag of potatoes.

"That one's unconscious, but when he comes to you can ask him how serious we are." Victor adds, with one of his trademark shit eating grins.

Mom and Dad step back, looking down at the discarded body with surprise as Jameson and his Beta crouch down to assess their pack member to make sure he is in fact still alive and breathing.

"Where are the rest of them?!" Jameson demands as he gets to his feet.

"Depending on your next words, you might find out." Victor says as he dusts snow from his hands.

"Seriously, Baxter." Marisol interjects before Jameson can spew more retorts. "Just leave Conan and his family be. All of you." She says, making eye contact with each wolf surrounding him. "What he and his mate do is no one's business. The ridiculous prejudice against vampires is outdated. Who are we to judge who his wolf decided was his true mate?"

"Well said, Alpha Gonzalez." Cairo says as Caspian nods in agreement.

"Do any of you really want a blood bath that can be avoided by simply minding your own fucking business?" Zayn challenges, lifting his chin as he dares any wolf to respond with anything other than compliance.

"Wait, aren't these bloodsuckers breaking the law by being on your territory, Jameson?" an Alpha asks, elbowing his way to the front of the crowd, his Beta in tow.

"Actually, no." Silas speaks for the first time, stepping forward as he clasps his hands behind his back. "I was actually present for the laws of this territory being made over a hundred years ago with Alpha Jameson's grandfather. The law simply states that a vampire may not hunt, be it human or wildlife, on this territory. Since no humans or wildlife are being harmed, no laws are currently being broken. All attacks on Jameson's wolves have been in self defense," Silas cocks his head to the side with a grin as he holds up his cell phone, "which we can prove to The Ravens if need be. But you're more than welcome to check your trail cams as well."

"Look at your being old as dirt coming in handy." Draken says with a smirk.

"Bite me, Fox."

"Sorry, I'm happily married."

"Are the leeches telling the truth about the laws of this territory?!" Alpha Dwayne asks angrily.

"The name callin' is entirely unnecessary, ya know! Didn't your Mama teach you better than that?!" Alice calls out with a scowl, placing her hands upon her hips.

"Don't you dare speak about my mother, you filthy—" Dwayne quickly shuts his mouth once Alice gives him a pointed look, simply raising one perfectly manicured finger in his direction, sparks momentarily popping off from the tip of it. I honestly don't know who is scarier, her or Draken. The look alone without the threatening fire powers would make any grown male tuck his tail.

Jameson crosses his arms, the veins bulging on his head visible from a mile away as he grinds his teeth. His eyes flash to gold then back to their normal dark blue.

"Unfortunately, yes they are correct." He reluctantly grumbles.

Victor asks Alice a question in Romanian, to which she rolls her eyes and nods. Reese and Heath chuckle at whatever he said.

I seriously need to download a translator app or find one to just learn the damn language.

"What are they saying?" a wolf calls out.

"Is that Russian?" another asks.

"That's the famous one, Dracula's grandson. It's gotta be Transylvanian."

"You mean *Romanian,* you moron?"

"Hey! Don't—"

Victor claps his hands loudly together and smiles toward the crowd of wolves.

"I also speak English and am right here if you'd like to ask *me* any questions about *me.*" He says, his voice layered with thick sarcasm through a smile.

"Enough of this foolishness!" Jameson's voice thunders and the wolves talking amongst themselves quickly shut up. He turns to face me and his nostrils flare as he exhales, the cold winter air making him remind me of an old cranky dragon blowing smoke through its nose.

"Fine," he spits out. "Get the hell off my territory."

"Does, 'fine' mean that you'll leave me, my mate and her family the fuck alone?" I ask, my eyes darting over to my parents. It's a question for them, mainly Dad, too.

"Yes, no more blood will be shed on my pack grounds tonight." Jameson snaps.

"Conan," Dad says, taking a few steps toward me while ignoring Marisol's wolves who creep forward to stand in front of me, "just keep in mind that if you go back with *them* —" he gestures toward the Foxes, Victor and Silas, "—you can *never* come back to my pack or my territory."

"Luther!" Mom grabs his arm, her face a mixture of horror and disbelief.

I scoff, shaking my head as I smirk down at my boots.

As if that's even a threat.

"Fine by me if it means I never have to hear your bullshit ever again." I say with a shrug. Dad gapes for a moment, and then kicks a pile of snow before turning around to stomp off. Mom looks at me and it seems like she's struggling on what to say before trailing off after him.

"Luther, *wait!* You can't do this!" I hear her shout as she catches up with him.

"I don't know about all of you, but I'm ready to go home." I say to Draken. He gives me an apologetic smile and claps me on the back.

"Let's." He says as he turns to walk away.

Jameson and I lock eyes once more, then I turn away to follow Draken and the twins through the woods. My heart is heavy at how upset and conflicted my mother looked, but what more can I do?

Maybe after things settle down I'll call her.

Rider, Marisol and her wolves trail behind me, forming a protective circle around the vampires and wolves in human form.

"You okay?" Victor asks, jogging to catch up with me.

I grunt in response. It's a loaded question that I really don't know how to answer right now.

"Yeah," Victor nods in agreement, "it's never easy to stand up to your family. I know that all too well."

I sigh, and look down as I place my hands in my hoodie pocket. Crystal has told me a little of how Victor doesn't get along well with his family, and there's always been a rift between him and his parents.

"Yeah." I reply quietly. Normally my first instinct when it comes to Victor is to ignore anything he says, but he's genuinely been helpful with all of this and seems to actually be trying to connect with me, not tease me. It's not much of a response, but he knows I'm not much of a talker anyway.

The crunching of snow beneath our feet is the only sound

we hear for a few minutes, then he reaches out a hand holding a cigarette in front of my face.

"Smoke?"

I give him a half smile and take it from him.

"Thanks."

"Figured you'd need one after all that." He replies as he hands me his lighter.

"That's an understatement." I chuckle dryly. I slow to a stop, using my hand as a shield from the cold wind as I light my cigarette. Victor playfully shoves his shoulder against mine as he keeps walking ahead. I catch up to him, then bump his shoulder back with mine. He blinks in surprise, then we both burst into laughter.

It feels good to laugh when I feel so empty inside.

ALICE

As the wolves disperse, I notice Conan's parents hovering by a large black truck. His mother is crying as his father spews profanities that I think are more to himself than to her. I patiently wait a few minutes for more wolves to disappear, and watch that Alpha Jameson guy stomp back into his house, yelling into a cell phone.

I glance at my smart watch to see a text from Draken.

Fang Daddy

You coming?

. . .

I quietly reply with speech to text for him to give me a minute and that I'm safe. I know he won't go far without me and I feel confident that I could defend myself with my fire powers alone if needed. This might be the dumbest idea I've ever had, but I slowly walk toward Conan's parents.

"Camilla?" I say softly and she stiffens before turning to face me.

"What more do you blood suckers want?!" Luther snarls at me.

"Rude. I wasn't talkin' to you." I say with a huff. I ignore whatever insult he throws back at me, placing my attention solely on Camilla.

"You're Conan's mother, right?" I know she is, but it feels right to address her out loud.

"Yes?" she asks suspiciously, her red, watery eyes pulling on all of my heart strings.

"From one mother to another, I can see how much you miss your boy." I say softly, holding my hands over my heart. "If you want to meet the grandchild we share, please do reach out to Conan. I'd be more than happy to help arrange it."

She blinks in surprise, her mouth opening and closing as she struggles to respond. Even Luther shuts up, even though he's still eyeing me as if I'm some sort of pest.

"Just thought I'd offer since you don't seem like you agree with any of this mess." I say with a shrug. "And I know how much Conan misses you." I offer a small smile, "He talks about you all the time."

"He does?" Camilla asks, barely above a whisper, eyes filling with fresh tears.

I nod.

"He does. I love him as if he were my own son. He's a

good boy." I say with what I hope is sincerity that shows. "Your love shows in him, and now that I've met you up close I can see he has your eyes." I say with a grin, hoping she knows I'm saying that as a compliment.

Camilla claps a hand over her mouth as another sob escapes her, and Luther's face softens a bit. Just the tiniest bit. But enough for me to notice.

"Just think about it. Our door will always be open for a peaceful visit." I say, then begin my walk to catch up with the others. Her tears are breaking my maternal heart. Anyone can tell she loves her son, and I can't imagine being in the situation she's in. I'd fight Draken tooth and nail to see any of my kids, but I try not to judge. I can only hope she does the right thing.

"I will." I hear her softly whisper behind me, and my heart warms with hope.

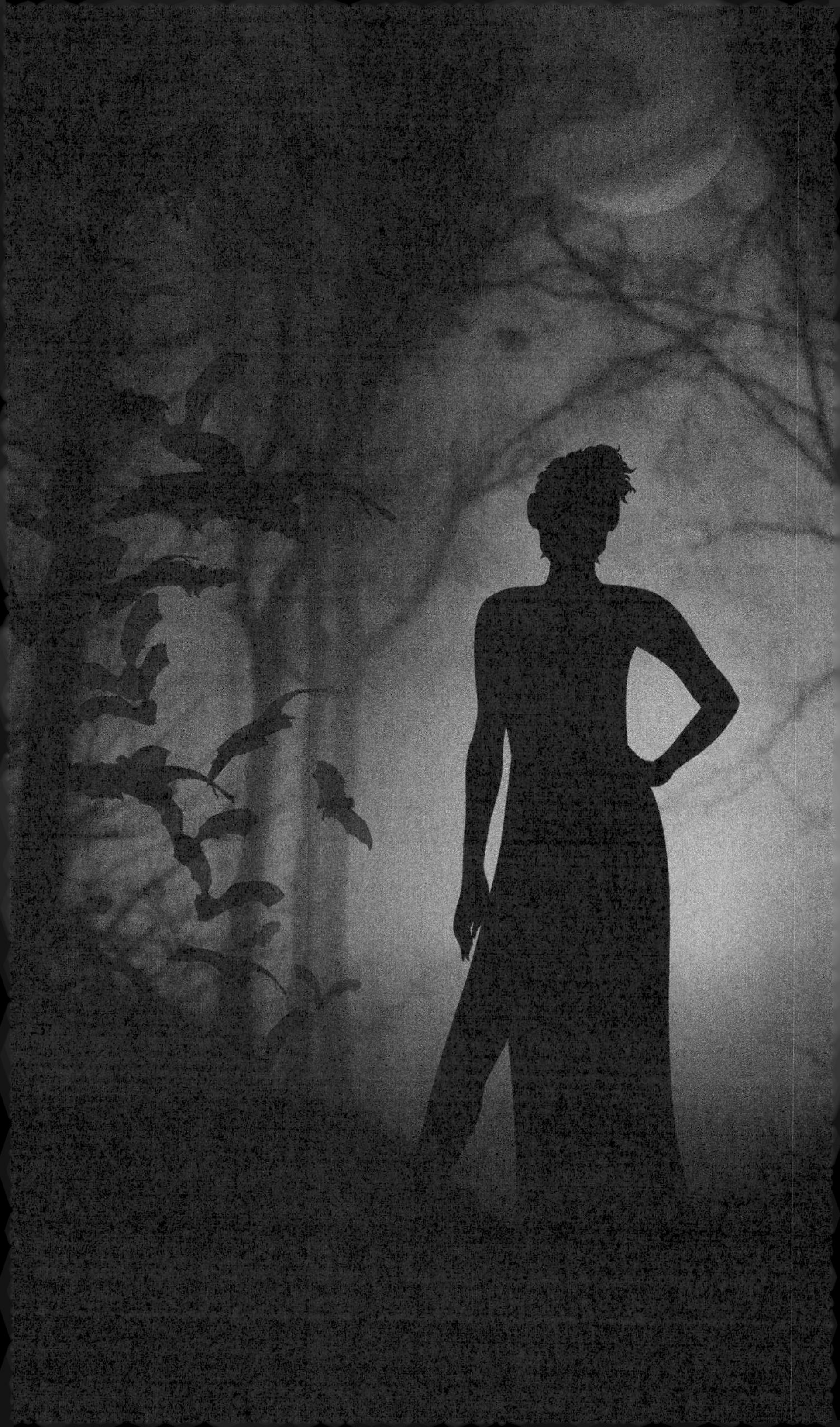

Twenty

CRYSTAL

"So, you're the little dhampir Carrot-Top here won't shut up about." Cadence says dryly as her aqua-blue eyes look me up and down, a bored expression upon her beautiful face. She has four nasty looking claw marks scarred across her cheek and a handful of smaller ones on her forehead, nose, lip and other cheek that in no way hinder her beauty, but enhances it. I also love the whole goth aesthetic she's got going on from her clothes to her black lipstick. Honestly, if she wasn't such a bitch, we'd probably be best friends.

I hear Baylor sigh in defeat, even though he's the one that warned me she's a bit rough around the edges.

"Yes, I'm Crystal. Nice to meet you." I say with a polite smile.

"Eh, sure. Wanna cig?" she asks, offering me her pack. I have to admit, I absolutely love her New Yorker accent. She definitely grew up around the Queens area.

"Sure." I say, noticing her eyes widen ever so slightly in surprise as I take one. She quickly shifts her expression back to bored while handing me her lighter.

"Here."

"Thanks."

Now it makes sense why she wanted to sit outdoors at the coffee shop she requested us to meet her. The cold doesn't bother either of us too much, but I can see Baylor's teeth chattering as he lifts his hood.

"I thought you quit?" he asks before blowing into his hands for warmth.

"When I was pregnant, yeah." I reply with a shrug.

"Responsible parenting," Cadence says with a smirk, flicking the ash of her cigarette into an ashtray on the table, "nice."

I can't tell if she's being sarcastic or not, so I just smile and nod as I take a drag from my own cigarette.

"So, speaking of your little bundle of mystery," she continues, "I understand she's what you call a 'tribrid'?"

I exhale smoke with a nod.

"Correct, since I'm half human and half vampire and my mate is a wolf …" I shrug, "it's just a term I came up with while I was pregnant."

She hums thoughtfully while pulling a drag from her cigarette.

"You're half vampire and half werewolf, correct?" I ask.

"I dunno. You tell me." She says coyly.

I tilt my head in confusion, then watch her eyes flash from red to gold, then one eye red while the other stays gold, before finally fading back to her natural aqua-blue.

"Wicked!" I exclaim probably a little too excitedly.

"*Wicked?*" she wrinkles her nose. "What are ya, from Harry Potter or something?"

"No, but my dad's British and my mom's a witch."

"... You're just a little bit of everything, aren't ya?"

"Can we please get back to the point?" Baylor sighs.

"What exactly *is* the point?" Cadence asks, raising a pierced brow in annoyance.

"Well," I begin to fidget with my ring inside of my hoodie pocket, "I have a few questions if you wouldn't mind answering them?"

Cadence rolls her eyes in response.

"As long as none of them are too personal, of course!" I quickly add.

"Whatever, go ahead."

"I just want to know what possibly to expect from my daughter." I take a deep breath while Cadence studies her black nails. "Since she's part human I know it won't be the exact same as you. I'm also sure every hybrid is probably different in their own way ..."

"Out with it."

"Well, for starters," I reply, trying my best to not sound agitated by her rudeness. "Do you still have to drink blood? Do you have to recharge after you feed?"

"Yep. I'm guessing you do too, even though you're half human?"

I nod.

"What about your wolf? Do you shift every full moon?"

"Yep. I can also shift at will."

"Oh, really?"

"Yeah, my wolf is smaller than the average werewolf, though." She shrugs. "Not sure if that's because of me being a hybrid or genetics."

"Erm, speaking of genetics …" Cadence's eyes flick up to me almost as if in warning, the rest of her face still looking bored. "How did your parents get away with … you know, having you?"

With a loud sniff she looks back at her nails.

"Dunno. Never met 'em."

"Oh," I gasp, feeling heartbroken for her. "I'm so sorry."

"I don't need your fucking sympathy." She snaps, angrily shoving her hands into the pockets of her jeans. "You gonna ask me anything else, or what? I got somewhere to be." She mumbles around her cigarette.

This is going so horribly wrong.

"Sorry! I didn't mean to offend! Just, um …" My mind scurries for a way to fix this awkward situation as I snuff my cigarette out inside the nearby ash tray. "Why don't you come over to my place when you have more time to talk?"

"I'll pass."

"Please?" I clasp my hands together, and I swear I notice her gaze flit over my own black nail polish. "It would mean so much to me and my family if you could come by. We've been longing to meet a hybrid that could help us with the trickier—"

"Save it!" She abruptly stands, drops her cigarette into the snow then stomps on it. "Look, Blondie, I promised you and your red-head pest here a few minutes of my time. You got 'em. I answered a couple of your stupid questions. You drove all the way out to the shitty side of town to learn that I drink blood and can shapeshift. Congratulations." She says through a fake smile, showing every perfect white tooth in her head. "Now, I'll be on my way." She says while jabbing a thumb in the direction behind her.

"Fine!" I finally snap back as I stand to my own feet. "Thanks oh so much for your time!"

Baylor quickly scampers over to my side, nearly knocking his chair backwards in the process.

"Watch your temper, Cici!" he whispers loudly.

What was even the point of whispering?!

"Look," Cadence says with a smirk as she eyes me up and down, "you know how shitty it is to grow up not being classified as a pedigree, I'm sure." She tilts her head as her eyes lock with mine, "But you have no idea what kinda life you just set your kid up for."

"Excuse me?"

"Being half human probably sucked ass, being half of two species that hate each other is no walk in the park, either."

"Her father and I are working to give her the best life we possibly can away from all of that bullshit!" I shout, and Baylor shushes me again as he looks around for any human witnesses that might've heard my outbursts. I shrug him off as I feel my pulse quicken, my face growing hot with rage as I glare at Cadence.

I'm expecting her to come at me swinging and I prepare myself as I square my shoulders. To my surprise, she barks out a laugh.

"That's a cute dream. Inspirational, really." She says with a tone as if speaking to a child that just told her they want to be the Tooth Fairy when they grow up.

"Cadence ..." Baylor groans.

"I'm leaving, Carrot-Top. Don't sweat it." Cadence chuckles as she lifts her hood, then casually walks away as if nothing ever happened.

I feel my breath quicken as I clench my fists, glaring after her until her figure fades away completely in the snow.

"Calm down, Cici! Your eyes!" Baylor whispers as he clasps my shoulder.

I breathe slowly through my nose a few times, then slowly unclench my fists. I close my eyes, taking one more breath through my nose, then exhale out through my mouth slowly as I will my eyes to change back to purple. I open them to see Baylor staring at me with concern and I sigh, shaking my head.

"I get that she was probably bullied like I was for being a halfling, but that's no reason for unnecessary rudeness out of nowhere!" I say, exasperated. "We were trying to be as friendly as we could and she just—ugh!" I kick at a pile of snow in frustration.

"I know, I know." Baylor says, holding up his hands in surrender. "Don't go trying to run after her and kick her ass, now! The last thing I need is a supernatural cat fight breaking out to get me fired!" he exclaims as his grip on my shoulder tightens, as if he's terrified I'm going to bolt after her and demand a smack down.

"I'm not, I'm not! I've got more sense than that, geez!" I grumble, shrugging him off.

"I warned you that she was a little rough around the edges …"

I snort, crossing my arms in annoyance.

"Just give her some space. I'll text her later, okay? She might come around."

"Perfectly fine with me if she doesn't." I scoff.

"Come on, let's go." He says, looping his arm through mine as he leads me back toward his mustang. "The others should be getting back by now. Don't you want to hear how the meeting went?"

I sigh, and quicken my pace.

"You're right. Let's go."

"Who's the prettiest, purple-eyed cutie in the world?" I hear Ella say to Lila as I approach the nursery. She was kind enough to babysit both Lila and a still recovering Ruby, while Conan and I each went on our separate missions.

"There's my favourite girl!" I hear Reese say, and I roll my eyes as I come to the door.

Ella scowls at him, clutching Lila to her chest.

"What? I meant my niece of course!" Reese adds, holding his hands up with the most angelic expression on his face.

Ella's face relaxes and he ruins it by smirking.

"Unless you *want* to be my favourite girl …" he says slyly with a wink.

"I hope you realize that me holding this infant is the only thing keeping me from smacking you." Ella replies dryly.

"Cupcake, don't talk dirty to me while you're holding my niece."

"Would you go away!" I shout, smacking him behind the head.

Ella laughs as he winces, rubbing at the spot.

"You're the literal worst!" he spits back, slapping my arm.

"No, *you're* the literal worst at flirting!" I reply with a punch to his shoulder.

"*You're* the worst cockblock on the planet!" He swings back, but I dodge and offer him a grin in response.

"I try my best!" I say happily.

"*Anyway,*" Ella interrupts what probably would've turned into a wrestling match. "How did the meeting go?"

"Yeah, is Conan back? Everything went okay?" I ask.

"Yeah, he's downstairs. We made the whole lot of them shit themselves, basically." Reese says proudly.

"So I'm guessing we don't have to worry about them bugging you for a while?" Ella asks.

"Hopefully, if they know what's good for them." Reese says as he takes Lila from her.

"Thank you again for watching her." I say with a smile.

"It was my honor." Ella beams.

"Ruby's good?" I ask.

"She is! She even talked to me a little bit when I asked a few questions about Lila. She's just gone downstairs to meet your mom."

I feel my entire body relax in relief.

"That's wonderful. Please tell me you'll be joining us for dinner?"

"Yes, please do." Reese adds with a grin, and I elbow him.

"Don't scare her away!"

"The only thing that would scare her away is your breath!" He elbows me back.

"I wouldn't want to impose …" Ella says with a small giggle.

"Oh, please! We all want to thank you for watching the most precious cargo!" Reese says as he practically drags her toward the door.

"For once, I agree with him." I say as I follow them downstairs.

"Well then, I'd be delighted." Ella agrees with a nod before shaking herself free from Reese's grasp.

"What? I don't bite!" Reese says, looking insulted. "Unless you want me to … Just not in front of Lila."

"*Reese!*"

I see Conan's large form standing on the back porch, and I rush out while Ella and Reese continue to bicker their way into the kitchen.

"You're back!" I exclaim happily as I wrap my arms around him.

He chuckles as he flicks his now snuffed out cigarette into the trash, then envelopes me into a bear hug, lifting me off my feet as he nuzzles my neck.

"I am." He simply states into my hair.

"I'm so glad you all came back home safe to me." I whisper into his chest. "I know you were safe with Dad and everyone else but …" He begins to rub my back as I take a deep breath, trying to organize my thoughts. "I still wish I could've gone with you." Is the only thing I can think of to say.

"I know." He mutters as he sets me back onto my feet, then kisses my forehead. "But you needed to be with Baylor." He wraps his arms around my waist then rests his cheek on top of my head as he pulls me back toward his chest. "Besides, I didn't want you around all of that shit anyway. Your parents even agreed with me on that."

I roll my eyes as I hug him tighter.

"Yeah, yeah …"

"How did the talk with the hybrid girl go?"

"Ugh."

"Hm?"

"I'll tell you about it later." I grumble.

He pulls back to look down at me.

"That bad, huh?"

"It definitely could've gone better, that's for sure."

"Come on, we can talk more inside. There's a few wolves I'd like you to meet."

I nod, slipping my hand in his as we make our way back inside the house.

CONAN

Once we left Jameson's territory, Alice insisted on a "victory dinner" to thank all of our new allies. Of course Marisol and her pack took her up on the offer, as did Zayn, Cairo and Caspian along with their Betas, though they still are weary to invite their mates. I told Alice not to take it personally, it's just instinct for us. Even though they might trust the Foxes enough to stand up for them, bringing their most precious people around them is still uncharted territory. She and Draken didn't seem offended in the slightest, thankfully. Alice was just happy to cook, as I've come to find out it seems to be a stress relief for her.

The scents of meat and spices cooking, along with the sound of laughter and chatter almost makes this evening seem unreal. I look around at all of the wolves relaxing casually inside of a vampire's home and can't help but feel hope for the first time in … well, I don't know how long.

Change is happening. For the better.

I spot Reese holding Lila as he annoys Ella with his relentless flirting, and I make a beeline straight for him.

"I'll take her." I say as I hold my arms out.

"If you must." Reese says with a frown, giving Lila one last cuddle before handing her over.

"I must. I've missed her."

"Fair enough, I suppose."

"Thank you for watching over her, Ella." I say to the Ruby-sized female.

"Of course!" she replies with a wave of her hand.

"I really hope we get to see you more often." Crystal says cheerily. "I'd love to hang out with you when there are no looming threats or Raven duties."

"I would absolutely love to." Ella replies with an enthusiastic nod.

"You definitely should come around more often." Reese agrees.

"Ella, I love you and all …" Crystal says with a sneer, "but Reese flirting is gonna make me lose my appetite." She says before turning abruptly and walking over to Alice to ask if she needs any help.

I smirk as I follow after her.

"Poor Crystal." I hear Ella say behind me, and I stop by the kitchen island to adjust Lila's swaddle as I listen. "I can't imagine what horrors you and Heath put her through growing up." She continues.

"Why does everyone say that?!" Reese replies, feigning innocence. I snort to myself. "She grew up just fine!" he adds.

Ella chuckles then stops abruptly. I glance their way without moving my head to appear as if I'm still looking down at Lila. Reese has his hand under her chin, propping it up to look at him. He's maybe a couple inches shorter than me, so he has to be bending down quite a bit to close the gap between them.

"Have I mentioned I love that adorable little giggle of yours?"

Barf. Ella should be punching him at any moment now.

She pauses, then begins to pick at a thread on her sweater. Is Ella *nervous?*

What the fuck.

"What're you trying to accomplish, Reese?" she asks so quietly, I almost didn't hear her.

"Go out with me." Reese replies, all taunting vanishing from his tone. He actually sounds sincere for once.

What the actual fuck is going on?

"Do what?" Ella replies, clearly as shocked as I am.

"Just one date." Reese mutters quietly, his face expression so serious it actually concerns me a bit. "Just *one* date, and if you don't have a good time, I'll leave you be."

"It's pretty common knowledge that Reese and Heath Fox don't date." Ella snorts, but her cheeks are red with embarrassment.

"You're different."

"How?"

"If I could figure that out, maybe I'd finally be able to get some sleep."

"What're you going on about now, Fox?"

"Don't you get it, you silly girl?" Reese smirks and leans down so close, there's barely an inch between their noses. "Ever since I met you, I've not been able to get you out of my head."

"What?" Ella asks barely above a whisper, her eyes wide.

"I mean it."

She pushes his hand away and takes a step back. He frowns, but doesn't stop her.

"I'm not going to be your bloodwhore, Reese." Ella states adamantly.

"I would never ask you to." Reese replies, seemingly disgusted by the idea. "I mean it. A real, actual date." He steps forward then grabs both of her small hands in his, lifting them to his lips. "Please?" he mumbles against them, practically staring into her soul with his big, pleading eyes. The guy that recently committed murder for his little sister looks like a kicked puppy.

Ella eyes him warily then exhales sharply through her nose.

"Okay, fine." She grumbles.

"Lovely … Oh? Looks like you have something on your lips …"

I wrinkle my nose.

No she doesn't.

"How embarrassing …" Ella stammers as she turns a deeper shade of red as she pulls a hand free from his to reach for her face. "What is it …?"

"Me." Reese replies and quickly pulls her in for a kiss.

That was so fucking lame. I'm outta here.

I quickly pull Lila up to my chest and head toward Draken and Cairo, trying to erase what I just witnessed away from my memory.

"Hey," I say with a small smirk. "Just wanted to say thanks again for all of your help back there."

"Of course." Cairo replies, his eyes instantly darting down to Lila in my arms. "This is your daughter." He states instead of asks. A look of curious wonder on his face as he takes in Lila's purple eyes.

"Yes, this is Lila." I say, turning her so that he can see her a little better. Nero is *not* a fan of all of these newcomers around Pup, but I'm fighting off any of his urges. They need to see who they just protected for me. They need to see why all of tonight mattered so much to me.

"She's a cutie." Cairo says with a smile. He puts his hands in his pockets and I know that's his wolf's way of trying to show he's not a threat and not going to ask for her or cross any lines. I appreciate it more than he realizes.

"Isn't she?" Draken agrees proudly.

"I have a daughter about her age." Cairo replies.

"Oh, really?"

"Yes, she's my only for now. Being a Girl Dad isn't for the weak." He says with a chuckle.

"Isn't that the bloody truth." Draken says as he raises his glass of brandy, then takes a sip.

We both chuckle.

"Maybe one day we can arrange a play date of some sort, as long as both of our mates feel comfortable." Cairo offers.

"I would like that."

CRYSTAL

"Hey, Ru. Wanna taste this?" I say, offering a spoonful of stew I just added seasoning to.

Ruby nods then opens her mouth as I feed her. She nods happily and gives me a thumbs up in approval.

"Not too salty?" I ask, and she shakes her head.

"No." She replies softly.

"Thanks!" I say with a grin as I turn to continue stirring. She's slowly been talking more and more, thankfully. I'm grateful for every single word she blesses me with. I notice her look over her shoulder when Marisol walks in, and I wonder if she remembers that day Marisol met her. Ruby fidgets for a moment, then makes her way over to her.

Well, that answers that question I guess.

I see Mom pause from chopping vegetables as she looks over to watch Ruby as well.

"She just went over there on her own?" Mom whispers.

I nod, watching Marisol's face light up when Ruby approaches her.

"Ruby! You're looking so much better since I last saw you!" Marisol greets with a smile.

Ruby nods shyly.

"How'd you like the goodies we sent you? Me and the girls had fun picking everything out and—" Ruby silences her by quickly pulling her in for a hug. Marisol blinks, then hugs her back. "You're welcome."

I hear Mom sniffling beside me as a tear rolls down my cheek.

A badass Alpha female werewolf just hugged my vampire sister in my vampire parents' kitchen.

This is the kind of world we need for our daughter to grow and thrive in.

CONAN

M A

> I think I'm here.

I peek out the window to see my mother is indeed walking up to the Fox property and I feel knots begin to form in my stomach. I know how hard this was for her but I'm so happy she actually came. I'm proud of her for doing something for herself without Dad's approval.

I close my eyes as I grip the door knob and exhale slowly, trying to calm myself. Still full of the jitters, I open the door to greet her, raising an arm to get her attention.

"Ma! Over here!" She doesn't look at me though, instead I see her glaring at the side of the house and am shocked to see my father standing there.

"Are you crazy?!" I hear him whisper. "Showing up to the Ripper's home by yourself?!"

"You will not keep me from seeing my son or ... or my grandchild!" Mom snaps, her posture rigid and ready for a fight.

That's it, I'm going down there to tell him to fuck off.

"No. No I won't, I suppose."

I nearly fall off the steps when I hear Dad sound the calmest I've ever heard him sound in my entire life.

"Wait, what?" Mom stammers, clearly just as stunned as I am.

"Dad?" I finally blurt out.

They both turn to face me, Mom's expression clearly showing this was unplanned on her part. Dad just crosses his arms and stares at me, his eyes swimming with questions as his lips form into a tight line. He scratches at his scruff, clearly nervous about this entire situation.

Mom eyes him warily and he just looks at her for a moment. She nods, then turns back to face me. Dad rolls his shoulders then takes a step forward.

"Conan ..." he starts, then the distinct sound of a gun cocking has us all freeze.

Dad shoves Mom behind him as his head jerks in direction of the nearest cluster of trees.

"You cowardly son of a bitch!" he shouts, his eyes widening with rage and panic.

Adrenaline rushes through my veins as I try my best to see what he does. Even with my night vision I can't fully make out the figure standing there thanks to the porch light distorting my view.

"This is for the best." A familiar voice calls out before the deafening sound of a gunshot rings out through the trees, echoing throughout the property.

And just like that, in the blink of an eye, my world changes forever.

Who was shot?
Who did Luther see?
Are Conan and Crystal in more danger than ever?

Find out what happens next in the third installment of *The Blood Fate Series*:

BLOOD AND TEARS

... COMING SOON ...

Name Pronunciations

Conan – Koh-nuhn
Draken – Dray-kehn
Lila – Lye-luh
Zayn – Z-aye-n
Cairo – Kai-row
Caspian – Cas-pee-an

And finally, my name
Andalee – Ann-dah-lee

ACKNOWLEDGMENTS

Thank you to all my readers who have followed and supported me from Episode where Crystal and Conan's story first began.

A special thank you to Mikayla, Anna and Maranna for bringing Zayn, Cairo, and Caspian to life and trusting me with them. Everyone loves a good crossover!

And a special thank you to Ella for being the perfect cupcake for Reese.

I LOVE Y'ALL!

♥

ALSO BY ANDALEE BROOKE

THE BLOOD FATE SERIES

Fangs And Paws

Fangs And Paws (Mature Version)

Allies And Outcasts

Allies And Outcasts (Mature Version)

FOLLOW ME!

- x.com/andaleebrooke
- instagram.com/andalee.writes
- patreon.com/andalee_is_writing
- tiktok.com/@andaleeiswriting

Printed in Great Britain
by Amazon